The WitchSlayer

Witch Bound

Book One

Opal Reyne

Cover art: Sam Griffin
Internal Illustrations: Etheric Designs

Trigger Warning
Spoiler below

This book is <u>not</u> a dark romance. However, it does contain a trigger that may be unsettling for some readers. Please only read further if you have triggers.

There is a non-consensual sexual assault committed to the male main character by the female main character in this book. It is on page. I do skim over it as not to make it too unbearable. He is not afraid, only angry, so you will not have to experience any fear through him as that would have been quite distressing. I would never do something like this to my characters needlessly, so please understand that there is a legitimate reason for it and everything will make sense only a few pages later.

Also, as there are in many Witch novels, there are often Witch Trials such as burning at the stake, drownings, and cliff falls. The female main character endures one of these and is saved and healed by the main male character. Of course, she is suffering mentally from her trauma.

<u>Author's note on language</u>

I'm from AUSTRALIA.

My English is not the same as American English.
I love my American English spoken readers to bits.
You're cute, you all make me giggle, and I just wanna give
you a big 'ol hug. However, there are many of you who
don't seem to realise that your English was born from British
English, which is what I use(although a bastardised version
since Australians like to take all language and strangle it
until it's a ruined carcass of slang, missing letters, and
randomly added o's).

We don't seem to like the letter z.

We write colour instead of color. Recognise instead of
recognize. Travelling instead of traveling. Skilful instead of
skillfull. Mum instead of mom. Smelt is a past participle of
smelled. We omit the full-stop in Mr. Name, so it's Mr
Name. Aussies cradle the word cunt like it's a sweet little
puppy, rather than an insult to be launched at your face.

Anyway, happy reading!

This is a call to all my DragonFuckers out there,

This book is for you.

Where the girl gets the Dragon, fucks him as a human, and then also takes that big 'ol Dragon *Dick*.

Amalia would like to say she felt terrified as the storm raged outside with a vengeance. That its unbending will elicited fear as the screeching wind clawed its way around her little cottage, threatening to take down the four weak walls surrounding her.

A deafening *boom* rumbled. Lightning sliced often through the clouds and illuminated the small town in the distance. Angry and relentless, fire burst to life when it struck the tops of trees before the unending rain drenched the leaves and snuffed the flames out.

At least that is something, she thought.

The sideways pouring rain tried to fly into her home by the windows while puddles steadily formed anywhere there was an entrance.

The foundations rattled as though at any point, her cottage could blow over.

But instead of being terrified, the storm both calmed and infuriated her.

In between staring out the window, hoping to catch the lightning strikes with their odd red hue, she was mopping the water up to take back outside into the elements.

She'd already used the rainwater to her advantage,

cleaning her floors without having to refill her bucket. However, that task had been completed a while ago and it was now long into the black of night.

I do not think I have ever seen a storm this bad before.

It appeared that the Gods were angry tonight.

Fearing her house would flood if she slept, she stayed awake, cleaning and boiling herbs to make herself tea – one that she hoped would keep her awake. She often went outside, not only to empty buckets collecting rain from leaks, but to also shout into the deafening storm.

"Bala!" Amalia didn't think she had yelled this loudly yet, but she was starting to worry. "Bala!"

Where is that darn cat? It wasn't hers, but a stray who often found comfort in the warmth of her home.

He might as well be hers with all the whining he did for her to feed him. She often found him at the foot of her porch steps, tired from doing Gods knew what or meowing to come inside.

With another sigh, she took one last look into the shadows of the forest beyond her yard, before turning away from the freezing winds trying to make her eat her own hair. She found salvation back inside.

He probably found a hole to crawl into.

She'd bet tomorrow when he returned, she would have to bathe him.

Peering down at her hands, she pulled back the sleeves of her peasant dress and looked at the healed, but puffy red scars that marked her. They were the hazards of washing a stray who definitely hated to bathe.

He also hated the rain, which was one of the reasons she was worried about Bala being out in the storm.

She debated whether she would toss herself out into the storm to find him but decided against it... again.

The rain was pouring so heavily that along with the black

of night, she could barely see farther than three feet in front of herself. She knew she'd never find him, and with the howling winds, she doubted she'd hear him either.

Return safe, old friend.

Amalia heard quick fluttering, then squawking. She let out a frustrated groan when the sound of clawing feet and bumping started right before the squawking turned into shrieks. Then the angry growls of another animal started.

Quickly grabbing her broom, she shoved it repeatedly into the ceiling, hoping she didn't poke a hole through the straw.

"Hey, you lot! Share!" she yelled, eyeing the timber ceiling supports that kept the straw of her roof in place. All sounds halted. "Bloody ravens and racoons," she muttered to herself.

Animals flocked to Amalia.

Right now, the ravens and racoons sought shelter from the storm in a burrow the racoons created in the straw roof of her house. They weren't adjusting well to seeking refuge together.

I really need to fix that. Especially since the burrow was causing water to drip into her home and into multiple buckets she'd placed on the floor. Then again, she didn't like the idea of leaving them defenceless if another storm this terrible occurred.

She would've invited the animals inside, but the last time she did they'd wreaked havoc in her home. When they ruined some of her favourite herbs and spices, she'd tossed them all outside, despite enjoying the comfort of their presence.

Just as she sat down to return to her warm tea, something whined horrifically. It whined and screamed with demanding, unyielding calls. It grew impatient and louder with every second she didn't pay it any attention, stealing the peace she'd found within the angry storm.

Getting back to her feet, she went to the front of her cottage and ripped open the door.

"Stop that infernal racket, you annoying old sod!" The

whining didn't stop even when she narrowed her eyes downward. "It is not my fault you got caught in the rain. I thought you creatures were able to sense this sort of thing. Or are you just dull-witted?"

The noise finally calmed, and bright green eyes stared back at her as a sopping wet tail tapped the floor. Bala tilted his head down and picked something up with his teeth.

"That had best not be another dead rat," she threatened while moving out of the way to allow him inside.

They eyed each other as he pranced in like a royal prince with his head and tail held high. She couldn't see what he had in his mouth, but she knew she wouldn't have to wait long to find out.

It would either be a gift for her or his dinner.

"I will find a towel and dry you. You better not make a mess while I find one, handsome!"

Bala was, indeed, quite the handsome cat.

She didn't know what breed he was, but he was so fluffy that she'd mistakenly thought he was a fat pig of a cat at first. She'd shooed him away, thinking he was just a house cat wanting extra food.

It hadn't taken her long to realise he was homeless.

With a chest and cheeks of white, the rest of his coat was tortoiseshell with bright orange and red mixed in with the flecks of black. Bala hated children and was irritable on the best of days. She assumed this was why he was homeless.

All that pretty fur hid the cat's true, feral nature – except with her. Well, most days with her. *Definitely not at bath time.*

It didn't take long to find him a towel. She turned around and immediately yelled when she realised he'd hopped onto her bed sopping wet. He started pawing at the prey he had. She knew he only did that when he intended to eat what he found since he often liked to play with it at first.

"Oh no you will not! I will not have another bloody

massacre on my bed."

She picked him up and tossed him to the ground. Every time she did, he stared up at her like he was dumbfounded at the fact that she would. He was a very expressive cat.

Amalia didn't mind the circle of life; she just didn't want it messing up her home.

She knelt down on one knee and started forcefully rubbing the towel over the cat's fluffy fur, hoping to dry him as much as possible. He raised his head, enjoying the rub down with obvious happiness.

"Why were you out in the storm, Bala?"

She wasn't expecting an answer.

The townsfolk often called her a crazy spinster when they saw her talking to him or any of the animals she passed in the street. His feline head turned towards the bed, almost like he understood her question.

"You cannot tell me you wanted food. I feed you so much every day that I have turned you into a spoiled, rotten, little stray."

He opened his mouth like he was going to yawn, but then licked across his long whiskers instead.

With a roll of her eyes, she stood with the intention of picking up his prey and discarding it onto the floor for him to do what he would with it.

So, what is it this time? A bird, a rat, possibly another cat?

It wouldn't be the first time he brought something the size of himself into her home.

She tilted her head when she stood in front of it, a frown crinkling her brow.

What the... A lizard?

No, it wasn't a lizard. Well, maybe it was, but she'd never seen this kind before. She scooped it into both of her hands since it was too large to fit into just one.

It has wings?

Indeed, it did. Large, scaly wings.

"What in the heaven's name did you bring me, Bala?"

He came onto the bed at his name being called, and she quickly shoved him off. She knelt onto the bed while placing it against the sheets to examine it.

"What are you?" She gingerly lifted a wing in curiosity.

It had four legs, two wings, and a thick body with spikes jutting up its back before becoming larger around its big head. Its neck wasn't too long, and even without the wings, she knew she'd never seen anything like it. Its scales were such a deep purple that it almost appeared black.

It was also very warm, and still breathing.

As she did whenever Bala brought something into her house that wasn't dead yet, she took it over to her table and carefully rested it down upon it.

Amalia pulled on a wing and noticed that both were broken.

"Poor thing."

She'd take care of it, heal it as best as she could – and keep the cat's dirty mittens off it.

Once she grabbed a clean towel, she folded it and moved the scaly lizard to it so the creature had something soft to lay on. As she dried it, blood soaked into towel from the deep scratch marks across its back and belly.

"You sure did a good job on it," she said to Bala before she turned to her kitchen.

Her house was small and bore no rooms. Her bed was tucked near the front against the wall with a small wooden chair and table nearby so she could read. In the middle was the dining table where she had placed the little lizard.

The rest of her cottage, including the kitchen, was covered in shelving with every herb, spice, and crystal she could possibly find.

Herbal plants hung from the ceiling, while others were

pressed up against the walls or were sitting outside in pots if they weren't planted. She often had to push large leaves out of her way to walk around her home.

She pulled a leaf off a hanging plant and added it to a small cauldron pot with a little water before she placed the pot over fire to bring to a boil.

Grabbing multiple glass jars from shelves, she placed them onto the table next to the injured creature and started checking them.

She held up an empty one. "Dammit. I forgot that I used the last of the sapphire petals on that sick lady."

Unbeknownst to all within the town she lived just outside of, Amalia was a Witch.

The humans wouldn't understand that she didn't have many skills past herbal medicines and was just a healer.

Although she knew her kind could be deadly and wielded powerful magic, she'd never had any way to train herself to do so. All she had were the two books she'd been given by her mother which consisted mostly of healing spells and teas.

Well, that wasn't necessarily true.

The books held other, more dangerous secrets, but she'd never used those for much other than to create fire for her hearth or make her plants healthier.

Amalia had never harmed another being in her life, and she'd much prefer to keep it that way.

In secret, she helped the humans when she could.

She offered them healing teas as gifts or gave them ointments she'd tell them she found on her travels. She also helped as a midwife to ensure both child and mother lived through the gruelling task of childbirth.

She just wanted to live peacefully in secret.

But without the petals, she couldn't help the strange lizard creature heal its bones. She could only help with its scratches and the pain – not until she got more, at least.

Putting away the jars she no longer needed, she started brewing a tea that would lessen its pain. Once it was cool enough, she tilted its head back and used a spoon to pour the contents into its mouth.

It was unconscious, but it still understood when liquid was going down its throat because it swallowed. She also covered its scales with an ointment that would heal its scratches.

Amalia examined its wings again.

With them broken, she was unsure how they were actually supposed to lay, so she wrapped them around its own body until all the disfigured bones were straight. She then strapped cloth around its torso, making sure to keep both its front and back legs free, to trap its wings to itself so it couldn't harm them further.

The storm outside was beginning to quieten, and she rubbed her cheek in tiredness. Bala hopped onto the table and knocked into her hands, making her slap herself. Amalia glared before she shooed him when he came to inspect the lizard.

"I can never trust you, you little cretin."

It is a flying creature, so it will not appreciate this, but I do not trust that cat. With an exhausted sigh, she lifted the towel and then opened a small birdcage she had inside her home, locking it in and, most importantly, Bala out.

After removing the key, she cleaned up her mess, except for the tea she would rewarm in the morning. Then she crawled into bed and closed her aching eyes.

In order to help the creature, she'd need to get up at first light.

Walking through a merchant town a little ways away from her home, Amalia tightened the travelling cloak propped over her head whenever anyone made eye contact with her.

Clagmore was a half day's walk through Dawnbrook forest. It wasn't the town closest to her cottage, but she trusted she'd find the sapphire petals here. She also planned to grab some extra supplies while she was out.

Her pale green dress revealed that she was nothing more than a simple peasant, and her thick wintery grey cloak wasn't out of place among the other weary travellers that came here. As a Witch, it was best she didn't look out of place among the humans.

As always, she met every vendor with kindness, even when they were rude or brash, much preferring to not irritate them.

That didn't mean her thoughts were pure.

Fat toad, she cursed at the baker handing her a softer loaf of bread after she told him the first one was stale.

He'd been trying to get rid of the previous days' baking and didn't appreciate that she'd picked up on it. He'd called her a peasant bitch and told her to get out of his shop after she paid, worried that other customers would overhear that he was selling stale bread.

Putting that unpleasant encounter behind her, she continued on her way to the rare herb salesman's store.

"Hello, Darth," she greeted when the bell rang, entering the loveliest smelling shop in the entire town.

She took in a large, healthy breath through her nose, sighing with contentment at the different aromas of flowers, spices, and herbs littering the air.

"Amalia! My most beautiful customer," the older man greeted. "It is always a pleasure to see you."

He was a nice human fellow with brown hair that was becoming peppered with white from his age. His face was bearded, but it was always kept short and trimmed with a moustache that would put most to shame. He obviously took great care with it and liked curling the ends.

"Shush," she hissed, placing a finger over her lips with a smile. "We do not want your wife overhearing you complimenting the local girls again."

He gave a bellowing laugh while wiping his spice covered hands on his brown apron behind the counter. "My wife does not mind as long it is only her I lay with at night. What can I get for you today?"

"You are too jovial, Darth. Women get insecure in their older years."

"I hope not. Even as a wrinkly old prune, I would still love that woman."

With a roll of her eyes, she looked over the counter as she spoke, "I am seeking more sapphire petals."

"More? But you just got some a little while ago." He walked to the back of his shop where his more expensive products were kept. "Ah, here we go."

He didn't come out straight away, eyeing her from deep within the dimly lit room. When he did, he held two large jars instead of one.

"I also got a rare item in since you were here last. Knowing you, you probably already have it... But do you have any sun sap?"

She thought for long moments. She knew she didn't have any, but she tried to remember if she'd ever needed it before or if it was an ingredient in one of her medicine books.

"Now, missy. I know you keep a constant mental list of the contents in that home of yours, so you must not have it then. Because it is you, I will sell you a jar for half price."

"I do not know if I need it, though."

"I heard that it is hard to get a hold of and has apparent healing properties, if you believe in that sort of thing." Although Darth didn't believe he sold anything of magical value, Amalia knew better. "It also tastes like the sweetest honey you have ever tasted."

Always an up-seller. Darth could rob a person blind if they stood in his shop with a heavy pouch of coin.

"You know I have a sweet tooth, you cunning man. Fine, I will take a full jar of sapphire petals and half a jar of sun sap. Where does it come from?"

He took the single jar she'd brought with her and grabbed another, which she would have to pay for, from under his counter.

"A place high in the mountains somewhere. It comes from underneath the bark of a certain type of tree that only grows at that altitude where the sun can always reach them. I do not know if I believe that story, but I think it is actually named because of the colour of it." He placed the jars on top of the counter, and she exchanged coin for it. "There you go."

She examined the golden yellow, thick liquid. Sure enough, it looked like pure drops of sunlight.

"Thank you, Darth. I will make sure to visit soon."

"Careful out there, alright?" Her head perked up at his serious tone. "I heard some Witches are roaming these parts lately. You know what they can be like. Evil little wenches."

"I will be fine. You worry too much."

She gave a bright smile before placing the items in her carry basket. Covering it with a piece of cloth to hide its contents, she left his shop.

Once a good distance away, she let that smile fall. Amalia didn't believe Witches were good or evil, but the more harmful the source of their magic, the more corrupt they became.

Herbs, spices, plants – they were generally considered light magic. Anything that required death or blood was considered dark, and Amalia had drawn that line in the sand a very long time ago.

People often spoke about them in hushed whispers but had little information on them. That was beneficial for someone like her who just wanted to be left alone.

After obtaining everything she needed from the merchant town, she raised her hand to her brows to shield her eyes, checking the location of the sun before heading home.

Horse-pulled carriages passed her much slower walking speed, and she made sure to stay off the dirt road to avoid being hit or shouted at.

Amalia didn't particularly know how she felt about meeting other Witches. Just because of the overall hatred humans seemed to have for them, she didn't know if she could trust them. *But I want to learn more spells.*

She wanted to grow stronger, but she didn't crave power like many of them apparently did. That's all she really knew about them, though, since her mother had given her little information about her own kind.

All she was told was to avoid them unless she knew they were a light Witch.

With her lack of experience, how was she supposed to know the difference if she met one? She looked like an average human unless she wielded her magic.

Perhaps I should keep my head down until I know they are gone.

Nobody bothered her as she made her way back through the town closest to her cottage. The two towns, Lacmain and Clagmore, were connected by the Dawnbrook forest. Her house and woodlands were on the other side of Lacmain.

The townspeople knew she lived there. It was built by her father who had been a high-ranking human soldier. He'd been given permission to build in the woods by the nobleman who ruled this town, wanting a quiet life after the warring in the west was finished.

Unfortunately, after the last time he'd gone to fight, he'd never returned. There had been no quiet life for him to retire into. Still, her father's respect outlived his life. She and her mother had lived there until one day she just up and left, too depressed by her husband's passing.

Amalia had been heartbroken, but she knew how much her mother had loved her father. She truly believed their love expanded over time, and that they would meet each other in their future lives.

War plagued the lands to the west and south borders, and the Western King demanded every able body willing to fight. Although she was upset without her parents, it was what many of the people had to endure during these difficult times of war.

She wouldn't dare pity herself when others were fighting to live just as much as she was.

Her parents had been hoping for her to marry so they could have their little cottage to themselves, but they never got the chance to. Instead, she now occupied it.

Simple, sweet, peasant Amalia, who no one really knew.

Her life hadn't been easy, but she thought she had proven to herself that she could withstand anything.

She smiled as she opened the door to her cottage.

Bala, obviously hiding in the trees, ran in behind her and

almost knocked her forward when he bashed into the back of her knees.

"You feral little cretin!" she yelled, grasping her basket to her chest to protect it. "Why are you such a pest? If you cannot be good, go find some other sympathetic female to feed you."

She dumped her basket onto the dining table and checked that everything was okay. Bala jumped on as well and stood above her basket, pawing at the covering. He expected her to have something for him.

Which she did. *Smart cat.*

She opened a small paper bag to reveal the fresh fish she'd bought from the market.

Holding it by the tail fins, she held it above the ground, and he hopped to the floor while staring up. He pawed at the air, impatient as always, and Amalia threw it out the front door.

When he ran after it, she closed him outside.

She walked over to the long-dead cooking fire and held her hand above it. With a small, quiet chant, energy pulsated from her hand and fire burst to life.

She brought the saucepan pot of tea she'd made the night before over the fire and left it to boil. Then she started preparing the medicine she needed the sapphire leaves for. Although she knew the recipe by memory, she grabbed a spell book to check its other recipes for their ingredients and all their uses.

Darth, you brilliant man. He was correct, sun sap did have healing properties if it was mixed into ointment, oils, and creams. The person would need to sit in the sun with it on. If eaten, all it did was substitute for honey.

Grinding all the herbs and spices she needed for her potion with her mortar and pestle, she added a small amount of the sun sap and the morning dew she collected most days. It turned it into a thick liquid paste.

Once she was done, she placed a small cup with the tea and

a spoon on the table next to it. After pulling the key from the top drawer of her nightstand, she opened the birdcage and carefully reached in to grab the limp lizard.

Startled, it suddenly woke and stumbled to the back of the cage. It appeared disorientated; its eyes unfocused while its head lulled about.

"Shhh... shhh," she whispered to it.

She followed it with her hands, chasing it around the small cage. Then it bit her!

With a cry, she pulled her hand back to look at the muscle right below her thumb where it had bitten her. She gave it a foul glare when she realised she was bleeding.

Shaking its head as if to clear it, it returned her look.

"You stupid little thing!" She shoved her hands back inside the cage. "I am trying to help you!"

It bit her again, but this time into her wrist. She let it bite her so she could grab the sides of it, wincing when it shook its head to worsen the damage. As she pulled it to her chest, she cradled it while grabbing the towel it'd been laying on.

"You better not bite my tit." As if it understood her, it did just that. "Ow!"

Wrapping the creature in the towel so it couldn't run or crawl away when she put it down, it struggled against its weak bonds. She grabbed a rag from the kitchen to wipe the blood from her hand, and unfortunately, her breast.

Then, Amalia sat down at the dining table in front of it, plopping herself into the wooden chair with a *grumph*.

"Stop fighting. You will hurt yourself worse."

It snapped its mouth at her, revealing sharp pointed fangs. Then it opened its maw wide in her direction.

She thought it was yawning, but it closed its mouth and went cross-eyed while staring at its own snout. It was like it expected something else to happen. It tried again, appearing to yawn, and then looked at its own snout in confusion.

It did it against the table, and when nothing happened again, it glared at her. She knew it was a glare; a hateful, menacing little glare.

"I do not know why you are looking at me like that when I have done nothing to hurt you."

She placed her chin in her hand as she waited for the creature to finish having its tantrum.

"Are you not in pain, little creature?" she asked before carefully patting the top of its head with a forefinger.

It froze, its eyes wide as it turned to her. It looked horrified that she'd touched it.

With a sigh, she dipped a finger inside the tea to check that it wasn't too hot. Deciding it wasn't, she grabbed a spoonful and tried to get the lizard to open its mouth.

It gave a hissing squeal, and she giggled.

"That is a rather cute sound you have there."

She giggled harder when the contents of her tea spilt over its head because it knocked it away with its snout. She knew the tea wouldn't hurt its eyes, but it gave it a sweet bath. The second time, it grabbed the spoon with its teeth and pulled it from her grasp.

The wooden cutlery clanked against the timber floor.

With an exasperated sigh, she picked up the spoon, placed it on the kitchen counter, and grabbed a clean one.

"You are rather odd, are you not?" It stopped to stare at her. "I am not surprised that you are afraid of me, and you probably do not understand me, but I am sincerely trying to help you."

When it was distracted by trying to escape, she forcefully grabbed it around its fat head. Its eyes widened when she expertly squished the sides of its jaws to pry its mouth open.

She dumped a spoonful of tea in its mouth, pushed its head back, and forced it to drink. It squirmed, and she found it an honest struggle to fight it.

You sure are strong for something so tiny!

Before it could get out of her grasp, she gave it more.

Amalia released it and waited, still amazed at its strength. Eventually it ceased struggling, and its eyes drooped.

"See? Is that not better?" It turned to her with another foul glare. "Do not give me that look."

Then, to its apparent shock, she poked it in the head.

"What are you, anyway?" It frowned, staring up at her so defencelessly with narrowed eyes. "I do not think I have ever seen anything like you before."

She placed her chin back into one of her hands while she patted the top of its head with her other.

"I am sorry Bala attacked you. He is such a feral little cat, but I cannot help loving the stray. Then again, you might have drowned in the storm if he did not find you."

It was calmer now that it wasn't in as much pain, and it allowed her to drain more tea into its mouth.

"If I unwrap you, are you going to bite me again?"

That glare came back.

Only realising now that she was still bleeding, she wiped her hand with the rag again.

"You have quite the nasty bite." She shook her long hair around her shoulders. "It would be easier if I could talk to animals. I could explain to you that you are injured, and I am only trying to help."

She'd never taken care of something with so many sharp teeth before.

"Screw it. You are not the first animal to bite me while I care for it."

She laughed when she started to unwrap it from the towel. As soon as it was free, it ran. Amalia grabbed it by the tail and pulled it back before it fell off the edge of the table.

While grabbing its face, she held its mouth shut and a hiss resonated from it. She tucked it into her armpit so she had freedom to undo the cloth she wrapped its wings and torso in the night before. It tried to flap them, and struggled harder when she rubbed ointment onto each one. She also smeared it over its scratches until it was completely covered in a slippery film of medicine.

While she was still holding it, she walked outside and sat on the front step of her porch to hold it in the sun.

"Would you just stop struggling?" she groaned while digging her fingers in so it couldn't get away. "I have never met an animal as stubborn as you. Eventually you all calm when you realise I am not trying to hurt you, but you are just being a rude prick now."

It did, in fact, stop squirming to stare up at her.

"Once you are better, I can let you back into the wild where you belong. Until then, you need to start behaving or it's going to take longer."

It kept its body still, but tugged its head so she would let it go.

"Promise not to bite?"

She knew talking to it wasn't going to matter, nor was she expecting an answer. But she found if she talked to an injured creature, they would calm sooner.

She finally released its face and its head shot back before it turned it to her, like it was assessing her. Careful of its injured wings, she held its sides and let it bake in the sun. *I have never worked with sun sap before. Hopefully it helps to heal it faster.*

Bala came up to sit at her ankles to watch them. She should have known he was up to something because he swatted the lizard in the snout.

"You cretin!" She booted him away, and he hissed before running off. She tilted the lizard a little towards her face. "Sorry about that. He has absolutely no manners."

Figuring its back had spent enough time in the sun, she

flipped it over. It looked horrified and squirmed its cute, little legs in the air.

"Be patient. The ointment requires to be in the sun to work best. When the scratches underneath you are gone, we will only have to work on your wings."

It didn't care; it just kept squirming. Amalia rolled her eyes.

Once they'd spent enough time in the sun, she took it back inside and forced it to drink more tea.

"What do you eat?"

She kept a close eye on it on the table while she went to the kitchen to grab a handful of different food. After offering it some carrot, potato, and celery, to no avail, she tried fruit. It huffed at the food before turning its head away. At least it was behaving by staying on the towel.

"Perhaps you eat meat?"

She dug into the basket she'd taken into town for the other piece of fish she'd bought.

"This is a secret between me and you, okay?" It blinked at her with a lack of understanding. "Fish is Bala's favourite. He would be upset if he found out I was giving you the second piece I got for him."

It started to eat it raw, and a small smile curled her lips.

"So, you are definitely a carnivore. Tomorrow I will go into the town and buy some food for you."

It eyed her when she leaned closer to inspect its dark purple scales and, strangely enough, its silver eyes.

"Even with your mangled broken wings, you are rather cute, are you not?"

Only Amalia would find a biting, sharp-toothed creature adorable.

She went to pat it again, but it stopped eating and snapped its jaws at her, grasping the fish tighter in its foreclaws. It slid it closer to its chest protectively.

"Stop being a pain, Mr. Lizard. Or is it Miss Lizard? I cannot tell." It continued to eat again. "Hmm, since you are such a pretty violet, I am going to call you Lady Lizard."

She could only assume it was a girl.

She still didn't know what species it was. She'd already gone through the books on her shelf detailing magical creatures, and none of the illustrations matched the strange little lizard.

At its new name, it stared at her through the corner of its eye. Then, very slowly, almost with exaggeration, it continued to pick the fish clean around bone.

When it wasn't looking, she picked up its tail – which almost gained her another scar from its bite. Then she remembered her hand. She started lathering that same ointment she'd put on the lizard onto her wound.

Amalia crinkled her nose.

"You do not have a disease, do you? Last thing I want is to get sick because of some lizard." Then she gave a burst of laughter. "Would that not just be ironic? A Witch dying by a sickness."

It saw no humour in what she said.

"You are not laughing only because you cannot understand me. I assure you, I am quite hilarious."

And then it started. The pesky, annoying wailing that she could never, ever, ignore. Rushing to the door, she shoved it open and Bala sauntered in.

"Yes, your highness. Your bed awaits you."

He didn't often come to sleep in her home, but she always allowed him in when he wanted to. Actually, she found he'd been here more over the last two days than he ever usually was. Sometimes she wouldn't see him for days.

"Sorry Lady Lizard, but you are going to have to go back into the birdcage."

It started squirming in her hands. When she tried to put it

inside, it held onto the sides of the cage door for dear life, refusing to go in. There were a few moments of struggle where she pushed its back to get it inside, and it pushed away from the cage.

She laughed. She couldn't help it. She stood stuck, laughing while pushing its arse while its hands and feet had a death grip on the cage as it pushed back.

"I think this is the most fun I have had taking care of an animal, but I do not particularly want to wake up to a massacre because you became cat food. Now, in you go."

She shoved hard, forcing it in and immediately closed the door. Quickly locking it, the creature swiped through the bars with its front claws at her, hissing in rage.

"Come, Bala. I will make us both something to eat."

She knew the feral cat wouldn't be able to get to the birdcage while she slept.

Well into the next day, banging at the door brought Amalia out of a trance as she sat at the dining table watching the brooding little lizard.

It wasn't happy with her again because she'd bathed it so she could reapply the medicine, and it definitely hadn't appreciated her lifting its tail to rub its bottom from behind.

"You are just as bad as Bala!" she'd yelled when it scratched and bit her.

With the way it was reacting, someone would think she was trying to drown the thing.

Once it was calm, but obviously seething, she'd forced it to drink more tea and she put more ointment on its wounds. Then they lazily sat in the sun together.

She was a little concerned that the medicine had done absolutely *nothing* to start mending it. Its wings were in the exact same state they'd been in the day before, and even its scratches weren't healing.

It was odd. With humans, she couldn't explain why their bones or bodies suddenly mended without being accused of being a Witch, so she diluted the remedies she provided. But with animals, she could heal them as fast as she wanted with stronger ointments. Even though she knew the bones might take time, the scratches, at least, should be gone by now.

At the knocking, Amalia gave no warning and tossed the lizard into the birdcage so the humans couldn't see it. If they found she was harbouring such a strange creature, they might steal it and do unthinkable things.

She ran to the door when the person on the other side started yelling for her while bashing.

"Victoria, what is the matter girl?" she asked the child who was huffing like she'd just ran as if her life depended on it.

This was a child of one of the townsfolk who always greeted Amalia when she was in the town. With her long, beautiful, brown hair and wild freckles dotting her cheeks, Amalia always thought she looked cute.

"Miss Swafford, please come. Alesia's baby is coming!"

Amalia's eyes widened. She quickly rummaged through her home, shoving everything she needed into her basket. Within only a few minutes, she was rushing to the town with the young child next to her.

It was a long and painful birth. There had been much screaming and so much blood. Unfortunately, Amalia had been the one to share the terrible news with the father that the mother might not make it.

Amalia was tired, physically, mentally, and magically drained. Her clothing was covered in blood that was not her own, but she at least managed to remove her bloodied apron and wash her skin clean before she'd left.

That poor woman, was all Amalia could think.

She returned home with her heart paining her. All she wanted to do was bathe and curl into a ball on her bed.

When the door opened, she saw Bala hanging from the bottom of the birdcage and the creature inside swiping its claw at Bala's paw. Both were making angry, ferocious, hissing noises.

Amalia burst into tears and fell to her knees in the

doorway. She couldn't handle anything more right now. She hadn't had time to process the loss of someone she'd known for most of her life. Someone she had failed to save.

Immediately they both stopped. Bala let go to land on his feet while the lizard began staring at her like it always did. But the damage was already done. She lacked energy left to fight back her tears.

She was hoping Bala was coming to comfort her and she opened her arms so she could cuddle into him. *Please help me to feel better.*

Instead, the selfish cat just walked next to her and out the door with his head held up high.

"You are such a bastard!"

She slammed the door behind him with her boot. Then she folded her knees so she could hug her legs and cry into them. For a long while, she just sobbed her sadness away, wanting nothing more than to curl away from the disappointment in herself.

When she heard the birdcage creak as it swung on its small chain, her head shot up to see the lizard moving around.

It must be in pain. With a sniffle, tears still falling, she walked over to the cage and unlocked it.

"Please do not be mean to me right now, Lady Lizard," she begged while reaching inside.

She needed a distraction. She needed something to keep her occupied as she grieved for the woman she'd been unable to save.

It freely let her pick it up.

She placed it on the towel and started the cooking fire to warm the fresh tea she made earlier that day.

Amalia stopped crying by the time everything was warmed and ready, getting the lizard to drink the tea that would elevate its pain. She sniffled while she worked and, to her surprise, it did everything it was supposed to, putting up no fight against her.

It took healthy mouthfuls of the tea, but when she started putting the ointment on its mangled wings, her eyes darted wildly over it. The tears started again as though she was nothing more than a child who had no control over its emotions.

"Why are you not healing?" she asked it with a sob. She felt like a failure.

Unable to stop them, she carefully put the lizard down on the table and started crying heavily. She folded her arms and rested them upon the table, burying her head against them.

"Why could I not save her?"

Deep down inside, Amalia knew it wasn't her fault. Still, she couldn't stop blaming herself. Alesia had been heavy with twins, and no matter how much of the potion she had prepared and lathered on her hands, it made no difference. No matter how much she quietly chanted even with other midwives in the room, no matter how much she prayed for her life, she'd eventually lost the fight.

"I was not able to stop her pain. She just kept bleeding," she blubbered. "And now those poor babies are going to be raised without their mother."

Amalia had really tried *everything* in her power.

She turned up to the lizard, seeing it was watching her from the towel she'd placed it on. "I wanted so badly to save her. Why am I so useless? Why is my magic so weak?"

It twisted its head at her, those silver eyes glancing between both of her own.

"No." She gave it a fright when she scooped it into her hands. "There has to be another reason why I cannot save you either."

She started checking over it, lifting each wing carefully before checking its paws. Her check was thorough, and she knew it didn't like when she lifted its tail from behind.

"Have you been hexed by one of those pixie vermin?"

It darted its head towards her.

Pixies were just as small as fairies, and although most people rarely got the chance to see either of them, there was a big difference between the two. Fairies were sweet and playful, eating fruit and nuts. Pixies were naughty and mischievous, eating meat and bugs.

Both had magical capabilities and could cast minor spells.

A fairy would never harm another, but pixies went out of their way to. It wouldn't be the first time she'd experienced dealing with their naughty magic.

The lizard squirmed when she picked it up and walked over to the bookcase.

She pulled the book she wanted from it and tossed it carelessly onto the table, hearing it thud, before flicking through the pages. But it wasn't a page from the book she wanted but rather a piece stored in it from another, torn and put inside this one. It contained a spell that revealed hidden hexes or curses, and on the back was one that could reverse it depending on how strong it was.

She found it and memorised the chant. It didn't matter that the moon wasn't full, as long as she was bathed in moonlight it would reveal if there was a magical imprint on the creature.

Her determination made her tears stop.

"I will not fail you too."

She took the creature outside and stood in the moonlight, thankful there were minimal clouds.

Panic was obvious on its face when she started chanting while holding the creature out from her. She spoke the words carefully and focused her magic.

Closing her eyes, she felt the pulsate of warm essence pouring from her hands.

The lizard struggled harder, frantic now, but she knew the spell had worked when she opened her eyes. Then she blinked.

The spell was supposed to reveal the left-over magic on a being, whether animal or human. The entire thing was glowing!

"Well, that is strange," she whispered. "Why are you completely glowing? Only magical creatures glow like this."

It snapped its teeth at her multiple times while giving her that hissing squeal. She grabbed the back of its head and pushed it forward so she could examine the dark spot she could see.

"There it is. There is the hex. I was right!"

Right between the wings protruding from its back was a dark mark and symbol she didn't recognise. She figured the creature's magic was stronger than the hex, but it was unable to break it by itself.

Maybe it does not even know that it has been cursed.

She turned it, lifting the creature to her eye level so they could look at each other. It tried biting her nose, but she dodged it just in time.

"No wonder I was not able to heal you. Something else is at work here. Now, Lady Lizard, I have only broken a few hexes, but hopefully I can get rid of this one."

It paused its struggles to twist its head at her, so she moved her head the same way to copy it.

"Why are you looking at me like that for?"

There was nothing she could do for Alesia. She had tried everything, had maybe even risked her own life. Life and death were an inevitability, and she'd long ago accepted it after her parents. But one thing she would do was save this creature.

She worked tirelessly throughout the night to follow the handwritten instructions on the parchment. There was a special footnote, but it wasn't something she'd ever needed to add before.

Once she had all her candles ready after drawing the

correct symbols on the ground, she wrapped the lizard in the towel so it couldn't escape. She placed it in the middle of the circular spell drawing.

She started chanting. Amalia hated removing hexes because it made her lethargic afterwards, but that was a part of her job as a good Witch. The creature was still glowing and would continue to glow until the sun rose, but it meant she would be able to see if she removed the hex.

A swirl of magic came from the chalk circles she'd drawn on the ground surrounding the creature, and she sensed the energy pulsating all the way up to the very end of the chant. Then it burst out with a gust of wind, telling her the spell had completed.

With a smile, she picked up the lizard and unwrapped it.

Her smile fell when it bit her. Not because of the bite, but because she could still see the hex on it.

But I followed the instructions. I have always been able to remove a pixie hex. They always placed them on animals they wanted to eat. Bala would sometimes get to them first and bring them home. *Why did it not work?*

She eyed the parchment, making sure she did everything correctly. When she knew that she had, she eyed that footnote – the one she'd always ignored.

"I should not..."

Then again, how much trouble could she get herself into?
As long as nobody finds out... I should be okay, right?

Its eyes widened when she wrapped it in the towel again and placed it in the circle. Unlike before, she brought a knife with her.

She restarted the chant, but this time she brought the tip of the knife down her wrist to let her own blood drip into the circle she'd drawn.

Swirling energy started back up, pulsating with more magic than before since she had added her own essence into it. Along with that burst of magic wind at the end of her spell was a small burst of flame.

The circle charred into the wooden floor of her cottage, carving into it permanently with scorch marks. The sound of crackling was loud until the fiery glowing faded.

Without care for her floors, she scooped up the creature and unfurled it from the towel. It was far angrier now, refusing to allow her to hold it as it clawed and bit rapidly. She bit back her cry of pain when it latched on, trying to ignore the panicking animal as she searched its back.

The hex symbol was gone.

"It worked," she whispered with a shaky voice, immediately feeling queasy. "I lifted the hex. I should be able to heal you now."

The creature stopped its attack. It tried to look over its shoulder like it had an understanding of what she'd said.

She started lathering it in the ointment. Even without the sun, it should still work, and she'd add another layer in the morning.

"I do not feel so good," she mumbled when her vision began to waver.

She'd never felt like this before after a spell. Her sight split into two, and her ears felt like they were stuffed with cotton. Her knees wobbled, and she stumbled with the lizard in her arms, almost dropping it.

Her mind felt dizzy, her energy completely drained. She made her way to the birdcage and placed it inside to make sure it was safe from Bala. She didn't know how the cat managed to do it, but he would somehow get inside her cottage when she wasn't looking.

Just as she locked the cage door, she fell. Her eyes rolled back, and she knew she was fainting from the deafening sound that roared in the silence of her room.

She passed out before she even hit the hard ground.

Amalia woke with a start by the worst sound she'd ever heard. It was right there, right next to her ear, *screaming* at her.

"Bala, you absolute pain in the ass. Shut the hell up!" The whining cat stopped and instead hopped up to stand on her chest, like he wanted to weigh her down. She opened her eyes and picked up the big cat by cupping his chest. "Why? Why are you like this?"

It pawed at her head, smacking her with quick taps. She could barely defend herself as she threw her head side-to-side in a failed attempt to dodge.

Amalia sat up and found herself on the cold ground as she held him in one arm. She was still a little dizzy, but at least she remembered everything.

It'd felt like every ounce of magic and strength she'd possessed had been sucked away from her. Clenching and unclenching her free hand, she knew it was only temporary.

Her stomach gave a ravenous rumble, and she got to her feet so she could raid the kitchen for all the fruit she could find. She also fed Bala since he wouldn't shut up and then sent him outside to be the stray he was.

Eating while nursing a headache, her eyes fell onto the creature she currently had in a cage.

It was already watching her. She noticed it did that a lot.

"And how to do you feel, you lucky bastard?"

It appeared to glare, so she turned her sight down to her arms.

The cut down her forearm needed cleaning and medicine, and so did all the scratches and bite marks. They weren't small either. There were bruises around every sharp and deep fang mark, showing just how upset it'd been.

Since she waited so long to do anything about them, she knew they would scar. If she had put medicine on before she'd passed out, she may have been able to fix her skin completely.

Like a new daily ritual, she boiled the tea and collected the ointment she had ready for the creature. It wasn't happy with her, but it did let her freely grab it from the cage – once she found the key she'd dropped, that is.

She gave it the tea and let its effects start working before she lifted its wings.

"Your scratches are gone, and your wings are already healing. Maybe tomorrow I can free you. I know how much you want to be free of me." She poked its hard chest, and it snapped its teeth near her finger. "You do not like me very much, do you?"

Whatever. She lathered its wings and the centre of its back with the medicine before she took it outside to sit with it in the sun on her steps. Gently holding its underbelly, the warm light washing over them was refreshing.

"I still feel terrible that I could not save Alesia." Her shoulders slumped. "She was rather young, and her husband must be devastated. It is not very often I cannot save someone giving birth, but sometimes there is just too much damage."

She placed the animal on her lap, hoping it wouldn't scuttle away and she wouldn't be forced to chase it through the forest. It didn't, and she was able to prop her elbows behind her against the porch stairs.

She stared out at the thick brush of woodlands before her just past the small clearing surrounding her home. It was eerily quiet, except for the odd bird that squawked in the distance.

"I have never done blood magic before removing your hex. Which, by the way, I am rather curious about. That was no pixie hex. That was something much more powerful." It eyed her suspiciously with its snout bunching. She turned her head away from it to lift her face to the beautiful and welcoming sun. "But now I am left wondering... Perhaps if I had done it before, I may have been able to save her."

She curled her arms around the lizard, not to trap it, but to lean against her legs as she looked down.

"Is dark magic really that bad if it can be used to save people? Now, do not get me wrong, Lady Lizard. I think using parts of animals is the absolutely worst way to go about it."

Sometimes with the way this creature stared at her when she spoke, she felt like it was listening to her. It didn't seem as uncomprehending as other animals did. She thought there may even be intelligence there.

Like now, with how its emotions seemed to reflect her words.

Blank when she spoke of Alesia, but then it almost seemed angry that she had suggested the use of dark magic. Only when she added that she didn't want to harm animals, did its gaze soften.

"Why can I not use my own blood?" It tilted its head. "I am not harming anyone or anything if I use my own power. It would mean I could save more people. Why can I not do that?"

She checked the lizard's wings gingerly with her fingertips, lifting them to see they were healing further. She knew the longer they stayed in the sun, the faster it would heal, so she continued to sit with it.

"I probably will not do it again, though. It harbours far too much risk. I just want to live in peace and help those around me that I can. If I start down that path, the townsfolk may start to notice." Then she gave a small laugh which startled the wee creature. "They would probably run afraid if I just started cutting myself in the town. They could even throw me in the lunatic asylum for women."

She smiled down, and it twisted its fat head at her.

"Are you feeling any better?"

For the first time since Bala had brought it inside, the creature moved its wings. She heard cracking sounds as it stretched them, most likely popping the bones back into their rightful places.

"That tea works wonders, does it not? You would not have been able to do that on your own."

It snapped its head to her with a glare. That glare deepened when she started prodding its back while moving her fingers in a circle. When it tried to bite her, she tapped it on the snout. It looked at her in shock, like it was dumbfounded she had the audacity to smack it.

"It is called a massage, you ungrateful sod."

Since its back wouldn't be riddled with so much pain, she could do this now along with other things to help it heal.

Eventually, the stiffness the lizard had been holding in its body since it arrived started to loosen. It even sprawled on its stomach down her thighs with its back legs stretched back while the front seemed to reach forward.

She peeked over to see its eyes were drooping, barely blinking, like at any moment it might fall asleep.

Such a weird creature.

She has me trapped in this damn cage again.

Rurik growled quietly to himself while watching the Witch potter around her pathetic peasant home from the window outside.

He was angry that she'd made him fall asleep just by prodding his back with her nimble fingers. With the tea she was forcing down his throat, the ointment now actually working, and her fingers expertly getting at his sore and tense muscles, she'd completely relaxed him.

He hadn't even woken when she'd picked him back up. He put it down to being in too much pain to rest beforehand.

However, he'd definitely woken up when she'd pushed him into water, that was for sure. He was embarrassed by the fact she'd bathed him... again! He'd bitten her for doing it, and she'd tapped him on the forehead because of it.

Him! *How dare she treat one such as myself like this!* She kept smacking him, and the only reason he hadn't unleashed his fury upon her was because she was aiding him.

Until his wings were healed, he was stuck like this.

Well, that was not necessarily true.

He could revert back to his true size, but with his wings still unusable he'd be a sitting duck. Either a different Witch would stumble upon him, or a useless human would, starting a battle he didn't wish to fight in his injured state.

So, he allowed this filthy *Witch* to care for him in the hopes it wasn't a trap, and that she truly intended to release him.

After she smacked him, he'd held in his want to let loose every ounce of his fury and allowed her to bathe him. Then he had to deal with her slippery hands while she put something over his scales and tender wings.

He shuddered with disgust that this woman was touching him with her hands and magic.

Obviously, whatever concoction she was using required sunlight because she hung his birdcage outside so she didn't have to hold him while he soaked it in. He was offended she didn't want to! Like... he wasn't worth holding.

He felt conflicted about the pretty thing – and she really was a pretty thing, even for a lowly *Witch*.

She had long blonde hair that was straight near the roots of her head before spiralling into large curls that framed a very soft and easy to look upon face. Her long lashes were dark, like her eyebrows, but they framed spell-binding blue eyes – Azure blue, like a shallow lake.

Rurik didn't just hate Witches, he detested them all the way down to his soul. Yet, he could tell this one wasn't inherently evil. Actually, she appeared to be quite kind, very nurturing even. She had no reason to take care of an injured creature like himself, and yet she was.

He'd also watched her sob like a child over some useless human because... *Something about not being able to save her?*

He'd barely been paying attention since he had been plotting his escape. He'd been scheming as to how he could trick her so he could run away because she hadn't been able to heal him.

Then last night, he'd watched with abject horror at her using blood magic, *evil* magic, to remove the hex he'd already known was on his body. Not only had she done it, but she'd done it to him! *Blasphemy!*

He couldn't believe he'd allowed her to do such a thing to him, even though she'd removed what was stopping him from healing by doing so.

He didn't like her simply because of what she was, but he also didn't find her particularly... unpleasant. Although... her constant chattering to him was irritating.

She also did keep saving him from that blasted cat that tried to eat him.

He felt shame at the fact he'd almost been taken down by nothing but a house pet, but it's not like he was the one who'd delivered the hex. No, that was one of *her* kind.

He glared at the Witch again through the window.

They were hunting him, just as he was hunting them.

His glare softened when she came outside to check on him by pulling his wing up through the cage. He let her, knowing he would leave quicker if she knew he was healed.

"Look, Lady Lizard. Your wings are getting better by the hour."

She kept calling him that, and it grated on his nerves. He was not a girl, but indeed a male.

He was also not a lizard.

He could tell her, call her stupid for not knowing what species he was. But then, he'd be the idiot for revealing that to her, or that he could talk.

She might extract him for parts then like the rest of her vile kind liked to do to his. That's why he hated her, hated her kind.

Bloodthirsty, power-hungry Witches.

They scoured the land for his kind so they could pull them apart and use their wings, their blood, their scales, bones, horns, tail, *anything* to fuel their morbid and sick magic. Even his cock wouldn't be spared that defilement.

So no, he wouldn't be telling this female anything. He'd let her believe that he was some kind of strange flying lizard, and hopefully she'd let him go. He wouldn't abide by his kind's laws that dictated he help her or guard her now that she'd saved him. Technically, he had a blood debt to her.

He wouldn't hold that up for a lowly Witch.

His debt would be repaid by him not destroying her house and snuffing out her life permanently on his departure. *I also will not tell my kin about her.*

Rurik was thankful for her, though.

He'd be dead if it wasn't for her, or at least still hexed. He would have been a broken creature, fighting off vermin just so he could take his next breath.

His home was too far from here to return to safely without the use of his wings.

He growled again as he remembered the particular curse that had been bestowed upon him. It was to stop him from healing by taking away his regenerative abilities. It also stopped his ability to morph, not in size, but in shape, because of how damaged he'd been.

He wondered if he'd be scarred from what had been done to him. This Witch's magic might heal him seamlessly if he was lucky, of course, combined with his own.

Fear like he'd never known had coursed through him when she had revealed that he was radiating magic by making him glow. He thought then and there she might grow evil.

She does not seem to care, though.

That had surprised him. Actually, she kept surprising him.

He kept thinking she'd suddenly become vile, turn on him, and because of his size, she'd think he'd be at her mercy. Rurik didn't like being at anyone's mercy and definitely didn't like feeling weak.

If they didn't call him by his current title, they would have called him Rurik the Vicious, or the Destroyer, or the

Vengeful. He wasn't some weak defenceless creature, but a deadly, sharp-toothed soldier. A warrior.

She is a kind soul, though. He crinkled his snout at having to think that of a Witch, but he couldn't deny it when it was so apparent.

Where is her coven? That was another reason he wasn't comfortable here.

Eventually, one of her coven Witches might visit her peasant home. This woman might show him to her visitor without knowing what he was and how much value he held to her kind. Then he'd be forced to morph his size so that he could kill them and escape.

He already knew he didn't want to harm this woman. She wouldn't be much of a challenge, either. *There is no sport in hunting the weak.*

Laying down with his head resting in the palm of one of his front paws, he watched the female move the dining table she kept laying him on like some injured baby bird. She pulled a wooden tub to where it had been, and he cringed when she filled the tub with nothing but magic.

He also may not want to kill her because she was pretty. *Very pretty,* he thought when he watched her disrobe from his perch near the window.

She was more than simply pretty, but he refused to allow himself to think anything higher than that about her. Even when she stripped down to nothing and was facing him in the water, showing him everything she had under that boring dress of hers.

It wasn't the first time he'd seen her naked. She didn't know that he had the capability to morph into a human male if he wished to.

He'd laid with a few human females for entertainment, but he'd rather slit a Witch's throat than fuck one.

Still, he was free to ogle this one at his own leisure, who

had no idea she'd just grasped her own breast with a soapy hand in front of him.

Her breasts weren't particularly large, but they looked firm. Round mounds just above a tucked in waist. *Her arse looks great though. Too bad it belongs to one of her ilk.* He'd seen it enough when she'd changed each day.

She soaped her other breast absentmindedly before rubbing her neck while stretching it to the side. Like she could feel his eyes on her, she turned her head to him. Her eyes squinted – a very assessing squint.

Should I turn away? He had to force his eyes not to flick in another direction. *No, no. If I do that, it will make it obvious.*

Rurik very much found humour in this. He was sure she'd be mortified that a sentient being was watching her bathe.

If this had been the previous day, he would have been glaring at her and wishing for freedom. Now that he was feeling better and freedom was on the horizon, he was allowing himself to relax.

In due time, I will be able to leave without her help. Once his wings healed completely, even if she didn't release him, she'd find his birdcage destroyed and him missing.

Seeming to think better of it, she turned in the water to give him her back. She settled back in to clean her body without him being able to see.

Pity, it just started getting good. He looked elsewhere since there would be no entertainment inside for him. He found that cat staring up at him from the ground.

It hissed when he met its eyes, no doubt knowing he wasn't some mere creature.

"Watch it, cat, or I will make a meal out of you when I leave," he warned it, knowing she wouldn't be able to hear him from inside.

That seemed to anger it further and it jumped for the cage, hanging from the bottom of it. Now that the hex was gone, he was able to release a fireball at its paw. The cat made a horrible cry and let go to flee into the woods.

The Witch, who had her back to him, had no idea about what just happened.

That had also been bothering him, that he'd been unable to release his breaths of fire. He'd tried to blast her when she'd pulled him from the cage the first time, and he'd been completely dumbfounded when nothing came out. He was thankful he was able to breathe fire again.

She didn't seem to know, but he'd been hexed twice.

It wasn't long before he watched her rise from the tub, giving him a view of that pert arse. Then she ducked out from sight only for the curtain to close a moment later.

Once she was dressed, she came outside to check on him.

"I do not like the way you watch me, Lady Lizard. Even though you are a girl, you make me nervous."

I am not a girl, you nitwit. Before he could glare at her though, she started to pull his cage down from its hook in the roof and brought him inside.

"Since you are a lizard, you must like the sun."

She placed his birdcage back on the hook inside but unlocked it so she could reach in to pull him out.

He hated that she carried him around like some form of pet. *I am a Witch-eating beast! Stop treating me like some poor puppy.*

His anger quickly deflated when she popped him on the table and offered him some meat. Eyeing her, he allowed her to feed it to him with her fingertips.

I could bite the tip of her thumb off. I really should.

He didn't and was rewarded by her shoving that damn spoon in his face. The tea tasted just fine, but it was imbued with witchcraft, and that's what really made him detest it.

To his discomfort, she picked him up and turned him around so he was no longer facing her. He didn't like having his back to her, so he tried to turn around. She forced him forward and slippery hands rubbed over his entire body. *More of that concoction.*

He didn't think he needed it anymore. Sure enough, the bones in his wings were almost aligned and he'd be able to flap them as much as his heart contented.

Flap them far, far away from here and this woman.

"You have healed quicker than any animal I have ever helped," she said when she was done with the concoction.

She massaged his twisted back – a product of his broken wings. Deciding he deserved to be pampered for being the awesome warrior he was, he let her.

"You must be full of magic then." His eyes squinted with suspicion at her words. "The only creatures who heal as well as you do are the fairies that visit me."

He snorted with his eyes rolling. *As if fairies would visit a Witch.* None of them would be that suicidal.

Turning his head to her, he gave a bored look at her lies. She didn't understand that's what it was.

"Do you hide like them? Is that why I do not know what you are?" It still confused him that she didn't know what he was. He thought Witches were raised from birth to know what his kind were – and to hunt them. "They come to me when they are injured. Sometimes they bring me animals that need help."

It was like she spoke the truth. He stared at those spellbinding blue eyes as she rubbed the top of his head, too distracted to notice by the look she gave him.

"I swat the pixies away with my broom, nasty little things. I do not understand why they are so mean. Then again, I have healed a few when Bala gets his fangs into them and brings them to my home."

She takes care of something as foul as pixies? Even he hated them, simply because they were foul, irritating creatures who liked to come into his home and play tricks on him.

He could only imagine what chaos he would return to when he went back.

"Fairies are such strange creatures, not as much as you, but still quite odd. They bring me crickets to heal."

He noticed she was patting his head and neck now. It felt nice, though, since they were soft gentle touches against his scales and spikes. It concerned him that she might be using magic to calm him, but he didn't think that was it.

"They are the ones that taught me that every life is sacred no matter how large or small. They taught me that everything with breath deserves to live. I often agree with them, even when they brought me that venomous viper."

She pulled up the sleeve of her dress all the way to her elbow to show him the snake fang marks.

"I felt terrible that I had to milk its venom to save myself, but if I had not, I would have died before I saved it."

Rurik didn't take his gaze away from her arm. Not because of her story, but because of the many small and white scars she had marring her tanned skin.

Other than his marks on her, he'd expected her skin to be perfect, like the rest of her kind. Like perfect porcelain. They usually healed themselves straight away to prevent any permanent marks on their bodies.

He could only deduce that she tended to the animal before healing herself like she had with him.

You are really an odd Witch, are you not?

"Do you have a partner, Lady Lizard?" *Great, I am to hear of her love life.* He could only imagine how long this would last. *Maybe she knows, and she wishes to torture me with boredom.* "Or are you a baby lizard? You are awfully small, but you do not look round and soft."

She poked his underbelly, and he was so offended he snapped at her finger.

I am no hatchling, you–

"I have never had a suitor. Rather difficult when you do not have parents to offer any worth to your marriage with a dowry."

He'd never thought on if her parents were to turn up.

Good, they are dead. Less Witches to hunt for. Maybe even he killed them.

That idea made him grin.

"Then again, I do not particularly want to be bound to another."

That caused him to raise a brow just as she started petting him again. He let her, suddenly interested in this conversation.

Although Witches were hateful things, they did indeed love heavy and hard. He'd used that to his advantage on many occasions to kill them.

Rurik was cruel enough to use their loved ones in traps.

"Maybe it is because sex is quite terrible."

He almost wanted to laugh. *I disagree, Witch.*

She rolled her eyes at her own thoughts before she said, "Perhaps it was just the stable boy, but it was rather sloppy and unimpressive. It was not very painful, which is what I had been warned of for my first time. Perhaps he was not adequate."

If he wanted to, he could horrify her by talking back to her. She would realise she had just spoken something he thought she might find embarrassing to say to him.

"His mouth also filled mine with saliva, and it was rude and disgusting!"

That was it! He had to turn away from her before he gave away that he was laughing.

"I plan to release you in the morning." He hadn't realised the sun went down until she said those words. "Your wings should be healed throughout the night. I would stay up and release you, but I want to make sure you will be comfortable in flight. I do not want some hawk taking you down before you return from where you came."

She leaned over the table to rest on it with one elbow, beginning to stroke him from the top of his head to between his sensitive wings. They shuddered lightly from her touch.

Why am I allowing her to touch me like this? It was so pleasant he didn't feel like running away from it. He didn't even allow his own kind to touch him like this, didn't allow them to touch him this... tenderly.

"If you ever need a safe place to return to, you are always welcome to rest here. You do not understand me so you probably will not, but I would not mind seeing you again. Especially since you have stopped biting me. Well... mostly."

She gave him a small smile, the kind that anyone, creature, human, or Witch, would want to return. *A smile that innocent does not belong on the face of a Witch.* It was sweet, filled with love and care.

I could stay another day. He didn't know why that thought came to him, but it might be so that he could see that kind of smile directed at him again.

"To make sure you are not slippery for your flight, though, I will have to bathe you first."

Never mind! I would rather not endure too many more of those.

She would lift his tail and rub him in places that were rather precarious. No warrior like him deserved that kind of shame.

He would never tell his kind of the days he'd spent in this peasant cottage.

5

Laying in his cage, Rurik let himself fall asleep once his wings had fully healed and he bore no more pain. The next time he left his birdcage, he knew he would be freed and was gaining strength for his flight home.

She'd brought in that cat when it started making the most horrible noises at the door, begging to be let in and fed. He didn't know why she put up with it, especially when she called it a cretin because it would try to trip her or wail some more.

It refused to sleep on the bed with her, instead choosing to lay on some of her herb racks or squish one of her plotted plants. The cat watched him often.

The only reason Rurik woke was because the Witch started groaning. When he unfurled his head from its tucked away position, he saw Bala smacking her in the face to wake her.

"What do you want, you rude bastard?"

She has quite the tongue for a pretty face. She often swore at him and that cat. The rest of the time, she came across as pure innocence.

The cat jumped down and headed to the door, scratching at it with a whine. With an aggravated sigh, she got up in her nightgown and opened the door for him.

She stood in the doorway and waited for his return for a

long while, yet she eventually came back inside without him. He tilted his head when she laid her back against the closed door with some strange expression on her face. She appeared paler.

Then her eyes fell to him. Suddenly she was in motion, rushing to the drawer next to her bed to fish out his key.

She has changed her mind. She is going to take me apart. He gave a hiss. It was actually a growl, but he knew it was too quiet to her ears to make out the difference.

He bit her to let him go, harder than he had before when she held him. She trapped his wings beside his body with her hands, his legs dangling as he kicked them.

She took him to the kitchen, and her hand reached out towards a large knife on the counter.

Just as he was about to change his size, destroy her home and possibly her, she'd grabbed a cloth instead of the knife next to it. Silently, she shoved that cloth into some water and started wiping him down.

She was removing her concoction from him.

Once it was done to the best of her abilities without shoving him in water, she walked over to the window. Grunting with hard tugs, she managed to get it open with one hand.

"I know I promised to let you rest, but I have changed my mind, Lady Lizard. It is time for you to go home."

I do not understand. He turned his head to the dark sky outside, the stars glittering on a perfect, cloudless night. *She promised to let me go when the sky was bright.*

"Please be safe, okay?" His eyes grew wide in surprised when she kissed the side of his head. He didn't try to bite her for it, too shocked that she'd done it in the first place. "I am glad I was able to save you."

Then she placed him on the windowsill. She tucked his tail carefully out of the way before she closed it, not allowing him back inside even if he wanted to.

He turned to watch her disrobing and put on a proper gown. *Why am I hesitating to leave?*

A screech got his attention just before that fat cat leapt for him on the windowsill. He quickly unfurled his wings to take flight, and the cat chased him through the forest.

It didn't follow him forever, but he was far enough away that he could no longer see the cottage through the trees. He stopped to land on a low hanging branch and stared back at the direction he came.

Strange. Then again, he did find the woman rather odd to begin with. *She just let me go in the middle of the night?* She'd kept her promise to release him, though. He was free of her, of his cage.

It is not my business to understand Witches.

He turned from the direction of the cottage and took flight once more, heading towards his home so he could rest properly and plan for his next hunt.

He'd come to this part of the world for a reason.

But something nagged him on the back of his scales. It worsened the further away he got.

It was that face, the one she'd given him when he thought she was planning on gutting him for his entrails. After she slammed the door closed, it looked like the face of fear.

No, she is a Witch. I kill her kind, destroy them. He pushed his wings harder to leave, hoping distance would help him to clear his mind. *She has probably been called to be a midwife again so she can let that human die too.*

That nagging on his scales didn't diminish.

The moon shifted further down, telling him some time had passed since he'd been flying.

"Damn blood debts!" Rurik growled to the sky when he dipped one of his wings to turn around. "I will just check on her. She is probably telling that blasted cat off again!"

I cannot believe I am wasting my time on a lowly Witch.

Before Amalia could place her boots on her feet, a soldier kicked down the door.

She hadn't even gotten the chance to scream before she was gagged, while two sets of hands grabbed her wrists to bind them together with rope.

Her fingers were interlocked so she couldn't weave any magic, and she was pushed to the ground on her front. Metal shackles were not only placed on her wrists but her ankles as well.

"Look at the ground! She really is a Witch," one of the soldiers said to the others.

She turned her head to the charred circle and symbols on her timber flooring, the result of her using blood magic to remove the hex from the lizard.

"Has no one ever been inside her home?" another said, pointing at all the herbs and spices everywhere.

Their eyes scanned her simple home with anger and shock.

There were three of them. One held her down while the other two began to destroy all of her precious jars. Her home. They went through her small bookshelf and one soldier took her two spell books. He held the books up, and her chest began to tighten.

"This is enough evidence with Lady Marya's accusation."

Lady Marya was one of the midwives who had been helping with Alesia when she was giving birth.

She heard me chanting.

Fear tore through her as she tried to squirm away.

Tears fell before they had a chance to pool. She hadn't

known what the town guards wanted when she saw them coming up the hill when she let Bala out, but this terrible feeling had come over her.

She checked the window to make sure the lizard was gone.

They grabbed her by the back of the dress. "Filthy Witch! How long have you been cursing our town?"

That's when they started beating her with their fists, their boots. They hit her blindly in undeserving rage. She cried out and screamed against the cloth shoved against her mouth and tied around her head. Her own pain-filled grunts echoed their enraged ones.

When she was barely moving, they dragged her from her home with the backs of her bare feet scraping against the ground. They didn't set it alight, but she was sure in the morning they would come back to. They would probably make a grand show of it with the townspeople to celebrate its destruction.

It was a small party of men, probably so she wouldn't think much of it. Any other Witch may have attacked them, but Amalia didn't have that kind of magic – or the heart to.

Most of the townspeople had collected in the centre. They threw rocks and rotten food in her direction while she was dragged between an aisle of people, too hurt to be able to walk on her own.

One of the soldiers held up her books. "We found spell books!"

"And we found symbols burned into the floor of her house!"

"She is a Witch!" a person from the crowd yelled, making others shout it as well. Her face paled when they said the most terrifying words she'd ever heard. "Burn her!"

A wooden stake had been permanently placed in the centre of the town. It was always prepared in case they came across a Witch and needed to be rid of them as quick as possible.

When they started placing straw around the bottom of it, Amalia squirmed against her bonds as they dragged her to it. *No! Please, no!*

"She killed Alesia!" a woman shouted. Amalia turned to the voice and found it was Lady Marya. "I heard her chanting. She stole her soul!"

I did not! She tried to plead against the cloth in her mouth but all the came out was muffled snorts. *I tried everything to save her.*

"There are symbols at the back of my home. I found them when Marya told me she was a Witch!" another townsperson yelled.

They are protection spells to ward off evil and sickness.

Amalia could tell there would be no trial for her, no way for her to plead her case. They looked determined. They had already made up their minds.

It was true. She was a Witch. They were right.

But I have never harmed another in my life.

A metal shackle was placed around her throat. They pulled on the chain connected to the back of it, hanging her up by it until the tips of her toes barely skimmed the straw under her feet. She struggled to breathe against it.

They attached it to a loop of metal to keep her against the wooden stake.

They had to. A calm Witch about to be burned could still fight back once the fire started. They'd learned long ago that fire could give them energy, but if they were struggling, unable to breathe, they couldn't focus their magic.

I am going to die. She couldn't help crying harder when the soldiers from before carried lit torches towards the straw at her feet.

They were going to make sure she suffered before she died.

Gasping for air, she was able to draw in small amounts of oxygen. It was just enough to keep her going, to keep her alive so she would be able to feel the lick of flames painfully dancing across her skin.

The metal around her throat dug so deep she couldn't speak against it.

She pleaded with her eyes at the people she'd cared for, helped, had saved over her years of living here. Many of them would have died due to sickness or giving birth. There was little to no crime in this town because of the protection spells she'd placed on each home.

Instead of helping her, one threw a stone, and it pegged her in the temple. Dizziness assaulted her vision just as a trickle of blood dripped down the side of her cheek.

I just wanted to live in peace.

The fire burst to life under feet, and it didn't take long for her to start screaming. Whenever she lifted her legs to escape, the shackle around her throat made it impossible to breathe as she hung there.

She knew what she feared most. She feared the flames that had already engulfed her feet and set the skirt of her dress on fire.

Hot agony shot up her legs.

Amalia allowed herself to hang there by the shackle, desperately seeking death. No matter how far she weakly lifted them, the fire was already surrounding her.

Unable to do anything with her arms and legs bound, she trembled and shook at the pain she felt. Her body was so dry she could no longer produce tears. *So hot.*

She also didn't want to smell the foul scent of her own skin burning anymore. The stomach-churning aroma of charred, burning meat was there on every intake of her final breaths.

I want to die. I want to die. She wanted to escape this torment. *Please! Let me die!*

She couldn't take much more of it.

Her chest was tight without breath. Her eyes rolled back

with blurry vision when her heart slowed. Something shadowed the moon for a moment, but it was too late.

Amalia's heart was about to stop beating.

Rurik returned to the Witch's home and landed on top of it. Something squawked from inside the straw of her roof, some flying creature, but he ignored it as he climbed down.

He crawled against the outer wall of her peasant cottage until he grabbed the wooden frame of the windowsill. With claws digging in, he held on so he didn't fall.

He slyly peeked his head around to see through the glass to avoid being seen. *She is gone.*

He could see the devastation inside her house. Dirt, spices, and plants were scattered across the ground, her books were thrown without care. Even the table she often rested him upon was on its side.

She has been taken.

Jumping back from the window, he flapped his wings and took flight.

Unsure of which way to go, unable to scent her out with his body so tiny, he looked around to think. He noticed a bright light coming from the town, and his brows drew together before he headed in that direction.

The closer he got, the more he understood what was happening.

A Witch's trial. And it appeared he was too late.

She was burning, flames already eating at her feet. *She is still moving, though.* He could see her struggling.

With an irritated growl, he chanted while he flew, and his size grew exponentially bigger.

What he was doing was a risk to his own life. If there were any Witches nearby, they would see him. Still, he continued to fly towards the town, doing one circle above it to slow his approach while he thought on how to best handle this.

His snout puffed with a growl when the Witch stopped struggling. Her body went limp, and her feet dropped back into the flames.

Dammit. He'd been hoping he could shift to a man to save her. Instead, he was going to have to reveal himself to these humans.

He swooped down above her, making all the humans scream or gasp in some form. The gusts of wind his heavy wings created while he hovered above her pushed the fire down and away from her.

He hoped they thought he was some form of demon she'd conjured rather than what he really was.

I cannot believe I am saving a Witch! Me!

Soldiers drew their swords, but Rurik ignored them as he curled both his back paws around the wooden stake she was attached to. Then, as if it was like nothing but plucking a long splinter from under his scale, he pulled the stake out of the ground and lifted off.

Unsure of where he was in this part of the world, he took her back to her home so he could land in the small clearing in front of it.

He didn't fit in the space. He uprooted trees by knocking them over as he gently placed the wooden stake on the ground and touched the grassy dirt himself.

It wouldn't be long before the humans made their way here, so he quickly blew a ring of fire and then chanted the single word he needed before it dissipated.

"Shift."

That ring of fire drew back and started making its way over his body until he was encased in flames, almost as though his scales were covered in flammable oil.

When the flames died, Rurik was human – and naked.

He knelt beside the Witch and crawled around on his hands and knees to break the shackle around her throat with his bare hands. He made quick work of the ones around her wrists and ankles.

Rurik pressed his ear to her chest. *No breath or beat.* For a short moment, he stared at her as he contemplated on what to do.

Then, with a disgruntled growl curling his upper lip, he bent over her face.

Imbuing his own magic into his breath, he breathed into her mouth. When he pulled away, he placed his hands on her chest and started pumping his arms.

"Come on, Witch. Count yourself lucky I am doing this for someone of your ilk," he said with disgust and anger mixed in his tone.

She didn't take a breath. He bent over her face again so he could spread his magic and breath into her, before Rurik pumped his hands to massage her heart.

Does she no longer want to live? She had to have will for life for this to work.

With one last attempt, he gave her another one of his breaths, and a gasp followed before he even got his hands back to her chest.

There. She breathes.

His blood debt was paid, and he could leave.

Turning from her, he walked back over to where he had shifted into his human body. After he released that ring of fire again, he chanted the single word he needed to, and he was once more back in his beast form, waiting for the flames to die down.

His face pointed to the sky when he spread his wings to take flight. In that position, with his wings raised and one swoop away from taking him into the air, he froze.

My blood debt is complete. Why should I care what happens to her now?

He'd given her life. He'd given her his breath.

They will come here for her. They would try to kill her again. *Blasted!* With a snarl, he picked her up in his forepaw and finally took flight.

He forced magic to fill his skull and closed his eyes for a moment. When he opened them again, the spell of sight he cast allowed him to see the tendrils of magic he wasn't able to see before.

When he followed them, they took him deeper into the woods near her cottage until he came to another clearing. Sparkling magic glittered everywhere here, and he, once again, landed. This space was large enough to fit him.

His eyes scanned the ring of trees around him as well as the ring of mushrooms at the bottom of those trees. The area was dark, and to those that wouldn't know better it would appear as if there was no life here.

"Fairies, I am in no mood. Stop cowering and come."

"Why do you bring a Witch here?" A small voice said to him – easy for his large ears to pick up.

He turned his scaled face to the female who spoke. A tiny fairy, no bigger than a human's palm and fingers, floated towards him. Her wings shimmered as glitter seemed to fall from them.

"Because, Fairy Queen of these woods, she said that your kind often visit her home, and she is no longer safe there."

"And why do you care what happens to a Witch?"

He gave a snarl while snapping his jaws right in front of

her, expertly missing her.

"Do not question one such as I, or I will smite your entire tiny fairy kingdom."

Heads peeked out from around branches, leaves, and those mushrooms around the clearing. It was slow at first, a head here and there popping up, until eventually he had a swarm of eyes on him. They wanted to watch what was happening between him and their queen.

"I do not know or trust this Witch." She waved her hand dismissively while giving him her side. "Take her away from here."

He turned his large head down to the unconscious woman in front of him. *Did she lie?* His lips drew back over his fangs. *Deceiving Witch.*

A small handful of fairies approached him. Well, not him but the woman at his feet.

"Queen Starlight," one of them said, a male. "A few of us have been bringing injured animals to this Witch for quite some time."

"How dare you do something so reckless! How dare you break our laws! You are never to reveal yourself to Witches or humans," the queen yelled. "You know better. They are dangerous, treacherous beings."

A female near the Witch spoke this time, her voice soft. "She saved my life. A pixie attacked me, and her cat brought me to her home. She mended my broken wings and leg. I thought it was so that I was able to be of value, but then she released me."

"You mean a Witch healed you and then freed you?" the queen asked, her anger vanishing on a small gasp.

"Me as well," another fairy hovering with the small group said, this one male as well. "I did not know anyone else had been visiting her, but after she saved me, I started bringing her animals to heal. Ravens and racoons that now refuse to leave her roof. I speak to them, and they tell me about all the good she has done for others."

"Has she ever...?"

The queen turned her gaze down to the woman while hesitantly flying a little closer.

"She has never killed another from what the animals have told me, or from what she has said to me."

"You have spoken to her?!"

"Hard not to when she talks to you while she heals you," he said, and the queen's eyes narrowed. *So her chatting is not uncommon.* "I have also seen her release a pixie in her care."

"She takes care of them too?"

"She feels awfully bad when she smacks them with her broom," he laughed. A few of the fairies hovering over the Witch's chest giggled in return. "She is rather sweet."

"I did not think there were any pure-hearted ones of her kind left."

"Is it settled then?" Rurik finally cut in. "May I leave her here?"

"I do not see why you would bother," the queen answered. "She will most likely try to kill herself when she wakes."

He was just about to ask why, but then the small collection of fairies that had pleaded her case fluttered down to her ankles.

"She will never walk again," one of them whispered.

Rurik hadn't cared to look at the extensive injuries on her until now. It was true, she'd most likely never walk again and would live the rest of her life in pain.

Her skin was coal black with the toe bones easy to see around melted skin. The fairies would never have enough magic to heal this kind of wound.

"You would be better off putting her out of her misery," the queen said. "Right now, she is in peace. Give her the mercy of a quick death before she realises what kind of pain she is truly in."

He'd never hesitated in killing a Witch before. This should be easy for him to do, and yet...

"I do not wish for this one to die. I have a blood debt to her. Is there nothing you can do to fix her?"

The queen shook her head. "No, and you already knew that before you asked that question."

That he did.

He stayed quiet for long moments, before his thoughts eventually made his lips curl back over his sharp fangs.

"Curse you all to the fiery pits of damnation!"

He knew what he needed to do and wasn't happy about it. Rurik picked her up in his forepaw and knocked away all the fairies closest to him with a gust of wind when he flapped his wings.

He couldn't believe he was doing this. Anger seethed inside him. *What am I doing? I should just drop her from the air and let her fall to her death.*

Instead of doing just that, he was heading towards his home, to his cave.

I am taking her to my lair. A Witch!

He'd seen her magic, had watched her. Without blood magic, she'd never be able to heal herself. Even with it, he doubted she'd fully recover.

No, he was going to have to save her. Him! *Not only did I save her, but I am going to have to care for this... this silly woman! Blast her!*

Instinctually, his kind always knew which way to go to get back to their own lairs.

I better not run into any of her ilk along the way.

He had a hateful fury he would just love to unleash.

The flight was long, a whole day in fact. It would have taken longer if he hadn't pushed his body to the point of exhaustion. There had been no Witches to fight in his journey, and he'd become relieved by that when he realised just how long it was taking.

The sun is going down. I do not have much time left. That was his thought when he nosedived for the entrance of his cave lair. He whooshed inside as he glided through the entrance tunnel, feeling his wings scrape against the circular walls.

Slowing his flight, he stopped in front of a carved alcove and pushed his large body through the opening. Carefully, he laid her body down on a stone table he often used for various reasons.

He blew a ring of fire above him. "Shift."

The flames encased him, and his body vibrated while it morphed into a human.

Without bothering to put clothing on, or to do anything else, he approached the Witch. He pushed her flat onto her back, moved her arms beside her body, and then straightened her legs. Then, thinking better of it, he quickly ducked out of the alcove to run to another not too far down from the one he put her in.

Sprinting back with shackles and a spike, he clasped her hands together above her head. He shoved the spike into the side of the stone table with his strength and hooked the shackles to them.

The last thing he needed was for her to use magic against him while he healed her.

Rurik lifted the ruined skirt of her dress higher and assessed her legs. From her thighs all the way down to her feet were burnt, and where her skin remained around it was red and boiled with blisters. The worst of it stopped past her knees since her thighs had little damage. Still, he thought it was best he healed her completely.

Gripping his palms around the top of her thighs where the burns ended, he let magic, strong magic, fill his hands.

I cannot believe I am doing this. He breathed deep, and in an ancient language, started to speak the words required.

Her body stiffened and then started shaking when he felt searing heat underneath his palms.

Rurik was reversing the burns. The process would become harder the further he went down her legs, and it would also become more painful. The Witch would have to relive her burns, every lick of them.

It was not for the faint of heart, but he'd done it on himself enough times. His kind, fire wielders, had learned to take away the damage of their own kind when in their human form.

When Rurik came to her knees, where flesh had truly melted away, her eyes snapped open and she let out an ear-splitting scream. She filled the cave tunnels with her pain.

His hands held her legs down with a tight grip as he continued to sweep them with his magic. He had to remain on her shins while he waited to feel her body heal and the warmth to fade, telling him he could move on from that area.

"Please! I was only trying to help everyone!" she screamed

as her body contorted.

She was squirming and struggling against him, flailing like a fish out of water. He let her vent, knowing there was nothing he could do or say to stop her pain while he did this.

The noises she was making were distressing, even he felt for her – especially when he got to her feet.

The Witch couldn't even scream. Her body just bowed and pulled taut as he worked his magic into her. The pungent smell of burning flesh assaulted his nostrils. He could see the line of coal flame through the gaps of his fingers while her muscles, tendons, and skin grew back.

She passed out when he'd gotten to the exposed bone of her toes, no longer able to withstand the agony she was in. It made it easier, and he was able to heal this and the bottom of her feet in blissful silence.

Once he was done, he checked her entire body to make sure there were no more burns. There was nothing he could do for the bruises and cuts on her face and torso in his human body.

He didn't particularly feel like licking her with the healing agents in his saliva in his beast form.

He could only fix wounds of fire like this on another, and he could only do it within a certain amount of time of obtaining them. Others of his kind, those who had stronger magic, could do this no matter the length of time. But he wasn't one of them, and they were exceedingly rare.

The last place he checked were her hands once he unshackled them.

He healed the burns on the tips of her fingers and then left to obtain some cool water from the stream deeper in his lair. *She will be dehydrated.*

Rurik also went to one of the many alcoves that had his treasure hoards, climbing over gold and jewels to find what he wanted.

He'd never needed a cup before since he mostly stayed in his beast form when inside his home. The large bowls he had laying around were more like buckets in comparison to the size of her body.

A jewel encrusted chalice? It will be the nicest thing she has ever drunk from, that is for sure.

He returned to her and dipped that chalice into the water he'd collected before leaving it on the floor. After disrobing her of her destroyed clothing, he placed her body in the porcelain tub he'd filled with cold water.

He had to sit behind the tub with his legs spread around it and put his arm around her shoulders to keep her head above the water. Her body was so limp she kept sliding in. He grabbed that chalice, tilted her head back, and slowly poured the contents inside her mouth.

He gave her little sips, making sure it went down first before adding more.

Would be awfully terrible if I did all this only to drown her.

Keeping his arm around her shoulders to keep her upright, he stayed with her for a long while to let her peacefully rest.

Now what am I supposed to do with her? He couldn't take her back to her cottage, there'd simply be no point. *I could take her to the human town nearby.*

No, he'd much rather not have this Witch so close.

There were also laws he needed to consider.

A Witch that had seen the inside of their lair wasn't allowed to be free. It was for their own safety. The Witches could bring others and take down their protective wards and kill them.

But she will not remember anything of the past day.

Once he thought she'd been in the water for long enough, he took her from it by cradling her in his arms. She felt so small and light in them.

Now, which collection of my treasures have those chests?

It was difficult to remember where he'd put everything and what all of his hoards contained.

When he found the right one, he cradled her legs over his knees while he held one arm around her. He opened the chests until he found one with dresses of the highest quality.

He'd intended to gift these to someone, a female – he wasn't quite sure who just yet – at some point.

Instead, one of them was going to be a parting gift for this woman. He dressed her in a blue one. He didn't know why the colour was important to him.

Now that everything was done, he walked her up the main tunnel of his cave that led to the entrance of his lair.

When he greeted the clearing that bordered onto a large, expansive forest, he was just about to shift to his beast form when a soft hand touched the side of his face. It was a gentle caress, barely a whisper against his skin, but it caused his head to dart down with mortification.

Azure eyes stared back at him. They weren't filled with pain, but they were dazed with lazy lids.

"You have a lovely face," she whispered, before both her arm and head went limp. She was still awake, but he could tell she just didn't have the energy anymore to hold them up.

His face twisted into a snarl as his nose crinkled tight in rage. *You just had to open your fucking eyes.*

With a growl, Rurik turned from the cave entrance and headed back inside.

Amalia's eyes fluttered open. When she found herself lying on something rather soft under heavy furs, she turned to the side to look at what she was lying on.

It was a large bed, probably the grandest bed she'd ever seen in her life. There were torches lit with fire along the stone walls of the room she was in, and they gave her the ability to see that pillars on each corner held a canopy above her.

With a few aches and twinges, she managed to lift herself up on one arm to look around. Her jaw dropped.

All around her laid riches. Gold coins and jewels were scattered against the ground. They came to the centre of the room, right next to the bed, to make a mound that reached a height above her head.

Her gaping eyes looked up and found a rocky ceiling.

I am in a cave? Indeed, she was. She examined the rock walls, and it appeared like a creature with sharp claws had gouged this space for itself.

She could see the exit, but a large boulder was mostly blocking the path unless she climbed over it.

"What is going on?" she whispered, placing her fingertips against her temple.

She crawled to the side of the bed so her feet could find the floor. She thought it may be a dream, hoping her feet might touch air. Instead, she felt the cold of golden metal as it clinked and moved when she placed them down.

My feet! She quickly lifted a foot to inspect it, wondering why she wasn't in pain.

"I am dead. I have to be dead."

Is this some kind of rich heaven?

"Not quite," a deep, rumbling voice answered.

Her eyes widened before they fell to the exit to see who spoke to her.

Amalia let loose a scream when whatever had been blocking the exit moved. A monstrous face with dark purple scales stuck its fat snout inside like it intended to enter.

"Stay back!"

She crawled backwards, scooting on her backside, until

she accidentally crawled off the bed. It halted as it watched her scrambling back on all fours, ignoring the riches around her to flee to the furthest corner. Her heart was almost in her throat when her back met the wall.

Will it eat me?

It blinked cold, silver eyes at her. It seemed to wait for her to calm down as if it wasn't some mindless beast.

Moments bled between them as she tried to settle her breathing – to think. All she could remember was burning at the stake and some handsome stranger's face in her dreams. She remembered pain, searing, unimaginable pain. She remembered wanting to die, wishing to die, anything for the agony to stop.

The creature, whatever it was, slowly crept its way inside. She curled her knees to her chest while whimpering, trying to scoot back further against the wall.

She knew she was visibly trembling. All her joints felt like they were shaking.

Her eyes panned over at the sheer size of the thing. It was three times as tall as she was and more than double that in length!

She looked over the long spaded-shaped tip of its tail, the spikes jutting up its back, and its wings folded neatly against its side. Her gaze fell back on its eyes, cold predatory eyes that were narrowed behind a glare.

They seem familiar. Actually, somehow this beast seemed familiar.

She frowned. *Wait...*

"Lady Lizard?"

"I am not a female, you half-brained twit!" he yelled.

It yelled at me?! It spoke! She dug her fingertips in her skull. It felt like it was going to explode, unsure of how to process this thing in front of her.

"I am not a lizard either, just to clarify that."

Amalia, unsure of what to do, stared at the ground with her eyes wide. "It is not real. This is not real. I am dead," she whispered, rocking back-and-forth.

"I can assure you, Witch, that thanks to me, you are far from dead."

I am not dead? It took her a moment to stop rocking and keep a hold of her sanity. She feared at any moment it would slip away.

Slowly she met his eyes again, still holding her head like she needed to hold onto it or it would spin off.

"W-what are you then?"

"I am a Dragon." He sat down and lifted his head as if he was proud of his statement. When she didn't say anything, his spikey brows furrowed deeply. "You do not know what that is, do you?"

His voice was filled with surprise, and his spiked brows raised this time when she shook her head.

"A Dragon is a reptilian creature which has the ability to fly, create fire, and use magic. My kind is the forefather of yours. You should have been told of your origin from birth."

She tried to digest what he said, to understand what was even happening. She hardly believed she was alive, let alone having a conversation with this creature.

"I do not understand. How is that possible? You are a monster. How can my kind come from yours?"

His snout bunched with irritation.

"We have the ability to take on a human form. Witches are the product of Dragons and humans mating over a thousand years ago."

Amalia's brows drew together. She'd never known such a thing. She'd never heard of Dragons before this day and always believed that humans always had the potential for magic.

"The fact you have not been told of your own heritage is

disrespectful. You do not deserve the magic gifted to you by my kind."

"My father was a human, though."

The Dragon rolled his eyes like he thought she was stupid, and a spike of anger hit her. It wasn't her fault she didn't know these things!

"Somewhere in your bloodline, most likely your mother's, if the truth of your father is real, is Dragon lineage. I doubt your father was a human, though. Your body harbours too much magic for it to be part human."

She stayed silent, unwilling to correct him. She knew the truth. Her father was a human and died as a soldier in the war.

"Your parents truly never told you any of this?"

She shook her head in response. "No. My father died when I was sixteen, and my mother disappeared not long after."

"Perhaps it is good that they had not informed you. It may be the reason you never became a *Dark Witch*," he sneered the last two words. "You never became a bloodthirsty Witch who pulls apart my kind just for sickening magic and power."

She saw the hate in his eyes and the disgust-filled crinkle in his snout. Amalia trembled with fright at the look he gave her – like at any moment he might snuff her out with one of his large paws tipped with razor-sharp claws.

They glinted in the firelight like a deadly beacon.

"I know you saw it. That the very essence of my being is magic, every bone, every drop of blood, every scale." He lowered his head and showed her his rows of fangs. "Do you want to pull me apart now that you understand? Pull me apart like I am sure you know other Witches do to pixies, fairies, humans, animals, and anything living they can get their hands on?"

"Are you going to kill me?" Her voice was shaky, wanting to know if he healed her just so he could torture her himself.

He stepped closer while stretching his short neck across

the pile of riches between them. "Answer the question, *Witch*."

She curled away to hide. "N-no. I would never harm another."

She felt his warm breath slide over her entire body like a curling, gentle wave. Deep as they fluttered over her, they lifted her hair slightly and billowed her dress around her.

"I know," he finally said, and her eyes opened as some of the tension in her body lessened.

She quickly turned her head to find two silver eyes directly in front of her, and they were so large that she could see the way his irises had formed around circular pupils. His puffy snout was so close to her knees that if she moved at all, she'd touch it.

He pulled his head back to tower over her, but it wasn't menacing. Instead, he appeared to be looking down at her with an assessing gaze.

"I can tell you do not want to harm others for power."

"Then why did you-?"

"Why did I ask? Simple. I wanted to know if the words you said to me on the steps of your cottage had changed. I can see that they have not."

"How do you know I am not lying?" The dangerous question fell from her mouth, but she was so curious she couldn't stop herself from asking it.

"There is no cunning or scheming note to your eyes, no determination. All I see is confusion and fear."

Her cheeks heated in embarrassment, and she averted her gaze to look at the room again. "If you hate Witches, then why am I here? All I remember is the stake."

"Because you saved my life. I had a blood debt to you, which is now paid in me saving your life and giving you the use of your legs back."

Amalia held her feet to wiggle her toes against her palms.

"You took away my burns. How?"

"Old magic. Dragons are fire breathers, and we often hurt our own kind. We also war with each other for territory. Although our scales are impervious to fire, we needed the ability to heal ourselves of burns when in our human bodies. I used that same magic on you because your wounds were of fire."

"Thank you," she said while squeezing her feet. "If your blood debt is paid, does that mean you want me to leave your home?"

"No. You will never be allowed to leave my lair, unless it is by death."

Her jaw dropped, and her hands stilled at his words.

"So, I am a prisoner? Why?"

His jowls lifted into a snarl.

"Because you just had to open your blasted eyes!" She squealed at his shout and then covered her head when he roared. He even stamped his large paw! "I have to keep a blasted Witch in my lair because you could not just stay unconscious for a few more minutes!"

He was so furious he roared to the ceiling this time.

While he was distracted, she darted for the exit with terror that he would turn on her. His tail slammed down in front of her before she could reach it.

He growled in warning at her.

"You can try and run from my lair, but you will be unable to leave. There are wards in place to keep Witches out, and therefore, you in."

"I do not want to be trapped in this cave with you!"

She jumped over his tail and darted down the tunnel, thankful more fire torches lined the walls.

She heard him turn in the room she'd been in by the sound of coins sliding against each other. There were also the sounds of his heavy paws hitting the ground as he gave chase.

Amalia had no idea where she was going, but it didn't matter. Before long, he grabbed her in his forepaw, lifted her into the air, and made her face him.

Their positions had been changed. She was no longer the one handling a tiny lizard. Instead, she was the small prey he held captive.

She pushed at his scaled fingers to free herself, yet they barely budged.

"What was the point in saving me if I will not really have a life?"

"Because you saw my human face," he puffed at her, obviously seething in his anger and barely able to rein it in.

"I do not remember seeing anyone."

"Think, little Witch."

So, she did. She paused to think on what she could remember. Her brows drew together into a tight knot while she recollected everything.

"Wait, you are the handsome stranger? I thought he was a Witch who had taken away my pain as I died." She wished she hadn't added that last part, because his eyes went wide, and then one horribly twitched. "I am sorry! I did not mean to offend you. I just did not know about your kind at the time."

That seemed to placate him. He took in a long draw of air and released it as the tension left him.

"I did not mean to look at you. I will not tell anyone."

It was a sincere promise.

"That does not matter. By the laws of my kind, you are not allowed to know my face or where my lair is. I do not want you in my home." He gently placed her down on her feet with his face softening. "But regrettably, I also do not wish to kill you."

"I hardly call that a mercy." His soft look morphed into a sharp scowl. "I released you once I healed you. Can you not do the same for me?"

"No. Even though I do not think you wish to cause me any harm, there are ways other Witches can get you to talk or see your memories."

Her knees gave out and she fell to her bottom, understanding that he truly intended to keep her here.

"I would much rather you kill me then."

"Excuse me?"

His eyes blinked rapidly, utterly dumbfounded.

"What kind of life would I be able to live? Imprisonment does not seem like a life that I would be able to enjoy, or anyone, for that matter."

"You told me that you wished to live in peace. In my lair, so long as you leave me alone and never use your magic, you will have peace."

Her eyes fell to the cave walls of the large tunnel they were in. She felt the dirt beneath her palms and fingertips, the coldness of the stone.

"I wanted to live in peace as myself. I wanted to help people, heal the wounded or sick whether they be human or animal." She turned her head up to meet his gaze with a beseeching crinkle in her expression. "You are asking me to no longer use magic or be anything of what I was when you found me. You also told me I would never leave your cave. That would mean I would never be able to touch the sunlight or feel the grass beneath my feet."

"You would be alive," he answered, like that was enough.

After this conversation, she no longer felt so frightened, just upset that she would be imprisoned here.

She wasn't some feeble human that was desperate for life. She wasn't afraid of death. It would come for her one day, and although she had wanted it to be of old age, she didn't want to live a life of misery.

He glared when she snorted a laugh.

"I would be as much alive as you were trapped in that

birdcage."

"This is the end of this discussion." He tapped a single claw against her torso, forcing her to fall back against the hard ground. "You will live, and it will be in my lair. If I find you using magic, I will lock you in the prison alcove I have available. Be thankful I am allowing you to roam."

Then he left her alone, disappearing down the tunnel.

8

While Rurik wandered his lair, he thought he might find the soft-hearted, trembling Witch crying in a corner, like some blubbering, defenceless little girl.

That is not what he found.

After some time apart, he instead found her crawling through one of his treasure hoards. He didn't know what she was trying to find, because it obviously wasn't the coins and jewels she carelessly threw behind her as she dug.

He tried not to admit that her arse pointed towards the ceiling while her feet dangled in the air behind her was cute. He really did, especially when he was trying to figure out what she was up to.

Does she think something here will help her escape?

The sounds of someone grunting as they struggled echoed in the alcove she was digging through. It was smaller than the one she'd woken up in.

He hadn't been able to remember how he'd gotten that darn bed into that treasure room, but he'd wanted to put her somewhere safe and soft so he'd eventually just laid her down on it. Rurik had half-expected her to froth at the mouth at waking surrounded by treasure.

It seemed as though she hadn't cared.

She must not care for gold.

"Witch, what is it you are doing? I do not like my treasures moved."

She gave a startled yelp before falling back and sliding down the small pile of coins.

"I am bored. I saw there was a book in here and thought there may be another."

"How can you be bored? You have not wandered my home yet. Is that not entertainment enough?"

She plopped her back against the riches to lay against it like it was a bed. Her face was towards the ceiling, and she raised her arms above it to gesture to her surroundings.

"Your home is a cave." Seeing he was about to snarl at her rudeness, she quickly followed with, "Also, if I am to live here, I have plenty of time to explore our home."

He blinked, taking in the fact she'd called it *their* home.

"Well, you adjusted to that rather quickly. I expected to find you crying or trying to escape."

She tilted her head forward, and her eyes met his. "What is the point? I am guessing with that large nose of yours, you would find me if I ran."

That is a very fair point.

"You do not plan to escape then?"

"I never said that." He scowled at her response. "I am hoping I can find your merciful side and get you to free me in due time."

"Telling me of your plans makes them near impossible."

She laughed, and he couldn't help frowning at her for it. *Why is she not broken?* She'd been trembling earlier like a spooked animal, so he thought she may have been weak-hearted.

"Does it? Then perhaps I will annoy you so that you may rush me out of our home. Do you have a large broom for those large paws of yours? Perhaps I can get you to swat me away like I used to with those pixies near my cottage."

"Once again, you have told me of your plan."

"I doubt seducing you is a possibility then."

Rurik reared his head back with his eyes wide.

I brought a crazy person into my precious home.

Her lips tightened while the corner of her eyes crinkled. He realised she was trying her absolute hardest not to giggle.

"Do not play games with me, Witch," he sneered, unsure why his voice held no malice in it. "There is nothing you can say or do that will free you from your imprisonment."

"Is there not?" She sighed, letting her head fall back against the riches she lay upon. "Are you not well read then?"

"What is that supposed to mean?"

"I asked you if you had books. Do you not know how to read to have any other than that one?" Without looking, she pointed to a thick bound book on the floor.

"Did you just call me stupid?!" This time his anger flared like a hot inferno in his chest. "You never asked me if I had books, only mentioned you were seeking them."

"Well?" Her head lifted again, seemingly unafraid that she'd angered him.

His eyes trailed to the rock wall with nonchalance.

"Yes. I have books, many. You would have known that if you had taken the time to wander *our* home."

"Will you take me to them?" She bounced to her feet, ready to follow.

"No, find them yourself. Get used to your surroundings."

Rurik turned from the treasure room.

He'd only wanted to make sure she wasn't trying to escape. Now that he knew she wasn't, he didn't see the point in being in her presence.

He shook his head while he walked. *I have a captive Witch in my home, one that does not appear to be right of mind.* Oh, how his kin and kind would laugh at him. They would believe he'd gone mad, *him*, housing one of her ilk.

He assumed the further he walked away from her the more her scent would fade from his senses. A scent he found rather delicious. It wasn't that it was delicious to his stomach, but rather other parts of him.

Now that he was large and wasn't covered in the Witch's concoction and swallowing sickly sweet tea, he'd managed to finally pull her aroma in. It tingled his nostrils with pleasant sweetness.

He didn't like that one bit. He already found her quite beautiful.

He frowned at himself. *When had her looks gone from just merely pretty to beautiful?* He shook his head again.

The last thing he needed was to think of other aspects of her as nice. No, she was nothing more than his prisoner. A prisoner he didn't want here.

Rurik didn't like others in his lair. He preferred silence and to be left alone. He hadn't spoken to his own kind in quite some time, and he'd prefer not to speak a word to another being for a few weeks... or even months. That seemed impossible now with this woman in his cave.

Why can I still smell her? He'd been walking for a while.

He quickly turned his head behind him, and a wisp of yellow-white ducked into one of the alcoves.

"Why are you following me?"

She came out from her hiding place with her lips pouted. "I wanted to know more about you."

"I told you that while you are in my home, you are to leave me alone."

"You are just as bad as Bala. So rude and mean to me when I have done nothing wrong to you."

Her hands were clasped behind her back, almost as if she wanted to feign innocence.

"Are you not afraid of me?" His voice rang with confusion.

Rurik didn't understand her at all. His interactions with humans were very limited, and he'd never had an extended conversation with a Witch.

"I cannot be afraid of what I do not know or truly understand. All I know is that you said you do not wish to kill me."

With a growl, he turned and came up to her quickly.

"You wish to know about me? You should be very afraid. My name is Rurik the WitchSlayer."

She took an unsteady step back at his closeness and the glare he gave her. The innocent expression she'd worn faded to fear, and the scent of it worsened as he skulked closer, following her when she retreated.

"I have been hunting and killing your kind for many years, and I take great pleasure in it." Then Rurik lowered his head and bumped her body with his snout so she'd fall. "And you would do well to remember that."

Their kinds were enemies, and had been for centuries.

He turned, allowing his tail to swipe just above her as he stormed his way further inside his lair and, hopefully, away from her.

Rurik was angry because he found this woman... disconcerting.

In truth, her lack of fear of him, he somehow... liked? Yes, he must like it because it showed she had bravery. It meant she had strength in her personality he hadn't seen before.

He was also becoming increasingly fascinated by her with every moment he spent with her, and he didn't like that whatsoever. Even in her cottage he'd felt this way.

She obviously found humour in the strangest of places, and she had no problem with trying to share that with him already.

When she'd mentioned she'd might try to seduce him, his head had nearly spun off. He hadn't expected it. When he realised she had only been teasing him, he'd almost wanted to laugh at her.

Maybe with her. He wasn't sure just now.

No, he didn't need to get closer to this kind Witch that he found attractive, with a pleasing scent, and sweet voice.

Rurik growled at his own thoughts.

His list of her positive attributes was growing.

Amalia wasn't adjusting well.

She was horribly confused and felt cornered and upset. She had no way of letting these emotions out without screaming and crying, which she didn't want to do. Eventually she would start letting them out, but she would rather them seep slowly, over time, so it didn't feel like it was ripping her apart.

She wanted to distract herself before she slipped into a daze. Amalia had always read when she felt despondent to escape her reality with books.

Alesia's death through childbirth had been too much of a shock to her system and Bala and the lizard, *uh... Dragon?* It had all thrown her over the edge that night. Usually, she didn't allow herself to become such a blubbering mess, but she'd been grieving and had seen it as her fault.

Usually, Amalia would read or daydream on her bed, letting her tears come slowly and silently. She didn't feel comfortable enough here to allow herself that sweet peace since she didn't want him to find out she wasn't coping well.

She thought he may not care either way.

She was pretending with her emotions, letting him believe that she was fine, lying with her laughter. Some of her words had been funny to her because she knew she'd confused him, but mostly it'd been empty.

If he thought she accepted her new imprisonment with strength, she may figure a way out of it sooner. She needed to be logical about this.

It wasn't that she hated him, she couldn't really. He'd saved her life, and she'd woken without pain. Actually, she was rather thankful that he'd done that for her when it was obvious that he detested her.

She just didn't want to be trapped here.

With a sigh, Amalia got to her feet once the Dragon went around the tunnel corner with his tail flicking to the side.

Am I really to spend eternity with a moody animal? She sincerely hoped not.

She knew it wasn't eternity, but Witches lifespans were still two hundred years, nearly double or triple a human's life. The idea of spending another hundred and seventy-five years inside this cave didn't sound appealing.

Not with an unpleasant Dragon, at least.

Amalia thought perhaps the Dragon and her could be friends since he was forcing them to occupy the same space. They had saved each other, after all.

That seems like a farfetched reality.

Deciding to take up his advice, she wandered the tunnels to distract herself. She peeked her head inside each alcove, finding them mostly less than boring.

Many held treasures. They did appear somewhat organised, though. Piles of gold and jewels in two. A room filled with chests of clothes. Another with furniture. There was a room with different kinds of armour bearing crests of kingdoms and noble houses she'd never heard of.

She stopped when she came to an alcove of weapons.

If only I knew how to fight, maybe I could fight him and flee.

Curious, she stepped inside and picked up a claymore sword. She had to use two hands because it was awkward, and she'd never held a sword before. The tip stayed against the ground, and she wasn't able to lift it much higher for more than a few seconds. *I cannot use this.*

She picked up a bow and pulled the string back as best as she could. Pushing her head into the space she'd created, she pretended to aim it across the room.

Then she let the string go.

It slapped her in the back of the head and then the long handle smacked her in the face. Instantly she felt blood pooling in her nose.

She placed it on the ground with her eyes darting around, thankful that the Dragon hadn't seen her do that. Her cheeks grew hot. *That was embarrassing.*

She then picked up a mace. It wasn't as heavy as the claymore, and she twirled it with two hands. With a smile, she then spun in a circle with it.

The spinning momentum was quite exhilarating.

Oh, I very much like this weapon. She twirled the mace and then slammed the ball into the ground with a loud thud. She did it repeatedly. *I wonder if I could use this.*

She spun it again in a circle around her body – only to realise she was now being watched. She cringed when she accidentally let it go.

It sailed in the air, eventually copping the Dragon in the snout.

"My apologies."

She winced when he huffed at her and walked away, but in the opposite direction he'd gone before.

Deciding that being in a room that she'd managed to hurt them both in was no longer a good idea, she left the weapons alcove. *I doubt I would win if I fought him anyway.*

To her relief, she happened across the many books he'd been speaking of.

In a large alcove, the only one matching the size of the one she'd woken up in, were towers of books. They were neatly piled on top of each other, and she could barely reach the tallest ones with her fingertips.

There were also chests here. When she tried to open them, she discovered they were locked. *I wonder what books lay inside them.*

She started going through the stacks while creating herself a small pile she would come back to read. The number of books in this alcove was daunting, and she knew it would take her a long time to sort through them. It was perfect to allow her some time to process what she was going through.

I want to go home...

Amalia didn't know how long she'd been in there, going through all the books, but she barely made a dent. Yet, there was something she couldn't ignore, hadn't realised she'd been ignoring for quite some time.

"Lord WitchSlayer!" she yelled, walking down the tunnel in the direction she'd seen him go last.

"Did you honestly just call me Lord WitchSlayer?" he called back groggily, a note of humour in his tone.

"Well, what else am I supposed to call you?"

She followed where the voice came from to an alcove of treasure she'd visited earlier – one only of gold and jewels.

She didn't see him inside.

"Hey, where did you go?"

She gasped when the treasure shifted and his head ducked out, coins cascading from him to allow him through. A red carved jewel spun on his snout before just resting there right behind one of his flared nostrils.

"Rurik will be just fine. Why are you shouting in my cave when I am trying to slumber?"

He rested his head against the ground littered with coins, his eyes lazy, like he might fall back asleep any moment.

"I require food. I have not eaten today."

"Was wondering when I would have to feed my *pet*." He didn't get up, instead choosing to curl his head towards where the rest of his body must be under the pile of coins. "You must wander my tunnels some more if you seek food. I have collected fruits and vegetables from the town nearby for you. There is also a cow carcass in the same room."

Her stomach grumbled loudly, as if the mention of food gave it a voice.

"Will you not show me?" When he didn't respond for a long time, she slumped her shoulders. Her heart radiated with a tender ache, and it worsened with every second he didn't respond. "Please? I do not remember the last time I ate or drank any water."

Rurik turned his head back to her with the intention of telling her *no* once more. His eyes were still lazy, and his body was beyond comfortable and relaxed. Then he saw the crestfallen face she wore, the kind where she looked tired and emotionally worn.

"Fine!" He stood, letting everything fall off him as he gave his body a small shake. "I will show you."

She showed me kindness in her cottage, fed me and made sure I had water. He could at least do the same for her.

He led her towards the entrance of his lair. She must not have gone this way if she hadn't come across it yet.

Motioning his scaled hand towards the particular room, he waited on the outside for her to enter. If he wanted to, he could have occupied the space with her, but he didn't want to get in the way nor be particularly close to her.

"Thank you."

She surprised him by nodding her head in his direction before she entered.

Sitting down with his head inside, he watched her check all the different baskets of food available. His lips curled in humour when it was obvious she was not only ignoring the cow dead in the corner, but was pretending it didn't even exist.

Her eyes often found his, like she was wary of him. He wondered if he'd managed to give her a scare earlier.

He also realised the once chatty female was now silent.

"You have yet to tell me your name," he commented, tilting his head in question.

"Amalia Swafford," she answered, pulling the skirt of her dress forward to pile different vegetables into it.

He waited for her to continue.

When she didn't, he asked, "Do you not have a title?"

She stopped to frown at a potato in her hand. "Why would I have a title? I was considered a peasant."

He twisted his head the other way.

"I mean among Witches. What did your coven call you?"

"What is a coven?"

His head shot up, his gaze assessing the woman in his keeping.

"You are jesting, right?"

"No." Then she gestured to everything she collected in her skirt. "Should I be collecting food for you as well?"

His spiked brow creased. "Why should you?"

"Am I not to cook for you?" She looked around at the many different baskets of fruit and vegetables. "This seems like an awful lot of food for just myself."

Rurik was taken aback by her kindness. She was his prisoner, but she willingly offered to feed him.

"I do not eat anything other than meat in my Dragon form."

"But you do in your human one?"

He was unsure if he noted the sudden pinkness in her

cheeks correctly.

"Well, yes. There are times I venture through human towns, and if there are no cattle available, I may find a tavern to eat at."

He travelled often in hunt of her kind and would rest in small towns when he needed to – if there wasn't an empty cave nearby, that is.

"Does that mean you do not want me to cook for you while I am here?"

"No. This food is for you." Rurik scratched a claw at the tip of his snout. "Perhaps I overcompensated since I was not sure how much you ate."

He'd collected it while she'd been unconscious and asleep.

She gave him a small smile. The same one she had once shared with him. It stole his breath as it did before. It was sweet, innocent, and showed that the person wearing it was truly kind and thoughtful.

The scales around his face warmed in reaction to it, which would show more of the purple that the cold air around him had darkened. Her captivating blue eyes watched him, her lids flickering like she noted the difference.

"Could you perhaps show me where I can cook this? I am not sure I want to eat raw vegetables."

He cleared his throat, just realising then that he was having a moment there. "Yes, follow me."

Rurik took her to another room that had a cooking hearth he'd never used before and a table he'd never sat at. He left her there to collect water into a pot since he wouldn't allow her to fill it with magic. He also dragged in a chest he knew contained cutlery and plates before leaving the room to stand just on the other side of the entryway.

With fascination, not with her task but with her, Rurik watched her peel and cut vegetables.

She was once again quiet. After spending all that time with

her in her cottage where she refused to stop incessantly speaking to him, he found it rather odd.

"Do you truly not know what a coven is?" She affirmed with a single no. "How can this possibly be? How can you not know of your origins, of Dragons, or what a coven is?"

It seemed everything he'd ever known about Witches, he had to toss out his cave entrance with this one.

"My mother warned me of the dangers of being a Witch," she answered dully as she peeled a potato with a knife, being careful not to slice her thumb. "She refused to tell me anything about them and only gave me two spell books when she discovered I was using my powers in secret of her. So, she told me to heal without letting others know. Told me that if I wanted to grow my abilities, it should only be to help others. I believe my mother feared our own kind as much as she feared humans discovering us."

Her mother must have been a White Witch as well.

"She was right to. Your kind is vile."

"Appreciated." He noted the sharp tone in her voice.

"I did not mean you," he said, realising he'd offended her. "Just the rest of your kind."

A small smile curled her lips, but she was staring at the carrot she'd started peeling.

"I have always known my kind was bad."

She dumped everything into the water. He'd lit the hearth for her a while ago, and the water had boiled in the time she'd peeled and cut her food.

He frowned, his head tilting as he watched her move about. "You do?"

"Yes. I have heard about the things they do from the humans, and they are feared for good reason. I discovered what blood magic was on my own, how horrific it is." She lifted her eyes to meet his. "Apparently once a Witch tastes the power of magical creatures' essence, it will turn them, make them crave more. I have always avoided it because I do not wish to be like that. I do not want to be corrupted."

"So, you are not completely incompetent."

"Naïve, the word you are thinking of is naïve." *Excuse me? Did she just correct me?* At the look on his face, she continued, "Incompetent means that I am not capable of doing something or obtaining knowledge successfully. Naïve means I am just not told of it and never knew the information existed begin with."

Rurik grumbled since she was correct.

She leaned against the table to wait for her food to cook, and the area was filled with silence. She walked over to it, stirred it, and checked to see that they were still firm before reassuming her place by the table. The Witch had also stopped looking at him, like she no longer cared to check that he was there as she had in the previous alcove.

"You are not as talkative as before," he commented.

He wanted her to go back to the way she was in her peasant cottage, where she had irritated him by never shutting up.

"You told me to leave you alone."

She pushed off the table and stirred her boiling food, giving him her back.

He quietly growled. He knew what he said, he just hadn't known he wouldn't like it.

"I changed my mind. You are welcome to talk to me." She didn't say anything, didn't start rambling like he expected her to. "Well?"

"Perhaps I do not want to anymore."

She turned her head away with her chin lifting, and he narrowed his eyes.

"I demand that you talk to me," he snarled, stepping forward into the smaller alcove and slamming his paw down.

He bared his fangs when she didn't, and a growl began emitting from his throat. *I will not allow some Witch to disobey my commands in my own home.*

Before he could do anything, she gave him a mocking snort – almost like a short laugh. "You are awfully moody, are you not?"

His head snapped back in surprise. Because the room was intended for use when he was in his human form, he smacked his head against the ceiling that was lower in this alcove. He winced, hitting it hard, and shot his head down to the ground to rub his paw over it. *Ow!*

"Oh my, I am so sorry," she quietly giggled. "I did not mean to make you hit yourself."

Hands grabbed the side of his large head.

He stopped looking at the ceiling, instead his eyes widening as they fell on her. She was directly in front of him, seeming to check for some sort of injury that wouldn't be there.

He'd only knocked himself, yet her face held real concern for his well-being. He wasn't sure if she was aware that she was leaning against his snout, her body soft as it pressed against his face.

"You are not bleeding."

He knew that.

What he didn't know was why he wasn't pulling away from her. His eyes became heavy-lidded when she carefully, almost soothingly, rubbed the top of his head with her whole hand, like she once had with a finger.

"Are you okay?" she said when he felt his chin brush the ground, like it was too heavy for him to hold up under her tender caresses. She pulled away and put space between them. "Sorry, I did not realise I was leaning on your face there." Then, with her eyes widening, she quickly exclaimed, "My food!"

She sighed with relief when she scooped up a vegetable with the wooden spoon she had been using to stir with and shoved her blade in to check it. One-by-one, she pulled each piece out and placed it onto a plate from the chest he'd brought in.

She sat at the table and picked up her cutlery.

"Once I finish eating, I was wondering if you had some sort of tub I can wash in?"

"I do, and yes, I will prepare it for you."

Just as she brought pieces into her mouth to chew, she startled him when she dropped her knife and fork. She looked absolutely mortified.

Her eyes slowly slipped from her food to stare at him.

"What is it? What is the matter?"

He lifted his head, almost smacking into the rocky ceiling again. *Has she somehow poisoned herself?* The idea did not bring him joy.

"I bathed you!" She shoved her reddening face into her hands – even her ears turned pink. "I thought you were some lizard. Oh my, I rubbed you in places I definitely should not have!"

Did she only just realise?

Rurik laughed out loud.

He couldn't remember the last time such a sound had left him. He couldn't remember what it had felt like as it filled his chest, crinkled the scales around his eyes, and then burst from him.

"That you did," he chuckled, making her go deathly pale.

Amalia watched the Dragon walk back into the room he told her to wait in with a porcelain tub full of water in one forepaw.

When he'd placed it down, he'd been upset with her when she'd told him it was too cold for her to bathe in. She barely had time to duck out of the way when he unleashed a string of flames against it.

Amalia couldn't stop herself from cowering.

Sweat dotted her skin. Not from the heat, but from the fear that cut through her so quickly her lungs tried to seize. *He truly breathes fire.* She'd been hoping he was joking.

"Is that warm enough for you?" he huffed, a note of anger in his deep voice.

She'd thought because he'd told her that he didn't find her vile, only her kind, that he might start being nicer to her. He'd also revealed that he'd changed his mind about her talking to him. His words had calmed her because she thought she may not be stuck with someone who hated her.

She'd guessed wrong.

Taking a moment to swallow her fear now that the flames were gone, she walked back to the tub on shaky legs.

She dipped her fingers into the water.

"Yes, this will be fine," she said with a tremble before she cleared it.

"Good, because I am not a servant. Now that I am aware that you require your baths warm, we will organise for water to be heated beforehand." *Such a moody male.* He scowled when she looked up to him with a dull look. "Now, enjoy your bath. I am going to rest. I have not since I brought you here, and I have used up a lot of energy in healing your wounds."

She blinked at the space he'd occupied once his tail flicked past the entryway of the alcove. *Oh, is he only behaving like this because he is tired?*

Amalia hadn't known he was exhausted.

Ducking her head down the tunnel to make sure he wouldn't return, she removed the dress she wore, uncomfortable knowing it wasn't one of her own. She hopped into the water and quickly wiped herself down, wishing she had some soap to truly cleanse her body.

She couldn't handle the putrid smell of charred meat wafting from her hair, like the smell of her own burning skin had permeated it. Pulling the wet strands over her face after she rinsed them, she was thankful that the fire hadn't managed to singe the ends of it too badly.

Do not cry. Do not cry, she thought, covering her face with her hands at the memory of being burned.

Gritting her teeth, like that would help her stem her emotions, she hopped out of the tub. She crinkled her nose at having to put on the same dress.

Amalia felt overwhelmed as she ventured through his home. She hadn't realised just how large it was until she truly ventured through it without getting distracted by the different alcoves. Some held many items whereas some were empty or had very little inside them.

She'd long ago passed the room that held the books, deciding to come back to that task later.

Thankful that all the torches were lit with flames, she

walked down a long and wide tunnel that didn't have any rooms for some time. Eventually, it opened up to a large area.

Although there was no furniture inside, tapestries hung from the walls. They didn't appear of human design, but rather like someone the size of a Dragon would have created.

They seemed to tell stories of Dragons.

Dragons fighting each other. Dragons fighting humans wielding swords.

She stared at the tapestries depicting Dragons fighting Witches for longer. Some showed Dragons killing them, some were the other way around, but each time it ended with the Witch encased in flame. Amalia shuddered.

But there was one that depicted the story of a Dragon and a human together. After the woman gave birth, she was no longer a part of the story, but it continued like it wasn't over.

It showed the Dragon father and what she figured was his daughter, learning and living together as a family. It showed the child's progression of learning magic, and her father teaching her to wield it.

A different tapestry showed more humans and Dragons together, giving birth to what she guessed were Witches and living in unison with them. There were hundreds of them, showing that it became a regular occurrence. Humans and Dragons mating to give birth to offspring that couldn't change form but could wield magic.

Then the images turned dark.

One child started to eat fairies and pixies, realising it could grow stronger by eating their parts. The child then turned on their shape-shifting parent by eating the heart of its kin.

From that point, the tapestries showed the Witch child teaching others to do it. Eventually, they all turned on the Dragons and horrific images of the deaths of the scaly beasts as Witches began to grow in numbers.

The tapestry ended there.

Is that truly the origin of my kind?

Each section of wall in this massive, towering room was covered with stories – a history of his kind and their different tales. Some were pleasant, most were not.

After examining each one, she stood in the middle of the large alcove. She could see the direction she came from, but there was another exit. She walked down it.

Amalia came to a fork in her path. One way was dark with no torches lit, while the other was dim. She walked down the one that had some light.

She was able to make out the sound of rushing water even before Amalia came upon a barely lit cavern. There was a stream here. It was slow moving due to a small waterfall that would keep the water fresh.

Exploring this area with much more enthusiasm than she had anywhere else in this cave, she lifted her hands to the waterfall. The rush of cold-water over her palms and fingertips caused her skin to break out in goosebumps.

There was a small space between the waterfall and the rock face where the wall dipped in. Curious, she squeezed herself between that space while trying to avoid getting wet. The tiny spot was only big enough for someone of her size to be able to sit down and rest.

Amalia spent some time there. The movement of nature, whether it be streams of water or the living of earth like plants and trees, always made her feel invigorated.

If she wanted to, she could harness the power of the rushing water here, but she decided not to. It wouldn't do much other than give her energy, and although she was emotionally worn, she felt physically rested.

She couldn't help finding this stream and cavern peaceful. She already knew this would be her favourite place inside of his lair.

His home is not too bad. Now that she knew of this spot,

she felt a small amount of peace.

Amalia had been thinking of her imprisonment. She wanted to leave, wanted to be free.

I am also afraid.

She did admit to herself that she was afraid of his flames. The fact he could wield them with such ease wasn't a comforting thought after what she had been through, but she was more afraid of leaving. If she was truly protected and safe here, it was a much better option than the outside world. Even though she didn't know where she was, people from the town near her cottage may travel. If she did manage to escape his cave, she could be recognised and captured.

Does that mean I may not want to leave if I find a way to? All Amalia wanted right now was to feel safe, and she didn't know if she felt that way. *Outside is fire, inside is fire.*

Even though the air was cool, sweat coated her flesh. She wiped her slick palms on her dress, wishing just the thought of burning again didn't give her such an intense physical reaction.

How do I live in peace while also still being myself? She didn't know the answer to that question. *Maybe if the Dragon lets me be myself, allows me the freedom to come and go as I please?* She doubted that would be a possibility.

She wasn't against this place being her home, she just didn't want to be trapped inside of it, powerless.

When she decided she'd spent too much time with her thoughts, she emerged from her hiding place. There was no other way out of this cavern, so she walked back up the tunnel.

She stopped when she was presented with that same fork in her path, one path would lead her to the entrance of this lair and the other shrouded in darkness. Amalia thought the second path may be dark because he didn't want her to travel down it.

Amalia puffed out her cheeks in annoyance.

She refused to allow him to keep secrets, so she pulled a torch from the wall and walked into the darkness. Along the way, she found two rooms on each side with large, rollable boulders next to the entrance ways. Inside were only furs and a chamber pot. They appeared to be prison cells. She figured these were the places he warned her he would lock her inside of if he discovered she used magic in his home. She imagined he would roll the boulder against the exit so she couldn't escape.

Passing them, she continued to move forward.

At the very end of the tunnel was another, larger alcove. She couldn't see the walls or the high ceiling because of the darkness, but in the middle, there was a firepit on a stand.

She wanted to see the room, so it didn't take much for her to decide to light the firepit. It was slow, but the flames grew over time.

The first thing to be illuminated was a long, red hanging tapestry directly in front of her on the other side of the pit.

It was the tale of a singular Dragon, one who hunted Witches. It depicted him fighting and destroying them one by one. By the end, it showed him roaring with his wings raised and flames coming from his mouth. He was standing above a pile of dead bodies, like he had killed dozens.

Her face paled at the ending of the story. She turned away from it to look around now that more light filled the room.

Amalia's heart leapt to her throat, clogging it, as a gasp tore through her.

Skulls.

The walls were lined with human-shaped skulls as if someone had carefully glued them there. They were neat, each spread apart at the same distance. But there were so many, dozens, in fact, all staring towards the pit of fire.

She felt like they were staring through to her very soul with the hollow bone of their eye sockets. Amalia fell back, suddenly losing the use of her legs. *What is this?*

Bumping into something large and very much alive, she twisted to find the Dragon standing above her. His silver eyes glinted as they looked over the walls.

"Was wondering where you went off to," he said before turning his head to her. "Noticed light coming from this tunnel."

"What is this place?" she asked with a tremble. "Why do you have human skulls?"

"Not human, but Witch skulls. They are my trophies." His voice was filled with pride, his chest bowing with it.

Then he stepped over her to walk further inside and around the pit to look over what could only be almost a hundred skulls.

She didn't think she could be more terrified until he told her that they were the skulls of her kind. Frozen in place against the ground, her face paled further as sweat collected over her skin.

"I am the WitchSlayer, and these are the proof of my strength, of my power."

Her eyes fell to the tapestry on the centre wall and realised the story was about him.

He has killed so many. He didn't seem to notice that she was on the ground about to hyperventilate as a dark grin formed across his monstrous face.

"I cleanse their bodies once I have killed them." He motioned to the firepit in the middle of the room, and that's when she noticed the femur of a leg bone sticking out. It must have jutted up when the wood was placed down. "That is if I have not killed them yet. Screaming often comes from this room, and when the flesh has melted, I take the head and mount it on the wall."

Her skin crawled as heavy drops of sweat dotted her brow. Her hands suddenly felt wet and slippery, and her gut twisted with nausea.

It was only now, while the warmth of the fire seemed to make his scales turn brighter, that she could see the scars that marred his body. She hadn't noticed them before, but now she couldn't see past them.

Since he was no longer a dark purple, the scars swiping across his back, across his fingers, near his throat became more noticeable. There was even a blast scar right near his side.

The deepest gash was across his snout right below his eyes. It started just below one eye, ran across to the other side, and then marred his entire cheek. There were many others that looked like puncture wounds.

"No other Dragon has achieved such a collection. Most do not live many battles of fighting against your ilk." He looked at his paw while he slowly clenched his clawed fingers. "I am even feared by my own kind because I am not afraid to cause harm to others."

Before he could continue, she bolted from the room, from him. She ran down the tunnel to escape, to run and hide.

He will kill me. He will turn on me. She felt it all the way down to her bones. One day, this creature would no longer have mercy and would try to take her life.

Amalia didn't look back to see if he followed.

I am not safe here.

At the cave entrance, she could see sunlight just past it. She wanted away from here, from the creature who could too easily kill her. She'd seen the look on his face. It was one of pride, of determination, of *hate.*

Just as she was about to greet the blessed outside world, she ran face first into an invisible barrier. The air in her lungs knocked out of her, and she bounced back before tumbling to the hard ground.

Amalia started bashing on the invisible wall with the

bottom of one fist while scratching at it with the other.

Something inside her skull felt like it was cracking, like her mind was breaking apart. *I cannot handle anymore.*

Too much had happened over the last few days. Amalia was beginning to spiral, no longer able to contain her emotions.

She'd learned of things she had never known, had seen and felt things she had never wanted to experience. And now... now Amalia just discovered that the person who had saved her life and legs from fire would most likely kill her the same way.

He burns Witches alive. She thought she may have been safe of that here. Sickness rolled in her stomach as bile rose. She swallowed thickly. *I do not wish to burn.*

Rurik knew he'd terrified her when he watched her scramble from his trophy room. He let her run, knowing she was unable to escape his home, and turned to the skulls on his walls.

She needed time to digest who she was truly being kept by. To understand not only the creature he was, but the person he was. She would eventually calm when she realise he didn't intend to harm her.

And he didn't.

Rurik had no want to kill this small and defenceless Witch, this kind and gentle woman. She didn't hold evil inside her. But he wouldn't pretend he hadn't slaughtered her kind by the dozens.

At any point, and he'd been waiting for it, she could have struck him down. Or at least, *tried* to.

When he first brought her here and laid her down to rest after he healed her, he'd filled his skull with magic. It was an easy spell, but it changed his sight and allowed him to see the tendrils of magic and its essence in the air.

What he thought was a weak Witch was actually one full of potential. Strong magic flowed from her in the same way it flowed from him.

He was unsure if she didn't know how to access it or if she

just didn't want to, but at any time she could have used it against him. She hadn't. She hadn't even tried, even when she'd been frightened of him.

His eyes fell on the tapestry.

When the Elders heard about his exploits and victories, they had this tapestry woven and finally gave him a title.

Rurik the WitchSlayer.

When a Dragon received their title, they were also given a tapestry explaining it. This was his glory. He was the first to receive what many of his kind considered to be one of the most glorious titles.

There was Glag the WitchEater, who, if the title didn't give her away, ate many Witches before she was killed by one.

Then there was Deik the Cunning, who wasn't strong of claw but of mind and helped others kill Witches.

And of course, Keela the FaceStealer, who learned that if she wore the face of a Witch or human, she could steal their identity – nobody else seemed to know how to do this.

There were many more, but Rurik was the only one famous for his collection of death.

He wasn't the only one who hunted her kind. Others had similar rooms to this, but none came close to the number of skulls he had mounted on these walls. They would die before they even reached a quarter of this.

So many of my kind have died because of hers.

There were so few of his kind left in the world compared to the Witches and humans. Every egg that hatched was to be celebrated, but there had always been less females than males. If he didn't eradicate the Witch vermin who hunted his kind for parts, they would cease to exist.

He wishfully stared at his title for a long while. All he wanted was to die with the knowledge that his kind would live on without him.

How many lives have I saved?

He gazed roamed across the skulls around him. *Many.* He had saved many.

All Dragons wished for peace and would rather live in harmony than in bloodshed. He shook his spiked head. He just didn't see that as a possibility. Her kind wouldn't stop hunting his to gain power.

Yet... His gaze turned down the tunnel. *Why does this one give me hope?*

If there was one of pure heart, there must be others. She couldn't be the only Witch who didn't seek power.

But, if white wielders were to fight dark, he knew the white would never win. They would never have enough strength against the vast power that came from corruption.

Rurik brought his head over to the firepit and sucked in his breath, drawing the heat into his mouth until the fire snuffed out.

He left his trophy room with the intention of finding the female.

He hadn't intended for her to come across this place yet. It was too soon for her to discover it, which is why he'd purposefully kept this tunnel dark.

Instead, she had bravely walked down it.

He may hate what she was, but he didn't despise who she was inside. As long as she never used dark magic, she would always be safe in his home, from him, and from others of his kind that may come here.

It wasn't hard to track her scent to the entrance of his cave.

She was seated on the ground staring out at the last tendrils of dusk haloing the trees, night soon to fall upon them. Her back was against the wall right next to the ward keeping her inside, her knees curled into her chest.

"Have you calmed?" he asked.

He could still smell fear mixed into her scent.

"Yes." Her voice was a whisper, soft but thick with

emotion.

He came up beside her and sat down to stare outside just like she was.

"You are afraid." Her arms wrapped around her legs tightened further. "You fear I will turn on you." When her scent deepened with it, he sighed. "As long as you do not use dark magic, I will not. I have no intention of harming you."

"Why?"

She didn't lift her head to him, nor did she meet his eyes when he directed his face to her.

"Because I can tell you are kind. You have a gentle soul that does not wish to harm others for power. I will not harm someone innocent who saved me."

He may want to scare the ever-living shit out of her and punish her for being a Witch, but he wouldn't hurt her.

She rubbed her nose as she gave a singular sniffle. "I do not believe you."

His lips curling back over his fangs as a growl emitted from his throat. "Why not? What I have told you is the truth."

"That is why," she answered. "You are filled with too much hatred. You are always angry with me, and you have already shown me that you do not want me in your home. One day, you will realise that you no longer want your enemy here, and you will kill me. I have many years left. You will not want to spend them with me."

He hadn't thought on how long he would have to keep her here. It is true he didn't want a lowly Witch in his lair, but her presence didn't truly bother him.

"Are you young then?"

Just as it was hard to tell with his kind, it was also difficult to tell with hers.

"I have only seen twenty-five winters."

Her kind naturally lived two hundred years – a mere fraction of the length of his own life. The only way a Witch could extend their lives further was with blood magic.

He hadn't expected that she was so young. He thought he may only have to deal with her for sixty years or so.

"That does not matter. You helped me, so therefore, you will be safe from me." When he was met with silence, and she still didn't turn to him, he said, "You are not as quick to adjust or joyful as earlier."

"I no longer wish to pretend."

Her scent changed. It still held fear, but it was shrouded in another emotion, something deep. He wasn't sure what. It grew the longer they sat there and didn't speak.

She obviously needed more time to process, and he didn't want to sit here with her if she wouldn't speak to him.

"I will not kill you," he sighed, getting to his feet. "I will not harm someone who helps others."

Just as he was turning to leave, she whispered, "They burned me."

He stopped and tilted his head. "Yes, the humans do that."

Her arms tightened further, but he wouldn't hold his tongue to the truth. Rurik knew just how merciless life could truly be, had experienced it for himself. Humans weren't as malicious as Witches, but they could be undeniably savage when it came to things they didn't understand or feared.

"You burn Witches, they burn Witches. You are all so cruel." Her voice was soft, but there was anger in it. "They put me on the stake."

Is she turning hateful? Has what happened to her corrupted her heart?

He hadn't thought about this possibility. That what she went through may cause her to become evil and spite-filled. She may want to seek revenge.

"And your kind pull apart others! While we are alive Witches pull our scales off one-by-one." He snarled, not liking that she may no longer be filled with innocence. "They strip us back until we are nothing but skin and flesh while we breathe, while we *bleed*." He took a step forward and let his paw hit the ground hard enough to shake his own forearm. "It is so painful that we pray for death while they laugh at us."

"There it is again, that hatred you are telling me not to fear."

"Because it is deserved! Your kind is vile! Every scale they pull, every bit of human skin they peel, is deserving of a lick of flame."

Finally, she turned her head up to him to give him a glare. *She dares to give me a look of anger?!* He who had saved her life when he should have let her die?

Her eyes were filled with tears that had yet to fall.

"Has this ever happened to you? Is that why you hate us, because we took your scales?" Her question was filled with such a quiet rage that it unnerved him. He'd never seen such hatefulness in her eyes before.

"No. I have never allowed such a thing to happen to me," he sneered. "I am not some weak creature who cannot stop someone from dragging me from my own home."

She suddenly got to her feet. He hadn't known she was holding a rock until she threw it at his face.

"Then shut up, you arrogant bastard!"

His lips curled back over his fangs in a vicious and deep snarl. "How dare you-"

"They put me on the stake!" Her scream held so much emotion; was so loud, raw, and powerful that it caused his head to rear back in shock. "You have not lived pain, whereas I have!"

Then those tears finally slipped down her cheeks, heavy, with more following. She covered her face while her knees buckled, and she fell to them directly in front of him.

"They burned me!" she cried with her hand-covered face resting against her knees. Her chest heaved in shuddering bursts as she struggled for breath. "I did nothing to deserve it!"

Rurik's anger vanished as he watched her.

Her head shook side-to-side as a distressing sob escaped her, one that sounded like she was in agony.

"I have never hurt another being. As I saved you, I saved them. From death, from sickness, from themselves, and they still burned me."

She is wounded. Wounded in a way no one could heal. Wounded on the inside where no kind of magic could touch.

Her hands moved from her face to hug her midsection as she rocked over her knees. She screamed out her sobs.

"I felt fire. I felt it eating me. I stared at the faces of the people who I cared for, and all they did was watch me squirm in pain with glee. I could hear them laughing."

Rurik thought she had moved past it.

She has been holding this in?

"I still smell it on my hair. I can feel every flame upon my skin, even now. I was in so much pain that I wanted to die. I held my legs up so I would, so I could escape it."

She no longer smells of fire. He couldn't smell the burning of flesh on her skin or hair, which meant it was a figment of her imagination, her trauma not allowing her to escape.

He didn't know what to do with this woman crying on her knees. He didn't know why she was releasing this in front of him, but he thought perhaps seeing his room of skulls had finally pushed her over the edge.

She has gone from betrayal and fire to imprisonment with a Witch killer. And he knew he hadn't been truly welcoming to her. What he had mistaken as a hateful look was actually a look of deep sadness.

"All I feel is pain in my heart, and it will not go *away*." Her voice broke on the final word.

With no idea what else to do or what she wanted from him

right then, he tentatively moved his paw towards her. He felt for her because he couldn't imagine how she must be feeling or how she must be hurting.

I would pity any Dragon who had their scales removed. The pain is the same.

"What did I do to deserve fire?"

Nothing. You did nothing to deserve what the humans did to you. Even he could see this.

With the back of one large forefinger, being careful of his claw, he brushed against the back of her knees and the top of her head.

She reached out and clung to it tightly.

"Please do not burn me," she begged, her body heaving harder as her sobs seemed to worsen. "I do not want to feel fire again."

She continued to cling to his scaled finger as though she needed something to hold.

I have brought a female who is now afraid of flames into a Dragon lair. Inside his chest, he now held the worst of her fears.

He pulled away from her, his own chest swirling heavily with sorrow for her. Rurik, who usually only felt hate and anger, felt tribulation because of this woman weeping in front of him.

All Amalia could do was cry as everything she'd been trying to push away finally crashed over her like a wave and threatened to drown her.

She was riddled with pain, and her heart was filled with so much agony that she could barely breathe. Her legs were hot, and she worried that any moment they would combust.

Her tears wouldn't stop falling, even when she knew she distressed him enough that he pulled his paw away from her grip. She held on, desperate to feel *something* other than herself and what she was feeling. When he pulled too far, she held onto the cold ground beneath her as small droplets wetted the dirt.

Why me? Why did I have to suffer such a terrible fate?

"Why do I have to live with the memories?"

She didn't want to anymore.

All she wanted was to forget, but she could always smell it in her hair. It lingered, reminding her.

She wanted to apologise for doing this in front of him. She didn't know why he still remained, or why he was choosing to watch her when she thought he might not care that she was suffering.

At any moment, she knew he would leave her alone to be a crying, sobbing mess. She wanted him to so that she could do this privately, but she didn't want him to leave because she didn't want to be alone.

Crawling loneliness swept through her, and she just cried harder. She was suffering alone and had no one to turn to.

She flinched when heat billowed over her, but thought it was just her mind playing tricks. She couldn't see beyond her forehead pressed against the soothing coldness of the ground.

Then shock cut through her when someone grabbed her shoulders and lifted her so she was upright on her knees. They slammed her body against theirs.

One arm wrapped over her shoulder with the hand pressing into the back of her head, and her face was squished against their neck. The other arm crossed over her back, pulling her tightly against them.

"Why are you-?" Amalia stuttered over hiccupping breaths.

"Cry, Amalia," Rurik said, in his human form rather than his scaly one. He pulled her tighter. "It is fine."

It was the first time he had said her name, called her something other than Witch. With a silent sob, she raised her hands and dug her fingertips into the bare skin of his back to accept his comforting hold.

I feel so alone.

Her body heaved against his, but he was strong enough to stop her from shaking him. The crook of his neck become wet with her tears, but she held him tighter, her fingernails digging in, as she released her pain.

Amalia didn't know why he was choosing to do this for her, to hold her in his big, muscular embrace, but she appreciated it. He even started patting the back of her head.

They stayed like that, both of them on their knees, while the sounds of her sobs echoed off the stone walls of his cave.

I do not want to remember anymore.

He stayed with her, even once she settled and limply held him. Her body was completely drained of energy, like the power of her outburst had sapped away all her strength.

He was so unbelievably warm, and it soothed her muscles that had been tight with tension. He continued to pat her head, causing her mind to go more and more quiet the longer he did it. Her painful memories ceased as she went numb.

She languidly laid against him, her eyes drooping now that her tears had finally stopped. He didn't move away when her arms dropped, nor did he pull them apart when she finally felt true peace for the first time since she arrived here.

The sounds of his breaths and heart, his scent and warmth, it all lulled her further.

He pulled her forward while he slowly fell back to rest against his ankles, no longer keeping them upright on their knees. He still didn't release her, and his hold was firm and comforting.

"Sleep. You are safe here."
And in that moment, being held by him, she felt that way.

11

Amalia woke lying on softness and found herself on the bed in the room filled with treasure.

She lay there for a while, curled on her side, watching the firelight catch against the pile of riches as the gold and jewels glittered. Her eyes trailed along the walls, then to the pillars at the corners of the bed.

Moving her head slowly, her gaze travelled until she saw large, silver eyes peering at her from the entryway.

In his Dragon form, Rurik was laying in the entry, facing her. His jaw rested in one of his paws while the rest of his scaly body was outside the room.

He didn't say or do anything when their eyes connected, allowing her to wake fully in her own time. Her cheeks heated, and she averted her gaze to the riches in the room.

I fell asleep in his arms.

She was embarrassed that she did, and ashamed that she allowed herself to cry in such a manner in front of him.

Yet, Amalia felt lighter, like a weight had been lifted from her shoulders. Not completely. No, the pain in her heart was real and continued to linger, but it just wasn't as prevalent. The memories weren't as clogging to her mind.

Amalia had vented hard and for a long time. He held her

the entire time, and she guessed he must have carried her to the bed once she fell asleep.

She was still a little surprised that he turned into a human to do so, or that he chose to comfort her at all.

She could barely remember his human face since she'd only seen it once before, and she'd been in a daze at the time. She hadn't seen it when she had been crying. He never pulled them apart for her to do so.

Her eyes fell back to his. *He comforted me.* Her, a Witch, his enemy. He'd taken away her suffocating loneliness by doing so, and given her someone to desperately cling to.

Amalia had needed to hold someone, to feel an embrace of safety when all she could remember was her skin melting.

"Why were you watching me sleep?"

She knew the first words out of her mouth should have been of gratitude, but she didn't want to remind him of her behaviour.

"To make sure you were well when you woke," he answered, his head lifting slightly to respond before he laid it back down.

She hadn't realised she'd needed someone to make sure she was okay until he said those words. That she needed someone to care for her while she was injured internally in the same way she cared for others physically.

She sat up to rest against the pillows and headboard. She didn't want to leave the warmth of the furs just yet. That seemed to be his cue to permanently lift his head up.

"I also wish to ask you something." She waited for him to continue, but he thought for a long while, eyeing her cautiously. "It may be a difficult question to answer, tell me now if you are not prepared for such a thing."

Amalia sighed deeply. "Ask it." She didn't think she would cry again.

"Why did you not run? You knew they were coming, but

you allowed them to take you."

"I was intending to." She averted her gaze again, this time to her hands folded on her lap. She brushed the furs with her fingertips. "I had a terrible feeling when I saw the soldiers walking to my home, and I knew something was wrong since they had never done so before. I had a suspicion that Marya may have overheard me chanting, but I was not sure. I did not have the time to flee."

"You freed me instead. You made sure that your concoction would not hinder me, and you freed me instead of fleeing."

"Yes, that is what I did."

She looked back up when she noticed his head did a puzzled tilt.

"Why? I know at the time I was nothing more than some strange lizard to you. Why did you put my life first and allow yourself to be captured in doing so? You did not know I was sentient. Most would not put a mindless animal before their own safety."

"What right do I have to decide that a creature's life is valued less than my own?" He tilted his head the other way, confused by her question. "I did not know you would be able to escape from your cage, but I was worried they may have burned my cottage with you inside it or taken you. I feared they would torture you because you were an odd, unknown thing."

"Would you have done the same thing if you knew what was going to happen to you?"

He raised his brow with an assessing hint to his eyes.

"I do not know," she answered truthfully, letting her head fall. "If I knew what awaited me, I may have just run. I may not have cared for your wellbeing if I knew I was going to be put on the stake. I may have also just grabbed your cage and freed you later."

"I expected you to have this grand speech that you would always put another's life before your own." His tone wasn't accusing, but she wondered if she noted the hint of humour in it correctly.

She let her eyes capture his with a boldness this time. "I will not dissimulate myself with innocence to appease you."

"And yet, with your honesty, you have just affirmed it more so."

It was her turn to tilt her head, her brows furrowing deeply. "How so?"

"You chose not to lie with pretty words. There is no harm in self-preservation, but you proved through your actions that your first thought is not for yourself. You showed bravery, then when questioned on it, you did not pretend that you would endure something that now terrifies you just to appear strong." He stood to walk inside the large alcove and sat in front of the bed, towering over as he stared down. "In doing so, you have not only shown that you would prefer to stay pure of lies by speaking truth, but you have also revealed strength of character."

"You are making it out that I am some pure, innocent woman of grace. That is not what I am."

"Oh no, do not mistake me. I am quite aware of the acid tongue you have, that you are not afraid to smack an injured lizard in the head when it bites you, and that you are not pure of body."

A knowing grin with sharp-jagged fangs spread across his features.

Her cheeks heated, only just now remembering that she had told him of her first time with a man. *I told him things I should not have!*

"But you have shown me that you are guiltless in the ways that matter."

"Why are you telling me this?"

He sighed as his grin fell. "I have not been fair to you since I brought you here. I realise I have pushed and terrified an already terrified woman."

"I did walk into that room of my own volition," she rebuffed. That wasn't particularly his fault.

"Yes, but I made sure I frightened you while you were in it. I wanted you to understand the kind of strength and power that I have, even against your kind. That, if you angered me, you may be added to my collection, when it had mostly been an empty threat."

Oh. That was different then.

"You can be a right bastard."

He lightly chuckled while nodding his head. "Yes, that is often said about me. I am known for being spiteful. My behaviour towards you is not out of character."

"So, you will continue to be a moody prick?"

His eyes narrowed into a scowl, but it didn't hold any real malice to it.

"Most likely." Then his face softened, as if he wanted to appear sincere. "I truly do not intend you any harm, so you no longer need to fear my flame or claws."

She rubbed the pad of her thumb over the small bite mark scar she had on her other hand.

"You did not mention your fangs, though."

"I often bite. I can make no such promises." A small smile pestered her lips, only because she could tell he was trying to be humorous.

"Then I make no promises that I will not smack you in the head when you do."

Once again, his face morphed into a scowl. It left him as quickly as it came, but he held her eyes with a seriousness.

"I will tell you, though, that I will be angered if you use magic in my home, yet I will not harm you. But I do not know what I will do if you use blood or dark magic." A lump formed in her throat when he continued to hold her gaze. "If, for some reason, you choose to escape, I may put you in my prison rooms. If you attack me or try to kill me, I will do the same. Do you understand?"

There was no wrath or bite to his tone. It was just a simple warning for her to understand the confinements of their situation and that anything he did was a reaction to her actions.

"Yes, I understand."

He gave a singular nod at her agreement.

"Good. Now, do you still smell burning flesh?" She shuddered, the smell suddenly wafting from her hair like she'd been ignoring it until now. "By your reaction, I am assuming that you do. However, it is a figment of your imagination. The scent of your burning no longer lingers on you."

"But-" She lifted a few strands to smell them, and found they smelt worse now that they were closer.

"Come, we will find something to sweeten the bathwater until it is gone."

It was considerate that he was choosing to help her rather than let her deal with something that was obviously bothering her.

She walked beside him when he led her down the tunnel. He stopped at an alcove with an assortment of high-quality housing items.

"Inside the chests in this room there should be perfumed solutions made by the humans. Although I find them foul to my senses, you may use them until you no longer smell burning flesh. When you do, I ask that you stop using them. Find one that is to your liking while I fill the tub with water and heat it."

She entered the room and then paused to turn around, making him pause as well.

"Thank you." She smiled to show him just how much she

appreciated it, noticing the scales around his face appeared a brighter purple.

He said nothing before he left, and Amalia went through the chests. When she came across a perfume that smelled similar to roses, she took it.

Going down the tunnel to the room she previously bathed in, she found him already partially inside. He must have heard her, because he backed out of the small space to allow her in.

"How did all these rooms come to be here?" she asked while stepping around him.

"Dragons find a cave to their liking and then shape it by claw to suit them," he answered from the entryway. "I liked this one because of the waterfall and stream."

She dipped her fingers inside the water, finding it was warmer than last time and would be soothing.

"How come some are smaller than others?"

She quirked a brow when he sat down on his hindlegs.

"Because I do not need them bigger. Some are just for storage. Some I use when I am not in this form or this size since I can mould myself at will, if I choose to. The larger rooms are the ones I prefer to occupy."

"Oh, that makes sense."

Then she stood next to the tub while holding the perfume bottle in her hand. She intended to add a few drops at a time until all she could smell was roses. Since he told her that he found the smell of perfume foul, she didn't want to saturate herself in it.

"Well? Is the temperature not to your liking?" He motioned his snout to the tub.

"I was waiting for you to leave."

"We are talking. Why would I do that?" His tone had been nondescript, but there was a certain crinkle in the scales around his eyes.

"I will not strip or bathe in front of you!"

He lowered his head to bring himself further into the alcove.

"Why not? I have seen you naked plenty of times. I also changed you when you arrived here."

She covered her breasts with both arms protectively.

"You could have told me that you were not some mindless creature instead of watching me! I knew there had been a hint of thought in your eyes."

"I had not trusted you then."

Her arms loosened but didn't fall away. "And now?"

His spiking brows drew together as his eyes danced over her. "I do not know."

She guessed that was better than him telling her he didn't.

"Regardless of the fact you have seen me naked, although I was not a willing party to that, I will not prance around naked in front of a male *anything*."

"Dragons have no concept of nudity. Currently, as we speak, I am naked."

"It is different. You are not human formed!"

He raised a clawed hand to his face to tap at his chin. "I have also never worn clothing around you while I have been human."

Her face paled, realising she had been holding a naked man when she'd been crying. Then that paleness faded into a roaring red, and she shoved her hands against her face in embarrassment.

"Come now, your kind is not known for being shy. They often have rituals of sex that are viewed by others."

"Get out, you perverted scamp!"

She threw her hands away from her face to yell, wishing she had something to toss at him.

"It appears I have been caught," he said, making her realise he indeed had been wanting to gaze at her in a lecherous manner. Before she could say or do anything, he turned from her. "Fine, I will leave you to your modesty."

He was lucky she didn't toss the perfume at his nose.

Rurik found entertainment in teasing the pretty thing. He was rewarded with her sharp tongue, and he happened to like it. Much more than her tears, at least.

If she hadn't cared, he would've been delighted to view her unclothed. He was awfully fond of the idea.

Now that he knew she wasn't turning hateful because of what happened to her, he was hoping she would return to the way she was before. The chatty little Witch who had taken care of him inside of her cottage.

Her presence didn't annoy him like he thought it would. Perhaps if they continued to conversate in the way they were now, he may come to think of her as a companion in his home. Although she was a prisoner, with the fact he was allowing her to roam around inside his lair, it was more like she was a guest.

A very attractive guest. He shook his head of that thought.

No, Rurik would not bed a Witch because she was pretty and conveniently in his home.

Although the idea didn't disgust him as it had before, he would never allow himself to get that close to her. He would be distracted, and she could harm him. *But she will not harm me, will she?*

She still didn't have violence in her. He could sense this.

Rurik hadn't liked seeing her pain. He still didn't fully understand why he changed into a human and held her. He'd been wary of her the entire time, wondering if perhaps she was waiting until he was in a more vulnerable form to attack him.

She didn't.

Then instead of merely seeing and hearing her sadness, he'd felt it. He'd felt it against his chest as her body struggled to breathe against her own sobs, and her warm wet tears that had soaked the side of his neck and shoulder.

He'd felt it in her fingertips as she clung to his body.

He'd known she'd sought physical comfort when she clutched his scaled finger.

Pity had swelled in his chest for the kind woman who took care of him even though he'd bitten her and tried to unleash fireballs at her. Yet in doing so, in holding her until she passed out in his arms, something small had shifted inside him.

When she had finally stopped crying and had trustingly fallen asleep against him, he understood that he no longer wanted to lash out at this female because she was born a Witch. Rurik no longer wanted to take his anger and hatred out on her because she was there for him to do so. She hadn't asked to be in the situation she was in, and he wouldn't torment her needlessly.

Rurik would never be able to release her even if he wanted to. Not when she had the knowledge of his home and human face, but he did feel regret that he was the one trapping her.

No matter. There is not much I can do about it.

If the Elders found out he released her, they would punish him. They may also punish him because he was keeping her alive, but he believed he may have figured out a way around that issue.

Rurik continued to walk, deep in his own thoughts, until he came to the entrance of his cave. He stared outside, realising he'd made a grave mistake in coming this way. Everything he could use to entertain himself was the other way.

He headed back. Since she was bathing, he thought he may do the same. One thing his kind preferred was to be clean so that dust and grime didn't imbalance their wings in flight.

They often tried not to fly when it rained.

"You better not be peeping, Dragon."

She must have heard his loud footsteps.

"Only passing through," he answered while he passed the room she was in.

He did, however, look inside to find her back towards him. With one knee bent, she had the other leg straight in the air while she was rubbing her hands up it to wash it. A long and slender leg covered in tanned skin with water sluicing down it.

Her calf looks as though it would yield if bitten. His walk slowed, mesmerised by her action.

She sharply snapped her face towards him. He quickened his step with his tongue pressing deeply against the back of his fangs.

The stream at the back of his lair was just big enough to slip his body into. He flapped his wings, stretching them so that they could catch the heavy drops from the waterfall and wash over his body.

One thing Rurik was very curious about was whether or not she liked his lair. He was very proud of it. He'd spent many years shaping it to what it was now and filling it with everything that caught his greedy eye.

Like most Dragons, he'd stolen things that took his interest to fill his hoards or anything he may possibly need for the future. Sometimes he even killed for them.

He collected tapestries because he liked seeing images of history. Not just of his own species, but of others as well. The others were somewhere lying about.

She hadn't reacted in the way he thought most would. Even the few Dragons that visited him had more interest in his hoards than her. The only treasure rooms he knew she had spent an extended amount of time in was the one with the bed and the one with his collection of books.

There was no greed for riches or interest in lovingly gazing at baubles.

She'd gone through the room filled with chests of clothing that were woven of the finest material and felt like silky flower petals against his calloused human fingertips. Yet, she hadn't taken a new dress for herself.

There was one room, however, he knew she would adore.

He hid it with magic when he brought her here since it contained almost anything a White Witch like herself could need or possibly want.

If she was to glide her hand down the walls of his tunnel, she'd realise a particular part of the wall was an illusion.

He hoped she never found it.

The Witch is digging through my collection of books again.

Rurik noticed she'd already compiled a small stack for herself in the corner. He considered picking one up to see what reading material she preferred but decided against it.

Currently, she seemed very interested in a particular book since she was already going through it rather than placing it on her designated pile.

"I already told you that I do not like my hoards rearranged."

He'd moved these books into particular stacks so long ago that he barely remembered the ones at the bottom.

She yelped with her back to him and turned swiftly. He winced when her arm smacked against a tall stack and it came tumbling down, making others tumble as well. She covered her face as they dropped on top of her.

He waited for her to dig herself out since he'd most likely squish her if he attempted to assist.

"Your hair is also wet. You will damage them."

She glared at him when she resurfaced.

"I will go through your hoards as I please, Dragon," she said, pushing books from on top of her chest. "You cannot keep me here and expect me to keep my hands to myself."

"Yes, I can. These items are not yours!" *She ignores my commands in my own home!* He wouldn't tolerate it. "Even though I share my home with you, these treasures remain mine."

"Which would you prefer? Me living here quietly or for me to annoy you?"

He reared his head back with a pouted frown. The answer to her question was obvious. "I would prefer you did not annoy me."

"When I am bored, I become awfully irritated. Since I have no one else to lash out at, you will most likely become my target. Especially since you are keeping me from things that will entertain me."

He tapped the side of his jaw with a claw. He hadn't thought on if she was unhappy or how she would treat him.

She is rather good at convincing me to get her way.

"Fine, you may go through them. Though, if I discover you are hiding items from me, I will be angered."

She rolled her eyes. "And just where would I hide them?"

Fair point, he thought.

His eyes fell onto the locked chests in this room. *I will have to remove those before she figures out how to get inside them.*

"Have you read all of these?" She picked up a random book and flicked through it, bending it so that the pages would quickly brush against her thumb.

"Most, yes. Although I much prefer to leave the more... feminine books for females to read."

"Do you often have females in your home then?"

"Well, no. I do not have many visitors. Although Dragonesses have come to spend time with me and have sought me out." He looked down the main tunnel of his home towards the entrance before bringing his focus back to her. "They do leave rather quickly when they realise I am ill-tempered."

"They seek you out?" She tilted her head, her eyes trailing over his scaled face and chest. "Does that mean you are a handsome Dragon then?"

Rurik blinked, a frown forming across his features. "I believe I am quite magnificent. I thought that was obvious."

She laughed at him!

"You are very arrogant, are you not? You have many scars."

He touched his face and let one of his claws slip against the large and deep scar across it. Then he gave a short and sharp growl, his lips curling back to reveal his fangs with lethal anger.

"We Dragons are not like you. Scarring shows that we have faced hardship and have prevailed. They do not make me ugly."

How dare she be so impudent!

Instead of being upset that she'd deeply offended him, she smiled softly with a small glint of humour in her eyes.

"That is not what I said. I was only stating that you have them." That was true, she never said his scars made him hideous. "I did not notice them when you were small, so I was curious about them. Will you tell me about some of them?"

She is curious about me?

He stared down at this odd woman who was allowing books to blanket her while they spoke.

"They are mostly tales of me killing your kind. I do not think these are things that you wish to hear of."

"Once again, you are treating me as though I am some weak-hearted damsel."

"You did cry."

"Because I was upset!" She tossed one of the thick bound books at him. "I was terrified and hurting, you stupid bastard!"

He snapped his jagged teeth in her direction.

"I do not understand why you are angry." She threw

another book. "Do not throw things at me!"

"I am embarrassed, you silly idiot!" That's when he noticed her cheeks were redder.

He didn't care if she was embarrassed of the truth. With a huff, he turned from her. He didn't like this conversation.

Stomping his heavy feet up the tunnel, he muttered to himself. *She disrespects me in my own home.* He wasn't usually a tolerant being, and he'd needed to leave before he'd gotten any angrier.

He touched the scar on his face again.

After their conversation, he wasn't sure what she thought of him.

Does she think me unsightly? She never truly clarified.

Rurik bore his scars not just in his Dragon body, but also in his human one. Witches and humans could be such fickle and vain things, finding ugliness in the weirdest of places.

Although he had no intention of bedding her, he found her quite lovely to look at. He didn't like that he thought this way about her, although she was considered his enemy, when she might find him revolting.

Did he want her to find him attractive? *Do I want to bed her?* He thought for long moments. *No, no. I have just been without a female for quite some time.*

With a glower, he decided to find a place to nap since he hadn't slept throughout the night. He'd been waiting for her to awaken to make sure she wasn't going to go into another horrible fit of tears.

A bit later, Rurik found her crawling through one of his piles of riches. Well, in reality, she found him.

He felt and heard the shifting of coins and jewels as she climbed to the top of the pile. He didn't think she was aware that she was climbing on top of him as well.

He waited for her to leave in hopes she would just take what she was interested in and go. He eventually felt her sit at the very top of the pile, doing whatever she pleased. The soft humming noise she made grabbed his attention, informing him that she was no longer upset.

Rurik slowly brought his head out to see what she was up to. He moved quietly enough that she didn't seem to notice, and he found her staring at a tiara in her hand. Then, with much glee, she placed it on her head.

"Would you prefer to be a princess rather than a Witch?"

Her squeal of surprise painfully pierced his ears as she slid down the pile and came to a stop beside his face.

"You are so big. How do you keep coming out of nowhere?"

The tiara had dislodged. It was now sitting crooked on her head and was horribly tangled in her hair.

"Well, considering you are sitting on top of me, I believe you are the one disturbing me."

She dug through the pile on her knees to find she'd been sitting on his shoulder and before that, on his back.

"Why do you sleep like this?"

She untangled the tiara from her hair, her cheeks slightly pink at being caught, before she tossed it onto the pile.

"I like the weight of it. The heavier it is, the better it feels. It is also so that if some human came into my lair and went through my hoards, instead of finding some sleeping Dragon to kill, they will wake me, and I can make a quick meal of them."

"Do you often eat people?" She gave him a wary look.

"Yes, I eat anything of meat." He expected her to be horrified, but she just shrugged, making him frown. "You are not bothered by that?"

"I am aware of the circle of life and that it is to be observed without bias rather than with disgust."

"You say this," he said as he rose to stand, letting his riches fall from him. "But you saved me from your cat."

"I would prefer to preserve life when I can, but if you had been dead when he brought you inside, I would not have batted an eye." She looked around the room. "Why do you sleep here if the other one is bigger? Would you not prefer the larger pile?"

Although many of his hoards were organised, only two consisted of coins and jewels.

"This was my first pile. When I realised I did not have enough room, I carved the other. I just have not moved these yet, and your bed occupies it."

She nodded with her hand on her chin as if she understood the ways of his kind.

He expected her to stand when he stood, shaking the last of everything off his body, but she didn't. She continued to have a thoughtful look.

"I have been meaning to ask, how did you end up in Bala's mouth?" She turned her gaze up with a deep frown across her face. "You are not some poor, helpless animal."

Rurik sat on his hindlegs. He'd known she would eventually ask on how he came to be in her cottage.

"Do you know of the Witch, Strolguil the Vast?"

She shook her head. "I have never met another of my kind other than my mother."

He was no longer surprised or shocked by these kinds of admissions.

"Strolguil the Vast obtained his title by obtaining power through taking parts of magical creatures. He has killed many Dragons in pursuit of corrupted magic." He held her gaze as he said, "He is also the first Witch who turned on his Dragon parent."

She turned her eyes away to think on something.

"But you said that Witches came from Dragons over a thousand years ago."

"There is evil magic, dark power that can give Witches the

ability to extend their life by taking certain parts from mine. He has been doing this for centuries." When she looked up to him, he noted that her face had paled. "He is old and very powerful. I have been hunting him for many years. The storm from that night was not natural. When he realised I caught up to him, he created it in order to hinder me as I chased him in the air."

"Witches cannot fly," she scoffed.

He lowered his head so that he was closer.

"They can if they steal our wings. Steal a Dragon's wings, and it can give you the ability to use them. Take our scales, and they can be used as armour. Take our bones, and they may give you strength. Take our eyes, you will see better. Take our tongue, and you may breathe fire. Take our blood, our essence, and you will obtain unimaginable power."

"I am surprised you are telling me these things."

He knew why she said that.

He was revealing why his kind was so sought out by hers. He was giving her information that she could later use to kill him.

Rurik shook his head. "I can see you will not harm me, nor do you know the spells in order to do these things or have the knowledge of how to fight against me. If you were like the others of your kind, you would have broken my neck when I was small and injured. You would not have released me."

"So, this Strolguil the Vast created the storm while he flew with stolen wings," she said, wanting him to continue.

"Yes. I did not know he obtained the ability to create a storm, and I was blindsided by it. Although I managed to tear at him, he redirected the lightning of the storm to hit me. I felt the blast to my wings and knew that they were broken. Unable to do anything as I fell, I knew he followed me when I felt him hex me."

She listened to the story silently while bravely keeping her eyes on him. Whereas most Witches would have sneered with joy that he'd been injured, her face softened into one of care.

"Before I hit the ground, I had the strength to change my size in hopes he would not find me if I was to be knocked into unconsciousness. It is a defensive ability. I managed to stay awake, but I was not well. As I crawled for a place to hide, not knowing I would not be able to heal, your blasted cat stumbled upon me. Not wanting to change my size so that Strolguil could find me, I stayed small. Unfortunately, I hit the ground with my head, and when I fought against your cat, he managed to throw me against a tree when I tried to kill him. With my head already wounded, I was knocked out and woke up to you grabbing me from your birdcage."

"Well, you are very lucky then."

"How so?"

If he told the tale correctly, he'd been anything but lucky.

"You were lucky that Bala often likes to play with his prey before he eats it." She gave a heartfelt smile as she said, "And that you were brought to my cottage so that I could help you."

As it usually did, that smile warmed him. With her long, curling blonde hair, her soft and gentle facial features, and mesmerizing azure blue eyes, it made her appear unbelievably kind.

I very much like it when she looks at me like that.

To his dismay, her smile fell and changed into one of deep sadness as she gazed down at her hands. She didn't say anything for a long while, her eyes flickering side-to-side. Even her shoulders slumped.

He stepped one of his front legs forward to lower his head and bring himself down to her level.

"What is the matter?"

"I miss that feral cretin. I miss my home with my own bed and clothing, my herbs and spices. I miss sipping on calming tea as I sat in the sun watching Bala catch bugs."

She is homesick. He turned his head to stare at the pile of treasure around them, but also towards the direction of his entire lair. *She is not comfortable here.*

He wouldn't be able to take her back. She couldn't leave, and it was likely that they'd already destroyed her home. Although he wanted to kill that cat when he left, it had been her companion.

Why do I care if she is sad or not? Strange emotions swirled in his chest at the woman sitting quietly on top of wealth who wanted nothing more than to live like a peasant.

Then she seemed to snap out of it, bouncing to her feet like nothing had been the matter a moment before.

"I am hungry. Since you will not allow me the use of magic in your home, will you prepare the pot and water so that I may eat?"

Rurik blinked at her abrupt change of behaviour.

Amalia stood over the cooking hearth, boiling the vegetables she obtained in the alcove close to the entrance of his cave.

Her eyes often found his watching her from the entryway. She was rather surprised that he didn't just dump everything she needed into this room and leave.

She noted that he often found her and then stayed with her. *I must be a source of entertainment for him.* That should bother her, but she would rather this than for him to be hateful and mean.

At least she knew he didn't disdain her presence. With the way he watched her, she had an inkling that he may actually like it.

"Do you have any herbs or spices? Food is often bland without them."

"I will not allow you to have anything that will allow you to use magic in my lair if I can avoid it."

She sighed while rolling her eyes. "I just want it for food."

"Yes, but once you have it, you may want to play with it."

"It is like you wish for me to be unhappy in your home," she grumbled.

Rurik frowned, his head tilting to the side. "Are you unhappy?"

"Well, no, but I am not content either. You keep telling me not to touch things. There is nowhere other than this table and chair for me to sit." She pointed to furniture she was speaking of in the middle of the room. "And you will not allow me to use magic even though it will not cause harm."

His gaze fell to the dining table she gestured to and then back to her. The look on his face was clear. *He does not understand.*

She half-expected him to tell her she should just be thankful she was alive, but he didn't. Instead, he rolled his eyes and swiftly turned from the room like he no longer cared for the conversation.

Great, I have been dismissed.

With a pout, Amalia sat at the table eating the array of plain vegetables she cooked. *Am I not even allowed salt and pepper?*

He didn't return, and she didn't go looking for him. She went to the front of his lair and sat in the middle of the exit to stare at the outside world, unsure if she would ever be allowed to touch it again.

She missed the tickle of grass under her feet, the touch of rough bark against her fingertips, the warm sun washing over her skin.

At some point, she wanted to wake early enough to see if

the sunlight came into the mouth of the cave. The mountain caused a shadow across the land in the evenings so she thought the cave entrance may be facing east.

It is quite a beautiful view. Although the ground was rocky directly in front of her, she knew that she was only halfway up the mountain.

Not too far away was a small clearing that turned from rocky mountain into grass. It spread between the single tree here and there before it became a lush green forest. On one side, she could see a river that ran through the forest some distance away. She bet the stream in his lair connected to it.

She couldn't see any towns or buildings, but the area just seemed much more peaceful because of it.

Scraping noises and the sounds of rock shifting against rock from behind her grabbed her attention.

She looked down the tunnel to see the tail of the Dragon coming towards her. He was walking backwards slowly with his forearms sweeping often against the ground.

"Move it, Witch," he demanded.

She quickly had to scramble out of his way before he stepped on her.

Standing by the wall, she watched as he walked backwards out of the cave while pulling different size rocks with him. The larger ones came with ease, but he constantly had to grab the smaller ones that rolled away. He took the rocks outside to the side, and she wasn't able to leave to see where he went.

Because he so rudely called her Witch, she pretended she didn't care what he was doing when he came back inside. She tilted her chin up, ignoring him in the same way he ignored her.

She sat back down to stare at the sky bright with light, soft white clouds passing over the sun. *I would really love to walk this land.* She'd often strolled through the woodlands near her cottage to talk to the trees and wind.

Not too much later, the Dragon came through again with more rocks. Instead of telling her to move this time, he pushed her out of the way with his tail, making her squeal.

"Stay out of the tunnel," he said when he came back inside.

"What are you doing?"

Okay, he had officially piqued her interest.

"Leave me in peace while I work."

Moody prick.

If she wasn't able to find peace at the mouth of the cave, then she would go elsewhere.

I will have to go through those books again. She thought she might have been halfway through them until all the stacks tumbled.

Now the area was just a mess.

Since the books were in one of the last alcoves in the tunnel, she had to walk next to where he was working in order to get there. She swore she heard the sound of claws scraping against rock walls.

He stuck his head out and growled at her when she travelled by. She lifted her chin again to snub him even as her eyes tried to peek around him to see what he'd been up to.

For most the day and late into the night, she heard him moving around his lair by his large footsteps pattering around.

She stayed away, going through the books until she was most of the way through them, and her own pile had grown. She hadn't been able to find the book she saw earlier, and she was desperate to.

She constantly eyed the entry to the alcove.

Amalia had found a spell book in this collection and knew he wouldn't like that she had. She intended to hide it in plain sight with the other normal ones she'd put aside for herself to read.

It'd been a simple one filled with remedies and teas, but there had been chants and spells as well – ones she didn't know. There had been a spell to create a shield, a way to protect herself. Everything inside the spell book had been harmless magic.

She'd just started reading it when he gave her a fright earlier.

The chests in this room had been taken away. She wondered if they had also been full of spell books, and this one had not been put away like it was intended to be.

There it is! It sat at the very bottom of the pile.

She started flicking through the pages.

"Come," that deep voice said behind her, and she gasped, shoving the book to her chest to hide it. Amalia eyed him warily while he stood in the entryway. "Come."

"No. I am busy," she answered, snubbing him with her shoulder. Amalia crawled over to her pile of books and shuffled them around to hide the spell book. "Go away."

With an irritated snarl, he turned away, his tail swishing into the room. Then, to her surprise, he grabbed her with it!

She let loose a small scream when he picked her up and dragged her from the room in the air. His tail had a heart-shaped spade at the tip and looked awfully sharp near her face.

"Put me down!"

She struggled to free her arms, and her legs dangled as she kicked them like she was running in the air.

"When you do not do as you are told, I will make you."

He stomped his way up the tunnel and then flung her inside of an alcove. She immediately turned around, heading straight for him to bash her fists against one of his arms. She uselessly beat against him.

"I am not some pet you can pick up and do with as you will!"

With a sigh, he picked her up with his other paw and pushed her into the alcove. Just as she was about to turn back around and yell at him again, something caught her eye.

The bed has been moved.

Instead of being practically on top of a pile of riches, it now lay in a different room with the backrest placed against a rocky wall. Her eyes fell onto the large paintings of nature that hung high on the walls above furniture.

There was a wardrobe with multiple chests in front of it, and a vanity table with a glass mirror. There were chests of drawers and an empty bookcase next to a plush chesterfield sofa. There was also a long, full body mirror that was cloudy along the edges, weathered by time, standing near the wardrobe. She couldn't see the cave floor because carpets had been laid down. In the very centre of the room lay the metal tub.

Amalia could remember what this room had been, and it had been much smaller before, not as tall, not as wide. It'd also been filled with very little.

The Dragon was seated, watching her take everything in.

With her lips parted and a deep furrow to her brows, she said, "I do not understand."

"You have been walking around my lair without a place to comfortably return to." His eyes scanned over the furniture and all the work he had done. "You miss a home that no longer exists to you so... I have created a new one."

He did this for *her?* That's when she realised that he'd been rude to her because he wanted to keep this as a surprise.

"That is very considerate of you. Thank you," she said, unable to keep the tender feeling of warmth from spreading through her chest.

She also couldn't keep that feeling from her face, a caring smile showing for him. She watched the scales around his face become a brighter shade of purple.

"Is that a blush, Dragon?" she asked with a giggle.

His eyes widened in horror.

"No."

He fled, and she chased after him.

"Yes, it is!"

She grabbed the tip of his tail and pulled it. Instead of halting him, she ended up being dragged forward against the ground.

He stopped, his head turning slowly with unmasked shock.

"Did... Did you pull my tail?"

She knew at any moment he would explode with rage, and she fell back onto her bottom with a laugh. "Oh, do not be mad. I only wanted to stop you from running away in embarrassment."

"You dare pull me?!" he roared. "After I do a nice thing for you? I worked all day for an ungrateful cow!"

He didn't appreciate that his anger was met with more giggles. She covered her mouth when he growled to hide them.

His lips curled back over his fangs, and he lowered his head to snarl right in front of her with his snout so close that his breath fanned over her. His eyes were narrowed, and he looked as though he was a moment away from biting her in half.

Amalia didn't feel fear.

Instead, she leapt forward and wrapped her arms around his scaly neck as best as she could with the differences in their size. He froze.

"I wanted to spend time with you to thank you," she said with sincerity. "I did not expect you to show me such kindness."

The angry tension in his body lessened before one of his paws wrapped around her torso – almost like he was returning her hug.

It had been two weeks since Amalia was brought to the Dragon's cave.

After he showed her the room he'd created for her, he told her she may go through his hoards and collect anything that may be of interest to her. When she'd asked him why he was suddenly okay with her doing so, he explained that technically, since they would not leave his lair, they were still a part of his treasures.

She changed very little about the room although he told her she may rearrange it as much as she liked, only adding a candle here and there and filling the bookshelf. He never said so, but she knew he liked that she didn't change the way he'd decorated it.

The chests he had placed in front of the wardrobe were filled with dresses and clothing. Once she went through them and hung the ones she liked, he took the chests out of the room when he saw her struggling to do it herself.

The Dragon tried to convince her that she should have a small pile of coins and gems in the centre. When she refused, not wanting such items, he'd given her a bewildered face.

And as the two weeks passed, like he had warned her, he was often ill-tempered and easy to anger.

Still, they often spent time together.

One day, she found him laying down in his largest treasure-filled room that once held the bed. He'd been sorting through it like he was trying to find something in particular. A coin, perhaps, or a piece of jewellery.

They'd had pleasant conversations earlier in the day, so she walked in and sat resting her back against him to read a book in her lap. He hadn't asked her what she was doing, nor did he tell her to go away, but he did stare at her for long moments.

Then he went back to his task, barely moving since she was there against him. She didn't know how long they had spent together, but it wasn't the last time the situation occurred.

He also often came to lay outside of her room. Most of the time it was to talk to her. Sometimes, very rarely, he just laid there watching her move about or read.

Amalia had settled into her new home.

Since the day he'd given her the room, she no longer smelled burning flesh, and she stopped using the perfume like he'd asked.

Unfortunately, that same night, she started to be plagued with nightmares of burning, of running, of being captured and being tortured while the word 'Witch' was screamed at her. Each time, the nightmares were of humans, and she would shoot up in her bed covered in a layer of sweat.

She never woke screaming, never woke crying. Mostly, she was able to ignore it.

If she were ever given the chance to be free, Amalia knew deep down to the very essence of her being that she wouldn't live near any humans again. She would have to become a wanderer. That in itself presented problems since women on the road were often targeted because they were alone – taken as slaves, beaten, raped, or murdered.

She didn't know how to wield a sword or a dagger. She

had been studying her hidden spell book in secret, practising her magic without him knowing so she could protect herself.

She already learned how to shield herself as well as how to hide small items on her person. She'd taken a singular, large gem from his hoard and practised the illusion in front of him – he hadn't noticed.

She wondered if she could use the same spell to make herself invisible, but upon trying it out, she discovered it only worked on inanimate objects.

There were others, but they required natural ingredients like raw crystals, herbs, or spices.

Overall, her life had become calm. Between the Dragon who roamed these tunnels and the books she had to read, Amalia had found peace. Sometimes boring peace, but safety, nonetheless.

Except on this particular morning.

She'd been having a mostly calm sleep, trying to recover from already having a nightmare, when she heard strange noises. She'd been slow to wake at first, but she hadn't been able to escape the subtle feeling of weightlessness.

When she finally opened her eyes, little flying creatures were holding her in the air, lifting her off the bed by the corners of her sheets.

Tiny snickers came from them. When she realised what they were and what they were doing, she struggled to get free. They'd callously dropped her, and the bed hadn't been underneath her.

Amalia hit the ground and the wind knocked out of her. She gingerly got to her feet to fight them off, but they had already started pulling on her hair and lifting the outer skirt of her nightgown to blind her.

"You feral little pixies!"

As she tried to swat them away with her hands, they bit her with sharp teeth – not enough to draw blood, but enough to hurt. Then they swarmed her and picked her up onto her side, floating her around the room.

"Put me down!"

Heavy and large footsteps came from the tunnel before they stopped at the entryway to her room.

"How did you vermin get into my cave?" the Dragon snapped, quickly ducking into the alcove to give chase.

A few went missing when he snapped his jaws around them.

Eventually he grabbed her from the air, pulled her to his chest protectively, and unleashed a rush of flames. Most of them to disintegrated. He held her upside down, and she was thankful he'd grabbed her around her legs so that her skirt didn't fall.

The rest rushed from his lair with tiny shrieks. He let out a loud, ear-splitting roar behind them, watching them scatter as the troupe fled.

"Blasted vermin! Why do they return to my cave when they know I will kill them?"

"Uh, could you possibly put me down?" Preferably before he squeezed his paw any tighter in anger and possibly crushed her to death.

Growing dizzier by the second, he lifted her to blink at her face that had reddened from the blood rushing to her head. He carefully transferred her to his other paw, right way up, so that he could place her down on her feet.

"Wretched pixies. They manage to sneak past my wards because they are so small and dishevel my home," he said as she stumbled from light-headedness. "They usually try to steal my treasure. I did not think they would attack you."

She put her hand up to indicate it was okay.

"I was surprised. I have never been attacked by so many before. The ones where I lived, although mischievous, have never tried to harm me because they knew I would help them if they were injured."

She rolled up the sleeves of her dress to double check they hadn't broken skin. It would bruise, but mostly she was fine.

"This will most likely happen again."

His expression crinkled into a glower.

"Do you happen to have a broom?" She pushed her sleeves down before putting her hands on her hips.

His spiked brows crinkled into a frown. "You wish to clean?"

"No, silly. So I can swat them away next time. You have never seen action like an angry Witch with a broom," she laughed.

He gave a chuckle in return. "That would be an entertaining sight to see."

Amalia liked it when he laughed.

He didn't do it often, but it was deep and warm and very soothing to her senses. Every time he did it, it made her feel as though she was truly safe from him. She didn't think he would laugh with someone he hated.

"It is quite early." Thanks to her rude awakening. "I am going to go sit by the entrance."

It was her way of extending an offer to him to join her. Though, she thought she should've been more direct when he nodded and left her on her own.

Amalia had been right when she thought the sun would come into the cave mouth in the morning. She decided that each day she would try to sit in it.

After the sun faded from her reach, she went back to her room to read, sitting upon the couch he'd brought in for her. Licking her thumb and using it to swipe the page, her head turned up, like it did every time she heard movement. She glanced up at the entryway.

What she hadn't expected to see was a human man walking past her room while tossing something into the air, only to catch it a moment later.

She does not see past my scales, Rurik thought as he dug through the basket of apples in his food storage alcove.

He grabbed the two that appeared to be the ripest and most firm before leaving, placing one of the apples in the pocket of his black leather breeches for later consumption.

She does not see me as anything more than a creature.

He knew it was the truth as he walked down his tunnel, on two legs instead of four.

Although he didn't have an issue parading around naked in his own lair, he was aware that she likely wouldn't approach him if he did.

He constantly readjusted his pants until they eventually sat right, finding them uncomfortable. They were tight around his muscular calves and then looser around his thighs. *I do not like wearing trousers.* And yet, he often did when he travelled around the humans.

So, barefoot and shirtless, he made his way down the tunnel, tossing his captured prey, the green apple, into the air as he thought.

She does not feel desire for me. He hadn't seen it or scented it from her, and that had started to bother him over the two weeks she'd been in his home. Even though she didn't feel this way, he did, and he didn't appreciate the unrequited desire.

Rurik found this woman, an enemy, alluring and he was insulted that she didn't think the same of him. Realisation dawned on him that she saw him as a creature when she'd been sitting next to him one day and started petting his side like a dog.

She treats me like I am a mindless animal.

He thought it may be because he hadn't spoken to her or spent any time with her as a human, something that is the same shape as her.

Today, he decided he would rectify that and start showing this side of himself more in hopes it might pique her interest.

It wasn't to bed her. *No, I would never bed a Witch.* It was just because he hadn't appreciated it when he'd felt desire for her, apparently, so easily. *Pretty little thing.*

He wanted them on the same level so they could suffer together, by themselves.

However, he thought his desire may not be just because of the way she looked. There was something else about her that drew his attention.

Sometimes he was mean to her, he often growled and snarled. They bickered a small amount because she wasn't afraid of him, and therefore, she was willing to use her acid tongue and call him all manner of names. Her reaction would anger him, and he'd storm off in a huff.

Yet, this female already seemed to know how to handle him.

When he was truly angry and he hadn't done anything to upset her, she didn't argue back. Instead, she would try to redirect his thoughts by distracting him. He could tell it was because she truly didn't want to fight with him.

Perhaps it is her kindness that draws me to her?

The reason he and many Dragonesses didn't get along was because when he showed anger or irritation, they would mirror him. He was short-tempered, and they would fight. It would start with words and then, being the beasts they were, it would sometimes get physical. He'd be thankful when the Dragonesses would storm from his home – and generally never return.

Instead of arguing with him, Amalia would leave it be.

She would lash out when she thought he deserved it, but she didn't fight for fighting's sake. She wasn't some pushover, either – even though he indeed pushed her over a few times with the back of his claws because he could.

She was caring and soft, radiating an innocence that he didn't see in most. Whether it be her own kind, his, or humans.

An innocence he'd seen when she had cried in his arms.

Rurik often reflected back on that moment. The delicate broken woman who desperately needed someone to hold.

Not once had they spoken about it, and he knew that was because she was ashamed of herself for it.

But what had been a simple attraction to her had grown into something darker because of it. Her emotions had been strong, powerful.

He realised she had passion inside her.

Sometimes when he thought on that tender moment, he would remember what had happened. Then, other times, his mind would twist it into some sort of image. A dark fantasy.

An image of a woman whose cries of pain turned into cries of sex. A woman whose struggle for breath from a sob was a struggle for breath from a thrust. A woman whose desperately clinging fingertips turned into nails scoring across his back in deep strokes, and whose shuddering from heaving breaths of sadness became trembles of a woman lost in the throes.

It burned hot in his mind, especially when it would end with her giving him that beguiling smile that made his chest feel tight.

His desire deepened with every moment he spent around her, and he wouldn't have it! He wouldn't allow himself to be the only one who felt this way.

Rurik entered the main room of his lair, the one with the tapestries that depicted the histories of his kind, and picked up one of the many claymore swords he'd brought in here earlier. He'd done so when he was large and could do it in one go.

With one hand, he swung it to get a feel of it, with the other, he bit into the apple in his hand, letting the juices fill his mouth.

Too light. He tossed it carelessly to the side and picked up another.

Taking another bite of his fruit, he swung the new sword around. Since the weight didn't feel terrible, he propped it up in front of him like he was holding it with two hands.

He rolled his arm and wrist to get momentum, the blade swinging by his side before it cut downwards through the air, mimicking a downward attack on an enemy. *The handle is uncomfortable. The guard is too sharp.*

He tossed it to the side.

Bouncing a new sword in his hand, he checked that the weight was to his liking. Then he gave a downwards swing of his arm. When the handle felt just fine, he spun in a circle like he was gutting an invisible enemy.

Weight is fine, handle is fine. Then he flipped it over to double-check the blade itself by ghosting his fingertips along one of the edges. A yellow crystal in the guard caught his eye, something he hadn't noticed before because of the gold handle.

With a roll of his eyes, he tossed the sword behind him, and it clattered as it bounced precariously. *Witches will notice the jewel and use it against me.*

Swords wielded by him couldn't have simple earthy materials such as gems and stones. They would be able to direct power to it and harm his hands.

He picked up another sword, checking it for jewels and then its weight. As he was grabbing it, he noticed a scent from nearby.

She is watching me. He took the last bite of his apple and threw the core to the side.

Swinging this new sword around, he immediately disliked it. Off it went, scattering on the floor with the others around him.

He hoped one of the last two would be suitable, otherwise he was going to have to hunt down some human soldiers to steal their weapons.

Rurik knew where she was. She was peeking inside to watch him while trying to stay out of sight.

Since he had two hands available, he picked up both the swords left. Both were claymores – his preferred weapon. He checked them and then swung his arms around, trying to get a feel for them.

Both seemed good. He switched hands to make sure.

Making his decision, he tossed the lighter one away. But he didn't just toss it, he threw it in her direction. She yelped when it cut through the rock next to the tunnel entrance she was hiding behind, the sword jutting out from the floor. It eventually fell from its own weight.

She stared at it for long moments before peeking her head inside the room. He was facing her, and their eyes connected.

Now that she knew she was caught, he expected her to step out. Instead, she ducked away, and he shook his head. She wasn't usually against approaching him, and he'd expected her to berate him for throwing the sword in her direction.

With a shrug, he began to practise with the weapon in his hand. *She will approach in her own time.*

After a while, she did eventually come out of her hiding place.

"What are you doing?" she asked over the distance.

"Picking a new sword," he answered as he pretended to fight an invisible enemy.

"Why?"

"I do not always have the luxury of fighting as a Dragon. I

often wear a pouch with weapons." It also carried clothing in case he needed to stop off in a human town. "I lost my previous one in my fight with Strolguil the Vast."

Rurik wasn't sure how this female would react, but he would have to go Witch hunting again at some point. He was preparing himself for when he felt comfortable enough to leave her here. She'd made no attempts to escape as of yet, but he was sure once he was gone that she would try.

Happy with his choice of weapon and relieved he wouldn't have to steal another, he started piling the rejected ones to the side to deal with later – when he was larger and could carry them all.

"You tossed a flail at my face. Do you not know how to use a weapon?" He checked the blade of his chosen claymore, seeing it needed sharpening.

"No."

"Would you like to learn to?"

"Not particularly."

His head shot up to her with his brows drawing together.

"Why not? You should know how to defend yourself without magic."

He placed the weapon off to the side of the others.

Although he knew she would never need such skills while trapped in his home, if he were to die his wards would disappear. She would have the opportunity to leave.

"I do not think I have the heart to harm another."

What a silly admission. Rurik strutted towards her, closing the large space between them to stand in front of her.

"What if someone threatens you with fire?" She'd already taken an unsteady step back from his approach, but it was his words that made the colour drain from her face. "There is no time to care for righteousness when faced against someone who wishes to hurt you."

She gave a shrug while averting her gaze.

"Then I would run."

"What if you cannot run?" Her head lifted, and she took a step back when he took a step forward. Then another and another until he was following her step for step. "What if no matter where you go or how fast you run, you cannot get away?"

He was slowly chasing her, directing her path by stepping to the side so she would retreat the opposite way.

"What if, no matter what you do, you become cornered?" Her body met the wall. Her back tightened when he shoved his hands against the rockface beside her shoulders to trap her there. "With nowhere left to run or hide."

Her eyes were wide, not with fear but with something else as he held them with his own.

"Then I do not know," she whispered softly.

The pulse in her jugular was quick and her breathing shallow. He squinted his eyes like that would help him to sense what she was thinking or feeling since he couldn't pick up anything by her scent.

They stayed in place while he had her cornered.

Her eyes are such a strange colour of blue. They appear like lagoons.

He'd her cornered, and he was waiting to see what she would do while he closely inspected her face.

She seemed to be doing the same.

Her face looks sweet. She reminded him of a tiny bunny – soft, gentle, and defenceless. It often made him forget what she really was, that he could sense strong, untapped power.

As if she couldn't hold his eyes anymore, they drifted down his body and the arms caging her in. Her eyes flicked over his torso for long moments.

Then she did something he didn't think she would do.

She reached forward and tentatively touched one of the many scars marring his body. He knew the one she was gently caressing her fingertips over without needing to look. It was the palm-sized blast scar he had just above his hip.

"You have been hurt very deeply."

Her fingers tickled a different scar, one that ran across his abdomen. The muscles tensed in reaction. His brows drew together at her touching him like this. He was unsure if he wanted to pull away or not.

Although he'd received many injuries in the past, anything that didn't go past his skin or scales wasn't deep enough to scar his body. With the natural regenerative abilities his kind held and the magical healing properties in their saliva when in Dragon form, only certain, deep injuries would be lasting. Even smaller bones like his wings could be spared any permanent damage.

She peeked up to him to see if what she was doing was allowed.

Whatever she saw made her duck her gaze to watch herself touch the one on the left side of his sternum, just below his heart. Rurik had almost lost his life obtaining the one she was touching now.

"Did these all happen in your Dragon form?" she asked when her fingers lingered over his neck.

His blood rushed faster, apprehensive of her being so close to somewhere vital. He had many there, some deep, others barely noticeable. It was the place most targeted because of its vulnerability.

"Mostly." A few he gained in his human one.

Mainly the blast scar and the one she was reaching up to touch, the one across his face.

"How did this one happen?"

She ran her fingers over the length of it and the tips of them tickled his face. It ran from the middle of his cheek beneath one eye, trailed over his nose, and then slashed across his cheek all the way to his ear.

The injury had been deep, cutting through bone.

"I had been hexed to remain human. Even though I killed the person who did it, the hexes remain until they are removed. As I was returning home so I could remove it, I was ambushed by a troupe of rogue soldiers."

"So, you do not just fight Witches?"

Her hands retreated.

"I am temperamental. I fight with everyone."

A quirk of humour twitched on the corners of her lips, and he tilted his head.

She does not find me appealing in the same way I do her. Rurik thought he would have sensed something by now considering their close proximity and the fact that she'd touched him. *Did she touch me because she truly finds me unsightly?*

He didn't understand the swelling inferno in his chest, but he didn't like it. He could feel anger prickling on the back of his neck, could feel it warming his skin. *She had not even been hesitant in touching a man.*

Her eyes fell away from his face to his jaw, then neck, slowly making their way to his chest and biceps. He dug his fingers into the rockface of the wall with his jaw clenching.

How dare she treat me as though I am insignificant. Him! A male who Dragonesses and humans fawned over.

Just as he was about to pull away, his nose crinkling with rage, her cheeks darkened and her lids flickered.

It was slow to build, pink flushing her chest as if she was getting hot in the cool space they were in. Her pulse fluttered heavier, before her eyes quickly darted up to his. They continued to dart, from his jaw to his lips, bouncing across his features. He even recognised when they trailed across the scar marring his face.

Then he scented it, subtle desire coming from her skin.

Rurik couldn't help the grin that formed across his

features, which seemed to make the scent deepen. *Ha! I knew it was possible.*

Now that he obtained the reaction he'd been seeking, he lowered his arms and leaned back. She started and brought both her hands to her chest to cup them.

"Your hair is strange," she said before clearing her throat.

Distract yourself as much as you like, but it is far too late. Now that he had made her cross that barrier, it shouldn't matter what form he took, she would still hold it.

However... he was sure his hair *was* strange to her. It was black, but flickers of light gave it a purple tinge, much like his scales.

"Is it now?" he answered with a quirk of humour.

"Um, yes." She quickly averted her eyes, and he frowned when she stepped to the side. "Excuse me, but I must go."

But I just started having fun.

Before he could speak, she fled.

Trapped against the wall, Amalia felt apprehension with someone being so close to her – not just him, but anyone.

He'd been asking her distressing questions. Questions she didn't know how to answer while he tried to convince her to change something she didn't know if she wanted to change.

In order to protect herself with a blade, she would have to hurt another. She would have to make someone bleed or take their life. Amalia felt no aspiration to see or do that.

Amalia would prefer to use magic to protect herself, but she knew if she told him this it would anger him. So, before he could say anything more, she touched one of his scars to distract him from the conversation.

That had borne curiosity in her.

Curiosity about his scars, how he had obtained them, and what kind of battles this person must have endured to be marred so heavily. *He must be so strong.*

They appeared deep and were scattered all over his body. Some even appeared as though they should have been fatal, like the one across his stomach and the other near his heart.

She'd noted, at the time, that his chest was broad. That the brawny muscles of his abdomen were easy to see and twitched when she brushed over them. That his defined pectoral muscle bunched when she touched near his heart.

She'd been surprised that he had let her touch his face, but it was like she hadn't been able to help it. She had wanted to touch it while he was in his Dragon form, but he often didn't let her touch his snout. He wouldn't let her stroke him there.

She tentatively caressed her fingers across it to feel the raised skin. Even from the distance when he'd been swinging his sword earlier, she'd been able to notice it.

It made him appear rough, almost like a thug, with the fierceness his silver eyes above it always seemed to hold. His eyes bore cunning intellect when he was a Dragon, a hunter's observational glare.

She hadn't expected it to appear the same when he was human.

She pulled her hands away when she thought she was making him uncomfortable. Then he'd humoured her, and it took away the apprehension she'd felt from him questioning her. Her curiosity had still been there, and she'd once again looked over the marks on his body.

As her eyes drifted down his torso, she wondered what other scars he had and where they might be. She couldn't see his back, and even though the bottom half of him had been clothed, her eyes had fallen to his breeches in wonder of what scarring marred his legs.

It was when her eyes came to the centre of his hips, where his groin was, that her eyes darted up to his.

She had just been touching a half-naked man! And awfully low on his body too.

Instead of seeing the scars, her mind registered other parts of him. The sharp clip of his jaw and chin, his wide cheekbones. The curve of his nose to his dark eyebrows. He had strange hair that appeared black, but there was a purple tinge to it. His hair was only a little longer than an inch in length all around his head, but it was unruly, tossed, and spiking without a care.

He is exceptionally handsome. She'd only vaguely remembered what he'd looked like since she'd been dazed the only other time she saw him. Even then she'd found him striking, and that had only been a peek.

This was a full examination of him up close, and her body subtly reacted to the pleasing man before her. Immediately, she realised she found him attractive, and his scars did nothing to diminish it.

Actually, she found that she liked them, like that there were places where her fingers could always trail.

The subtle feeling of desire had almost been fleeting because his face had started to crinkle. His nose had bunched, making that scar seem more prominent.

But then he'd smiled.

A large, teeth exposing grin – one that seemed of triumph.

She noticed, although his teeth were white and mostly straight, the human canines he had were twisted. They tilted forward towards his middle teeth, making them appear as though they were jagged.

She hadn't known why seeing them or seeing him smile made her body blossom more, but she immediately wanted to flush in embarrassment.

Although she knew the Dragon well enough, she felt as though she barely knew the man standing in front of her.

She'd been trying to calm her heart rate when his arms fell. It spooked her, and Amalia fled to the only place in this cave where she felt comfortable... her room.

She hid next to the entryway with her back against the wall. Her hand shot to her chest in hopes of calming her breathing from running and whatever emotions were crawling up inside her.

How can I feel desire for someone who hates me? Well, not her, but her kind.

He is also not human. But Rurik wasn't some fumbling stableboy either, like the one who had made her turn away from such thoughts and desires.

How can I possibly feel this way towards someone who has me trapped here? She knew the answer to that question.

It was because she didn't feel trapped here.

In the small time she had spent in this cave, she begun to feel safe. Not free, not content, but safe.

The outside world had become scary, and when he gifted her this room, he'd given her a piece of tranquil calm. Because he held her while she wept, she had begun to feel secure when he was around.

Whenever she felt unwell about her past, sadness and pain crawling in, she often sought the Dragon out. It was as though being in his presence made the feelings go away, like he guarded her from them.

Do... Do I like him? Had Amalia turned pure feelings of trust and sometimes playful banter, into something it shouldn't be?

He will not appreciate this.

She could picture him becoming enraged that one of his enemies would feel this way towards him. She ran her hands down her face, her eyes darting around the room. *I must clean my mind.*

Her gaze fell on the tub in the room.

Perhaps if she cleaned her body of its reaction, it may also cleanse her thoughts.

Seeing no other way to free her mind of impurity, she filled it and disrobed before hopping inside of it. She sat with her knees up, unable to stretch out because of the size of the tub, and leaned back to dunk her head, scrubbing at her face in frustration.

I touched a half-naked man I am attracted to. Then again, she didn't particularly know that at the time.

I am not right of mind. She almost laughed when seeing her own naked body seemed to deepen the way she felt. *Perhaps the flames have truly unhinged me.*

She stayed in the tub, waiting for it to go away. She knew it would. She was just too flustered at the moment, too embarrassed with herself.

When movement to her left caught her eye, she quickly covered her breasts and brought her knees closer to her body.

"What are you doing?!" Amalia yelled when he walked to stand in front of her.

He leaned his human body against the tall chest of drawers, his shoulder resting against it as he folded his arms. He took a bite of a fruit, chewing it for a moment.

He stared at it like it was more interesting than her.

"Eating an apple. They are my favourite when I am in this form." Holding it in his fist, he pointed his index finger and shook his hand up and down as if to punctuate his next words, "But only the green ones, that is very important."

"Not that! Get out, I am bathing!"

"How did you fill the tub?" There was an accusatory hint to his tone, but his eyes remained on the apple as though he didn't have a care in the world. He even turned it side-to-side.

Her eyes widened with horror.

"There is a bucket."

She waved her hand towards the wooden bucket she had in her room, the one she usually washed her clothes with.

It wasn't a lie. She didn't say she used it to fill the tub with water.

"The bucket is dry." He took another bite of his apple with a slurp. He chewed and then pushed what was remaining in his mouth between his cheek and teeth to talk. "How did you heat the water then?"

Biting her lips together, a small lump formed in her throat. She said nothing.

Amalia hadn't been thinking clearly because of her flustered thoughts. She'd filled the tub in the way she did back in her cottage, how she had done all her life – with magic.

"You know," he said, shaking that finger towards her. "I have been waiting for you to slip up. You think I have not known, but I have been able to sense you using magic in my lair. I have been unable to catch you in the act. I have had no proof until now." His fierce silver eyes finally slipped to catch hers with a ruthless, narrowed stare. "How did you fill the tub, Witch?"

"Okay, fine! You were not in your Dragon form, and I wished to bathe. I cannot carry the water myself. It is too far. I filled the tub and then heated it with my magic."

She eyed the apple core when he threw it behind him, glaring at it since she knew she would be the one to clean it up later.

Then he approached her, and she wanted nothing more than to shrink away. He placed both his hands on the edges of the tub she was in and leaned above her.

His face crinkled into one of rage.

"You used two spells in my home when I explicitly told you never to use magic here!"

It was a snarl, a hate-filled glare.

"Well, why not?!" she yelled back, not liking being cornered naked like this. "Why can I not use magic?"

"Because it is witchcraft, and I do not like it."

"You said that my kind comes from yours, yes?"

His anger didn't fade, but he did frown. "So?"

"Then do we not share the same magic?" His face gaped in horror right before he growled and came closer. Amalia had deeply offended him. "If my magic comes from Dragons and humans mating, then it is the same."

He backed away, shoving himself by using the sides of the tub to stand straight.

"No, it is not! It smells different, looks different. Your magic is foul. Mine is not."

"But I am not harming anyone! I have seen you use magic in a similar way. All I did was fill a tub with water and warm it for myself. Why can I not do that?"

"Because it is not dragoncraft, but witchcraft. Mine cannot be corrupted, it cannot be used as evil or dark magic. There are properties in witchcraft that make it twisted." He was seething like he might explode at any second. "And you will not use it again in my home!"

"Only moments before I felt something, and this has made me realise why it should not matter." He cocked his head at that before his brows furrowed deeply. "And I will not allow you to think you have me cornered here to yell at me for no reason!"

Amalia, still covering her breasts with one hand, reached for the edge of the tub and stood. She snapped her face away from him when he reared his head back, surprised that she would allow him to see her naked body when she never had before.

She wouldn't allow him to think that he could push her into a corner because she was unclothed.

She swiftly walked over to the bed where her dress lay and pulled it over her body. Just as she finally popped her head through the neck hole, her arms slithering down the sleeves, hands grabbed her wrists and held them up.

"I am angry for good reason. Do not tell me otherwise," he snapped. "I told you that I would not tolerate it."

Amalia tried to twist her arms from his hold but was unable to free herself from his strength.

"Let go of me!" she screamed at his face, bringing them closer without a shred of fear.

"No." He pushed her, making her legs catch on the edge of the bed. They both went tumbling onto it. "Now promise me you will not use witchcraft again!"

Rurik was between her thighs with his body pressing deeply between the centre of them while pinning her hands to the bed. Her face grew hot, her chest flushed, and not even his snarling face did anything to make her forget that, not long before, she had held desire for the angry man above her.

"No, I will not make such promises. I will not lie to appease you!"

She twisted her head side-to-side, thrashing as she tried to pull from his hold. Amalia even arched her back to escape, and it caused her body to rub against him. She struggled to hold onto her own fury when his thighs deeply pressed against the centre of her hips and put pressure on her folds.

"It is the same as if I asked you to stop becoming a Dragon!"

"I would never allow anyone to tell me not to take that form, it is who I am. I was born in it. I cannot live without that side of myself."

He is too close. Amalia arched her back deeper so she could wiggle up the bed and away from his body pressing against her. It shifted their bodies.

Her eyes widened when she felt something long and rigid now pressing against her. She looked down his body. *Is he hard?*

It was impossible to see with their bodies meshed against each other's, and she dared not believe what her body told her was pressed against her. Yet, her core reacted to the idea, and she struggled harder.

"Let me go!" When he didn't, she continued, "If you cannot live without your Dragon form, then you should know I cannot live without my magic."

"Yes, you can." His hips moved against her, and she wasn't sure if it was only to lift himself higher above her or not. "And you will if you want to be free here."

Amalia halted as understanding dawned. Then she gritted her teeth while giving him her own filthy glare, refusing to be afraid of him.

"Then throw me in your stupid prison. If it means I will be free to use magic in it, then I would rather live there."

He gave her an assessing eye while she huffed beneath him, her chest rising and falling at a rapid rate. *Did I finally convince him how much it means to me? That I truly cannot live without it?*

Finally, he pulled back to stand.

She thought she'd won, but a moment later, he grabbed one wrist and curled her body while he bent over. Amalia yelped when she was suddenly tossed over his shoulder.

Then he took her from the room and down the tunnel.

Amalia beat at his back. "Put me down, you loathsome cad!"

He ignored her, taking her further inside his lair, past the room with tapestries to the fork in the tunnel. He headed down the more darkened path.

"I will hurt you," she threatened, placing her hands against his back.

She could. She could unleash the fire she usually used to light her cooking hearth in her cottage.

"You do not want to hurt me," he said with a dark laugh that was completely shaken with fury.

Dammit, he was right. She continued to beat at his back while kicking her legs. His hand was firmly grabbing her arse, and she wasn't sure if he did it simply to hold her steady.

When they passed the two large boulders, he turned into one of the alcoves and popped her onto her feet. He pushed the centre of her chest to force her into the room and put space between them.

"You are to promise not to use magic, or this is where you will stay."

Her eyes roamed on the mostly empty room. There were two torches to allow her light inside, a chamber pot, and a fur rug on the ground for her to sleep.

"All I want is to be able to use simple magic, things that make life comfortable. To cook my own food without your help, fill my own bath, fight off pixies."

"Make the promise, Witch!" It was a yell, but it no longer held anger, it held frustration. It seemed like he desperately wanted her to submit, like he truly didn't want to do this. "Do not make me lock you in here."

She didn't understand why he wasn't just moving the boulder already.

Amalia turned from him, walked to the centre of the room, and sat down cross-legged. Then, to prove her point, she held both her hands up beside her with her palms flat towards the torches. With determination, she held his gaze and mentally chanted the words she needed. Two fireballs released from her hands to fly across the room and light the torches.

His eyes widened with horror that she had done it in front of him. She just folded her arms and waited for him to lock her in with her chin tilted up.

She watched his rage build.

His hands clenched into fists next to his ribs. His arms shook with a terrible quake. His face screwed so tight she thought his head might explode as it reddened.

Then he roared, a loud, wall-rumbling roar that she didn't think anything human could produce. It was monstrous, bone-chilling, and it immediately sent dread through her.

Even her face paled.

"FINE!" he yelled, turning from her to kick the boulder he was standing next to with the bottom of his foot.

It rolled slightly from his strength before he stormed away, roaring and yelling and snarling as he went.

Her arms loosened as she gaped in shock at the open

entranceway of the prison. She hadn't thought he would give in. She truly expected him to close up the cell and leave her to rot.

She bested me! Rurik growled to himself as he stomped around his cave.

He let loose a ring of fire. Shifting back into his Dragon form, he took his anger out on the cave walls in the cavern that housed his waterfall.

I let her win! He dragged his claws along the walls before he let loose another roar. It was louder in this form, deeper, booming in this spacious area as it echoed off the walls.

His body shook while he tried to release the wrathful fury inside him. He stomped his large paws while swiping at any large, loose rock he could find so it would fling and crash into the walls.

All because she feels desire for me. He'd scented it when he had pinned her against the bed, small whiffs of it. He'd seen that she was not afraid of him, even as he snarled and yelled at her, and it had eventually made his cock harden.

I wish I had not played this trick on her. He may have been more determined to lock her away if he knew she didn't hold lust for him.

Now she will freely use witchcraft in my home. And because he'd given her permission to do so, he couldn't yell at her for it.

He placed his forepaws against his face. *Why does she tempt me?* Why was he giving in to this female who was a Witch? Giving her gifts such as her own room and freedom in his lair? Why was he allowing her to touch him and speak to him rather than treating her with cruelty like he would any other, even his own kind?

He'd always been intolerant, which is why he generally avoided everyone, no matter their species.

Why does she have to look the way she does? He thought about taking his claws to her face to rid himself of her beauty.

He paused with that idea in his mind, contemplating it.

It would not matter. Even picturing her with gouging marks, whether healed or bloody, didn't take away his want of her. He also knew he'd be angry with himself if he maimed the kind woman. He would deeply regret it if he harmed even a single, glossy hair on her head.

It is not her fault I want to fuck her.

Rurik stilled at that thought.

He had just witnessed her use witchcraft right in front of his very eyes, had seen it, smelt it. And instead of being disgusted with her, his mind had finally told him what he'd been ignoring.

I want to bed her?!

Rurik roared, unleashing a row of flames at the ceiling, no longer sure he wouldn't allow such a thing.

15

Amalia listened to the Dragon unleash his fury inside the cave, his roars echoing against the tunnel walls. She sat in her room, trying to ignore it.

She'd never seen or heard him this mad before, and she wasn't going anywhere near him until he was done... and maybe for a little while after that.

If he is so upset by it, why has he not changed his mind?

It had been going on for *hours* now.

The sounds of yelling and rocks being thrown made it all the way to the entrance of his cave. She feared it would collapse against his anger.

I cannot concentrate with all the noise he is making. Amalia tossed the book she'd been trying to read to distract herself with.

She laid back against the sofa and rolled her eyes when she heard yet another roar. *Will it ever end?* She'd seen children end their tantrums quicker than this adult male!

With a huff, she jumped to her feet. If she couldn't rest or read with all the ruckus, she would make herself something to eat.

After she obtained food, she went to the cooking alcove and lit the cooking hearth before filling a pot with water.

Great, here he comes. Perhaps she shouldn't have used magic when he was having a tantrum over her use of magic.

He didn't stop at the cooking alcove, but he did turn his head and growl towards her when he passed it. The Dragon left his lair, and he didn't return in the time she'd finished eating.

He has left to get himself food, she thought while eyeing the entryway. It wasn't the first time he'd ducked out for a short amount of time. She gave a shrug. The wards wouldn't fade away just because he wasn't here.

If I am allowed to use my witchcraft, does that mean I may not want to leave? Being unable to use her magic had been the main reason she hadn't want to remain here. He would never allow her to use it to the degree she once had, but even being able to cook her own food brought her much joy.

I want to stay here then. She gave herself a small smile. Maybe one day she could convince him to let her roam the forest, knowing she would return. *Maybe he may even walk the trees with me.*

It was a pleasant thought, Witch and Dragon feeling the earth and the energy of life that came from woodlands.

Just as Amalia was cleaning her plate, she heard him return with heavy footsteps against the ground. She stayed out of the tunnel, but stood near the entryway to let him pass, knowing it wasn't a good idea to get in his way.

A bright green snout emerged a second later before a large scaly creature ducked its head inside the alcove.

"I thought I smelled a Witch," a Dragon sneered – one that wasn't Rurik.

Amalia let loose the most terrified scream when it grabbed her and brought her out of the alcove.

"Unhand me!" she yelled, beating on the Dragon's fingers wrapped around her torso.

"Where is he? What have you done to him?" His top lip

curled back over his fangs. His eyes were a dark shade of yellow and the closer he brought her to his face, the more she hated the stare of them. "Have you killed him and stolen his lair?"

He walked her down the tunnel with his head searching each room for Rurik.

"I have done no such thing."

His head snapped to her. "Liar!"

Then, to her absolute horror, he threw her so that he could grab one of her legs and dangle her above his head. She tried to stop her dress and undergarment shift from falling and revealing her bare backside.

"Tell me what you have done, or I will cook you."

He licked at his jowls, showing her that he was serious.

"I tell the truth! I have not harmed him."

The concern over her modesty vanished when a distinct sucking sound came from his mouth – the same one she'd only ever heard from Rurik when he lit the cooking hearth for her. This Dragon was about to spew fire from his maw.

His mouth opened, and he dangled her higher.

Amalia didn't wish to wear flames again. Just when the sound worsened, she threw her hands forward in the direction of his throat. She mentally chanted the spell that allowed her to fill her bath, and water spouted from her hands.

A gurgling choke came from him before he dropped her, coughing as he spit the water away.

Amalia got to her feet as fast as she could to quickly run back up the tunnel. When she got to the entrance of the cave, she bashed her fists against the ward keeping her in, desperate to escape.

That horrible sucking inhale was right behind her, and she quickly dove to the side just in time to miss being burned.

The Dragon's head followed her when she ran down the tunnel next to him. She was unsure of where to go or hide as he gave chase.

She didn't make it far before she heard that noise again, the one that sent chills through her. Sweat dotted her skin, and it wasn't because she was hot or from exerting herself; it was from fear.

I do not want to burn again.

She had nowhere she could go that would save her. If she ran into an alcove, she would be trapped. She couldn't fight him.

What do I do? The answer came when she sprinted past the entry to her room and saw her bookshelf.

Amalia began to chant out loud. That sucking sound stopped, and she managed to duck out of the way of flames, just in time.

It broke her thoughts.

She started it again just as he was preparing to unleash fire once more. His fire was so hot she could feel her skin drying because of how close she was to him.

She had just chanted the last word when he unleashed his flames. She dropped to her knees, awaiting agony. When no pain came, Amalia turned onto her backside with wide eyes.

He looked confused until he realised what she had done. He growled, quickly drawing in air to release more flames.

The magic shield around her grew smaller. It wasn't strong enough to withstand the power being unleashed.

Fire. Amalia's chest heaved, barely able to breathe against the anxiety filling her soul. *Burning.* Her legs felt hot from memory, and her toes and feet ached in a way she desperately wanted to forget. *So hot.* The heat of it billowed over her, and her skin crawled at the memory of it searing her skin, lick after lick.

Melting. Bubbling. *Boiling.*

Orange and red encased her, the shield getting smaller and smaller by the second. The smell of burning flesh assaulted her nostrils even though no flame had touched her skin, and tears began to fall.

The Dragon stopped to breathe in and let loose again.

Amalia curled onto her side, knowing this time the shield wouldn't last, and she would have to suffer the torment of her skin burning. She sobbed, crying out loudly. While wrapping her trembling arms around her torso, she brought her knees up.

The flames abruptly stopped before the shield gave in. A heavy thud rang in her ears, but she was too terrified to lift her head. She didn't want to turn, fearing that she would be greeting her flaming death head on.

Rurik landed outside of his lair with a cow carcass hanging from his maw.

As he started to walk in, he saw the scaly green back and tail of his kind in the tunnel. When he also saw and smelt fire, he quickly dropped the dead cow to gallop down the tunnel.

Without a second thought, he grabbed the flicking tail of his uninvited guest and used it to throw him against the wall.

Am I too late? Rurik grabbed the snout of the other Dragon by wrapping his fingers around it to force his jaw shut. Then he slammed his head against the wall when he tried to rise, using his other paw to push his body down.

His eyes quickly scanned over the tunnel to find her.

There she is. Relief washed over him when he found her huddled on the ground with the tiniest shimmer of magic surrounding her.

Still holding his snout, Rurik turned his head to the Dragon with a *beastly* growl.

"You dare come into my lair and attack my property?"

Although Amalia wasn't property, per se, she was still his prisoner and that made her his. His to guard, to protect, just like he would his treasures.

He pulled his hand back while still holding onto his snout, and then slammed the Dragon's head back into the wall.

The other Dragon gave a snarl and wriggled from his grasp while slashing out with his claws. Rurik dodged them and slashed his own, cutting him across the jaw.

"Why do you attack me when there is a Witch in your home?!" he yelled, his wings flapping wildly in outrage.

Then he lunged, and Rurik allowed him to wrap his arms around his body so he could do the same. He was stronger, a seasoned warrior, and he threw him to the ground onto his side before crawling on top of him to keep him down.

Rurik brought his own head closer to the Dragon's. "Because I follow the laws, whereas it appears you do not."

Rurik knew this Dragon, he often visited him.

Glov the Traveller obtained his title because he was a wanderer and never often left the skies. He had no home, no lair. He knew many secrets and always had more information about the outside world than other Dragons who preferred their own lair and hobbies.

Glov was the main Dragon that visited Rurik, and it was usually to tell him of the location or dealings of Witches so he could hunt them. Occasionally, Glov sought a place to rest. After too many days, Rurik would chase him out while snapping his jaws close behind his back feet.

"A Witch found in a Dragon's lair is to be dealt with by the one that owns it," Rurik told him.

The recited law fell on unlistening ears as Glov struggled to get him off. He wiggled like a pinned snake, limbs and tail flailing.

He dug his claws in harder to stop him.

Glov wasn't a strong Dragon. With Rurik on top of him the way he was, he wasn't able to get away.

"And what of the laws of her? Should we not be focused on killing her rather than fighting with each other?"

Glov's yellow eyes trailed to where Amalia must be, but Rurik refused to take his focus off the threat below him.

"I have a blood debt to this Witch." Glov stopped moving, coming to the realisation that she was not here by mistake. "She is not to be harmed, understood?"

He gave a single nod, and Rurik released him. He stepped back to give him space to stand.

He spun to check on Amalia, but the moment he found her pale-stricken face, she bolted down the tunnel. *She is terrified again.*

Rurik knew she felt safe here, and everything he did to make her feel so had just been undone.

"I do not understand. Why is she not in your prisoner cells?"

Rurik turned to him.

As he usually did when angered by his own kind, Rurik smacked his paw across Glov's face. The force made his head slam sideways into the wall with a thud.

"You dare question me, the WitchSlayer, as to why I have a loose Witch in my home?!" Rurik was offended that Glov would think he didn't know what he was doing in his own lair. *I am not a fool.* "She is a White Witch and intends no harm."

Glov steadied himself back to his feet while cupping the side of his jaw.

"How is that possible? I did not think there were any pure-hearted Witches left."

He raised his head dismissively to the words. Rurik had thought the same at first, but he knew he'd indeed found one.

"I would not be alive if it were not true."

"You let her roam free? *You* of all people?"

"She saved me and has proven to me that she will not attack anyone."

Glov stamped a foot forward with a guttural snarl. "She tried to drown me!"

Rurik rolled his eyes. He highly doubted that.

"You threatened her, and she reacted in fear. If she were truly like the rest of her ilk, she would not have tried, she would have succeeded."

"You are defending her when I tell you otherwise?"

Rurik snapped his jaws in warning, a sharp, chomping sound coming from his fangs. "Yes, I know she would never harm another purposefully."

"Are you sure she has not tricked you?"

He'd asked himself this question many times, and he always came to the same conclusion.

"I am sure she has never used a charm against me to enchant my mind or to make me think illusions."

Although many Dragons had fallen to this kind of trickery, his senses were too keen. He would've been able to smell the tendrils of witchcraft wafting around him and nagging him on the back of his scales.

He'd had no kind of inkling.

"I am certain of this."

That made Glov pause and tilt his head.

"Unbelievable. You trust her."

It wasn't a question, but a statement.

"To some degree, yes. Although she is imprisoned in my lair, I trust her enough to let her roam free inside of it."

Glov's jaw dropped in astonishment. "You, one of the most unsociable of our kind, allow a Witch to walk your tunnels when you cannot even stand our own kind for merely a day?"

"Why are you here?" Rurik bit out before he lost his temper again.

Glov eyed him warily before sighing.

"I bring big news. Witches have been seen heading this way. Quite a few of them."

"How is this unusual? They often travel in a group with their covens. I would have heard of them when I next scout the lands."

"Strolguil the Vast is leading them."

Rurik's brows furrowed and brought a paw to his snout to tap his claw against it.

"Well, that is strange. He travels alone in search of power. I have not known him to be with a coven for a hundred years."

"That is my point. They are up to something." Glov shook his body free of the dust that had collected on him from Rurik throwing him around.

"Yes, indeed it would seem that way." And they were heading in Rurik's direction.

A large, sharp-toothed grin spread across his features. This may be the opportunity he was waiting for.

"How far?"

"Half a day's flight southwest." Glov touched the claw marks Rurik had given him to check the depth of the gashes.

It wouldn't be enough to scar, but it had been a sharp warning not to anger him again otherwise he may do permanent damage. He was known for being ruthless.

"Have you told Mahesh the Flightless yet? His lair is closer, and he may not be aware Witches are at his rockstep."

"I just came from there. He was the one who told me."

Rurik nodded, pleased that he was already informed.

Mahesh lost his wings long ago, but he was a powerful Dragon. He didn't fight any longer, but if he was aware of the potential threat, then he would go to the necessary lengths to keep himself hidden.

"Have you told any others? If Strolguil is using a coven and is plotting something, we may need multiple Dragons to take them down."

Rurik was fierce, but even he knew he wouldn't be able to fight the strongest Witch with a coven supporting him. He often had to get them alone or attack when there was only one or two of them to fight.

"No, not yet. I knew I needed to tell you first since no one else has the formidability to defeat them."

"Once you know more, tell me, and I will formulate a plan. Let others know that I may call upon those willing to fight." Glov nodded his head in answer; he would do as he told him. "Is there anything else?"

"No, that is all I know for now."

"Good, now get the fuck out of my lair," Rurik demanded, already sick of seeing this green Dragon's face.

Only a handful of his kind were dark like him, mainly the few brothers and sister he had left. Dragons came in all shapes and colours, from blue to gold, even white. Some had horns and even hair – he was ever thankful he didn't share those traits.

Glov scowled. "I will have to tell the Elders about her."

A growling cringe twisted Rurik's face, but it held no bite to it. It was more of a show of irritation than anything else.

"I am aware."

He wouldn't ask Glov to keep his secret. He wouldn't ask something of him that could possibly get him in trouble with the Elders of his kind. They had laws, and they needed to be respected.

"They will not like that you let her walk your tunnels. They may come here."

His eyes found the wall, wondering what he would do if they did.

"I have a blood debt to her. They cannot touch her."

It was a lie, the blood debt to her paid, but Rurik saw no other way to keep his kind from her.

"They may take her away to imprison her if you will not. Law also states that a Witch may only be alive in one's lair if they are bound and locked away. Are you sure you wish to let her walk freely? They may punish you."

When his eyes fell back to Glov's yellow ones, Rurik knew the truth.

He wanted to protect this precious thing he found, the soft and gentle woman. This tiny piece of purity that was a rare thing in this world. She was like a gem he had added to his treasure hoards. *She has become my friend.*

In the small time that he had come to know her, he started to think of her as his companion. Although he found her attractive and held desire for her, his feelings didn't reach any real depth other than friendship.

And Rurik would protect his new friend.

"If they try to take her, I will fight them. She has done no evil. She does not deserve true imprisonment."

He would not allow this spark of light to snuff out in a dark cell.

A booming laugh echoed from Glov.

"You are lucky that it is you that has her then. None of the Elders will truly want to fight you, not alone at least. I will tell them all of what you have told me. However, I may lap it on that she is a pure-hearted Witch and try to convince them to let you handle it."

He turned to walk from Rurik's lair, sensing he was running out of patience with him already. If Glov hadn't angered him, he may have been able to stay, but the wanderer knew better, knew that Rurik was in no mood to house a guest.

"You are the WitchSlayer after all. You perceive them better than anyone else."

Then he was gone, flapping his wings to lift off once he was outside.

Rurik knew Glov would make this his priority, and that he

would see him very soon.

Witches are coming, led by Strolguil. He could only imagine what this meant. *What is he planning?*

Something big. Something dangerous.

Unfortunately, until he had more information, there was nothing he could do about it. He didn't take action without calculated thought first.

Rurik decided to give Amalia time to herself. She was frightened, possibly even frightened of him again. *She will need to approach me in her own time.* How long that would be, he didn't know.

Returning to his cow, he took it outside to cook it, knowing if she smelt it, it would worsen how she felt. He picked it apart, carefully cracking bone with his paws to get to the juicy meat and organs.

Then he laid at the entrance of his cave facing the world while using a splintered bone to pick at his teeth. It was his way of letting her know that he wasn't roaming his tunnels, so she was free to move about.

It was while he was staring up at the stars and night sky that he heard her soft footsteps. She didn't come to him.

She has returned to her room.

It meant he could now go inside.

Considering the hour, he went to his biggest treasure room. *I really must move the rest here.* He dug underneath it, wanting the cold pressure against him while he slept.

After much thought, he let his snout peek out fully, only letting the riches cover his eyes and top part of his head. He did this so she would see where he was in case she wanted to avoid him.

I do not foresee her leaving her room for quite some time, though.

He allowed himself to fall asleep. He was tired from venting his anger, hunting, and then dealing with Glov.

After what he could only imagine was many hours later, she disturbed him from his slumber by digging through the riches he lay under.

The sickly-sweet scent of perfume permeated the air around her. *The figment of burning flesh has returned.*

He lifted his head slowly as not to startle her, wondering if perhaps he'd moved while he slept and covered himself completely in treasure.

She didn't stop digging. She also didn't say anything even when he looked at her. Instead, she dug lower until she had uncovered his arms, the curvature of his neck, and top half of his chest.

What is she doing? he thought when she crawled into the space between his arms and curled into a ball. Using his arm as a pillow, she tucked her face against him and clasped her hands tightly against her chest.

She looked tired, her face a tear-shed colour of pink.

"I cannot sleep," she explained.

He figured it was so that he wouldn't ask her to move.

She is afraid. And the fact she was seeking comfort from him meant that she still regarded him as something safe.

Something stirred in his chest, some unknown emotion. He moved the arm she wasn't laying on so that it would curl around her body. Then he lowered his head so that his neck would lay across her to give her warmth.

Rurik remained awake even when she fell asleep, and he watched over her as she did. It was fitful and she woke often with the stench of fear coming from her.

She immediately calmed when she realised where she was.

16

A week had come and gone since the incident with the green Dragon, and Amalia had gone back to feeling comfortable in Rurik's home.

Since that day though, the other Dragon visited infrequently and in short bursts. She knew his name now to be Glov. Amalia wasn't as trusting of him as she was with Rurik. She often stayed away and avoided them when they spoke together, which to her relief, was usually in the main room of the cave that could fit them both comfortably.

There had been no apology, and the only words he'd ever spoken to her were given the only time he wasn't greeted by Rurik at the entrance of the cave. It was the one time he'd been alone to do so.

He'd walked his scaly body down the tunnel in search of Rurik, but he'd given her a warning when he was passing her room. A warning not to harm the Dragon who was allowing her to live.

He didn't like it when she had rolled her eyes and propped her book up so she didn't have to see his ugly, green face.

But Rurik had assured her that she wouldn't be attacked by another of his kind again in his lair. She felt comforted by that.

He never confronted her about why she'd chosen to sleep

against him that night. She also didn't plan to speak of it.

She had needed to, had needed to be beside him. She'd been unable to rest as nightmares of her time on the stake had riddled her sleep. Anxiety gripped her throat so tightly that she sought comfort and security from the one being available for her to do so.

She also did it because of the times in the past when her memories had been bothering her. He may not have saved her from obtaining them, but he saved her from death and healed her wounds.

Mostly, her life slowly returned to the ebb and flow as it had before while living in this lair – except for one change.

She would see the human side of Rurik more often.

The first time she noticed him in that form was when he'd been laying against the wall in the alcove that held his collection of books. He'd been quietly reading with his ankles crossed and one meaty arm behind his head.

They'd traded glances.

Amalia had become flushed and immediately fled.

The next time she saw him human, he snuck up on her.

She'd been going through the food so she could make herself something to eat, and when she stood up, she bumped into him. He'd steadied her hips with a firm grip so she wouldn't fall and drop her food, but she'd felt her arse grind against his groin

She'd stepped away quickly with a blush heating her cheeks.

He'd told her he was interested to know what her cooking was like since its scent often filled the tunnels. So, by his request, she cooked him a meal. They'd spoken as they ate at the table, although barely, and she'd fidgeted often in her seat.

Then he complained that it was rather bland, and she'd yelled that it was his fault because he wouldn't give her any herbs or spices! She'd stormed off in a huff.

There were other times he would appear around her in his human form. She wasn't sure if she was becoming more comfortable because she was getting used to seeing him like this, or less so because of the way her body reacted whenever she did.

"Why must he visit?" she asked her Dragon companion who was moving the smaller pile of riches to the bigger one.

Glov visited earlier and had only recently left. She'd been unhappy about it because she hated being stuck in her room while he was here.

"I have asked him to return when he has new information on a possible threat," he answered, walking with one paw full of treasure against his chest.

She trailed behind him, picking up the odd coin and jewel that fell between the large gap of his fingers.

"What kind of threat?"

He eyed her as he scooped his paw forward and let the riches in his hand fall on top of the pile. The look he gave her was one where he wasn't sure if he wanted to give her the answer or not.

"Strolguil is on the move, directing a coven of Witches."

He turned from the room when she dumped her own handfuls.

"Does that mean you will be adding to your collection of skulls?"

Looking at her through the corner of his eye, his answer was slow to come.

"Most likely." She gave a nod, placing her hands behind her back as she continued to follow him. "You are not upset by this knowledge?"

His head turned to assess her face when they got to the smaller alcove.

"Well, are they bad?"

"If Strolguil the Vast is leading them, then yes."

"Then why should I care what you do to them?"

He tilted his head in the way he did when he was bewildered by her.

"But they are of your own kind. Do you not care for them?"

She gave a shrug.

"If they use blood magic or dark magic, then they cause harm to others. What happens to them is then deserved." His spiked brows drew together in a deep frown. "I am not the one hurting them, so why should I care?"

"I was not expecting that answer."

She could tell that he liked that she was casual about this with him, and that she wasn't asking him to stop. Amalia didn't see the point. She knew even if she asked him to stop, he wouldn't.

She brought her hand up to her chin and rubbed her index finger against the seam of her lips.

"I do ask that you not burn them alive while I am here. I do not think I will be able to handle hearing such a thing." *And definitely not smell it.*

As it usually did, the memory of her own burning plagued her thoughts. She did her best to ignore it while staring into the sharp silver eyes peering back at her. Amalia very much liked looking at them.

They were so large that she was able to see the way his irises were formed around his round pupils, the lighter and darker swirls and pools of silver. They were mesmerising, and she thought she could explore them for hours.

"I will attempt to refrain from doing so."

He walked into the alcove and swept his arms to bring the last of the pile together. They'd already transferred most of it over.

"Why are you doing this today?" she asked, following behind him once again to pick up the pieces he dropped.

"Thought it was time. I usually do not spend an extended

period in my lair. Since I am here, I have no excuse not to."

He scooped his hand forward and placed the last of the riches. Then he started moving around the massive pile while sweeping everything that had rolled to the edges of the room into the centre to make a mound.

"You could make a human very wealthy with all of this," she laughed.

He gave a chuckle in return.

"Alas, they will have to kill me to do so, and I do not see that forthcoming. My death will mostly likely not be by a human."

The Dragon laid on top of the pile, shifting his body like he wanted to squish it tighter to the ground. When she realised he didn't plan to move, she came to sit on top of it with him.

"Do your kind live a long time?"

It was a question she'd always wanted to ask.

"Depends on the Dragon." She cocked an eyebrow, waiting for a proper answer. He rolled his eyes like he was exasperated that he had to explain it further. "We live to roughly eight hundred years, but most do not achieve such a length of life. It is believed that ten human years equates to one Dragon year. It takes a long time for us to age and die."

She sat with her legs straight, her hand covering her mouth in thought. "How old are you then?"

"I have seen two hundred and ninety-three winters."

Her eyes widened, and she looked around the room.

"No wonder your pile is so large then!"

Another chuckle rumbled, and she smiled at the sound. It was warm and deep, and she often found it pleasing, especially when she was the cause of it.

"It would be bigger if I were not set on hunting the way I do. I would like much more, but it is enough that it gives me a pleasant sleep."

She nodded as though she had any understanding of what

it was like to be of his kind who liked to sleep the way they did.

"Does living for that long not become tiresome?"

"Not particularly. Our minds are not the same as humans, and we perceive time differently. We often spend periods thoughtless and asleep."

That sounds horribly boring. She shrugged since it wasn't her place to judge.

Her eye scanned over the length of the Dragon and the large spikes jutting from his body. They were long and fanned out around his head before they became smaller between his shoulders, his back, all the way to the heart-shaped spade of his tail tip.

Amalia stared at his wings.

"I was wondering. How would one mount you in order to ride you?"

"By my hips, I would imagine."

It took a moment for the words to register.

She immediately became flustered when she realised. The image of sitting on top of this Dragon's back turned into one of her sitting on top of him when he was human... and facing her.

The desire she wished her body wouldn't feel swiftly coiled in her belly, causing her face to pinken. Her head turned to his to find he was grinning mischievously.

"I meant to fly!"

She grabbed a handful of coins and threw them at his face.

"That is the only way I would allow someone to mount me. I will not parade around in the air like some flying horse to be used for travel."

"But it must be so beautiful in the sky."

She gave a loving sigh, picturing what he must see when he flew. To be able to see the world from so high up, towns and forests and people who didn't know you were there. To feel the rush of wind and feel it against her skin.

"Are clouds soft? They look like pillows in the sky."

"They are made of water."

Her jaw dropped. "You lie! They float too delicately to be made of something so heavy."

The Dragon shook his head, but his chest was moving like he was silently laughing.

"There is much humans do not know, and therefore, you do not know."

"I will not believe you unless I see it for myself."

She folded her arms with a huff, pouting.

He gently flicked her back, not hard enough to make her go flying across the room, but enough that she went tumbling down the pile.

"Do not flick me with your claws, you scoundrel."

She bent over and picked up another handful of coins to toss them at him. When he closed his lids to avoid being hit in the eyes, Amalia hiked up the skirt of her dress up and scrambled up the pile.

He knew when she stepped onto his forearm because he immediately stood. It was too late. She grabbed a hold of one of his spikes jutting from his back.

"Get off me, Witch."

She gripped a higher spike, and then another, climbing up his side until she was on his back.

She gave a squeal when he spun in a circle while bucking to get her loose. She held on firm and eventually found a spot where she could sit. It was hard to do so. She kind of had to kneel with her legs far apart otherwise she would have to do the most uncomfortable splits.

He continued to move to get rid of her. She held onto two spikes jutting above where she was seated right between his neck and wings.

"If you do not hop down this instant, I will roll over."

She gave a laugh. "No, you will not."

He wouldn't kill her by crushing her to death.

He stopped moving and turned his head around to give her a quiet snarl over his own back. She already knew he had a very flexible neck.

"See, it is not so bad." She pressed her lips together into an innocent pout, fighting the humorous curl in them. "There, I have mounted you in a way no one has mounted you before."

He squinted his eyes. Then, he began to stand up on his hind legs.

She struggled to hold on, but eventually had to let go and tumbled down his back. She was lucky that she rolled against his wing otherwise her body would have been impacted by his hard spikes.

Eventually her back lay against the riches, and he stood over her with a foul glare. He was angry, most likely furious, but Amalia couldn't help laughing. She lifted her hands until her palms cupped the scales of his jaw.

"That was fun."

Her joy seemed to deflate the worst of his anger.

"I would have to disagree. I have never been treated so disrespectfully in my life."

He pulled away from her touch.

"Then lock me away forever so I may suffer the consequences," she said with a flare of dramaticism.

"I have said this often, but I find you rather odd."

Her punishment? He placed his paw against her and pressed down, forcing the air out of her lungs so she couldn't breathe. He didn't do it for long, and he was careful to make sure it wasn't painful.

"Henceforth, I shall be known as Amalia the Odd. World, fear my strangeness as this Dragon does."

"That is not an appealing title, and I do not fear something as defenceless as you."

Amalia folded her arm against her chest while blowing a strand of hair from her face. "I am not defenceless."

"You speak as if it is not true, but you will not learn to fight to save yourself."

He often tried to convince her to learn how to wield a weapon. She always refused.

"Why should I... when I have you?"

She smiled for him, but her words made him tilt his head.

The scales around his face turned a brighter shade of purple.

Today, I will bed the Witch, Rurik thought as he walked through his lair human, shirtless, and wet from the dip in his stream. He didn't know how he was going to achieve this, but he'd decided that this day he would figure out a way under her skirt.

Rurik had spent enough time around her in his human form to know she readily held desire for it by the arousal in her scent. He also sensed it occasionally when he was in his Dragon form, her mind thinking about it.

The more time he spent around her, the more he wanted to feel his body sink inside hers. It worsened when he knew she was aroused, his mind wanting to seize the opportunity.

He wanted to know what her skin tasted like upon his tongue, how she felt against his palms. He wanted to know the kind of lewd sounds she would make. He needed to how she would feel when she came, what that sweet, innocent face looked like when it was filled with wicked pleasure instead.

Would she cling to him or arch her back? Would her thighs tighten around his hips so he couldn't escape, or would they spread to feel him deeper?

Constantly, the thoughts plagued him, the questions he wanted answers to. A gnawing need.

He thought maybe if he found out, if he knew, then they might stop. That perhaps once he had sex with her, his curiosity filled, that he would stop feeling desire for her.

Then, he could be her protecting companion and nothing more.

He saw no other way to rid himself of this fascination of her, and he was fascinated by her. He constantly sought her out, craved to be in her presence so she would speak to him.

She didn't ramble like she once had in her cottage, but she spoke wildly enough to entertain him – sometimes of the strangest topics.

She also did things that often made him raise a brow.

She once attempted to sneak up on him, which she wasn't able to do because he could hear her quiet footsteps and smell her wherever she went. He'd pretended he didn't notice her as she stalked him, then she tackled his tail to sit on the spaded tip.

When he told her to remove herself, she had gripped him firmly and demanded that he slide her around his lair. He'd spun to remove her himself, but she'd made this adorable squealing noise. He'd enjoyed the sound so much he complied and was rewarded by her stroking his cheek afterwards.

It was something that always made his eyelids feel heavy.

He also once found her sitting on the ground in the main tunnel of his lair, watching a large spider crawl over her fingers and knuckles. Rurik tried to convince her to put it down since it was deathly venomous, but she refused, telling him she knew it wouldn't bite her – as if she sensed it.

It hadn't, even when he returned much later to find her walking around with it moving through her hair.

She often made friends with the bugs that would enter his home.

Rurik was fascinated by this woman who had brought laughter and oddness to his usually quiet lair. She also brought yelling, but her anger didn't linger, often forgotten or easily managed.

On this particular day, he found the beautiful woman sitting in the sun that spilled inside the entrance of his cave.

She did this most mornings. She would come to feel the sun upon her skin with her face turned upwards to the light, soaking it in with her eyes closed.

Something Rurik had noticed was that if she didn't greet the sun once a day, the shining brightness her hair held would dim. He didn't know if she was aware that her body was drawing energy from it, but he found her prettier on the days that she did. He even thought he could almost smell the sunshine in her hair.

He joined her, sitting beside her while she sat hugging her knees. Her toes were bent and pressed against the ward keeping her in.

His legs went straight through it.

She didn't turn to him, but she said, "The view is quite lovely here."

With his eyes still on her, he answered, "Yes, it is."

Her dark and long eyelashes twinkled from the sun. She kept her lids closed, and they created shadows against the soft tan across her high cheekbones. Her full lips were such a bright shade of pink and looked so incredibly soft that he wanted to reach across and feel them for himself with his own.

His tongue dabbled out to lick the seam of his lips. He was sure he would find out, in due time.

Rurik often sat next to her in his Dragon form while she did this, but he'd never done so in his human one before.

When she finally peeked her eyes open to look at him, her brows immediately furrowed. Then she shifted to her knees and reached over to pull the short length of his hair up.

"Your hair has turned more purple."

She may not have realised, but she put her breasts

precariously close to his face. He held back the urge to close the small distance and bite into one of the firm-looking, medium-sized mounds.

"It does that," he answered, unwilling to remove his gaze from the dip of her cleavage.

His cock tingled at the idea of them pressing against his face. *Just a little closer...*

"I have never seen anything like it. I have noticed that your scales get brighter. Why?"

She tugged more strands into the light to see.

"I am dark when the air is cold. I become bright when I am surrounded by warmth. It is believed that the changing darkness is to help with camouflage, although we are not quite sure. Our hair usually mirrors our scales."

"You must find it difficult to walk among the humans."

She finally pulled away. Facing him, she rested back to sit on her calves with her hands in her lap.

She was still in the sun, and the side of her face showered in the light made the eye on that side appear a lighter shade of blue. They both appeared like two different bodies of water, and Rurik wanted nothing more than to swim in them.

Yes, he definitely needed to bed this Witch in order to stop these fantastical thoughts about her. *I must dim them.*

She is comfortable with me today, that will make it easier. The question remained, how? How did Rurik lure the side of this female that desired him out? *She is not like my kind. I cannot be forceful.* A Dragoness appreciated dominant males dragging them around. Amalia would not.

"Dragons wear cloaks when we walk about outside our lairs. We do not like our faces to become known."

"And you have a very distinguishable face." Her words were followed by a smile as her eyes ran over the scar across his face.

"That I do."

His own lips twitched when he smelled the hint of desire mixing into her scent. But then she stood, like she was done with the sun and talking to him.

She often did this, ran when he was human, and she felt this way.

She wasn't aware that he could sense this from her. That he could smell the delicious warm scent of arousal that made him want to pant.

Unwilling to allow her to escape, Rurik followed when she went to the alcove that held the food. He'd obtained more of the foods she preferred when the supply had started to run low, but he used magic to keep it fresh for as long as he wanted.

So as not to crowd her, he leaned against the entryway once he obtained a green apple to eat, and he calmly watched her. She also seemed to be in the mood for fruit because she piled different ones into the skirt of the dress.

He noticed she grabbed an apple for herself. "You prefer red over green?"

She crinkled her nose as she walked her haul down the tunnel. "I find the green ones sourly sweet."

That was exactly why he preferred them.

She cut and peeled the fruit before placing them into a bowl.

He leaned against the side of the table while she sat at one of the ends of it. His eyes scanned the walls before they eventually fell to her, like he was unable to keep them away from gazing upon her.

I already grow impatient. Especially when their eyes met and the bridge of her nose pinkened, causing his cock to jerk in his trousers. She fidgeted in the chair.

"Why are you in your human form today?"

He couldn't help noticing that her gaze trailed from his face, down his naked chest, and then quickly back up like she had caught herself doing it.

Sometimes when she asked this, he answered her that he had tasks that required smaller hands. Most of the time he didn't respond because his answer wasn't one he wanted to share.

When he shrugged, she averted her gaze to her bowl. Usually he found blushing, bashful females annoying, but with Amalia, it was almost his undoing. Every time she placed a piece of fruit between her lips, he was tempted to lean down and steal it straight from her mouth.

One thing Rurik was curious about was why she never tried to approach him or touch him when human. Already he'd come to learn that she wasn't afraid to be herself, to do as she pleased like climb his back or grab his tail. If she was aroused, why didn't she do anything about it?

She didn't hate his kind like he did hers. He had refrained from doing so in unwillingness. He was curious to know why she was restraining herself.

Could be because of the terrible stableboy story she told me. He would show her that one sloppy male wasn't representative of them all.

Once she was done, she rose to her feet to move her plate away.

He followed next to her when she left, but their footsteps were heading to her room, like she was planning to retreat into it. Mostly Rurik stayed out of it, knowing she needed a comfortable place where she felt secure, even from him.

I tire of waiting. If the moment wouldn't present itself, then he would try to create it.

He grabbed her wrist gently and pulled until she slammed against his broad chest. His other hand shot up to hold the side of her face to keep her still.

He crashed his lips upon hers.

She froze with her free hand against his shoulder, her eyes wide. He moved his lips once to see if he could spur her into returning the kiss. When she didn't, he pulled back to give her time to process. Rurik flicked his eyes between hers and then her lips, before licking the bottom one of his own.

After a few breaths where she didn't say or do anything, and more importantly didn't run from him, he used the hand still cupping the side of her face to pull her in.

Rurik brought their lips together. He only needed to move his once before she returned his kiss, then the aroma of desire saturated her scent.

With a quiet snarl, he moved his hand to the back of her head to protect it when he slammed her back against the wall, squishing her body between himself and the rocky surface.

He kissed her hard, moving his mouth in time with hers until he tried to pick up the pace.

Her lips cave under mine. The softness and silkiness of them left a tingle in their wake. Rurik hungrily ate at them.

Letting her wrist go so that he could place his hand against the wall, he brought their bodies closer and tilted his head. *Have to taste her.* When her lips separated, he slipped his tongue inside her mouth to stop them from closing.

Her body flinched, but not even a moment later her tongue swept back against his. *She is not resisting.*

Deepening the kiss, he grabbed the back of her thigh and lift it so that her knee sat against his hip.

She tried to pull away.

He brought his lips down the side of her face while he forced her chin to tilt up by using the hand on the back of her head. Once he exposed it, he brushed his lips over it, occasionally flicking his tongue out.

The soft breath she gave made the hairs on the back of his neck stand on end.

"Why?" she asked, her voice so quiet that he could barely hear it over the wildly pounding beat of his own pulse.

Another little breath left her when he drew his tongue

but it felt like he had doused her with cold water within an instant. The warmth in her chest turned into a spike of gut-wrenching regret.

Her eyes didn't pool with tears, but she could feel them dotting along her eyelashes. With her hand clutching the top of her dress to keep it from falling down, Amalia turned to storm in the direction of her room.

His hand grabbed her wrist to stop her and forced her to turn around.

"Why are you angry with-"

He didn't get to finish.

As he spun her, Amalia let her hand fly, and she purposely slapped him across the face. She wrung her other hand out of his hold.

His shock caused him to let go.

Before she could even get a step away, he lunged forward and grabbed her hair into a tight fist, pulling her up to her toes by it.

Yet his voice was a menacing kind of quiet as he said, "Do not strike me unless you want to be struck yourself."

His nose was bunched into the snarl she was used to seeing and could usually make fade. Amalia didn't care right then, not with the way she felt. She managed to get her hair loose by prying his hand away, but she knew she ripped a few strands in the process.

She fell back a step when free.

"I am not some whore that you can use because I am convenient and mistakenly felt desire!" She wasn't sure if it was a scream, a yell, or a screech, but it sounded like a horrible mixture of all three.

He reared his head back, his snarl turning into a wide-eyed, shocked stare. Probably from how she said it, rather than what she said.

Then she walked to her room, half-running between certain

steps.

Amalia wanted distance from him to deal with this terrible emotion that had risen inside her when only a moment before she had felt something wonderful and tender. She wanted to wash herself of this so she could no longer feel its evidence, especially since she could feel semen and her own orgasms trickling between her thighs.

18

After her bath, Amalia laid under the furs spread across her bed. She didn't feel like reading, or sleeping, or anything for that matter. She wanted nothing more than to lay there quietly. To hide from him, from the world.

That was until she heard the crack of thunder echoing loudly, and then the sudden outburst of heavy pelting rain shortly after.

Like any Witch who was feeling misery, she eventually felt called by it and rose from the bed. She didn't even care to duck out to see if the Dragon was around when she entered the tunnel. She just walked until she could see the sheen of the ward that wouldn't let her outside to greet the storm.

She sat down a little behind it to watch the rain fall and quickly pool at the entrance of the cave. The spark of lightning filled the sky right before it gave a bellowing roar that would make most shriek in terror at the loudness.

Instead, Amalia was relieved in seeing and hearing it. It was like the sky was mirroring how she felt, angry and miserable.

She wasn't the cause of it. She didn't hold such magic to change what had once been a beautiful, sunny day into this cold and miserable storm.

She didn't know what she'd wanted Rurik to say to her afterwards. And even though she had hated the answer he'd given her, she was thankful for it.

He'd shown her how wonderful sex could be, but she didn't think she would want it from him again. *I am not some harlot.* And no matter how good it had been, she wouldn't allow it to happen again.

She wouldn't allow him to use her body simply because she was conveniently in his lair. *If he wants to have sex, he can go find some other random female he does not care about.*

She wasn't some weak-willed woman who would seek the pleasure of sex only to feel something as ugly as she did afterwards.

She hadn't allowed herself to shed a single tear in regret, refusing to. She didn't want to be some sniffling girl who had gotten herself hurt by a male who probably didn't even know what he'd done wrong.

Instead, she focused on trying to forget it ever happened. She'd liked how they were before, and she would like to return to being that way.

Something in her peripheral caught her attention, a moving object. It was small, a creature shifting its weight on its little legs.

She took her eyes away from the raging outside world to see what it was.

There lay what she could only imagine was a ferret huddled against the wall and ground just inside the cave next to her. She wasn't sure what it was because it had been rained on with mud and blood covering it.

It is injured.

Times when she took care of the racoons, birds, and other manner of creatures she found, or Bala brought to her cottage, flashed in her mind. It was the first time since the Dragon had given her the room that she truly felt homesick.

It must have come here to seek shelter from the storm. It didn't appear as though it would have the strength to find shelter.

The injured creature was staring down the tunnel, shaking in fear.

It must know it is not safe further inside.

Amalia slowly rose to her feet as not to startle it.

Here little thing, let me help you. Perhaps caring for something would make her feel better.

Before she could reach down to grab it, it looked up to her, turned, and then bolted out of the cave. Without a second thought, she chased after it, knowing it wouldn't be safe on its own.

She kept her eyes firmly on the animal as it darted around, and she was surprised by its speed with its injuries. Rain pelted her face and soaked her dress while she chased the stupid thing. She slipped forward.

It seemed her falling had worked in her favour because it threw her forward, and she was able to grab it in time. It struggled in her hands as she made her way to her knees while holding it and then continued to her feet.

There, now I can take you ins- It bit her!

With a hiss through clenched teeth, she dropped it by mistake when it latched onto her hand. It'd bitten deep enough that blood welled. *Another scar to add to the others.*

"No! Wait a sec-" she started while taking a step forward.

She watched it bolt up a tree right before something yanked her back.

The Dragon's clawed hand wrapped around her torso, and she beat at his fingers, wanting to get back to the injured creature. Rain stopped pelting her when she was tossed inside his lair. He'd tossed her hard enough that she was thrown against the ground.

Amalia didn't care that he was angry with her because she

had slapped him. He'd deserved it!

She was just about to stand when he yelled, "You tried to escape!"

Her brows drew together, and she looked up to his face that had water sluicing from it. Her eyes widened when she realised she'd been outside in the storm.

How did I get past the ward?

"I-" His growl cut her off.

His head lowered to the point it was almost touching the ground as he stomped forward.

"After everything I have tried to do, you dare to flee?!"

His snout crinkled into the hateful scowling snarl he only wore when he was completely enraged. The kind of rage she wouldn't be able to calm him from, no matter how she tried.

"Wait."

Instead of letting her speak, he roared, jumping both his front paws up to slam them around her body.

Amalia threw her hand up, not in fear, but to ward him away. She didn't think he would hurt her, but it was still unnerving to have his large body stomp around her in uncontrolled anger. *He is too close!*

All of a sudden, she was thrown to the side by some unseen force. She knew it hadn't been him. She didn't know what it was since they both flew apart, but she heard the crack of bone when her back met the wall. Unconsciousness blacked her out as quickly as someone snuffing a flame.

Amalia woke in suffocating darkness.

There wasn't a shred of light. It was the kind of voiding darkness that she couldn't even see if something were inches from her face and about to poke her in the eye.

She couldn't move, dazed. She lay there on what must be her side.

Am I dead? No, she couldn't possibly dead, not with the pain she felt in her hand and the back of her head – although it was a small pain, throbbing enough just to tell her it was there.

She didn't feel like rising since her mind was so foggy.

Where... am... I? The question rung slowly in her mind, but it was like she no longer remembered how to use her body or how to think properly to figure it out on her own.

She could hear nothing other than her own breath and heartbeat.

It was like she had been cut off from the world.

I do not feel well. Her eyes could only open a sliver since they were too heavy for her to use. Her head spun, and that seemed odd since she didn't even know where she was to know if she was upside down or not.

The air was cool, the ground hard and freezing against her rain drenched body. She was unbearably cold, but she couldn't shiver. She felt the want to tingling in her knees and fingertips, but nothing came.

Eventually she heard a scraping noise before light filled the room. Everything she saw was hazy, but she could tell the Dragon had moved something so she could see.

There were multiples of him. She couldn't count how many, the images moving too fast, but it seemed as though there were three to six of him. He stared at her before closing her off from the light again.

She wondered if he wasn't able to tell she was awake because her eyes were barely open.

I am in the prison cell. That's all she knew, but she couldn't connect the dots enough to be upset or think as to why she would be there.

A long time passed, but she did eventually find the strength to move. It was only enough that she half sat up with her side leaning against the wall with her legs partially under her.

She was once again limp and unable to move.

Amalia had bundles of energy. She could feel it radiating

inside her, up and down beneath her skin and mixing into her organs and bones. It didn't belong to her and the parts of her that did, were drained. Her magic felt drained, her body felt useless.

Her new position made her stomach woozy. She couldn't handle being upright. Her body tried to fight nausea, but it won out, and her body heaved while she made no other sounds or movements in distress.

Nothing came out, her stomach empty.

Something is wrong with me.

Rurik walked around his tunnels restless and seething.

Not only had she struck him across the face, but she attempted to flee!

He'd been laying in one of the alcoves of his lair in his Dragon form, his body off to the side while his head laid in the tunnel, watching down the long length of it.

He'd been both angry and confused that she had slapped him. He hadn't understood why she did. He knew he hadn't hurt her physically, and that she had enjoyed being intimate with him. He had felt it.

He'd been watching his tunnel to see if she would emerge while he thought on how his words may have upset her, because he had been able to tell that was what had caused it.

Because you are here... He wondered how that could have upset her. It was true, she was here, tantalising him with her laughter, bewitching him with her beauty, tempting him with her desire. He truly didn't understand how she could mistake his words, so he thought on what else he had said.

And I can scent your desire... She hadn't struck him in

embarrassment because he was able to sense this. No, it was something else. He could scent her desire. It had given him the knowledge that she thought about him in the same way he did her.

If she hadn't felt it, he wouldn't have pursued sex with her.

So, while he was trying to understand as only a creature could.

He'd known the storm was going on and he lifted his head when he saw that she wanted to watch it. For a long time, he observed her until he saw he get to her feet and then, to his shock, literally bolt out of his cave.

She is trying to run away. And he'd immediately chased after her, knowing she wouldn't be able to get too far with her little legs.

His first emotion had been disappointment that she had tried to run away from him, hurt by it. He'd also been shocked that she had managed to get outside at all when he could still see his ward was in place. And then a blinding anger had gripped him that she'd struck him, then tried to escape his lair.

The lair that he had changed for her, had tried to make her content in, safe in. That he had watched her flit around in and captivate him with her beauty in while she had planned to escape all along.

He'd been furious, and he'd roared and stamped his feet simply because he had no idea on how to vent it without hurting her. Rurik usually maimed things that angered him, but he couldn't, *wouldn't*, do that to her.

Then she'd used blood magic against him.

He'd smelt the foul and wretched scent of it, saw it when a ball of energy formed between them and sent them both flying. It had glittered with the tell-tale red that blood magic always produced.

I have been tricked. She uses dark magic. It hadn't been a small spell, but a powerful one, a strong burst of energy hitting him so hard it flung him back against his own tunnel wall. That kind of power couldn't have been an accident. *She tried to injure me so she could flee.*

And all the trust he had in her came crashing down.

She obviously hadn't been able to handle the use of it because it had sent her flying as well. With a growl, he got to his paws and stormed over, readying to fight her, only to find that she was unconscious. *She stupidly knocked herself out.*

Rurik took her to the only place he felt comfortable putting her now, his prison cells.

He checked on her once so he could sneer at her about her new home, but she still hadn't woken. Then he roamed his tunnels with a hateful swirl in his chest, seething and growling as he waited for time to pass.

Hours later, he was now heading back to check on her again. *I will laugh at her stricken face when she realises she will never be able to leave.* She had failed in her attempt.

The boulder was heavy enough that unless the Witch trapped inside was powerful, if they did not have the right tools to assist them, they couldn't move it.

The extra wards in place were just a precaution.

He rolled it out of the way and prepared himself for a possible fight, expecting the torches to be lit. Instead, he saw her curled up against the wall, barely sitting in the dark.

Her eyes flickered enough to tell him she was awake, but she didn't greet him. Actually, she appeared deathly pale, unmoving even.

Is this a trick? He waved his paw in the air to see if she would follow it while taking a single step inside.

She did nothing. She didn't react except for her flickering eyelids.

Something is wrong with her. His first reaction was to assist her, to check on her.

Why should I care how she is? He cared because he wanted

to fight with her. He couldn't do that with a dazed person.

That was, at least, what he told himself.

He was unsure of what to do. He couldn't physically check her in this form, but he didn't feel comfortable in his human one with her any longer.

How do I truly check if this is a trap?

Fear. She would react to fear.

Breathing in deep, he filled his lungs with air and then released flames against the ceiling. It wasn't enough to reach her, but it should make her scatter.

She didn't even flinch.

It is not a trap.

Rurik blew a ring of fire. "Shift," he chanted, and he did, that ring coming back to encase him in flame.

He quickly approached her and smelled the places on her that had blood.

He checked her hand, expecting to find the slice of a knife, but found what he could see was the bite from an animal. Staring at it, he didn't quite understand why she would have used an animal to injure herself so that she could use blood magic.

Choosing to disregard it because it didn't matter, he pulled her forward to look at the back of her head.

He winced. It hadn't bled this much yet when he brought her in here. Actually, he hadn't even really checked on her wellbeing since he'd thought it was merely a knock.

Her hair was stained red, the blonde making it easy to see just how badly wounded she was.

She cracked her skull.

He didn't have the knowledge to heal such a wound. When his kind were injured terribly, they would burn themselves so they could regenerate with the magic he had once used on her legs.

He couldn't do that to her.

Not just because of her fear of fire, but because she may not survive him doing so. The skull was too vital, too delicate. But he *could* obtain the knowledge to help her if he really wanted to.

He laid her down and locked her back inside the room. Remaining in his human form, he sprinted up the tunnel to the alcove he'd hidden from her. He passed through the fake rock wall illusion to enter a room that was filled with herbs, spices, and crystals. Everything a Witch could possibly need.

Turning to the two chests in the room he brought in here from his book collection, he unlocked it using his magic and opened it. He rummaged through the spell books, flicking through the pages quickly to find something that would tell him what he needed to make.

Even though these were made for Witches for the use of witchcraft, his kind could learn the spells and potions if they wanted to. Most didn't, and he'd detested the idea because it was designed for her ilk.

After going through multiple books, he found something that would be of use and made the concoction he needed. Since a Dragon was making it, it would be imbued with dragoncraft, making it stronger than it was supposed to be.

He had all the right ingredients ready and available, so it didn't take him long to make it. Once he did, he went back to the Witch and applied it to the back of her head. He also applied it to her hand so it would heal as well.

Eventually it would bubble and then become a hard shell while the magic worked the area that it was applied to. The information on it told him it was capable of healing muscles and bone even after a length of time, but every hour delayed in applying it, meant that it may not heal to what it once was.

She will most likely scar. But as long as her brain was fine, he didn't mind.

Rurik then shifted back into his Dragon form and laid at

the entryway to the prison cell. He kept a close eye on her. He was concerned that she would bounce to her feet to attack him again so she could flee.

With quiet angry huffs, he waited.

I will yell at her, laugh at her, and then I will only open this cell to feed her.

The colour returned to her face, and he saw her eyelids begin to flicker more. She remained awake the entire time, unmoving, and he wondered if she understood what happened to her. She started to blink, her lids fluttering further open each time right before she sighed heavily with relief.

His muscles tensed in preparation when he saw hers bunch, right before she unsteadily pushed herself up to sit on her hip. She eventually sat up properly and turned to him.

What confused him was that she smiled before she muttered, "Thank you."

It was that same smile that always made strangeness stir in his chest. *Hate that smile.* It caught him off guard. How was he supposed to yell at someone who looked at him like that? *Why is she not upset that she is in here?*

She stared for a long time and silence bled between them. As if she couldn't wait any longer, she finally spoke. "Well?"

"Well, what?" he snapped.

"I am waiting for you to growl at me for being outside." She rubbed the side of her head, not where she had injured herself, but close by. "Try not to be too loud, my head still feels funny."

"You have the audacity to demand something from me? To stupidly push me further to anger when I plan to leave you in this cell?"

"I know how it must have appeared, but I was not trying to leave," she answered before groaning from what he could only think was of pain.

"Lies! You were running from my cave, sprinting towards

the forest. If you had not slipped, I would not have grabbed you in time before you ran off."

She shushed him, motioning for him to lower his voice with her hands, and his eyes widened before one of them twitched. She spoke before he could release whatever sound or words were going to explode from him.

"I was chasing after an injured animal. A ferret, I think." She fingered the potion that had hardened at the back of her head, poking it. "If you do not believe me then you may go to the beginning of your lair and sniff for where it had been. It was afraid to come inside and afraid to face the storm in its condition."

"Why should I believe such nonsense?" *She is only trying to make me leave so she can plot something while I am away.* "You want me to believe such a story when you used blood magic against me?"

She winced at the bellow of his voice before frowning deeply. She inspected her injured hand, ripping the hardened potion off it.

"Did I?" His head twisted sharply. She hadn't denied it, nor did she admit to it. "Is that what pushed us apart?"

"You would try to make me believe you did not know? Do you think I am an imbecile?"

That frowned deepened when she turned her head to him.

"You startled me. I threw my hand up to ward you away because you were scaring me and then I was tossed against the wall. I knew you did not do it, but I did not know that I had."

"It was powerful magic. It could not have been done by accident."

"I just wanted you to give me space." Her spell had definitely given them space, violently. "I have told you what happened, my version of what I was doing. I was chasing an injured creature, like I would have when I lived in my cottage.

It was hurt, and when I picked it up, it bit me. You grabbed me right after I dropped it." She lifted her hand towards him. "You would have seen the wound when you put ointment on my hand. I did not cut myself on purpose in order to attack you."

It was true. Her wound hadn't been inflicted by herself.

Rurik thought for long moments, letting his eyes flick over her. *I have always known that she has strong magic.* Was it possible...? Did she manage to tap into it unconsciously because she'd been in a startled state?

He realised that he wanted to believe her. Rurik didn't want to hate her or be angry with her. *How do I pull what I saw away from what she says she did?*

"How did you get past my ward?"

"Now that I do not know. Although, it does not matter."

"Of course it matters! You would have had to use a spell, would have had to chant. How am I to believe you when getting past that ward is near impossible for a Witch?"

She shrugged, bringing her knees up so that she could wrap her arms around her legs while they spoke.

"Like I said, I chased the creature. I was not thinking at the time, and I did not even know I was out in the storm until you tossed me back inside." Then she shook her head as she said, "And that is not what I meant when I said it does not matter. Although I wish to roam the lands here, I wish to do so with you."

Rurik's brows creased, trying to understand what she meant.

"Your wards do not matter to me. I do not feel trapped here, and I do not want to leave your lair."

"As if that is-"

"I am scared," she sighed, pressing her cheek against the top of her knees before staring at the wall next to her. "I am afraid to walk among the humans, to be recognised and put on the stake again. I also do not want to find my own kind if they are willing to pull creatures apart." Then she turned her head, resting her cheek on her knees again, but so she was facing him. "I feel safe here. I would not be able to feel that on my own."

"If that were true, why did you not tell me sooner?"

They sounded like pretty words to appease him.

"Would you have believed me?" She laughed, but it held no humour. "I have not been here for long, and I know that you do not truly trust me. You will not even leave me here for an extended period of time by myself. I was going to wait until you were comfortable enough by making the offer to me since you know I like to sit at the entrance of your lair. If I had really wanted to escape, I would have done it when you went to hunt for food, not when you were here."

That is awfully... convincing.

"With the fact that you were able to slip past my ward, I cannot let you roam free here."

To his surprise, the Witch shrugged.

"Shackle me to my room. Leave me in this cell. I would rather that than the possibility of one day burning again."

"You would be trapped." He wanted to make sure she understood what that meant. "You would not have any taste of freedom. Your life would be boring and lifeless."

"Then give me the mercy of a quick death. Anything other than me leaving to face the humans by myself."

She truly does not care.

Rurik stood, and she didn't move. He turned from her, leaving the cell open as he walked up his tunnel. Unknown to her, he kept his shield against it so she couldn't leave. He would be able to feel if she tampered with it, and it would tell him if she tried to leave on her own.

He needed proof, needed to have some physical indication that she was telling the truth before he made any decision.

When he got to the entrance of his lair, he didn't need to sniff around to find what he wanted to, it was clear. There really had been an injured animal here, and he followed its scent back into the storm, having to use his senses to better smell through the rain.

The path stopped going forward right where he'd grabbed the Witch, and then it changed to go up a tree. The injured creature was no longer there, but it confirmed her story of her leaving his lair.

He walked back inside.

She did not leave my lair with the intention of escaping, he thought. *The creature had bitten her, causing blood to well... Could she really have used such magic without intending to?*

Rurik's anger faded, but he didn't feel relief.

I still cannot let her roam free inside my lair since we do not know why she was able to pass through my ward. And now that he knew his anger had been unfounded, he didn't want to cage her in more, to lock her away. *I liked her roaming my tunnels. I like watching her.*

He knew in the morning she hadn't been able to pass the ward since her feet had been pressed against it while she sat in the sun.

What changed? He didn't know.

She was still seated in the same position when he returned to the cell.

"Come," he demanded, and turned back.

When she followed, he took her to the entrance of his cave. He removed the ward and then reapplied it, pouring his magic into it to make it strong. She would have to chant out loud in order to go through it.

It would show him if she lied to him previously or not.

"Can you still walk through it?"

She lifted her hands in front of her and walked forward. His eyes widened when he was met with silence, and she slipped right through.

He exited his cave as he kept his eyes on the entrance, trying to understand how it was possible, why the ward wasn't working against her. It was designed to keep Witches and pixies out.

"Although I now believe your story, I cannot allow you to be free if you can do this," he finally said, trying to think of a way around having to put her in the cell.

If the Elders found out, they would take her. They would also punish him, and he'd rather not deal with that.

Mahesh the Flightless was wingless for a reason.

Her shoulders slumped, but she nodded as if she understood, to which he internally cringed.

Eyeing the ward he could see was still in place, he eventually pushed her back inside and took it down so he could reapply it. He changed the ward completely.

"Try now."

With a sigh, she lifted her hands and walked forward. This time, she was blocked by it. Her brows knotted as she ran her hands along it to check that she was barricaded in.

Well, this is peculiar. He'd changed it so that it kept everyone out except for the person who created it. The only way to allow people through was to either have someone invite them inside, or he would have to lower it and reapply it.

It would keep everything out. Animals he let come inside so he could make a quick meal of them, fairies, pixies, Witches, and humans. Even other Dragons couldn't penetrate it.

Although it was strange that his other ward didn't perceive she was a Witch and keep her in, he grinned. This meant she was once again trapped inside the way she was before.

"Excellent, I have created a solution. One that shall be entertaining for me when Glov tries to fly inside."

He will smack against the barrier, and it will be hilarious.

She kept her hands against it. "Does that mean everything is fine now?"

He nodded. "Yes. You may continue to walk through my lair. Everything can go back to the way it was."

She turned her face up to him, meeting his eye.

"Kind of." He tilted his head, not understanding what she was implying. "Thank you for healing me and finding a solution. I am going to rest since I am still not feeling well."

She turned and went to her room, and his eyes followed her as a frown formed across his face.

What did she mean?

19

It didn't take Rurik many days to understand what the Witch meant.

All had been forgiven in the terms of her injury and being locked away. She told him that she understood it must have been easy to misinterpret what she'd been doing at the time. But things didn't go back to the way they were before that day.

When he was in his Dragon form, she had no issue being in his presence. She continued to spend time with him, but she didn't touch him as much, didn't stroke his scales like she occasionally had.

She also wouldn't be around Rurik while he was human.

If he came to her while in that form, she would immediately stop what she was doing and retreat to her alcove.

He could scent her desire sometimes when she was with him, but it was fleeting. It would come, and he would grin to himself, until moments later it would vanish, and her face would almost appear crestfallen.

Her avoidance frustrated him. Her no longer freely feeling desire for him was maddening because what he'd been hoping would curb his curiosity had only made him want her more.

She had tasted sweet on his tongue, had felt exquisite under his palms and against his body. The noises she'd made often caused his ears to tingle in memory. His cock would start to harden when he remembered what she felt like wrapped around it.

He wanted to bed this female again, and this avoidance was infuriating him. It was like his desperation for her was making his scales itch.

She has me under her spell. One that she didn't cast.

It made him unhappy. *She feels regret, and I do not like it.* Especially because his desire for her continued to grow by the minute.

He also still didn't know why.

He didn't know how to rectify the problem when she refused to speak about it. The only words she uttered about it was the one time she deigned to answer him, as if to reconfirm what she felt without explanation.

"I am not a whore," she'd muttered as she pushed him away when he had attempted to kiss her the only time he'd managed to get close to her.

He'd been hoping if he showed her that he desired her, it would once again birth it in her. It didn't. Actually, it appeared to make everything worse.

But I do not think this of her. It often made him scratch the scales on the top of his head in puzzlement. Just because he felt this way didn't mean he thought this lowly of her. *I want to touch her because she enthrals me, not because she is an easy target.*

"Your thoughts are not focused today," Glov said when it was obvious that he wasn't listening.

Rurik blinked, bringing his focus back to the green Dragon in front of him.

They lay about in the main room of his lair, the one he had carved so that he could have guests the size of his kind laze about comfortably when they visited.

Glov visited him today to inform him of what he'd learned, which was not much, as well as to rest from flying. He'd barely landed since the day he told Rurik of Strolguil the Vast.

"Yes, my mind is elsewhere this morning." It was on the Witch, and her moodiness and unwillingness to let him touch her again.

"Well, bring your ill-tempered tail back to the conversation." Rurik gave a soft growl in irritation before the green Dragon continued. "What are your plans for Strolguil if he comes this way?"

"If they are close by and we have not discovered where they are hiding or what their plans are, then the others will have to come here so that we can prepare."

"Are you sure that is wise with the Witch you have in your lair?"

Rurik scowled, his upper lip curling back over his fangs.

"If any dare to harm her in my lair, then they will feel the consequences of my wrath. I do not care what the others think, and I will not change the way I handle my hunts because she is here."

This wasn't the first time Rurik had others assist him in hunting Witches. He'd never needed to call on so many before, but he often had his kind prepare to fight an entire coven in his lair and rest here while they waited. It could take time to call upon them if they were not here, and he didn't wish to be forced to fight on his own.

"You are awfully protective of her."

"She has further proved to me that she bears no ill will. She has also shown me that she does not plan to escape if given the opportunity."

Glov raised a brow in questioning. "How can you be certain?"

"She is afraid to be burned on the stake." Rurik let his eyes fall on the cave wall as he thought on how to word his lie. "She has, uh, witnessed its brutally herself and now fears the humans will do it to her if she is to walk among them."

Glov nodded his head in understanding.

"Yes, they are often worried of being discovered." Glov's shoulders visibly lost their tension. "It truly does seem as though she is not an issue."

"Exactly. So cease questioning me on it!" he snapped, his scales raising in agitation.

Glov constantly pestered him about it, and it was beginning to get under his scales.

If I am trusting enough of her that I was inside her, then I know she is no danger to me. But he couldn't tell him that.

He rolled his eyes at Rurik's shout before getting to his paws to stand.

"I know you well enough to know that my time here grows short. I will leave before you claw me."

"Good. Get out of my cave, you infuriating snake."

A warm, light-hearted chuckle rumbled from Glov. "I am only infuriating to you because you are ill-mannered."

The green Dragon quickly walked from his lair when Rurik answered him a warning grunt.

Glov was planning on meeting with Mahesh the Flightless to see if he had more information on the Witches who were seen near his lair. It seemed as though they were searching for something, but Mahesh couldn't uncover where they were hiding to discover what that was.

I wish to spend time with her today, but in my human form. The more he wanted her, the more he wanted to be around her in the form he knew she may let touch her.

If Rurik really wanted to, he could bed Amalia as a Dragon by changing his size. As much as he would like to, with how she was acting, he didn't see that possibility forthcoming any time soon.

Everything felt different to him when he was human. They were both him, but the softness of flesh and the shape of his body differed, and therefore, his body reacted differently. He didn't like how weak his human skin was. That it was easy for a simple rock to hurt his foot when his paw barely registered it.

He went to the alcove that held the chests of clothing and blew a ring of fire before he entered. "Shift."

He dug through those chests until he found clean, black, leather breeches.

He went to his book collection, retrieved one, and then made his way into her room. She was sitting upon the bed, reading as she often did when Glov was here since she refused to leave this room until he left.

She looked up from her book when he entered, but he didn't say anything as he walked over to the sofa. He plopped himself down, put his arm behind his head, and opened the book with the intention of reading it.

She has to get used to me again because I will not stand a female who flees at the sight of me for much longer.

"What are you doing?" she asked.

He turned a page but didn't face her as he said, "I cannot read a book when I am in my Dragon form."

The points of his claws couldn't juggle between holding the book to carefully turning the page without damaging it. He'd accidentally ripped pages from some of his favourites in attempting to do so.

"Do so somewhere else."

Rurik looked at her from the corner of his eye with a deadly look. "Do not command me. You know it does not sit well with me."

His head was smacked to the side when the book she had been holding hit him. He hadn't expected her to throw it at him!

With a growl, he got to his feet and approached her. He usually didn't care when she threw things at him because he was usually in his armoured Dragon body.

"Do not throw things at me while I am in this form. It hurts."

She knelt on the bed so that she would be level with him instead of letting him tower over her. His cock jerked in excitement at her feistiness.

"Get out!" She pointed to the entryway.

He grabbed both her wrists and brought them forward.

"You will learn to be comfortable with me again." She twisted her arms to release his hold, but he held firm, and her face screwed into a frowning twist of concentration. "I do not understand why you are apprehensive of me. You are fine around me when I am a Dragon."

Which made little sense to him when he was capable of clawing her or biting her in half with sharp fangs.

"Because I do not trust you like this!"

"I did not hurt you. I do not know why you are against it when I can still sense you desire me."

As if to prove it to her, he pushed her against the bed and pinned her arms down. He brought his mouth to hers. He moved his lips over hers, and instantly the scent came from her skin, even as she fought him and didn't return his kiss.

Why will she not be intimate with me again?

He kissed her harder, and she lost some of her fight, not all of it, but enough that her body started to soften. She gave him the sweetest moan when he slipped his tongue into her mouth, allowing him the sweet taste of her. Her tongue lapped at his, finally welcoming his mouth, and he brought his body down more on top of her.

Her eyelids shut and she turned her head to deepen the kiss herself as another small noise of enjoyment fell from her. The kiss was warm, wet, and filled with longing.

I want to feel her again. He thrust his hips against her as he twirled his tongue against hers, nearly groaning into her mouth in desperation.

It seemed his thrust snapped her out of it, because she bit his tongue!

He gave a growl in reaction and pulled away. Her cheeks and chest were flushed with arousal, her breaths coming out in pants. She scented heavily of it. He could see the conflicting emotions in her. The one that wanted him inside her, and the one that absolutely did not.

And Rurik wouldn't force the side of her that didn't. He wasn't the kind of Dragon to take an unwilling female.

"Get off me." She said it with a glare and a huff.

Rurik released her and stood.

His emotions were beginning to spiral out of control, his lack of understanding getting to him. He roared at her, wanting to vent his anger at a target he would never dare harm before he stormed off.

Fuck! He shifted back to a Dragon and stomped his way through his tunnels, to his stream where he could dunk himself under the cold water to shock his erection away.

She rejects me?! Him! Someone who shouldn't even want to bed one of her kind, and yet was desperate to. He was also angry with himself that he couldn't figure out what the fuck he'd done wrong to fix it.

He didn't know how long he had been in his stream, fuming and seething. He'd planned to stay in it for the rest of the day and evening, until he heard his name being called.

When he didn't answer or come to his cave entrance fast enough, his name was called repeatedly. He scuttled low to the ground as he moved, his anger prickling down his scales and his tail flicking dangerously.

"Do not call my name so impatiently. I will arrive... when I fucking arrive!"

His yell echoed in the tunnel, booming and loud and revealing just how deeply he was seething with rage. When he reached the entrance, he shot his hand through the ward and grabbed one of the spikes on Glov's head.

He yanked him inside by it.

"What do you want?" Rurik roared, his lips curled back so tight over his fangs it put pressure around his muzzle, making it difficult for him to breathe through his slitted nostrils.

Glov's eyes were wide, his breaths short like he was either afraid or had exhausted himself.

"Witches are at Mahesh's cave," he answered. Rurik blinked, immediately letting him go as his snarl faded. "When I flew to his home, I saw Witches walking in the direction of his lair. Mahesh was not inside of it, so I could not warn him."

Rurik's eyes widened. *They know where his lair is. They are after him.*

What they had been searching for... was him.

"Go, tell the Elders. I will go to assist him," Rurik demanded, pushing him out of his lair so he could go past the ward.

He turned down his cave, and regardless that she was most likely angry with him, he entered her room in his Dragon form.

"Leave me alone!" she yelled from the bed, tossing her book at the footrest of it in a fit of anger.

"I must leave. One of my kind is in danger." Her anger dissipated as quickly as his did when he heard of it. "I will not return for some time."

"Okay." She rose to her feet to walk over to him. She lifted her hands so he would lower his jaw and rest it against them. "Trust that I will not leave, I promise I will not try to."

He shook his head, taking a step back from her instead.

"You do not understand. I am going alone to fight against a coven." He held her eyes when she frowned, seeming to search his. "Amalia, I may not return."

Her face paled and her hands fell.

"What do you mean you may not return?"

"Exactly what I said, I may not return. I may be captured or killed." If they did capture him, it wouldn't take long for them to remove his scales while he was alive and then kill him to take more parts from him. His eyes flickered over her and then around the alcove of her room. "If that happens, my ward will disappear. You are to run."

Her hands flew up so she could cup them against her chest. She often did this when she was anxious or worried.

"My kind will come here, and they will not understand. You will no longer be safe. They will kill you, Amalia." His eyes found hers again. "Take what you need and run. They may not chase you once I am dead since my face will no longer need to be a secret."

Before she could speak, he turned to leave.

"I have to go. I cannot waste any more time."

"Wait!" He didn't. He walked up his tunnel with the sounds of her feet chasing after him. "You have to come back."

It was a sweet demand, but he didn't give her any promises that he wouldn't be able to keep. He looked at her one last time before he left his lair and ran into the clearing in front of his rock step.

Then he flapped his wings and took flight, heading towards what could possibly be his own death.

It was half a day's flight to Mahesh the Flightless' home if one was to fly calmly. Rurik didn't. He flew hard, and he flew fast, making the trip in just over a quarter of the day.

He imagined Glov had done the same.

I will be too late. He knew it. He knew the likelihood that Mahesh was still alive would be minimal. Still, he couldn't turn his back on his brethren. He couldn't abandon him when there could still be a possibility.

Rurik landed out the front of Mahesh's cave. He could hear noises coming from deep within, could smell the deep, rich aroma of blood.

He galloped inside.

There was a stray Witch walking in the main tunnel, and Rurik startled him when he came up from behind. Just as he turned to fight, Rurik slammed him against the wall with his shoulder, crushing and instantly killing him. He clamped his fangs around his throat and bit his head off before he swallowed it whole.

He planned to regurgitate it later, if he lived, so he could add it to his wall.

It had been a surprise attack, but his presence would be known by the others in due time.

He checked each alcove to make sure he wasn't passing a Witch who could come up behind him as well as to see where his fellow Dragon was. They were still here, which meant they weren't done pulling him apart.

It was a sad day when a Dragon walked into another's lair to visit and found nothing other than blood and the tell-tale signs that they had been extracted. It was something they all feared would happen.

Mahesh's cave was similar to his own, but windier and longer since he was much older than himself. Being flightless, he wouldn't have had the freedom to leave his lair for a great distance. He'd spent his years shaping his home.

Rurik came upon another Witch who was going through a hoard in an alcove. He grabbed her in his large paw and bit halfway down her body before she could react. Swallowing her down so he could add her to his collection, he backed up just as a yell sounded.

He turned and found another female Witch. She looked horrified to see him, and she bolted down the tunnel.

"The WitchSlayer!" she screamed to alert the others.

Before she could get too far, he landed his paw down on top of her, picked her up, and threw her against the wall. He'd expected them to come after him when he collected her, but they didn't.

He moved further inside until he came to the first main room that Mahesh had created, having carved multiple areas for him to house Dragons in.

There they waited for him, four Witches and Strolguil. He paused to enter, all of them ready to fight him now that they were in a group and weren't easy pickings.

"WitchSlayer!" Strolguil chuckled, his hands raised up like he was greeting an old friend with a grand smile upon his face. "I wondered if you would turn up before we had the chance to leave."

Rurik glared at the long-haired male. It was as red as fire and came down to his waist but tied back as to remain out of his line of sight. His skin was pale, not whitely or sickly, just fair. Most of it was hidden behind leather soldier trousers, a chainmail skirt, a cotton brown sleeved shirt, and an intricate metal breastplate.

Rurik's eyes didn't remain on him for long because they fell onto the Dragon laying behind the five Witches.

Mahesh's mouth had been tied shut so he couldn't bite or unleash flames. His front paws were crossed with rope leading from his paws to metal spikes keeping his arms pinned down to the ground. The same had been done to his back legs.

He is still alive, but Rurik was sure he didn't want to be.

Most of the scales except for the ones on his shoulders, neck, and head had been removed. Blood was pouring from him to create a giant puddle while jars lay around him, half of them filled with the crimson liquid.

Their eyes met, and he could see that Mahesh was pleading with him. Rurik shuddered, only being able to imagine the kind of agony he was in.

Rurik stomped one of his feet closer to the Witches with his lips curling back into a vicious snarl.

"You dare torture one of my own!"

He quickly sucked air into his lungs and then unleashed flames towards the Witches to make them scatter and dive away. All except one. Strolguil stood there unharmed, having encased himself in a shield using a dragonscale to fuel it and make it stronger.

Knowing it wouldn't be likely that he would survive this fight, he charged forward and jumped over him to get to Mahesh. *I will end your life so you no longer suffer, dear friend.* He'd been pleading for Rurik to kill him.

When he reached him, he dug his claws into his throat while Mahesh presented it, then he ripped it apart in a spray of blood so that he would die swiftly.

A blast of fire was thrown at him uselessly, one of the coven Witches attacking him with something that would never harm his scales. Another charged with a sword coated in a transparent liquid of blue. *Poison.*

He jumped back and swiped the back of his paw to send him flying through the air.

Before he could lower his paw, he heard two of them chanting in unison, one following the other's lead. Both of were holding string with bones and stones dangling from the ends.

Sharp spikes of rock jutted from the ground near their feet, moving towards him like a wave. He rolled to the right, narrowly missing being impaled.

He let loose a string of flames in their direction. When he stopped to see the damage he'd caused, he could see dragonscales floating in front of them mixed with a shield of magic. Those scales crumbled into dust when the spell faded and the shields disappeared. They'd already extracted them from Mahesh to make their magic strong against his abilities. *I will not be able to touch them with my flames.*

Strolguil did nothing to assist the coven of Witches while they attacked, instead choosing to watch with a smug, humour-filled smirk. *I will have to fight him last.*

Something lanced the spade of his tail and trapped it to the ground. The fourth Witch had created a spike of ice to stop him from being able to use it.

The one with the sword was running for him again, and he turned just in time to grab him before he could sink that blade into his side. He wore a necklace of Dragon teeth, and when the Witch bit him, he felt the lance of fangs cut deep into his hand.

It looked as though he had been bitten by a large, ghostly Dragon maw.

His hand twitched in reaction, but it was enough for the Witch to free himself.

Mahesh is not the first Dragon they have extracted.

They each had a piece of a Dragon, something they could use to fight him.

The one with the sword had fangs to bite just as viciously as he could. The one who had spiked his tail had claws to scratch just as deep. One of the Witches who had chanted had small wings tied together into a necklace so he could fly, and the other had bones threaded through her clothing so her body would be unbreakable.

All of these were small because they used magic to force the Dragon into a smaller size so their parts could be worn. He knew they each would have vials of blood and a pouch of scales on them.

Not only was he fighting against a coven, but he was fighting against one who was using vile magic that made them stronger. He may have been able to defeat them if they were alone, but not as a group, not with four of them.

He wouldn't be foolish when he could see victory was unattainable.

Rurik pulled the ice from his tail and ran for the exit. They chased after him.

A wall of rock blocked his path, and he attempted to sidestep it.

Having to dodge the wall put him right next to one of them who drank a vial of blood and uncurled a whip from her side. She whipped it forward, and it caught around his wrist. Rurik tugged to pull her forward, but she remained steady on her feet while she continuously chanted.

She has increased her strength so I cannot trip her.

Before he could go to her, the one with the blasted sword came for him again, and the last thing Rurik wanted was poison in his system. He focused on him instead even though one of his front paws was trapped.

His magic must be weak if he was using a weapon.

He flung his body to the side so he could swipe him with his tail. The Witch jumped over it and raised his sword to bring it down into his back leg, but Rurik kicked it and sent him flying once more.

Both of the Witches who had been chanting earlier ran onto his back. They looked like twins, one male and one female.

The female placed her hand against his body, and he shuddered at the vibration of magic pinching him before she slid off. It was a hex; he didn't know what kind yet. The male threaded something around his neck and pulled, making his head arch back and his body bow as it cut off his circulation and airways. A strangled choke caught in his throat, and he raised his free paw to scratch at it.

In his peripheral, looking from the corner of his eye, he saw that he was holding thick tree root vines. *Stolen fairy magic.* They'd extracted other magical creatures as well.

Living earth magic was stolen from fairies, while hexes and curses were stolen from pixies.

Rurik tried to free himself, clawing at his own throat as the pressure tightened. He was pulled until he was on his hind legs. His other hand was then also trapped in vines, crawling up his forearm and pulling it away from his neck.

The two Witches holding his arms in place ran sideways until his arms were crossed in the air. Soon they would get him onto his belly and he would be in the same position Mahesh had been in; defenceless and unable to free himself.

No, I will not be beaten so easily. He forced his head forward, ignoring the fact he couldn't breathe and tried to pull his arms apart. His wings flapped behind him like he was attempting to harness strength from each whoosh.

The more he pulled his arms, the tighter the one covered in

vines felt until he knew they'd deeply cut into his scales. Rurik struggled, his body shaking while he fought against them. He was winning, but he knew eventually his body would weaken from lack of oxygen.

"He is getting free!" Strolguil yelled, running forward and unleashing something Rurik had only ever seen him do.

Red lightning came from his hands, sparking dangerously. The crackle of it echoed.

He clenched his eyes shut and waited for the impact, which could possibly break his bones and cut his flesh. The strike wouldn't burn him, but the magic was so potent that even Rurik didn't have the strength to withstand it.

Strolguil missed, and the Witch on top of him was struck instead. He went flying, slamming against the wall with a satisfying crack and thud. This removed the vines cutting the circulation around his neck.

The male Witch didn't get back up.

"How could you miss?!" The other male Witch shouted while still trying to pull Rurik's arms together with the vines.

The twin's sister screamed about her dead brother.

Strolguil's glare was menacing. "Lightning is hard to control."

And yet... Rurik had seen him wield it many times with accuracy. It seemed odd that Strolguil would miss when Rurik was so unmoving, and stationary in their trappings.

They are distracted.

He spewed fire from his mouth while moving his head sideways so he could unleash it towards both the Witches who had trapped his arms. While they chanted and brought those scales up to protect themselves, he quickly jerked his arms, and he was released.

Giving them no time to react to him now being free, Rurik bolted for the tunnel.

They followed after him once more, but Strolguil threw his

hand up to stop them. "Let him run. He is too strong for the three of you."

Rurik couldn't help noticing the wicked grin on his face.

Sprinting up the winding tunnel, he didn't look back. Rurik flapped his wings before he even made it outside and lifted off as soon as he could so he could get himself into the air.

The only one that would be able to follow him was Strolguil, who had long ago stolen his father's wings. The male who also wore such a necklace totem had been killed by the lightning.

He turned his head to check behind him to find he wasn't being followed. *They will finish with Mahesh before I can get the chance to return with more Dragons.*

Rurik roared, unleashing hate-filled fire in front of him as he flew. *They descaled Mahesh!* They forced Rurik's hand, made him kill his own kind in mercy.

A blinding rage Rurik had never experienced to such a high degree clutched him by the throat. *Vile abominations! Sick, twisted, demented creatures!*

And he'd almost allowed them to capture him.

He released another roar, feeling pain around his throat, arm, and tail. Blood dripped from his many wounds, and Rurik vented his anger to the sky because he had no idea how else to do so. It wasn't fleeting. It didn't fade, but instead grew inside him as he flew to his lair.

It was building, his body visibly shaking with it. He wanted to turn back and maim the Witches. He wanted to strike Strolguil down for what they had done, what he had seen they were doing to his own kind.

Rurik needed to kill, to vent this horrible bloodlust that filled his chest, but he couldn't go back to do it to the people who deserved it.

I am running away like a fucking coward! The only Witch Rurik had ever run from was Strolguil, and knowing that made his scales puff around his head.

Infuriated with himself because he hadn't been strong enough to defeat them, he also felt undeniable shame.

Amalia sat by the entrance of the cave waiting for any sign of Rurik. *He has to return. He cannot leave me to face the world alone.*

She didn't want him to die.

Her heart hadn't settled since he left, and she was too worried to be able to sleep. She'd been unable to eat, unable to read, unable to do anything else than to wait for him.

Her focus constantly switched between watching the night sky for the Dragon and staring at the ward, praying to whichever Gods may be listening for it not to fall.

Please do not fall. Please do not tell me he is dead.

Her head turned so she could cuddle into the nook of her knees while she hugged her legs, biting back the urge to cry. She feared if she let a single tear fall that it would be the reason he died, as if her sadness and lack of faith in him were what might get him killed.

I care for him. He is not allowed to leave me.

He was her friend, her companion.

She shook her head, taking in a deep breath before she looked back up to the sky, determined to see him.

The moon was waning, only half full and barely shedding light over his lands.

It was well into the night when a shadow finally crossed over it. She could tell it was a Dragon by the shape when it flew over that light as it headed away. Then it turned, banking to the left until it was heading straight for the cave entrance.

She didn't even have time to get out of the way before he flew over the top of her and into his lair.

Relief washed over Amalia, and she scrambled to her feet to chase after him. She ran down the tunnel as he landed in the main room of the cave. When he set his four paws down, one gave in. He tripped forward, righting himself before he shook his head.

"You are alive!" she shouted in relief. "I was so worried."

"Stay back!"

Her footsteps slowed.

It was only when she entered the space that she noticed he was snarling and digging his claws into the ground in fury. She paused when he shook his head again as his body quaked.

Something is wrong. She was just about to take a step forward when he roared, but not like how he usually did.

No, Rurik let loose such a bellowing, bone-chilling shout that he stood on his hindlegs at the power of it. His forepaws were clenched into fists, showing her just how much force he used, before flames followed behind it and covered the rocky ceiling with heat. She stepped back with a gasp.

It startled her, but she wasn't afraid of him or his fire, knowing he would never unleash it on her. However, it still made her skin pale and sweat at the sight of it.

"Disgusting, vile, despicable creatures!"

He landed back to all four paws before he ran forward and slashed at the wall, almost catching his claws on a long hanging tapestry. He dragged his claws down, rocks flinging away from underneath their points, while horrible, guttural sounds emitted from him. Rurik then slammed his spiked head against it.

"What happened?" What was causing him to be like this?

His head snapped to her.

Amalia froze. *Perhaps I should not have spoken.*

"What happened?! Your kind is what happened!"

He slithered forward low to the ground as he came towards her with his eyes narrowing. When she took a step back, his jaws snapped, creating a sharp sound that made her halt.

"Witches had already started taking Mahesh apart before I got there." He stood at his full height when he got to her, and his eyes narrowed further. His lips were curled back to give a hate-filled stare. "They had been plucking him, forcing him to bleed so they could steal both his scales and blood. And he was still *alive.*"

Amalia stood her ground.

He wouldn't hurt her, at least, she very much hoped he wouldn't. He promised her, and she hadn't done anything to deserve it.

He is hurting. She could see it in his eyes. Although filled with anger, there was also sadness, and it became more prominent when his eyes crinkled at the sides.

"They made me kill Mahesh. He was in so much pain."

As she stared up at him, she eventually noticed that blood had tracked from his throat. Her eyes widened. They quickly shot down his body to see his forearm was injured and still fresh, like he wasn't able to heal.

"You are wounded."

She stepped forward to touch his arm so she could inspect it. He pulled back sharply to keep it away from her.

"Do not touch me! Do not touch me with your revolting magic. They made me kill my own kind!"

He shook his head, twisting it side-to-side like he wanted to shake the memory of it. She wouldn't be able to do anything for him if he didn't calm.

"I have three to add to my collection, but there were more! I should have been able to kill them, but I did not have the strength to face them alone. And Strolguil did not even engage! I was almost beaten by nothing but a coven."

Amalia raised her hands in hopes he would lower his head

so she could cup his jaw. He'd never told her, but she knew he liked it when she reached for him like this.

He didn't lower his head, instead he bared his menacing fangs.

"Please," she said softly while taking a step forward. "Let me help you."

"Help me?! How can you help me? I will not allow you to touch me with your magic!"

Amalia shook her head. That wasn't what she meant.

"You are enraged, let me help calm you."

"I am filled with so much anger and hatred right now that your soft touches will not help me! I ran, like a coward!"

Amalia winced. She didn't think running was cowardly.

She took another step forward, ignoring the warning rumbles he gave her as he stepped back. She kept reaching.

"You did what you needed to in order to survive. You will fight again."

"That is not good enough! They used dark magic. They killed a different Dragon and used their parts against me! They have stolen wings, and bones, and claws to fight against my own kind." He took in a shaking breath that was strange and guttural, like he was trying to growl and breathe at the same time. "They have stolen from pixies and fairies. They used a hex against me to stop me from healing, to keep me weak."

She took another step forward. "It is okay. I can remove it if you cannot."

"You are just like them! You have the same magic and use illusions to lower my guards." She knew he didn't truly believe that. "You trick me into feeling desire for you and then strike me when I use it."

He is not calming. She lowered her arms, frowning as she thought on the last of his words. *I have not tricked him.*

He turned from her, and she quickly ran forward to touch his back.

"Please, let me help you. You have done so much for me."

She wanted to comfort him in the same way he had once comforted her. He held her when she desperately needed someone to hold, had let her sleep against him when she had been afraid. He healed her of her burns and saved her from obtaining more from Glov.

Amalia wanted to return his kindness.

The moment her hand touched his back, his head snapped to her. He slowly spun back around with his silver eyes narrowed on her.

"You truly wish to help me?"

He stalked towards her, and the look he gave her made her take a step back. She stopped herself from going further when she realised she was retreating.

Without hesitation, she said, "Yes."

He blew a ring of fire into the air above him.

"SHIFT!" he shouted the singular chant before the fire came back to encase his body.

She'd never seen the Dragon change before while lucid, and her eyes widened at watching him do so. When the flames disappeared, he emerged from it human, stalking towards her with a dark predatory gaze.

She didn't even have time to react before he threaded his fingers through her hair. Grabbing a hold of it with a tight fist, he crashed his mouth down upon hers.

Amalia froze and then gave a gasp of pain when he tugged her hair because she wasn't returning his kiss. Unsure as to why this was happening when he was obviously enraged, she kissed back in confusion.

Her hands were against his chest, but she didn't push him away. She was unsure of what to do. His free hand came down on one of her arse cheeks hard, causing her to squeak in surprise, before he lifted her to her toes by it.

His lips spread hers before he slipped his tongue inside her mouth.

She felt wetness pooling between her legs and clenched her eyes shut tight. *I cannot do this.* She wanted to help him, but not like this.

Amalia pressed her hands against his chest to separate their bodies. When he realised what she was doing, her head was pulled by her hair, and she released a soft cry. He broke from her mouth, pushing their bodies back together before he forced her head to tilt up.

His lips found her neck.

"How can I still want you so badly after what I have just seen?" He bit her, making her gasp. It wasn't hard enough to cause true pain, but she felt the twinge of it. His tongue ran across where his teeth had been like he wanted to soothe her flesh, and it sent a small shiver through her. "How can a Witch be this beautiful?"

She stopped pushing him away as she blinked.

He thinks I am beautiful?

He'd called her many things. Odd, strange, entertaining, but he'd never said something so tender, had never complimented her.

His lips and tongue were rough against the soft places of her throat, his mouth eating at her skin hungrily. His breath fanned over the wetness he left behind, and it caused goosebumps to prick down that side of her neck and over her shoulder and arm.

Amalia thought he had sex with her because she'd been convenient. That if it had been any other female, he would have done the same thing.

Does... Does he actually feel something for me in this way? Not just because she was a woman and available, but because he *truly* found her beautiful?

He ground his hips against hers right after she asked herself the question, sliding the hardened length of his shaft against her. She felt like he answered her thoughts.

"Why do I desire you so much? Tell me to stop, Amalia. Or-"

Hope made her desire blossom freely and she pulled his lips back to her own.

His hand gripped her bottom tighter, his mouth moving faster than before as if in reaction to what she'd done. The hand that had been pulling her hair now tenderly gripped the back of her head to help to push them closer.

His kiss was hard, forceful, and unyielding. She tried her hardest to combat it, to return it, to show him she welcomed it.

When she met his tongue readily, his hand shot up to grab the back of her dress. The material tore at her skin like a burn when he ripped the back of it from her shoulders all the way to her waist. He then grabbed the front of it and shoved it down her body until it pooled at her feet, leaving her naked and bared to him.

He grabbed the back of one of her legs and lifted it to his side. She had to grab his shoulders, so she didn't fall, when he lifted her off the ground.

He was gripping her tightly, his fingertips digging in as he dropped to his knees like she was his salvation. The heel of her foot slipped against the ground and forced her legs to spread around his hips.

Amalia flinched when coldness met her back from the rocky floor, the shock making her pause. Growling emitted from his chest, dissatisfied that she had stopped greeting his tongue while he moved to lay on top of her.

He pushed his hips to grind his cock against her.

This time she felt him slip between her folds and she knew she'd wetted him by how slippery he felt. She let out a soft moan when it rubbed over the apex of her clit, that naughty little nub that wanted to be pet, singing with satisfaction. She

when she slipped her legs over the side of the bed and got to her feet. She dragged the fur with her to cover her nudity.

"Are you feeling better?" she asked, and his lungs emptied on a stunned breath.

His brows drew together when she lifted a hand toward his head that was low enough for her to reach it. She stroked it once before ducking underneath his chin to check him.

"I see your wounds have almost closed up. I did not know you healed so well on your own."

It was because he'd licked them or used the back of his paw to spread his saliva. His saliva had healing properties for small wounds, like cuts, so healing them was a relatively short process. Unfortunately, it did little for anything like muscle or bone injuries.

He'd be spared of any scarring around his throat, but he was unsure if his arm would be unmarred.

Bringing his head back, he twisted it when he looked at her. She brought her eyes to him.

"You are not angry?"

Where is the yelling, the screaming, the acid tongue?

She held the furs tighter against her chest, but a small smile played across her lips.

"No, I am not angry with you."

I do not understand. The first time I was careful with her, this time I was forceful. He tried to think on what he did better but couldn't think of a single answer.

"Will you tell me why?"

She backed up a step, using her free hand to wrap herself completely since her back was exposed. Before she turned away from him, she tucked her long curling blonde hair behind a single ear self-consciously.

"You complimented me."

Did I? He thought on the words he could remember speaking to her.

She frowned at his expression.

"You do not remember, do you?"

His nose bunched in embarrassment.

Blasted. What did I say to her? She'd almost woken up elated and he worried that him forgetting would upset her.

She flitted around the tub nervously. He could tell she wanted to fill it, but didn't want to do it in front of him. While she wasn't facing him fully, she smiled to herself.

"You called me beautiful."

I did? he thought as a light blush heated against the bridge of her nose.

"Said that you wanted me. And then when you were calmer, you kept telling me I was soft, and warm, and good as you touched me."

He blinked, watching her fidget with the furs while averting her gaze. Her words *did* remind him, and he grinned triumphantly. *She is pleased with me.*

"I thought you only wanted me because I was the easiest choice. That, if it had been any other woman here, you may have done the same because you had not told me otherwise. I had not known you had wanted me... for me."

He was just about to open his mouth to tell her he did, but then closed it.

Then he actually thought about the words he had muttered to her after the first time. He'd known what he meant, but his answer had been short. He hadn't bothered to expand on them at the time because he hadn't thought he needed to.

She did not know how I was feeling.

Now that he had actually told her something, she was happy with him. *She may want to do this again with me.*

The idea of that elated Rurik to no end.

He rose to his feet while opening his mouth to speak, but her eyes suddenly narrowed at her hands.

She lifted one and inspected her wrist in close detail before looking at the other. Walking to the long, cloudy mirror, she spun the fur around and then opened the front of it to look at her own naked body.

"What did you do to me?!" she yelled, staring at the mirror in horror.

Rurik cringed before settling back down to his stomach – like that would help him shrink away. He'd been rough, not just with his hips, but also his passionate, hungry hands and mouth.

Her throat and chest were covered in bite marks that were deep enough to show that he had broken through skin. There were fingerprint bruises trailing over her thighs – both inside and out – her waist, her shoulders, and even her cheek right below her eye. The worst ones were on her breasts, hips, and arse. He'd gripped them the hardest.

She trailed her fingers over her wrists with her mouth gaping. They weren't bruised like the others, weren't brown. They were nearly black with such a deep shade of purple.

She winced when she touched them.

The Witch spun to him while closing the furs. "You hurt me!"

She is upset. I have to fix this. He didn't want her to shield her body away from his touch again because of this.

"I will let you heal yourself," he blurted out.

"Pardon?" Her glare fell as her brows creased in surprise.

"I will give you the herbs and spices that will allow you to heal yourself of these kinds of wounds for now... and future times."

If it meant he would be able to be intimate with her again, he didn't care.

"You will let me use more magic? Will give me the ability to create teas and ointments?"

Rurik nodded. "Yes."

Her face grew into one of the brightest smiles he'd ever

seen upon her lovely face. Then she quickly pursed her lips together.

"That does not mean you can get away with doing this."

She gestured to her entire body.

"I did warn you when I brought you here that I bite." That didn't placate her. "*Fine,* I will refrain from being so rough."

I will just bite... softer. He didn't think he would be able to do that, but he doubted he'd grab her the way he did again. He'd been enraged, his anger giving him strength.

When she lost the tension in her shoulders, he knew he'd won.

"Come, bathe. I will give them to you after."

He motioned to the tub with his snout, his tongue darting out to not-so-subtly lick at his jowls.

"Are you sure? I know you do not like to see me use my magic."

Right then, he was too pleased, too triumphant. He was also sure he would see much more in the future, and he would have to learn to separate what she did from what the rest of her kind did.

"Yes, it is fine."

She hovered her palm above the tub, and it began to fill with water. Once it was full, she placed her hand inside the water, and eventually, it began to steam. He could see her concentration and that she had been chanting in her mind rather than out loud.

Her magic glittered with white softly before it faded.

It didn't have the red hue or the other colours the rest of her kind had. It also didn't smell foul or corrupted. He still wasn't completely comfortable with it, but it wasn't as terrible to witness as he initially thought.

Rurik wriggled against the ground to make himself more comfortable while he kept his head up. She turned and stared at him. When he didn't do anything, she gave him a 'what gives' gesture with her hand.

He frowned at it.

"If you think I will be leaving while you bathe, then it appears you are sorely mistaken."

"But-"

His lids lowered halfway before he rolled his eyes.

"You are covered in the evidence of me touching you. Are you truly to tell me you wish to be bashful still?"

"You really are a perverted Dragon, are you not?"

He was still waiting.

"For you, yes. Now, lower the furs. I wish to see."

His words were answered with a pouting smile, the kind that told him she was happy with what he said. She dropped the blanket around her feet and tilted her head up defiantly.

Dear heavens. She is lucky I do not shift and take her again now.

Amalia sat in the tub facing the Dragon while she bathed. She tried to give him her back, but he'd been unhappy with her doing so and demanded she turn. Considering she was pleased with him today, she decided to comply.

He will let me use magic again, she thought while soaking in the warmth of the water.

She was a little nervous about washing herself in front of him, but his greedy stare was titillating to say the least. It grew when she raised a leg to wipe it down and clean the dirt that had collected over it, especially her knees from being against the ground.

The bite marks tingled with pain from the water getting to them, reminding her that she had them. Her nipples ached from rubbing against the rough ground from his hard thrusts.

The heat did soothe her bruises though, the many that she had.

When she lowered that leg so that her knee was bent, not being able to lay down in the tub because of its size, she extended the other. He lifted his head higher almost in amazement. *This is quite erotic having him watch me like this.* The fingers of his paws tightened when she ran her hand under the curve of her calf.

Although her core was quite tender, it still managed to thrum, making her realise she was becoming aroused by this. *Perhaps I am the perverted one?* She almost giggled to herself.

"Your body is much softer than it appears," he said, his eyes seeming to widen when she raised her arms to wipe them as well.

"Do you often watch women bathe?"

She was trying to redirect their conversation because he was obviously growing excited. He licked at his jowls with his head lifting higher. Even his forearms bunched.

"No, never. My kind dip in streams and lakes. It does not look like this."

"Sounds awfully cold," she answered, dipping her head so that she could wet the length of her hair and wash her face.

Her palms wiped the water away before she going over her neck and shoulders. His eyes followed her hands, and she couldn't stop her face from heating when she had to rub her breast. His entire body tensed when she did, and then he quickly stood.

He blew a ring of fire above his head before he chanted the word he needed, and it came back to encase him.

A moment later, he was human and walking towards her. He was hard, his thick shaft jutting from between his hips like a pillar of strength and proof of his dominating manhood.

"Wait."

He didn't. He leaned his hands against the sides of the tub and lowered himself to capture her lips with his own. His mouth was rough, and she released the tiniest moan when she returned it.

"Get out of the water," he said between hurried kisses.

Amalia curled her body in the tub to escape him, lifting one of her legs so she could place her foot against his torso. She pushed him away.

"I need to heal and rest, Dragon. You were very rough with me before."

"I do not think I will be able to wait that long," he muttered, licking the seam of his lips to taste her own.

Then his eyes trailed down her body, and she saw his cock pulsate and bob.

"Are you usually impatient?"

Her eyes didn't leave his shaft, inspecting it since she hadn't seen it before.

The head was broad and such a dark shade of pink. His cock was long, and she thought if she were to wrap her hand around it, her fingers would barely be able to contain the thickness of it.

Has that really been inside me? No wonder she felt the bite of pain each time he entered her for the first time.

"Yes, I do not like to wait for things that I want."

He gave a pant right before it jerked again, and a well of semen rose to the deep slit in it. Her eyes shot up to his. He had been watching her stare at it! Her face heated to such a bright shade of red at being caught.

"Maybe if you were not so rough with me earlier it may have been possible, but I am tender and sore all over right now."

His nose crinkled into a cringe, and the scar across his face puffed because of it. She liked seeing it do that, making it more pronounced – regardless of the face he held doing it.

Whenever it happened when he smiled, she had to stop herself from reaching out and touching his face adoringly.

"Fine. Hop out of the water and we will obtain the items you need to heal yourself."

He removed his hands from the tub and stepped back. When he didn't leave her room, she laughed.

"I do not trust you with that thing." She gestured to his obviously straining erection. "Leave and find clothing. I will do the same."

"You are a wicked tease." Her lips turned upright into a pouting smile, taking the compliment since she didn't know how often he would give them. "Fine, I will cover myself for *your* comfortability rather than my own."

He strutted from the room, but not before he absentmindedly wrapped his hand around his shaft and gave it a stroke. He quickly threw his hand away.

"Blasted Witch!" he yelled from the tunnel, and Amalia covered her mouth to hide the laughter that escaped her.

Amalia followed the Dragon as he led her down the tunnel.

He wasn't angry, but she could tell he was irritated with the breeches he wore since he was constantly adjusting them around his hips and the bulge of his shaft.

She followed until he turned and then walked straight through the wall! She quickly raised her hands to touch what she could see was rock, but they moved through nothingness.

Poking her head through, she realised that it was a hidden room. Her jaw dropped, and she spun in a circle when she was inside.

Runic symbols had been carved into the walls in a circle, running the entire length of the alcove. There was a stone bench with an array of bowls, cups, spoons, and a marble mortar and pestle. In the corner was a small cooking hearth, while next to it was a small table covered in raw crystals and stones and another with jars of dirt and clay.

What especially caught her eye were the plants, herbs, and spices on multiple benches in rows against the back wall.

"I have never seen so many in one place before."

She walked forward to gently cup a flower, the plant looking healthy and so very much alive.

"I have seen bigger," he sighed when she turned to a

different plant to touch a leaf and rub a thumb over it.

"Why would you have all this?" And how did she not know about it? This was like every Witch's wet dream. "I did not think you liked witchcraft."

He snapped his head to her while giving a soft growl. It immediately quietened when he understood she meant no offense.

"Dragons also have the ability to create potions. Anything you can do I can also do if I obtain the knowledge. We learn from each other, but we refuse to learn from Witches."

He said this, but her eyes widened when she saw two chests in the room, one of them open. Amalia ran to the open one and picked up a book, flicking through it with excitement bubbling.

"These chests were a part of your collection."

Before she could read anything, he grabbed the book she had been going through and tossed it into the chest. Then he closed it with a shadow of magic lighting in the keyhole.

"I will not permit you to go through these."

She tried to pry the chest open and found she couldn't.

"Why not? I could grow my magic with them."

"Because most of these books I have obtained from Dark Witches. Only a handful are remedies or protections. The rest are spells of evil and will teach you how to pull apart creatures in order to use them."

Her hands immediately flew away to land between her breasts as she cupped them together. *I hope I was not touching such a book.*

She noted he watched her reaction and was pleased with it.

"Why do you not destroy them then?"

"I have studied them. If I am aware of the chant or the mixture of plants that are in the potion they are about to use against me, I have more understanding of what I am being attacked by."

That is a very intelligent deduction. She could only imagine him sitting there reading it with disgust but pushing through so he was able to better defend himself.

With an appreciative smile towards him, she turned back to the plants to touch them before she examined the shelves with spices. She didn't even know what some of the items were in this alcove.

"So, I can take the ones I need?"

"No, nothing can leave this room."

"I thought you said I could use the ones I need to heal myself."

He came up behind her and pushed her hair out of the way so he could freely bring his lips to the nape of her neck. The fibres of hair in her scalp stood on end, and her skin pricked due to the attention.

"You may make the concoction you need to heal yourself from my touch and take it with you." His other hand came up to rub between her breasts before softly clasping around her throat. "But I will have to ward this room away from you unless I am with you."

A shaky breath fell from her when his head tilted so he could trail his lips against the side of her neck.

"Can I take some to season my food?"

She really was sick of eating bland vegetables.

He paused to think before his mouth settled back in. "If that will make you more receptive, then yes. Depending on which combinations you wish to take."

It was a compromise, and one she wouldn't hesitate or argue with to take.

Amalia turned so she could take his lips with her own, very delighted with the Dragon right then. She wrapped her arms around his head before licking across his lips so he would open them. When he did, she tangled her tongue against his to taste the inside of his mouth.

I am liking this side of him.

Then her eyes snapped wide when he sucked on her tongue, a moan coming from her.

He pushed her until her back was against the shelving and she found herself surrounded by plants and flowers as he thrust his hips. Her mind grew foggy, forgetting why he needed to show her this room in the first place. She was too elated, too excited by everything around her to remember.

He was just starting to slowly lift her from her feet when he paused his movements. Even his lips had halted in the middle of a kiss. She opened her eyes to find his were open and off somewhere else, like he was listening to something.

"I sense trouble," he said, before pulling away.

"A Witch?" The irony of that when he had one in his arms escaped her.

"No, much worse." He backed up as he let his arms fall. "Stay in this alcove. Do not leave or touch anything. The illusion will hide you from sight."

She followed him to the entryway and stood at it when he left. He blew a ring of fire above him when he was outside, but he didn't get the chance to say anything before he was tackled.

"Ru!" A very naked woman shouted as she attached herself to him.

She wrapped her arms around his neck and began planting kisses around his face and forehead. He struggled to free himself.

Amalia hadn't considered that he may have a lover, and her face paled.

"I was so worried that I would find your lair empty!" she cried, bringing her arms in tighter to hug him. "I was with the Elders when Glov arrived."

Something inside Amalia's chest twisted at watching them, especially when they started to stumble back. Rurik grabbed a hold of her by her shoulders.

She was rather beautiful, with straight black hair flowing down her cream-coloured body. Her body was slender yet held lovely curves.

Just when she thought it was a sweet embrace, he yelled, "Get off me, you horrible snake!"

He pried them apart and pushed her back.

She leapt to wrap herself around him again, and he struggled to get this naked woman off him.

"No! You are not allowed to leave me. You are not allowed to die until I say so."

Amalia couldn't help feeling dismayed at seeing this female act like this. She obviously cared and loved him.

"How dare you do something so reckless as fight against a coven and the Vast by yourself!"

Amalia took a step back, needing to rest her hand against the bench to support herself.

"Leave me in peace! I told you not to return here."

"But Ru-"

"Detach yourself, ugly vulgar woman!"

He got them apart again.

The female slapped him across the face, offended that he had called her ugly and vulgar, and Rurik's head snapped to the side with his eyes visibly widened in shocked outrage. To Amalia's shock, he slapped her in return. She slapped him again, so he did it harder.

The rumbling of large footsteps came from the tunnel.

"You lower my wards and then do not reapply them?! You allow another to disturb me?" he said, right before a green scaled paw became visible.

"My apologies, Rurik. I did try to stop her, but she had a head start," Glov said.

The female put her hands on her hips, seeming not to care that she was unclothed in front of males.

"Both of you, get out of my lair!"

"I am not leaving," the woman whined with a stamp of her foot. "I have not seen you in ages."

"I have to speak with you about the Elders and what happened. I was not sure if I would find your cave empty and have to search Mahesh's instead."

Rurik shook his head.

"Glov, you may stay to speak with me." Then he turned to the female. "And *you*, you may see yourself out." She gave a pout, so he growled in response. "You have disrupted my mood. Do not anger me further. I will come to see you when I am ready. The least you could do is assist me and tell the Elders that I am alive and not to send anyone to Mahesh's lair. It is currently unsafe."

The pout worsened as she stormed up the tunnel, and Rurik shook his head at her.

"Glov, meet me in the main room. I will be there in a moment."

With a nod, the green Dragon walked further into the lair.

Rurik shuddered as he walked towards the alcove Amalia was in while muttering to himself, "Vile woman will not leave me be when she knows I have been in danger."

He stepped inside and frowned at her expression. She cleared her throat and stood up properly, removing her hand from the bench. She didn't want to let him know she was upset with what she had just seen.

Perhaps I should not be intimate with him if he has others. She didn't want to face the wrath of a jealous woman, possibly a Dragon.

His eyes fell to her bruised wrists before sighing.

"I will allow you to make what you need while I speak with Glov. You may choose your seasonings later when I am here to watch. Do not take anything else besides your potion and do not make a different one. I will be able to smell if you do."

She nodded, and he left.

Amalia searched through everything in the alcove to find all the herbs and spices she needed to make the healing remedy she'd once used on him. It was the only one she knew by memory how to make.

"So here you are," a feminine voice said from behind, and Amalia jumped.

The female from earlier was standing in the alcove with her arms folded across her exposed chest, leaning against the wall.

Holding the pestle she'd been using to crush her herbs and spices together, it flew to her chest as her heart accelerated. She thought this woman had left, and if she was here with her, then the Dragon didn't know she was.

The female stepped forward to approach. "I was surprised when I heard he has been keeping a Witch in his home and letting her walk freely."

Amalia retreated until her back met the bench. She began to lift Amalia's hair up around her face, looking at it, inspecting her.

"You are rather pretty for a Witch, are you not? I was expecting some frail old hag with the way Glov described you."

Amalia didn't respond, unsure of what to say with her this close. She worried that this female might attack her like Glov once had.

Leaning forward, she sniffed at the air and her eyes widened in realisation.

"His scent is all over you."

Amalia tensed. Was she going to face the possibility of jealousy from this woman?

Her gaze then drifted over her neck and wrists that were showing. Amalia wished the bruises and bite marks would just suddenly fade, redness marring her cheeks in embarrassment at being caught.

"It appears my brother has been playing with you."

A stunned exhale swept out of her.

Brother? This naked woman, who had been kissing around his face and latching on to him, was his sister?

That's when Amalia's gaze fell to her hair and realised it was dark, but the torches in the room gave it a red tinge in the same way the light made his appear purple. Her eyes were silver like his, but they looked darker.

The woman laughed because she was still frozen against the bench.

"Do not worry, Witch. I trust in my brother's instincts. He would not let you roam around if you were a danger, and I do not care what he does with you in the meantime."

"You do not wish to attack me?"

She stepped back to give her space, and Amalia settled – at least a little.

"No. I can sense that you are a white wielder. I cannot scent the lingering smell of darkness on you." She looked around the room as she spoke with a raised brow. "I am surprised he would let you in here, though."

Then she shrugged as though she wasn't bothered.

"How can you tell if I am a White Witch?"

She turned back to Amalia. "Although nobody believes me because they refuse to, I have met others like you." Then her brows furrowed deeply, a sigh leaving her shortly after. "Even though some of them *have* turned in the past century."

The fact that she could tell that Amalia meant no harm to anyone, eased her. Her shoulders eased as she became less apprehensive.

"I am Nyotakara the Brash." She pouted at her own title. "I have heard that your name is something sweet."

"Amalia Swafford." She seemed to be awaiting something, much like how the Dragon once had. "I have no title."

She nodded like she understood and then turned to the chests in the room. Seeming to tackle one of them, she managed to pry it open.

"He hates it that I can move through his magic so easily. Most spells cannot hold family back." She retrieved a book and began to read it. "Would you like to go through them?"

"I do not wish to read dark spells, and he has told me he would not like for me to go through them."

Her face of interest faded. The female tossed the book inside and closed the chest once more, like she no longer cared about them. Amalia knew she was happy with her response because she grinned almost mischievously in her direction.

"I think Ru has wisely chosen to allow you to roam then. I wanted to check for myself since I did not want my favourite brother to be in danger."

"You trust him that much?"

"Of course. He may be dull at times, but he knows your kind better than anyone. I am more surprised that he has taken an interest in you when he cannot stand most. He gets his unsocial behaviour from our mother." Her gaze trailed over Amalia once more while cocking an eyebrow. "I must say, it does not seem like you are against it."

She couldn't stop her cheeks from heating further. "Uh, well, you see. It is-"

"What is in it for you?" She folded her arms over her bare chest. "What are you trying to seduce my brother for? You obviously do not plan to harm him. Is this your way of trying to escape?"

Amalia may be hesitant about this woman, but she wasn't a coward. She dully raised her chin. "Who says I am the one seducing him?"

"That male does not know how to seduce anyone. He takes what he wants by force, like most male Dragons."

"I would have to disagree. I am not doing this for any

reason other than what it is. I have no plans on escaping and I-"

"You like him," Nyotakara chuckled while shaking her head. Amalia's cheeks heated to the point she thought her ears might have turned red. "Silly woman, he has no interest in you other than having a wet hole for him to fuck."

Amalia narrowed her gaze.

"And he has a hard cock that feels good. I know that this is nothing more than what it is, and I have no intention of pretending that it is not."

She closed the small distance between them to grab Amalia by the cheeks. Then, to her uttermost surprise, she nuzzled her nose against her own.

Amalia did nothing but blink, unsure of what was happening.

"I like you. You are soft but not timid." She stepped back with a grin. "Then again, I think timidness would bore him."

She seemed to listen out as her eyes wandered. After a moment, she finally brought them back to her.

"Well, I better leave before he discovers I am still here and speaking with his pet. I would not tell him we spoke unless you wish to face one of his terrible temper-tantrums."

She twinkled her fingers behind her in a wave as she walked to the alcove entryway. She ducked her head out to check that the coast was clear and then ran up the tunnel, leaving Amalia to wonder about the strange conversation they just shared.

And he calls me odd.

In the main room of his lair, Rurik stood in front of Glov

with his hands on his hips and stared up at the green Dragon. He then told him what he found at Mahesh's home and the events that followed.

"So, you believe that the Witches are hunting for Dragon lairs?"

"Yes, I believe Strolguil has joined with a coven to increase his power, using them to help him gain it more easily." Glov nodded, but his face was screwed into a cringing frown. "I do not know if this is for a special reason or not since he has been set on power from the beginning."

"And he has already shown the others how to use Dragon parts."

"They are coming from the direction I fought with him last. Have you visited Borlag? His caves are not far from where I fell." It was where he would have gone if Amalia hadn't taken him in.

With a shake of his head, Glov said, "No, I have been too preoccupied with this to visit him since it is so far away."

"I fear he may already be dead. Although he is known for being slithery, he still may have been caught unaware."

"It is unlikely he has been killed. His lair is difficult to enter. Only those who can fly can access the entrance."

Rurik pointed a finger at him. "You forget that Strolguil has been using his own father's stolen wings for eons."

With a sigh, Glov sat and pawed at his face.

"If you truly believe they are heading this way looking for our kind, then the Elders have already told me they wish for those along their path to not be alone."

Rurik crinkled his features into a face of disgust.

"I will not have others parading around inside my tunnel because they fear I am unsafe. I am the WitchSlayer, after all. I just fought a coven and returned."

"I told them you may act like this if you were here when I returned. It took some convincing, but they have agreed to leave you be as long as I check in on you every so often. They also do not want others near your... Witch."

"What are you, some messenger raven for them now? Do not annoy me. Simply lie to them that you have seen me."

"It would seem that way for now, unfortunately. If that is what you wish, then I will check on you only when I have information. I would much prefer to not have my face clawed again." Then he eyed Rurik's small body. "Why are you human? I have not seen this form in many decades."

"I needed to show the Witch something."

Yeah, my cock. He wouldn't tell him that, though.

He didn't shift since he planned to hunt Amalia down when Glov left. *Hopefully she will have started healing.*

"I am surprised to find that you are not enraged considering your failure." Rurik gave a small, growling huff in response to his words. "The last time you were defeated by Strolguil, I could not approach your cave for weeks."

"I am learning to control my anger," he answered casually.

The Witch calmed him. She took his anger and turned it into lust instead, something he could navigate better.

Glov burst into bright laughter.

"That simply cannot be possible!" Rurik gave a scowl as irritation rose on the back of his neck. The green Dragon must have noticed because he quickly said, "Tell me, did you manage to add to your collection at least?"

Rurik nodded, commanding him to follow him deeper into his lair. The green Dragon didn't appreciate following his smaller, human-legged strides, nearly tripping over his own paws, but he said nothing about it.

He brought him to his trophy room and lit the firepit with a fireball from his breath.

"I obtained three skulls." He'd already regurgitated the heads and mounted them when Amalia had been asleep. "I have one more until I reach my hundredth skull."

"Amazing," Glov said in awe while shaking his spiked head. "You would be the first to reach that high of a number." Then he looked to him. "At such a young age too."

Glov was only a little older than him, but he liked to pretend he was eons older than others.

Rurik had killed his first Witch when he was a hundred and forty years old, the equivalent of a human teenager. He hadn't stopped fighting them since.

"And yet, there are still so many more of them out there." His collection barely made a dent in their population. "They breed like mice."

"It is because their life is so fleeting in comparison to ours. They quickly find a mate in order to spawn offspring while we carefully select one to keep."

"They breed by the hundreds in the time we have produced hatchlings by the dozen."

Rurik shook his head in dismay.

"At least you have ensured that many of us are safer."

He perused his gaze over Rurik's collection with admiration.

"I want Strolguil the Vast to be my hundredth," Rurik told him, his chest bowing with pride at the idea. "And I wish for his entire skeleton to be placed in the main room below the tale of him killing his own father."

Glov grinned, nodding his head as he brought his paw up to rub his jaw. "Yes, that does seem like an adequate tribute to all those he has killed."

"Are you to visit Falen next? Her lair is between mine and Mahesh's."

Rurik wanted him to leave.

"Yes, but I have a request." Rurik raised a brow as he waited for him to ask it. "Falen will not accept me into her lair."

"You tried to bed her and lost in the fight against her

because you are weak."

Rurik had tried in the past and succeeded.

The Dragoness liked to put up a heavy fight that could sometimes be entertaining. All consensual, of course, but it was a game she liked to play.

Glov pouted. "Yes, so she will not allow me to stay, and I am tired. I have not rested in quite some time."

"You are asking to stay? My answer is no."

"Come now, Rurik. Would you really push a tired Dragon away when he has done much to assist you in the last few weeks?"

He clenched his fists while gritting his teeth, his arms visibly shaking. The flare of rage then quickly died, and he ran his hand down his face in frustration.

"Your manipulation has succeeded. You may stay until first light." He wouldn't be unappreciative to this male. "If you are still here when the sun has risen, I may pluck a wing from you."

Rurik shifted into his Dragon form, seeing no point in remaining human with the green Dragon here.

"Then I would be forced to live here with you forever, unflying."

His eyes widened as the fire from his shift faded.

"Fine, I will remove your tail tip instead."

Rurik had once done that to his own brother's tail.

"Much better," Glov grinned. "It is a shame that you demanded your sister to leave. I could have spent the evening with her."

A puffing guttural sound fell from Rurik. "If you wish to remain in the sky, I would stay away from Nyota." It was the nickname those closest to her used.

"My, my Rurik, I did not realise you were protective of her, considering how you are with her."

Rurik sharply turned his head to Glov's green face.

"I do not care whose cock is in my sister!" he yelled. "I was merely stating that she easily attaches herself."

"No female can keep me down by the tail." Glov gave a quiet laugh. "Perhaps if you spent more time fucking than fighting, you may not be such a horrible prick."

"Perhaps you are right, Glov." The green Dragon blinked his eyes, no doubt confused as to why he was agreeing with him. "Perhaps once you are gone, I will adhere to your advice," he answered with an evil hint to his grin.

Amalia sat on the sofa in her room reading while her skin healed.

It had been about an hour since she applied the healing ointment, and already the bruises on her body started to lessen. The ones on her wrists and the bite marks, however, had not.

She heard heavy footsteps making their way up the tunnel, and she expected it to be Glov leaving. Instead, Rurik poked his scaled head inside her alcove. She closed her book to give him her attention.

"It is with deep regret that I must inform you that Glov is not leaving until tomorrow at first light."

Her nose crinkled into an obvious cringe. It was still early in the afternoon, and she usually stayed in her room when he was here to avoid him. She didn't want to do that for so long.

"Glov has grown accustomed to you in my lair, so you are welcome to move about." He closed his mouth for a second, thinking before he added, "Once your wounds have healed."

She lifted her arms to inspect her wrists before she looked up to him through her lashes. *He does not want the other Dragon to know that we have been intimate.*

Even though she was completely on board with that idea, not wanting to reveal it to the world, she wanted to know *his* reasons behind it.

"Why?"

"I do not wish to complicate things with the Elders. They are prying and already do not approve of you being allowed to roam free."

"What will they do?"

"Although I will not permit them to tell me what I can do in my own lair, they will try to take you."

Amalia nodded. That seemed a fair reason to keep it a secret then.

Should I be worried that his sister knows then?

"I understand. I will stay here until the marks are gone." Her eyes fell on the tub. *Perhaps I should bathe again since she told me I smell of him.* The fact that his kind could smell these kinds of things was a little alarming to her. "Should I not use my magic while he is here then?"

"I do not care what he thinks of that. If he complains, then I will make sure he does not again." She smiled in response. "He is one of very few that visit me, and he does so the most. You should both learn to be comfortable around each other."

Once again, Amalia cringed. "I will attempt to converse, but I make no promises to be pleasant if he is not."

He shrugged, seeming not to care.

"I will not be available for most of the evening." His nose bunched in irritation. "I must play host like some lairmaid."

"I will try not to disturb you."

Rurik blinked while tilting his head. "Please do. I would prefer not to be left alone with him."

He backed away to leave Amalia to herself.

She continued to read, reapplying the ointment whenever it dried. She also bathed again.

When her skin healed to the point that it was barely noticeable, she couldn't stay in the room any longer. She hadn't eaten that day because of the green Dragon's presence.

After obtaining everything she needed from the food alcove, she went to the one with the stone dining table, cooked, and then ate. She was hoping it would take up more time, and that she may want to sleep afterwards.

She found she wasn't tired.

Ducking her head into the tunnel, she tip-toed her way down it while trying to be as quiet as possible. When she reached the main room where they were, she overheard them talking about one of the tapestries on the other side, facing it as they spoke.

Perfect, she didn't want to be noticed. Keeping a close eye on them, she silently crept past. Both were too distracted to notice she was there. Perhaps they didn't care.

Clear of the main room, she ventured further into his lair until she came to the cavern with the stream. She slipped her hand through the cascading waterfall when she walked next to it and crawled into the hiding place behind it.

As much as she wanted to sit by the entrance of the cave to look at the night sky, she didn't want to be alone and exposed like that. The rushing water was exhilarating to her. The sounds rang in her ears pleasantly, and the smell was refreshing.

She sometimes came here to be with the only nature she really could. *It is still one of my favourite places.*

Dipping one of her feet forward, she let the coldness of the water hit the top arch of her foot as she raised a hand to it.

Her head snapped to the side when she heard the sound of heavy footsteps coming from the tunnel. Amalia crawled deeper into the shallow and small hole in the wall.

Covering her mouth with both her hands to hide the sounds of her breath, she could barely see through the cascading water. Still, she could tell the Dragon approaching was green rather than dark.

She watched Glov make his way inside the cavern alone.

Her heart leapt to her throat when he went to the stream to smell it. He was close, only a few feet away. Then, to her horror, he slipped inside the water. It was barely wide enough to fit his body, but deep enough that it came to the top of his legs.

She curled up when he came towards her.

I just wanted to be alone!

Unfortunately, she was now alone with this Dragon who didn't seem to know she was there.

She almost laughed with horror-filled embarrassment when he ducked his head into the waterfall to let it fall over his body and came face-to-face with her.

"Whoa." He jumped back, startled. Then he slowly slipped his head forward through the water again. "Having a private moment here. You should not be watching someone while they bathe."

Her cheeks flushed bright. "I believe I was here first."

He paused, thinking for long moments.

As if he couldn't come up with a good enough rebuff, he said, "Fair point." He tilted his head to the side. "It seems you have found yourself a hiding place. I did not scent you were there."

"You could not?" She only thought she was out of sight and that the water would muffle any sounds she made.

He shook his head. "No, the water washes your scent away from the air."

Her eyes narrowed. So, she'd truly found a place to hide.

"Where is...?" She hoped Rurik would notice she was no longer in the tunnels and come save her.

"He has left to obtain me some dinner." He gave her a grin of a fangs, one that made her heart race. "It is just me and you here."

Amalia quickly scrambled to leave, but he put his paw out to cut through the waterfall and block the tiny path behind it.

"Do not fret. I have been explicitly, and violently, told not to harm you. Speak with me, I am curious as to why he thinks you are harmless."

Slowly, she backed inside the shallow hole to sit with her knees to her chest.

"Will you tell him of my hiding spot?"

"Perhaps, but I do not see the harm in him not knowing. You are still inside his lair, and if you go missing, he will follow your most recent scent to this room. He would eventually find you if he wanted to."

That wasn't comforting, but she also didn't think she would ever have a reason to hide from him. Others yes, she had come here to hide from this very Dragon.

"He says you are pure-hearted. Does that mean you have never used dark magic?"

"No, I have used it twice. I used my own blood to break the hex on his body when I healed him in my cottage. The second time was an accident. I had injured my hand, and he startled me."

"That was an honest answer." Glov raised a brow. "Why would you not lie? Telling me such things is not positive for our kind."

"Because I have not intended to cause harm and, therefore, have done no wrong."

"You tried to drown me," he bit.

"No, I stopped you from rendering me to flaming ash. I merely wanted you to release me. You choked on the magic I use to fill my bathwater. That was your fault for not unhanding me."

He pursed his lips in response.

"Tell me about his stay in your cottage then. He has not told me of it in detail. He only complained about some feral cat and that you put him in a birdcage."

Amalia's brows creased into a frown. "If he has not told

you, perhaps he does not want you to know."

Glov gave a bright laugh, and despite her uncertainty of him, even she found it warm. "What he does not know will not harm him. Come, tell me what happened."

"No." His laugh fell into an abrupt scowl. "I would rather not betray his trust, even in secret."

"But it could possibly mean that I trust you more."

She shrugged and lifted her chin slightly. "I do not care if I have your trust."

"You care if you have his though?" He tilted his head while seeming to assess her.

"Yes. He has been kind to me, which I have learned is against his nature with Witches. I do not wish to betray it."

"Interesting. Instead of attempting to gain any form of my trust with pretty words and possible lies, you have done so with your actions."

"How so?"

"It is to my dismay, because I truly am curious, but you have chosen not to tell me for his sake. He has told me you have not tried to escape, but I do not believe him. Tell me, little Witch. How do you plan to flee?"

His lips curled back into a grin to reveal sharp fangs.

Amalia puffed her cheeks in irritation.

"I do not wish to leave." His grin fell to scowl once more while his brows narrowed in disbelief. "Do not mock me with your looks! You do not know what I have seen, nor experienced, before I was brought here."

His head turned slightly to the side, his eyes trailing to the cavern exit. It was like he was thinking about the inside of the lair.

"He has given you a room." His head turned back to her. "He has offered you safety. You would prefer to be safe, rather than free?"

"There is freedom in safety. I spent very little time outside of my cottage. I only left it when I needed to buy food, which he obtains for me. I am used to being inside. I do miss being able to walk the forest near my cottage, though. I miss the earth under my feet."

"He will never let you walk the forest here."

She gave herself a sad smile.

"I know, but that is fine. I can see it. In the mornings, I seek the sunshine that comes through the entrance, and when it rains, it sometimes blows in. There is nature in this very spot that I sit." She motioned to the waterfall and let her hand duck through it. "I was not content until he allowed me to use the small amount of magic I know."

He inwardly cringed. "And what kind of magic is that?"

"Small things. Things like filling my own bath and heating it. Letting me light the cooking hearth. It has allowed me independence, so I do not have to ask him to do these things for me."

"Ah, so he allows it so that you do not bother him constantly." Amalia smiled, knowing that wasn't the truth, but she wouldn't correct him. "What was your life like before you were brought here?"

"It was peaceful, much like it is now. I would take in injured creatures such as animals, fairies, and pixies. I would heal them until they were well enough to be free. I would also help the humans near my cottage without them knowing. I helped women give birth, gave an old man whose back was hurting a tea that would lessen his pain."

"Are you to tell me you have spent your life helping those which the others of your kind would pull apart?"

He sounded astonished, like it possibly couldn't be true.

"Yes. That is why when the Dragon was brought to my home by my cat, injured and unconscious, I had not thought twice about healing him." Then she giggled, "I did not know what he was though, and he was not like how you are now. He was small."

She figured since Rurik told him of the birdcage then he at least knew this much already.

"It is a defence mechanism. Being able to change our size helps us to hide, if we need to. I must know, is there more of you then? Were your coven white wielders?"

His face softened, like he hoped for that very thing.

"I do not know. I did not have a coven."

"You were a lone Witch? That is rather strange. What of your parents? Did they not show you magic, teach you?"

"My father was a human soldier who was killed when I was sixteen. My mother disappeared shortly after she was told."

"Ah, so you are only the way you are because you have not been shown yet."

"You are trying to find evil in me."

She stemmed the want to fold her arms across her chest, but she did glare at him.

"It is hard to imagine that you are incorruptible. At least you will not be able to learn dark magic here, so hopefully you will never turn. But if you do, I hope Rurik does not fall prey to your hands."

Amalia gave him a mocking smirk.

"So, it is not that you do not trust me, but you actually lack faith in him."

His head reared back slightly, making it duck through the water. He brought it back with a growl. "Excuse me? How dare you say something so offensive to me."

"Is it not true? Should it not matter if I were harmless or not if you believed that he would be wise enough or strong enough against me? You do not trust me, but you also do not trust him in his decision."

He opened his mouth with a puffed snout in the same way Rurik did when he was growing angry.

"If you had faith in him, you would not be threatening me or trying to convince me that I am some form of evil monster. You would be mocking me, laughing at the fact I am trapped here. You would tell me that there is no way for me to escape, and that even if I did, he would find me and kill me."

Glov closed his mouth. She knew she'd gotten him to think on his own actions.

"I would like to leave now."

Amalia rose to her feet and was thankful when he didn't stop her, too stunned by her accusations to care. As quickly as her legs would take her, she retreated to her room.

Rurik felt the treasure mound shift when Glov rose from it to leave. Even though he hadn't wanted to let him, when Glov told him he wanted to lay under coin to rest, Rurik offered to let him sleep beside him.

He also had ulterior motives. It would have caused his brow to raise if Rurik laid at the entryway to the Witch's room to protect her from Glov while she slept. Allowing him under his treasure meant he could keep an eye on him.

Something had happened while he was gone obtaining food. His snout crinkled in memory of having to do so. The only reason he went alone was because they tried to keep the humans from knowing about them if they could.

Two Dragons in the sky was more noticeable than one.

Upon his return, he'd noted that Amalia was in a good mood, which was unusual when the green Dragon was present. Whereas Glov had been in a foul mood, which was odd because he often didn't hold onto his anger.

Neither would tell him what happened, but he knew they must have spoken. *He probably offended her, and she used that acid tongue of hers to yell at him.* That seemed plausible because that is what she would have done to him.

When Glov had been gone for a while, showing that he

wasn't intending to return for whatever reason, Rurik rose to his paws.

I have plans today, he grinned. *And they involve a certain female being naked.*

She'd healed when the sun had fallen. Instead of him trying to get under her skirt, he'd played lairmaid like he wasn't some ill-tempered, scornful warrior.

I must clean first. She will not appreciate the main room. He walked down the tunnel until he reached the room with the tapestries that depicted history.

He is such a messy eater. It made sense though. Glov wouldn't be on land for long to eat, so he would do so quickly. Rurik didn't appreciate the cow carcass pieces thrown about, rather than how he ate them, with care.

If a Witch does not get him then he will surely choke on a bone. Now that would be a shameful way to go. He would snicker, but he didn't think lightly on the death of his own kind.

He knew that the light-hearted female wouldn't like to see the bloody massacre. It may put her in a foul mood and be unreceptive to his touches, so he collected everything he could and took them outside.

He placed them in a shallow cave just around the corner he'd dug in the past. Then, he cooked them with his flames until they were dehydrated enough for him to crush into nothing more than dust.

Even though he didn't care about seeing bones lying about, he didn't leave them in his cave to step on, nor did he leave a trail or pile outside of his lair. He didn't want to make it obvious that these mountain lands possibly held a Dragon.

Unclean lands made it easier for Dark Witches to find them.

He headed back to where he knew his cave entrance was. He was able to see the tunnel whereas others would see the illusion of a rockface – it was the same magic he used to hide his secret alcove from Amalia.

Walking inside, he planned to shift, find pants, and grab one of the sour-sweet, green apples he liked. Instead, he noticed Amalia walking the tunnel. She appeared to be looking for something, ducking her head into alcoves before continuing down.

He didn't think she would be moving about yet.

With a grin, he ducked into the first alcove he could and blew a ring of fire above himself.

"Shift," he whispered before those flames came back to encase him. Once he was human, he slowly crept up behind her as to not be noticed.

"What are you doing?" he asked when he was right at her back.

"Eeep!" She gave a cute squeak of shock before quickly turning to face him.

"Looking for you. You promised me seasonings for my food."

She is wearing purple today. And for some reason, that pleased him. He didn't think too long as to why.

"Why are you human?" Her eyes swept down his chest and then widened when they went lower. They quickly ducked back to his face. "Where are your pants?!"

Her scent changed to indicate she liked what she'd seen, and it made him lick at his lips.

"Glov has left, and I am hoping not to need them today."

It took her a while to realise what he meant. What he hadn't thought she would do was bolt.

"No, no, no."

Yes, yes, yes, he thought with a chuckle as he chased her.

She didn't get far before he captured her in his arms, and she squealed with a giggle. Turning her, he brought his mouth down on hers. She gave no fight, immediately making a soft noise as she returned his kiss and leaned into him.

Up you go, he lifted her by the back of both legs so that they were around his waist. She wrapped her arms around his neck to hold on, her scent deepening the more their mouths moved over each other's with scorching, messy, wet kisses.

She always smells sweet. Already his shaft was hardening, and he deepened the press of his mouth before dipping his tongue inside. *And tastes it.*

She broke from the kiss when he started to step forward.

"If you put me against the cave, I will be upset."

He looked to the floor and then the cave walls he'd been intending to push her against.

"Where else am I to put you?"

It was an honest question from him.

"Somewhere soft, preferably."

He hadn't expected things to go this easily with her and thought he would have to coax her to be intimate with him. Rurik grinned since he knew exactly where he could take her. He'd been hoping to crawl into it at some point.

"As you wish."

He changed his direction to lead her up the tunnel. He brought their mouths back together, wanting to taste this delicious woman, to feel her soft and giving lips, the playful dance of their tongues.

Still holding onto her, he had to occasionally look away from her face to see where he was going, but he made it to the entryway of her room without issue. Freeing one hand to push at the rock frame to turn them, he headed to the bed and tossed her down on it.

"Do not dare," she demanded when he grabbed the front of her dress to tear it from her.

She started to push on his chest with her foot to separate them, and it caused him to frown deeply. *Why is she suddenly resisting?*

"If you hurt me this time, I will be angry with you."

Ah. He grabbed the ankle of the foot pressing against him and slipped his other hand down the length of it. He brought his head forward to lean over until he was able to bite into her calf. The muscle yielded under his teeth.

"I will be gentle." At least he would try to be. "Undo the front."

He nodded to the blouse ties.

If he did them himself, his impatience would make him rip them carelessly in his strength.

As she was untying the front of her dress to loosen it, he slipped his hands down the outside of her legs, over her hips, then her sides. Vibrating with want, he curled his fingers around the neckline sitting against her shoulders and pulled it down.

She lifted her body to help him as he removed it from her.

Excitement was already thrumming through him, and his cock pulsated when his eyes trailed over her body laying against the furs.

Her blonde, curling hair haloed around her head and shoulders, making her seem angelic. Those eyes of hers staring up were as blue as the skies the heavenly deities came from.

He let his gaze wander over the curvature of her neck, a craving to sink his teeth into it growing by the second. His eyes delightfully perused over the mounds of her breasts and the pink budding nipples that topped them before they drifted over the deep tuck of her waist.

She is quite lovely naked. Not even her hips and slender legs escaped his attentive gaze.

When he bent forward, he placed his hands around the back of her thighs and pushed her further across the bed so he could kneel on it.

She wouldn't open her legs for him though, and she

covered her breasts with one arm as the bridge of her nose and cheeks turned pink. She was suddenly turning bashful.

She is uncomfortable. He wasn't used to being around females who were shy. Although he stopped his eyes from doing it, he mentally rolled them.

I will have to be slow, at first at least. Gentle and slow. That was the last thing his lust-filled cock wanted with this woman.

He grabbed the leg that hadn't been pressing against his chest earlier and lifted it. Bending his head forward so he could bite into the calf of this one, he bit a little harder than he had before.

She made no complaint as she watched him.

He swept both his hands down the slender limb, parting her legs himself while his lips and teeth followed behind. Rurik lingered at her inner thigh, nipping it with his teeth before he kissed it while making a path from her knee down.

Right before he was where he wanted to be, she covered her intimate area with her free hand.

His eyes shot up to hers.

"What are you doing?"

"I am going to taste you," he answered, his eyes alight with the idea.

She frowned, as if the idea was foreign to her.

"You cannot."

With a dark chuckle, he grabbed her wrist and pinned it to her hip. "I can, and I will."

He lowered his body so that he was laying down between her pretty thighs and forcing them apart with his shoulders. He pressed his lips above her folds to kiss her pubic mound.

"Wait."

He didn't. He moved his mouth so he was kissing the crook of her inner thigh.

When her other hand came down, like he knew it would,

he grabbed it with the hand already holding a wrist. He held them both against her navel.

Before she could say or do anything else, he leaned forward and swept his tongue flat through her folds. She let out a surprised gasp until he sucked on the sensitive bud of her clit. He tongued it, and her gasp ended on a moan.

He released her hands, knowing she now understood that he could pleasure her this way. *She is unused to pleasure, but I will be more than happy to teach her.*

Pulling his head back, he brought his hands up and pulled the lips of her folds apart. He had wanted to see her and now that he was, he looked his fill.

She was a soft shade of pink, her folds like silky rosy petals. His tongue tingled with the want to taste that cream-filled dip not too far down from her clit.

Before she could grow more uncomfortable, he leaned back in to sweep his tongue against her again. Then he lowered his mouth and finally dipped his tongue against the entrance to her core. He almost groaned when the pooling wetness of her arousal collect on his tongue.

I knew I would like the way she tasted, but he didn't think he would like it this much. He couldn't stop himself from dipping his tongue against her for more of that sinful, decadent honey.

His eyes lifted to see her face, finding it was a bright shade of red and her hands were covering her mouth. It was like she was trying to hide her pants that he could hear clearly.

Why is it when she looks this soft, I just want her more?

His hands moved under her thighs and around her legs, so he could circle them from below, before he placed them on top of her waist. He pinned her hips to the bed so she couldn't escape him.

And then he was upon her, tasting quick sips of her wet arousal.

He drank from her like he was a man starved of water, his tongue occasionally ducking between the lips of her folds so he could suckle the sensitive bud. She moaned whenever he sucked her there, and he would look up to see that her stiffened nipples raised when she arched her back.

Unable to stay away, he brought his mouth back to her core. Her hands had fallen to the bed with her fingers gripping the fur tightly, her arms shaking with tension.

When her back would settle and she tilted her head down, she looked at him almost with awe and curiosity at what he was doing to her. If he came up to suck her clit when she did, he witnessed her become dazed, her head once more falling back as she released a strangled moan.

He thrust his tongue inside when one of her legs wrapped over his shoulder, almost like she didn't want him to pull away. He wouldn't, not until he took what he wanted from her.

He could feel he was already growing possessive of this sweet tasting, innocent woman's wicked desire in his mouth, mingling with his saliva.

Twisting his tongue, her leg tensed around him, the skin of her thighs shaking as her legs begun to tremble.

A quiet groan fell from him when he felt her core quiver around the tip of his tongue. Her breath hitched. *She is about to come.* Her hands tightened on the furs and started to pull. Her breath hitched again when he thrust his tongue and then curled it before bringing it back.

His cock pulsated while he waited, wanting to taste her orgasm, and his fingertips dug into the skin of her stomach when she didn't. He was growing impatient.

Growling, he lifted his mouth to the sensitive apex between her folds to give it a hard suck. *Give it to me!*

He wanted to feel and see her break apart while he did this, while he had his exploring tongue on her, while he tasted her.

She took a step forward and watched his muscles relax as a small smirk curled his lips.

Then she bolted out of the room with a giggle.

Amalia had her back against the bed hours later with the furs partially across her legs to keep the worst of the night chill away.

She convinced him to let her pick the herbs and spices she wanted for cooking after promising she wouldn't remove them from the cooking alcove. She didn't know what she could make with what she'd taken, so she didn't think she would ever need to steal any.

After she'd eaten, she hadn't even made it out of the cooking area before he'd taken her again, this time across the table she'd just eaten at.

He does not like to wait. She knew he was arrogant and impatient, but she thought this was becoming ridiculous.

They spent the remainder of the day in her room, touching.

She was enjoying it.

He wasn't being rough with her, so she felt like her body could keep up, and in between the bouts of sex, they would occasionally talk. This was new and exciting for the both of them, and they seemed to be making the most of it.

Amalia was surprised that she was filled with energy.

She expected herself to be feeling physically drained, but she felt alive with it, almost thrumming with it. It seemed to grow each time they had sex. Even though she would become limp afterwards, it wouldn't take her long to feel energised.

It was almost like energy was sparking under her skin and sending tingling waves through her bloodstream and muscles. It was an exhilarating, yet strange, sensation.

She hadn't told him this. Even when, once again, he was laying between her legs and petting one of her breasts like he was fascinated by them.

The energy seemed to radiate all throughout her body, and as much she was enjoying herself, was sated and feeling very well, she had questions and curiosities.

Playing with his hair because he was letting her, she mulled on which one to ask first.

"Why are you doing this with me?"

"Because it is immensely fun."

She rolled her eyes. That she knew.

He frowned deeply.

"Was that not the correct answer?" He thought for long moments. "I like your body and face, have already mentioned you are beautiful."

She shook her head, like she didn't understand.

"But I am a Witch. I originally thought you would not be interested in me in this way. I know how much you hate them."

His playful fingers paused as his eyes moved from her breast to her face. He didn't say anything, almost as though he didn't want to. Then he sighed.

"Your kindness and soft personality often make me forget what you are."

She expected him to pull away now that she reminded him, but he didn't. His fingers returned to their task.

"But I am still your enemy."

Her brows knotted as her lips pursed, not seeing how he could see past it when she knew, had seen, how deeply he despised them.

"*You* are very far from being my enemy. I would not allow myself to be so close to you in my human body if I did not trust you with it." He touched the tip of his finger to the pad of her nipple. "In the same way you would not let me inside yours if you did not trust me. You know I hold what you fear the most in my chest, can unleash it at will, and yet you do not fear that I will."

So, it is trust then and nothing more?

Her eyes wandered along the wall in her room, across the large paintings he'd probably stolen from humans.

His answer soothed her worries, but also disheartened her. She thought on why that may be.

Do I want him to feel more for me?

She realised she did. It was a foolish thought on her behalf, she knew it. Although he may lust for her body, he would never come to truly care for her. Not in the way she feared she was beginning to.

"Your arousal is fading, and your heart rate has increased."

Her muscles tensed, always startled when he made comments such as these about her body.

He grabbed her breast more firmly, thumbing her nipple and being rougher, like he was trying to combat her body's reaction to her thoughts.

"Your sister is... nice," she said, trying to redirect their conversation.

Nice was the best compliment she could give. She'd found the woman odd and invasive.

His nose crinkled into immediate disdain. "She is many things. Irritating and irksome are the words I would use."

Amalia smiled with humour. "She seemed very affectionate with you."

He gave a puffing growl.

"She does it because she knows it annoys me. If I am

human, she will shift and latch herself to me, kissing my face like I am some child. If I am Dragon, she will climb my back and lick my face. And no matter what I do, she continues to do so. It is worse when she knows I have been in danger." He gave a shake of his head. "Only our father appreciates her childishness."

He continued to hold her breast and swirled it in his palm. His other hand started trailing the under curve of her other breast. Then his brows drew together into a frown.

"How did you know she was my sister? I do not remember speaking to you about her."

Amalia cringed. She had brought her up to tell him, but she didn't think he would react well.

"Because she did not leave when you told her to."

With a gasp, she flinched when the hold of her breast became unbearably tight.

"You spoke with her?" His nose began to crinkle in anger while his eyes narrowed.

"I had not left your magical items alcove, and she cornered me." She hissed in a breath when his hand squeezed tighter. She grabbed his head and shoved it against the tit he wasn't grasping. "You can either play with me or be angry, but you do not get to do both."

After a moment, he released the tight hold he had and lifted his head with a huff. He kept his eyes on hers as his head slowly turned... before they fell back on her breast.

His fingers returned to being gentle.

She could tell he was still quite angry and was only hiding it so he could keep touching her.

"What did she say to you?"

"She heard I was here and wanted to make sure I was safe to you."

Rurik rolled his eyes. "Does nobody have faith in me? If I, the WitchSlayer, can see that you are harmless, then my opinion should be law about it."

"She said that she believed you because she has met other White Witches before."

"Could be true. Even though she is a thorn under my scales, she fights and hunts like me."

There was a long pause in between their conversation.

"Um." She cleared her throat, fidgeting slightly. "I had not made the ointment yet and was still covered in marks."

He froze, understanding what she meant as he brought his other hand to his chin in deep thought. Then he sighed once more before returning back to his task.

"She will not say anything. She is loyal to our family before she is loyal to the Elders." He nodded, like he was agreeing with himself. "And she would not be so stupid as to anger me by doing so. She would not be afraid to confront me first."

"You trust her?" With the way he reacted to her, she expected him to think otherwise.

"Of course, she is my family."

"You struck her."

He pointed his finger at her face. "She struck me first."

She gave him a mocking stare. "You called her terrible names."

"Because she is terrible."

"She is rather beautiful."

With that long black hair with a red tinge to it and tall, shapely body, Amalia imagined most men would fawn over her.

"She is disgustingly vile." He shuddered. "I once told her that I would claw her face to improve its hideousness, and she attempted to gouge my eye out."

Amalia's lips perked into a smile of humour before it faded. She tried to settle the blush that was forming across her face and averted her gaze.

"Do not misinterpret my next question," she mumbled. "But seeing your sister reminded me that I do not know you very well." She could tell his head lifted, but she refused to meet his eyes. "If your kind can so easily smell the evidence of, uh, this, should I be worried about potential guests?"

His head lifted more, and her heart picked up speed. She awkwardly squirmed beneath him.

"It is not my place to care what you do or who you have in your home, but women are often petty. I do not wish to be the target of a scornful Dragon when she is nearly four times the size as me and can unleash fire."

"You are worried that a female will attack you in my home?"

"Yes." Her face grew so hot she knew it'd be bright red. "You are rather handsome, in both your human and Dragon form. This is often cause for women to be possessive."

Amalia winced when she felt teeth sink into her stomach right below her breast. She sharply turned her head to him, wondering why he was biting her.

She noted his eyes were crinkled with humour.

Her brows furrowed as her face became crestfallen. She already felt embarrassed at asking this kind of question, but she truly didn't want to be blown to ash for a reason as silly as this.

"You are laughing at me."

She tried to get away by wriggling up, and he stopped her, releasing his bite to lift his head with a frown.

"You have never complimented me before. I did not know you found me handsome, and I did not know you felt that way about something that is not the same as you. I was laughing because I found that strange. I had not expected you to say such a thing about me as a Dragon."

Her eyes flickered between his silver ones as he spoke.

"And?" He still hadn't answered her question.

"To be quite honest with you, any female who has come to my lair for this reason has only done so once." He glided his hand between her breasts with a grin, like he thoroughly enjoyed his next words. "Most find me irritable and infuriating. I am ill-tempered, and they often bark back. I have had many claw fights with those I have bedded."

"You seem pleased with that."

She shook her head as the tension in her body finally faded. So, she would most likely not die by a jealous lover. That calmed her.

"I know who I am and have accepted it. It also means that I will not have a female attempt to become my mate."

"You do not want one?"

She assumed he meant partner, but in Dragon terms.

"Whether I want one or not, the likelihood that I will not is high." His hand traced over the top of her breast and the skin of the rosy peak that topped it. It sent a tingle throughout her body. "But no, I do not wish for hatchlings and a mate who I will leave shortly in my death. I am a hunter who often throws himself into dangerous situations against Witches. I hunt for Strolguil the Vast relentlessly. If I am not destined to be the one to kill him, then he will destroy me before long." Then he laughed to himself as his eyes fell elsewhere. "Plus, If I do manage to reach an old and frail stage, I doubt that I will find a female I can stand and one who will know how to handle me."

"You *are* a rather difficult bastard," she laughed, trying to draw away from this kind of conversation.

Amalia didn't need to know about his plans for his future since she likely wouldn't be a part of them.

He gave her a scowl. "Well, you are about to have this difficult bastard's cock inside you, so shut your trap."

He raised himself up to forcibly take her mouth with his own, and she couldn't help but giggle under his lips. She didn't know if he was truly irritated with her, but her laughter seemed to deflate what he'd been feeling.

Amalia woke to the most sinful warmth. The kind of radiant heat that she'd only ever felt when she'd woken in the sun after falling asleep outside in the middle of a cold, winter's day. The kind of warmth that was spreading and took away any chill to encase her.

She found herself still surrounded by Rurik's body as he softly played with the ends of her curling hair. She hadn't expected to wake still in his arms. When she turned her head to him, she noted he was awake.

Although his hair looked tousled, it didn't appear as though it was messed from sleep.

He was watching her, and when she faced him, his heavy lids flickered when his eyes came to greet hers.

"Did you not sleep?"

He shook his head lightly. "I have only slept in this form when I have needed to be in a human town and have sealed myself behind heavy wards."

Amalia blinked. *He did not trust me enough to sleep?* But she already knew that. She thought she would wake up alone or find him lying in his Dragon form near the entryway to her alcove.

She decided not to care. Perhaps because he had stayed

with her, she didn't have any nightmares of her burning. She had rested well and was at ease.

Actually, she was pulsating with energy.

Now that she was awake enough to realise it, the fibres of her hair stood on end on her scalp. A tingle trailed all the way through her spine, and it fluttered all the way along it, from the base of her skull all the way to her tailbone. Those tingles then spread all throughout her body, causing every part of her skin to prickle at once.

"You are becoming aroused," he said with a chuckle.

She could feel her body becoming slick, her nipples hardening. That energy seemed to make everywhere delicate throb, even the lips on her face, her ears, the sensitive bundle of nerves near her wrists. She even started to pant from it.

"I thought that I would have to combat you when you woke to stay in this bed with me."

Amalia had so much energy that she needed to release it somehow. She didn't feel embarrassed, didn't even think twice about it, when she jumped him and brought herself on top of him.

He didn't stop her. No, Rurik was smug as she tried to release something that felt like it was building.

It didn't seem to help.

Actually, it seemed to make that winding pressure pull tighter. She didn't know how long she'd tried. How long she hadn't let him leave the bed rather than the other way around, but she'd eventually become so animated that it felt like too much and she had to stop.

She didn't even feel like eating when she cooked and pushed food around on her plate. Her muscles twitched uncontrollably, even places she didn't know could spasm, like her shins and cheeks.

It must have been well into the afternoon when she sat at that table, trying to understand what was happening to her, when she heard the first crack of thunder.

She was beginning to become scared and confused as to why she was buzzed. Amalia was *tweaking* out.

The Dragon was off doing something else because she told him she'd needed to be alone for a while. It puzzled him since she'd just spent most of the morning desperately riding him to get this feeling out.

A second crack of thunder made her head shoot up in the direction of the entrance to his cave as, from the crown of her head, a wave ran down her body in reaction to the sound.

Perhaps the storm will calm me. She could hear the heavy pour of rain, and it made her ears ring like they were sensitive to it.

Pushing her chair back, she went to the front of his lair and knelt down in front of the ward to watch the dark and dreary grey sky.

The first hit of lightning she saw against the clouds made her gasp, and her breathing became shallow. The second made her put her hands against the ward, lifting her body so that she was kneeling higher. The third had her clawing at the ward, wanting out, to go into the rain.

The lightning didn't strike often. There were long pauses in between since the storm was light, but it caused every hair over her entire body to stand on end – even in places she didn't know she had them.

Like he was unable to stay away, or perhaps it was because she'd never knelt at the ward like this before, his loud footsteps came up behind her.

A fourth flash of light struck against the grey clouds followed by the loud crashing bang. She felt it all the way to the pit of her soul.

"Let me out," she whispered, trying to dig her nails into the magic that wouldn't let her pass.

She didn't think he heard her because he said nothing as

To see her later just sitting at his ward with her hands against it had caused him to frown. She'd never knelt or pressed her body against it before.

"Let me out," she asked of him, and he couldn't.

He couldn't allow her out there even when she seemed distressed to go.

Perhaps one day he could let her, in many, many years when the Elders truly knew she wouldn't run. If they discovered somehow that he let her outside now, even if it was with him, they would take her and then punish him.

She began screaming at him to let her, bashing on his ward, and he had winced at how much she needed it. He could see how badly she wanted to throw herself into the rain.

He still couldn't.

Then, to his wild shock, she passed through his ward. He watched her open it with her hand and saw her surprise.

Then, like she no longer cared, she bolted into the rain.

When Rurik tried to chase after her, his head smacked against it like his own ward wouldn't let him pass. That wasn't supposed to happen. Since he was the caster, he was the one person who wasn't supposed to be impacted by it.

His front paws leaned against it, now clawing to get through it in the same way she had been.

His eyes widened at the steady and strong release of power. Blue lightning shot from her and into the sky.

Smaller, thinner strokes of lightning branched out to touch the tops of trees, to touch anything alive. He flinched when one came to strike against his face.

His ward should have allowed it in. It was only when he opened his eyes to see why he wasn't being harmed did he realise that it wasn't his magic stopping him from leaving, but hers.

She had shielded him from the burst of power. Her magic glittered as it fought against the strike that was still trying to reach him.

His eyes wandered back to her. *That is not witchcraft.* The shield might be, he could scent it, could see that it was. What she was releasing, however, wasn't. But he knew what it was.

That is dragoncraft. It was his kind's magic.

The only other Witch he had seen produce dragoncraft such as this, that could release lightning, was Strolguil the Vast.

His eyes widened further. *How did she obtain this power?*

Yet, it wasn't red.

It wasn't tainted from the way Strolguil had obtained that kind of power, and didn't have the foul stench that came from blood magic. It hadn't been obtained by drinking his kind's blood by the bucketload for years.

It was pure.

When her scream finally died and the blue lightning ceased, she fainted. The shield keeping him in, faded.

Rurik galloped out of his lair to approach her, almost sliding in the rain next to her body with his speed.

Rain harshly pelted his scales while he gently used a claw to turn her to see she was truly unconscious. He stared down, dumbfounded by what he'd just seen and utterly confused by this Witch.

It was stolen magic she had used, a build-up of it. *How did you obtain it?* Where did she get it from, and why hadn't she needed to release it before?

Conflicting emotions spiralled inside of him, unsure of what to feel or do as rain poured on them. It hadn't been stolen viciously. It hadn't been taken by tearing apart his kind, but he couldn't stop himself from feeling unsettled that she'd gotten it.

She shouldn't be able to wield such power, and it was obvious she hadn't been able to contain it. She obtained so much of it that she couldn't hold it in.

Where do I take her? To the bed or the prison? He wasn't sure. First, he needed to think on where she'd stolen it from. Until he realised it hadn't been stolen at all but had been given to her... by him.

Rurik took an unsteady step back, bringing a paw up to rub it against his face.

I did not know this was possible.

And if he didn't know, then she didn't.

This had been an accident, although how she'd gotten it hadn't been. That wasn't her fault, but his own.

She stirred, and he carefully slid the points of his claws under her until she was resting in his large paw. He'd woken her further by doing so, and her eyes fluttered open before coming to look up at him.

Her eyelids flickered each time a droplet of rainwater pelted her paler than normal face.

She looked docile as he walked her inside while balancing himself on three legs. Because he was holding her, she was able to pass through his ward without issue, having been invited in.

"I feel much better now," she said, her voice small and lax. "Thank you for letting me outside."

He wasn't the one to allow her through, she'd done it herself. *Did she not know?*

With the dragoncraft she'd been filled with, she hadn't needed to think or chant her way through his ward. She wanted out and the strength of power let her.

That was no easy feat considering the magic in place was one of the most powerful wards known to his kind. The one she slipped through last time had been much weaker, only preventing Witches and pixies from his lair.

She has been holding this power for a while. And now that he knew where it came from, he knew how she managed to get through his magic the first time.

His ward had sensed his kind's magic the day she knocked her head and hadn't barred it from moving through it.

Rurik walked her into her alcove, understanding he didn't need to take her to his prison.

"You are not angry with me?" she asked when he laid her on the bed so she could rest. He could tell she didn't have the energy to be seated or moving.

His head moved side-to-side with a frown. "No. You have done nothing wrong."

Her eyes fell away to look at her hand resting against the furs. He stood back so he wasn't towering over her.

Her gaze came back to him as she spoke. "Do you know what happened to me?"

"Yes."

When he didn't elaborate, she worked up enough strength to frown slightly.

"Will you tell me?"

He didn't say anything for a long while, unsure if he should reveal this to her. His eyes assessed the female lying down in front of him. This gentle Witch who had never caused harm to others. This woman who had made him crazed with lust and want, had gained his trust enough to allow him to use it and accepted it from him.

"You released a burst of dragoncraft that your body could not contain and had most likely been overflowing from you."

"Is it all gone?"

Rurik allowed magic to fill his skull to change his sight. He looked down her body to see the tendrils of witchcraft that would always come from her.

He saw no other magic.

"Yes. It appears you have ridded your body of all of it."

She gave a sigh as if she was pleased with that, like she didn't want the awesome power he'd given her.

"Where did it come from?"

power?"

If the rest of her kind discovered this, he feared male Dragons may be tied down and robbed of their seed.

"Hmm?" she said around a mouthful of peach, eating more than he'd ever seen her before. She took a fuzzy fruit next, eating that as she spoke while licking at her lips "Not particularly. I do not care for power. I must admit though, it felt wonderfully exhilarating." A blush began to redden her cheeks. "I had so much energy that I was, uh, desperate to get rid of it."

He tried to think of why her face would heat at her words, and then it hit him. A warm chuckle left his lips.

Perhaps it was to his displeasure that he wouldn't allow her to obtain it again. She had ridden him with abandon throughout the morning because of it, and he'd thoroughly enjoyed it.

"But," she added. "I did not like having so much energy inside me. I feared that I was going to explode, and I worried about doing that in your cave, or next to you."

"Is that why you shielded me?"

She paused to look up at him. Her teeth were sunk into that fuzzy fruit before she removed them with a frown.

"I shielded you?"

He gave a nod. "Yes. I was unable to come to you because you barricaded me in my lair. Lightning tried to strike me but was unable to because of your magic."

She lowered her fruit with her brows crinkling further. "I do not understand. I keep doing things without intending to. I should not be able to cast shields or forces without chanting. I cannot usually."

"You appear to do so when you have additional help. You created the force that separated us that day when you cut your hand, adding blood to your magic. This time, it was because of dragoncraft."

"That still does not answer as to why I am casting spells when I am not thinking about them."

"Well... perhaps they happen because you are subconsciously doing so. I was too close, and you wanted away, so you separated us. You wanted through my ward, so you got through it. You feared harming me, so you protected me."

In her shielding him, she had further proved that she wasn't violent. Even on accident, this Witch didn't wish to harm others.

"I should not be able to do that."

"But many of your kind do." Her brows once again came together, and she looked up to him questioningly. It was strange that he often had to teach the Witch about her own kind. "Although many must pull apart creatures to gain such abilities where thought is all that is needed to cast, it is rare, but not unheard of, to do so without them."

Rurik nodded at his own words, agreeing with himself.

"Yes, that must be it. There are spells I can do that do not require chants. All I have to do is think and they happen. Such as, I can fill my skull with magic and direct it to my eyes, allowing me to change what I see so I can view the tendrils of essence in the air."

"It is very strange. I do not like not being in control." Her lips tightened. "I could hurt someone by accident."

"You have only done so in front of me when you have been stressed. Perhaps it is your fears that are the source."

She fell back to the bed with a disgruntled sigh.

"It does not help to know that. I am often startled and afraid."

"At least it is comforting to know that you will protect yourself even when you are in danger."

She rolled her eyes at him with a disgruntled, but light, sigh. "Once again, you bring up that I do not know how to fight."

"What if a Dragon tries to eat you?"

"If they do not cook me first, I do not think I will care. As long as it is quick and without suffering."

Rurik reared his head back, not expecting such an answer.

"Are you saying you do not fear death?" He didn't know whether or not to believe her since he didn't think she'd ever uttered a lie to him.

"I fear pain." She met his eyes with unwavering doubt. "I fear the agony of flames, I fear the stab of a knife, the suffocation of drowning. Death is an escape from worldly senses, and all I want is to not suffer or be afraid when I am living in this world – or dying in it."

"You do not worry if your life is cut short?"

"Why should I allow myself to care now when I will not do so on the other side?"

"You think in much the same way I do about death, and yet you do not throw yourself into danger to have such sombre thoughts."

She gave him a soft smile, the one he often liked seeing. "I wish to be at peace, and it comes in many forms."

As he usually did, he thought her odd. Her kind were obsessed with escaping their death and would extend their lives any way possible.

"Are you sure you are a Witch?" he asked, placing his paw across her body gently to squash her and knock the air out of her. She let out a giggle, squirming onto her side when he moved his hand. "Are you sure you are not some unknown creature to the world?"

"I have been lying to you, Dragon," she laughed. "I am secretly a powerful goddess who has come to trick you into believing I am some feeble Witch."

His eyes widened, and his head reared back. He raised his paw to look at it.

"Did I just step on a goddess?"

"I am jesting!" She laughed at his face, but he'd also been joking. "I am actually a troll."

He used his paw again to press down on her, doing it lightly a few times to bounce her.

"If you have energy to joke, then you must be feeling well."

With a grin, Rurik blew a ring of fire above his head just as she said, "Oh, no! I may be okay enough to speak, but I do not have the strength for that!"

Before he could ignore her and shift, he heard his name being yelled down the tunnel. *Just when I was having fun!* Rurik gave a growl as the ring of fire dissipated into smoke before it vanished.

He was still in his Dragon body.

"Glov has annoyingly returned," he told her, making her laughter die and turn into a groan of dismay.

"Must he return so frequently?"

"It appears he wishes to aggravate me regularly." Rurik ignored his name being called again and lowered his head to sniff Amalia's body. "You are very heavy with my scent. He will notice it."

She raised her arms to sniff her skin. "I do not understand how your kind knows these things. I cannot smell anything."

But his would. Although it wouldn't cause any suspicion on its own, they would be able to smell the musk of his body on her since she lived in his lair. But no, she also smelt of his seed, which would make it obvious as to what he had been doing with her.

"Bathe. I will bring him inside while you do, so that it is not as noticeable." She placed her feet on the floor to follow his command. "Do you need help?"

He extended his paw when it seemed she was unsteady. She righted herself using it and then released it when she felt she was stable.

After walking over to the tub, he watched her fill it and then heat it with her hand. He walked from the room before she removed her dress. He knew by the time they walked past her room she would be inside of it, and Glov wouldn't be able to notice.

Perhaps it is a good thing that I warded Dragons out of my lair because of her. Glov would have let himself in, otherwise, and Rurik would've been caught.

His Dragon body wouldn't smell of her since his flames would have destroyed her scent on him when he shifted.

He went to the entrance to let him in and noted that the sky was dark, informing him that Amalia and himself had been speaking for quite a while.

"Rurik! I am pleased that you are alive," he exclaimed even before Rurik finished making his way to the entrance.

"Why would I not be?" he asked, placing his hand on the ward to allow him to pass.

They walked down the tunnel.

"Witch." He nodded in greeting.

She was in her room with her back to them in the tub.

Rurik blinked. Not once in the time Amalia had been in his lair and this Dragon visited him had he ever greeted her. He was just about to ask him about it when they reached the main room of his lair, but Glov turned to him.

"Did you not see it?"

"See what? I have been inside my lair for most of the day."

"I had just been leaving Falen's lair when-"

"I thought you were not approved to stay in her home."

It was the whole reason he allowed him to stay here the night before last.

"Ah, so, she allowed me another chance to have a go at twisting her tail, and I succeeded."

His snout bunched in irritation. "I let you stay in my lair

for no reason? I played lairmaid like some fool!"

"WitchSlayer, calm yourself. I must speak with you about what I saw. It is urgent."

With a sneezing huff, Rurik shook his head once in an attempt to remove his anger. "Go on, speak."

"I had just been leaving Falen's lair when I saw this bright light shooting towards the sky. It was like nothing I have ever seen. Even from a great distance away I was able to see it."

Rurik's eyes widened when he understood he was speaking about the power Amalia had released earlier. He hadn't thought on whether others were able to see it. *My lair may be compromised.*

Rurik cringed. He didn't want to relocate.

If Witches try to go through my lands to find the source, it will mean I have a hunting ground. Even still, he didn't wish to have his lands scattered with Witches or humans. He had spent far too much time shaping his home to want to leave it.

From a distance, nobody would have been able to know that it was dragoncraft since they didn't often use lightning. Witches may be searching for others of their kind, ill-prepared to take on a Dragon instead.

"I came straight here because it seemed as though it was close to you, and I worried that Strolguil the Vast found you since you told me he has produced such power."

"No, I did not see it. Like I mentioned, I was in my lair for most of the day."

"It must have been loud though! Did you not hear it then, and go to discover what made the noise?"

"Why would I fly into a storm? I am not as imbecilic as you!" he snapped, eyeing Glov's wettened state. "I could not hear anything other than thunder."

He couldn't let the rest of his kind know what he now did, not yet at least. In many years to come, when everything settled and he could do as he pleased with the Witch in his home, then perhaps he could share this information.

I must tell someone, though. If he were to die, he would be taking this new information to his death. *Nyota...* His sister. She already knew what he was doing, and she would keep this information hidden. She may fight him on it, but in the end she would follow his wishes.

He gave a snarling cringe. She wouldn't leave him be with her twisted sense of affection, but she also wouldn't reveal his secrets. He could tell her and then upon finding out about his death, she could then reveal to others what he'd learned.

"Do you not worry that Strolguil may be close by?"

With an air of nonchalance, he asked, "What colour was this apparent power?"

"It looked blue." Glov shook his head, seeming both awestruck and confused at the same time. "Honestly, in all my three-hundred and twenty years in the sky, I have never seen such a thing. There is not much that can surprise me."

"Strolguil's lightning is red from blood magic. If you see red lightning, do not fly in its direction next time!" Rurik shouted at him for being stupid enough to come this way when he had feared the Vast was nearby.

"You are my friend, Rurik. I did not want to do nothing if you were possibly in danger."

His admission made Rurik's anger lessen.

"Yes, Glov, I feel the same," he sighed. "Which is why you are not to be so careless as to fly towards danger!"

Then he swiped him, catching his claws against Glov's face and making him bleed.

"One of these days you will scar me with your claws." He lifted the back of his paw to rub his face and wipe some of the blood away. Then he muttered, "What kind of person strikes their friends?"

"Do not whine like a young hatchling. I do not strike you hard on purpose." That was a lie.

He didn't care if he scarred Glov's face or hurt him.

"So, you did not see the light. Then what do I tell the Elders? I was hoping you might have more information because they will want to know what I saw. They will think me mad if I say I saw a strange light."

"You do not even know if it was truly near me. It could have been closer to Falen's lair or further behind my own. Do not bring the Elders down upon me when you are so unsure."

He didn't need them coming here for a further reason than the Witch he had in his lair. They would try to sniff around while they were nearby and meddle in his affairs.

"If you did not hear it or see it, perhaps it was not as close as I thought."

Rurik nodded, hoping it would help convince him to leave out the part where he thought it may have been near his lair.

"Perhaps your Witch saw something. When I arrive, she is often sitting at the entrance to your home."

Blasted. "She was with me today."

"All day?" Glov asked with a frown, tilting his head. "I did not know that you spent hours with her. I thought that she was an irritation to you that you merely dealt with."

"No, I did not spend all day with her."

"May I speak with her? She may know what it is and did not want to alert you that Witches are possibly coming your way."

Blasted! If he didn't allow Glov to speak with her it would be suspicious, but her bath may only have lessened his scent on her.

"She is bathing."

"Then I will wait until she is done," Glov answered, looking around at the tapestries like he often did. He couldn't recount the number of times they'd spoken about each tapestry, a constant source of entertainment to the green Dragon. "Also, I have been to Borlag. I was correct that he is still alive. He had not known Witches were nearby."

Rurik sighed, pleased to hear that Borlag was still breathing.

"Remain here. She will not appreciate it if we are to see her unclothed and will not speak with us if she is upset."

Glov nodded in understanding, and with a huff, Rurik walked to the Witch's room to find she'd already finished washing.

His nose twitched when a tingle in it made him want to sneeze. "Why are you wearing that foul perfume I told you I do not like?"

He'd only been able to tolerate it when it had been to ease her.

She gave him a smile when she heard his voice. "Because if your big nose does not like it, then neither will Glov's."

He opened his mouth to tell her to remove it but then closed it. Then he grinned widely. "That was very wise. He may not be able to smell through it."

"I have placed some on my wrists that I can remove when he is no longer here and then on the wall near the bed that I can wash later."

He turned his head towards the bed. "Why did you do that?"

"In case he stuck his ugly, fat, green head in here."

She laughed, and he would've returned it if he didn't have more pressing issues.

"You have been requested to speak with Glov about the lightning you produced, but he cannot know where it came from or that it was nearby."

"I do not wish to lie," she answered thoughtfully.

"I know, but you must do so. He will become suspicious if you do not speak with him, and he may give the Elders a reason to come here."

"Okay," she sighed. "I understand."

She nodded, and he led her to the main room.

When he stood next to Glov, he gestured his hand in Amalia's direction. "There, speak to her."

Glov took a single step forward and lowered his head so that he was closer to her. Rurik's scales puffed at him being so close, until the green Dragon sneezed and reared his head back.

"You smell awful." He scratched at his snout. "It is offensive to my senses, remove it."

"I will not return here to speak with you if I do so."

Glov sharply turned his head to Rurik who gave him a shrug. "If I put up with it in my lair, so will you."

"Fine, I will not need to speak with you long anyway." He turned back to her, but a safe distance away to keep the worst of the perfume from his nostrils. "I saw a light shooting towards the sky today, I want to know if you saw it as well."

"I saw a light today," she answered, and Rurik wanted nothing more than to claw his face off. *I told her to lie!* "Then again, I see many lights each day. Could you clarify?"

"I saw lightning."

"Yes, I also saw lightning." She placed her hands behind her back as she rolled on the balls of her feet. "The storm was rather heavy."

"No, I mean I saw strange, blue lightning shooting towards the sky."

She gave a face of puzzlement. "Like how it shoots down and hits the lands?"

Rurik began to frown in confusion just as Glov began to do so in vexation.

"Yes, but upwards, like it came from the land."

"That would be strange to see," she said with a thoughtful pout. "What do you think it was?"

It took Rurik a lot longer than it should have to realise what she was doing, but his lips eventually curled in humour. *She is far cleverer than I imagined.*

"I do not know, that is why I am asking you." Glov leaned forward ever-so-slightly while tilting his head questioningly. "Now, did you see lightning shoot up towards the sky?"

"I was inside for most of the day."

Her face appeared of one of pure innocence.

"Yes, but did you see anything when you were walking the tunnels? Did you sit near the entrance?"

"I did sit near the entrance, and I saw much lightning when I sat there watching the storm."

"Then you may have seen it."

Glov was growing agitated by the Witch's working of words. She frowned as if she was lost, bringing her hand up to her chin in a thoughtful gesture.

"Seen what?"

"The lightning!" he roared, stepping closer.

She didn't move, allowing him to roar in her face close enough that her hair lifted.

"Like I said, I saw lightning in the sky." Her hand came back to join the other behind her.

"Are you daft? Answer my question."

Rurik gave him a warning growl. He didn't appreciate him implying she was stupid when she was being fantastically clever.

"I have answered your questions. What else am I to do if you misinterpret me or are not listening?"

"Are you trying to say that you did not see the lightning that I saw?"

She smiled warmly. "Yes, that is exactly what I am trying to say." She had finally twisted the conversation to answer him without a single lie being uttered.

"Finally!" Glov yelled, darting his head in Rurik's direction. "How do you put up with this Witch? She cannot even answer a simple question."

"I often find her perplexing. Do not worry, you are not alone." Rurik had to hide his humour and pretend to be angry with her. "Leave, Witch. You have upset him."

"Do not bother, I wish to leave," Glov huffed, moving around her with heavy footsteps as he stormed from the room. "I will go to Kalagian's lair since he is also close by. Perhaps he saw it."

Once Rurik knew it had been long enough that he was truly gone, he turned his head to her with a large grin forming, his eyes alight with humour and pride.

"That was one of the most entertaining things I have witnessed. You must teach me how to irritate him into leaving."

"I did not want to lie, but you told me I could not tell the truth."

He nodded to show he understood.

"I must ask, have you ever done that to me?" Had she spun a web of conversation her way without him knowing?

"Done what?" She giggled, immediately making him growl. "Perhaps a few times."

His heart thumped a little quicker. "When?"

When had this amazing woman used such devious trickery against him?

It had been three days since Amalia released that strange power into the sky, and she felt much better since. She didn't realise she hadn't felt like her usual calm self until that energy was no longer inside of her.

Amalia had managed to convince him to let her rest for the night before he started trying, and succeeding, to get under her skirt.

The first time had led to a long pause afterwards, him checking to see if spending against her stomach prevented her from harnessing dragoncraft from him.

When he was sure that everything was fine, to both of their relief, her life inside of the Dragon's lair wasn't what it was like before.

She would spend part of her time entangled with him while he was human, and the rest of the time talking with him while he was scaly and spiky.

Their moments of intimacy were hot and intense, but it was always a bittersweet ending. She could tell he was unhappy about spending outside of her body and wasn't as calm afterwards as he was before. He made no complaint, knowing it couldn't be any other way.

She often spent time against him while he was a Dragon,

whether it be laying against him to talk or to read, and he didn't seem to mind.

He had many tales of his kind to share, most with a title and having a grand reason for obtaining it.

He'd also taken her to the stream of his cave.

He tried to convince her to swim while he bathed and spoke to her. She refused because she didn't know how to swim. Apparently, he was planning to rectify this problem in the future, and she wasn't keen on the idea.

The only reason she followed him there to begin with was because he was telling her, in detail, the tale of how her kind were created.

A thousand years ago when Dragons were the leaders of the land and were things known and very much feared, humans would give sacrifices to them. They believed them to be gods. To appease the Dragons, they would gift them a human to eat.

It was rather gruesome if someone were to ask Amalia. The Dragons knew they weren't gods but were more than happy to allow humans to believe so in order to obtain an easy meal.

One particularly beautiful sacrifice caught the eye of the male Dragon she was taken to. She willingly offered her life to be ended by his stomach, and he instead bedded her. No one cared that he'd done such a thing, and they hadn't known that they could breed until she'd fallen pregnant. She didn't die giving birth whereas most that followed did.

They'd birthed a daughter, and she was the very first human with the ability to use magic. They decided to call them Witches.

When others discovered this, they began to breed with humans over their long life and sired many witchlings before they found their own mates or died. It continued like that for seven hundred years, more and more Witches being born from Dragons. They also bred with each other until there were hundreds of her kind.

Strolguil wasn't the last to be born from a Dragon, but when he turned on his father and led others to do so as well, their numbers began to dwindle due to being hunted, and they stopped breeding Witches. They didn't want to add to the chaos they accidentally created.

The tale wasn't pleasant, and she'd been sitting beside the stream watching him in the water when it ended.

Now though, she sat at the entrance to his cave. She wanted to look at the night sky. Amalia sat between his forelegs with his paws around her to keep her warm as she rested against an arm.

They were speaking about some nonsense, as they often did, until the stars grew bright. She searched the sky for what she had truly wanted to see.

"It will be a black moon tomorrow," she commented, seeing the sliver of light against the blackness.

"Is that noteworthy?"

"I guess your kind do not care for such things, but each phase has meaning to mine. It is the start to the lunar cycle, and the black moon is representative of new life and new beginnings. The ending of one thing to move forward into another."

He turned his large spiking head up to it, and the light made his scales appear more purple as it reflected against him.

"That sounds like gibberish. The moon is nothing more than the moon. It has no power or control over what we do."

"I often feel quite lovely when I am bathed under the full moon, thank you very much," she answered with a snarky tone.

He turned his head down to face her. "You look better in the sun."

She smiled, unsure if that was intended to be a compliment or not.

"Do your kind truly not feel a pull with such things? I feel like everything gives me life."

He tilted his head thoughtfully.

"No, we do not feel things like this. Like I have mentioned previously, our magic is different. Our energy comes from within, and we use things like herbs, spices, and crystals to focus our magic to what we want, not because we need their aid. We do not do things that shift the world and unbalance it."

Amalia tapped her fingers against her lips. "I do not feel like I do things to unbalance the world."

"I am talking about dark magic. I have tried to use blood magic, but it does nothing because we do not need to. Our magic is usually stronger and therefore, it is a natural part of the world."

"But some spells do not require items, I only need to chant."

"That power comes from within, but if you wish to make those spells powerful, you must add to them."

"Which is where the discovery of blood magic came from? The need to find a way to make those chants stronger?"

"Yes, and, for some reason, that taste of power corrupts your kind to want more."

She continued to tap her lips.

"I must admit, having your magic inside me was quite energising, but I do not wish to seek more. Why does it corrupt others?"

He shrugged. "How am I to know the inner workings of your kind? Perhaps it has become a normalised thing and is not seen for how truly evil it is."

"I do not think my mother ever used dark magic, but she would often tell me to worry of the moon." This time she turned her face to it. "She said that sometimes new beginnings are not always a good thing, and if I did not want to get caught up in darkness, I should stay inside during those times."

"She sounds paranoid. I would not listen to her advice," he chuckled with a shake of his head.

"Do not be rude about her! What if she is right? What if the black moon is up to no good?" She reached for it.

He looked at her like he didn't understand her, before humour crinkled his large silver eyes. "Then let it be up to no good. No harm can come to you inside of my lair."

She sighed while slumping her shoulders. "I fear tomorrow I will wake with pixies upon me again."

"That... That I cannot save you from. I do not know how they always manage to get past my wards, but hopefully the new one I have in place will be better at keeping them at bay."

He startled her when he stood and scooped her up in one of his paws.

"What are you doing?" she asked when he began to carry her down the tunnel.

"You have been speaking of strange things, and the hour is late." He turned into her alcove. "You are to go to bed."

"But I am not tired!"

She squealed when he tossed her through the air onto it.

"I did not say you will be sleeping," he chuckled before blowing a ring of fire above his head.

The following morning Amalia woke alone, like she often did when she knew Rurik had clawed under his riches to sleep. She did wonder if he would ever rest beside her, but she knew trust like that would have to come with time.

He does not want to be caught unaware. It made sense to her. If he wasn't awake, his senses wouldn't be able to pick up that there might be danger afoot.

She would often wake when it was dark since she wanted to eat before she sat in the sun for the very few hours it was available.

She walked to the food alcove to collect an assortment of vegetables. She carefully picked the right ones for a soup she could make now that she had herbs and spices she could add to the broth.

It was while she was sitting down to eat that Rurik poked his scaly head inside.

"I see that you are eating. I am going to fly down to one of the farms nearby and find my own breakfast."

She smiled, appreciating that he often told her when he was leaving so she wouldn't go searching for him when he wasn't there.

And then he was gone, leaving her alone in his lair while

she ate, bathed, and greeted the sun just as it was peaking over the horizon.

She sat close to the wall with her legs crossed, knowing if she sat in the middle, she would have to move out of his way when he returned. Amalia closed her eyes, letting the warmth seep into her skin as she saw the orange brightness behind her closed lids.

It wasn't long before he returned.

She heard his wings swooping and felt the rush of wind they produced before he landed in the clearing. Rocks rolled and crushed into the dirt under his footstep when he walked over the stones of his lairstep, loudly huffing from his flight.

She didn't open her eyes to see the dead cow hanging from his maw and the likelihood that he had a second in his paw.

Once she knew he was behind her, she opened her eyes again to look at the land and sky, watching the world grow brighter by the minute.

I am always taken aback by this view.

She knew she would have to wait for him to walk back past her with his food mess before she could go to the main room of his cave. She didn't want to see him eating.

She also didn't want to hear it. It wasn't pleasant.

When the sun rose to the point it was barely touching her, the fleeting moment of sunshine gone, she was just about to get to her feet when something small walked into the clearing.

It was a cat, and it seemed to be searching for something. It sniffed the ground, scenting it before following a trail with its nose. It was walking in her very direction.

She frowned at its orange and black tortoiseshell coat and its white chest and cheeks. It looked very familiar, almost identical to an awful little cretin she loved.

That cat looks like Bala.

It sat in front of the ward and looked around at it with bright green eyes. No, it didn't just look *similar* to her feral cat. It looked exactly the same.

"Bala?" She couldn't help trying, missing that darn cat more than she was willing to admit.

It gave a soft meow, coming to where she was behind the ward and rub its neck against it.

"Bala, it is you!" she almost squealed with excitement. "How did you find me?"

She didn't think it was possible. Then again, she didn't know how far she was from her old cottage.

He started scratching at the ward to get to her.

"I cannot let you in. I will have to ask the Dragon."

But Amalia was afraid that if she left to ask Rurik to let him inside, he would be gone.

He placed a paw on the ward. She wanted so badly to touch it, to grab his paw and play with his little toe beans like she used to.

"You are still such a fat cat." She placed her fingers against the ward right where his paw was. "I am glad that you are well."

Amalia gasped with her lips parting when his paw came through the ward, his claws extending to clutch around her index finger. He wouldn't let go, and when she tried to yank her hand away, she ended up pulling him through the ward by accident.

Her shock that she managed to pull him through the ward didn't last when she realised he couldn't run away now. She gave a bright smile.

"Bala, I am so glad to see you!"

She scrambled to pick him up. That was until he started to grow, started to *change*.

The multi-coloured fur on his back began to turn brown and look like cotton and a metal breastplate. He started to stand on his back legs as they began to look like leather soldier trousers before a silver chainmail skirt appeared. Eventually, bright red hair grew from his head, long and tied back. His face and hands became more and more human.

Once the person finished transforming, on top of his head was a deflated looking cat who looked exactly like Bala, nothing about him solid except for his head – where it still appeared as though it had its skull.

Amalia stepped back in horror.

"Who are you?"

The stranger turned to her and reached his hand out. She quickly backed up.

"Are you pregnant?" he asked her, placing his hand flat against her stomach when her back met the wall.

What a strange thing to ask someone you've just met. She didn't answer, didn't do or say anything. She wanted to flee from being cornered by this stranger, but he followed her when she stepped to the side.

"I will check myself." He waved his hand in the air above her stomach, and a wave of magic washed over her. He frowned when he was done, his red brows crinkling. "I see, he has tricked you."

She looked down and saw that something was glowing from underneath her dress, right below where her navel was. She'd often felt a burning sensation there that was roughly the size of a thumb mark, but she never thought much on it.

"He has placed a spell on you. No matter, I will remove it." His grin, with his crooked and uneven teeth, sent a chill through her. "Let us go find your Dragon."

When he grabbed her hand in a tight fist, it painfully squeezed her fingers together since he didn't grab it properly. Amalia winced as he dragged her down the tunnel, forcing her to stumble behind him.

"Who are you? What do you want?"

He turned his head back to her. "You do not remember me? No matter, I will remind you, and you will remember your place in the world."

Who is this person? And where is Bala? She feared he killed her precious cat.

"Wait," she pleaded when they were approaching the main room to the Dragon's lair.

Rurik's head lifted from his meal when they entered, and he immediately got to his four paws with a growl. He took a handful of steps closer with his body lowering as though he was preparing to leap forward.

"How did you get in my lair?" His eyes narrowed into the hateful glare he only wore when he spoke of Witches that were not her.

Amalia's heart was beating frantically, unsure of what was happening as she stumbled and desperately tried to keep her footing.

"Why," he said with a gleeful tone before bringing her forward, so she was beside him. He gestured his free hand towards her. "She let me in."

Rurik's eyes flickered between this person, her, and their hands still connected.

"You did what?!" he roared, stamping his foot.

The stranger released her and stepped forward to approach him.

"Stay back or I will unleash my flame." Rurik's lips curled back further over his fangs with each step the stranger took.

"Well, you might hit her, so we cannot have that, can we?" he answered before he lifted his fist.

Rurik didn't seem to care when he took in a deep draw of air like he was preparing.

Just as he unleashed flames, the stranger threw whatever he was holding in his fist. It was tiny, something barely noticeable, but the moment it impacted against the side of Rurik's head he was sent flying.

The massive Dragon was tossed back with such force that

he didn't touch the ground before he hit the wall.

"Rurik!" she screamed.

She sprinted forward but was captured in the stranger's embrace from behind while her arms and legs flailed forward.

He is not moving!

"Come now, Amalia." She gaped at hearing him say her name. "The black moon is tonight, and we have much to prepare. We cannot waste time."

She pushed at his face as she tried to get him to let her go. She even kicked her legs against his shin and stomped on his foot – anything to get free.

"Let me go!"

"You will not fight me when you remember." She would never stop fighting! She squirmed harder. "Do you not wish to see your father, then?"

She froze. "My father?"

"Yes, your father." Then he released her, putting his arm out to make sure she didn't sprint forward. "Now stay there, I do not know if he will awaken, and I only have a short window to get him."

The stranger twirled his hands in front of himself as he stalked closer. A small ball of red liquid began to form, growing in size, like he was summoning something from thin air. Eventually it dropped into his hands. The red liquid washed away to reveal a large glass orb.

He placed it against Rurik and then stepped back to chant.

There was a swirl of dark magic, as if it was made of thick, black clouds. It came from that orb and the longer he chanted, the more it grew and slunk around the Dragon's unconscious body.

She could barely see him through the cloud, but there was enough of a gap that she saw Rurik grow smaller as he shrunk. Her lips parted in disbelief. He wasn't just shrinking in size... He was being sucked into that orb!

When he was gone, and the stranger picked up the glass ball. He brought it over to show her, and what had once been see-through now housed what looked like a tiny version of the dark purple male she had come to know and care for.

"What did you do to him?" Amalia reached for it.

He snatched it out of the way.

"This is the kind of magic I plan for you to gain. It is a rare and powerful spell, but I have sealed him in this orb so that I may carry him. Do not worry. I have not harmed your Dragon."

He reached up to cup her under the chin. It was gentle as his thumb brushed against her cheek.

"You have grown far lovelier than I had ever imagined. Everything is falling into place, and soon you will remember what I plan for you to become."

"And what is that?"

She didn't trust this man or the soft smile he gave her – one that appeared tender and caring. *What is he going to do to Rurik?*

Amalia quietly followed the stranger outside of Rurik's lair after he had spent some time at the ward and managed to lower it for them. Then he forced her to hop onto the saddle of a horse he'd hidden in the woods before he sat behind her and brought it into a trot.

She was complying. After watching what he did to render Rurik unconscious with little effort and then put him in some glass ball, she understood that this person was powerful and dangerous.

She still couldn't remember him, but she knew in time he would remind her of something... apparently.

Amalia inspected him in close detail. His face was clean shaven, which revealed wide jaw bones and sharp cheeks. His chin was indented, his nose broad with a rounded tip. Light lashes framed his green eyes. He was lean, but muscular, and appeared to be a similar height to Rurik since he towered over her slightly.

She couldn't tell if she thought him attractive or not, but even after examining him, she still couldn't remember.

And until she did, she had to figure out what he meant when he told her she may possibly see her father, and how to get Rurik out of the ball. *I cannot leave him inside it. There must be a way I can free him.*

Since she was in front of him, she was unable to grab it, even though he held it under his arm the entire time.

It wasn't long before he took her to a small, noblemen's castle. It wasn't far from Rurik's lair, and the sun only rose to the middle of the sky by the time they had arrived.

The mansion was grey and appeared as though it hadn't been looked after well. The building was mostly square with a flat roof, but there was a round tower on one side. Vines had grown over the side of it while dirt smudged underneath the windows. The grounds were covered in tall grass and the dirt road on the property had been plagued with holes.

"Come, I will help you down."

She didn't take his offer when he raised one arm while the other still held the orb. She jumped down by herself and almost fell.

"Where are we?"

The path to this place had been through a large forest with a thick density of trees. It was intended to be secluded and hidden, and they hadn't passed a single house or other building along the way. It wasn't comforting that she couldn't scream for help if she needed to or run to someone close by.

"This is a place I acquired many years ago in preparation for this night. I did have another one near your cottage as well."

Her face paled when he placed his hand on the small of her and pushed her towards the large, brown painted double-doors.

"How did you know I lived in a cottage?"

He gave a dark chuckle. "I have been your Bala for many years, my sweet."

She didn't know how it was possible, but her face whitened further. *I was spied on?* She had undressed in front of him, had bathed in front of him!

She covered her chest with her arms.

"Did you kill him to gain entrance into my home?" she asked when he placed his hand on the brass knob of the door and twisted it.

"I killed that cat many years ago before you met him. I needed his skin so I could morph into him." He said it as if it was meant to comfort her, but it did the opposite. "And it was smart thinking on my part to use his senses and appearance to enter the Dragon's home. The ward in place required someone to invite the other through."

"I really let you in?" She thought it had been a lie.

He gave her a stern nod. "Yes, you placed your hand where mine was, and it gave me access."

I let him in, and she wished she hadn't. She could tell this man wasn't good, even when he gave her a reassuring smile and held the door open for her like he was trying to be gentlemanly.

She found herself in a short corridor. There was a main room in the back that was obvious by the double doors that were in the centre at the end of the hallway.

As she walked down it, she looked inside both rooms she passed, one on either side of her. They appeared normal... dust covered, but normal. There were beds, wardrobes, tables, and even sofas.

"The others who are here with me will arrive shortly from the town. I asked them to leave so I could be alone with you," he said when they got to the end of the hallway, picking up a curl of her hair to play with it.

Amalia stepped back and put her hands to her chest to cup them in apprehension.

He gave a laugh, his smile bright yet jovial.

"Not like that, I would not get in the way of what is supposed to happen on this night, but... definitely in due time. There is much for you to remember, and I must prepare you for the black moon."

She still didn't know what he meant by that or why he kept referencing the moon cycle. When he turned to lead her somewhere else, she didn't follow.

"You promised me I may see my father."

He came back with a brow raised. "I did. You can do so tomorrow when everything is done."

"No. My father is dead. I want to know what you really meant when you said that."

His nose crinkled in thought as his head tilted to the side. "He is not dead. He is very much alive and has been my captive for nine years."

Amalia stepped back as her heart seemed to stop.

"But my mother told me he died on the battlefield."

"Battlefield?" His red dusted brows came together. "What, like some human soldier?"

"Yes."

He startled her when he grabbed the side of her head, pushing it so it turned one way and then the other. It appeared as though he was trying to see through her skull and into her mind.

"How badly has your memory been altered? For you to think your father is a measly human is quite impressive."

Her breathing began to shallow as anxiety picked up in her chest. *My father is not a human?*

"I can tell you are confused and do not believe me. Fine, I will show you him. Perhaps it will help me to unlock your memories if you know the truth. Knowing you are under a spell helps with breaking them."

He grabbed her wrist and pulled her along the hallway to the left of that main room door, leading her to a curving staircase. There were two windows on their climb, one low to the ground and another halfway up, giving just enough light to see each step.

At the very top, was a distressed timber door. He didn't open it, instead he turned to her.

"The door is unlocked, but I have my own ward in place." He motioned to the orb in his hand. "You may speak with him while I take care of the WitchSlayer. You have until then."

He left by walking back down the stairs.

Amalia faced the door with apprehension, her palms slick with sweat, as she slowly opened it. She peeked her head inside.

On the other side of the room, a man sat alone with his hands bound by chains. His hair was blond but was tight with curls, not loose how hers were. The moment he lifted his head up to see who entered, Amalia ran forward and crashed into an invisible barrier that shimmered when she was bounced back.

"Daddy!" she exclaimed with bewildered eyes.

He leapt to his knees to crawl forward.

"Amalia, you should not be here," he rasped beseechingly, his voice hoarse like he hadn't used it in a long time.

He placed his bound hands on the ward, and Amalia noted that he was covered in dirt and dust. His brown pants were worn while his white shirt tattered around his unusually lean frame. He looked frail and weak, as though he was half-starved.

"I was taken here." Then tears began to pool in her eyes before quickly falling. "I thought you were dead."

"No, sweetheart. I am not dead." His eyes were such a dark

colour of blue that it was easy to mistake them for brown from a distance. "I have been a captive."

"Why did she lie to me?" She placed one of her hands firmly on the ward while the other covered her mouth. She bit back a terrible sob. "Why did Mum tell me you died? She told me soldiers came to the house to tell us."

"She needed to in order to protect you."

"Where is she? Why did she leave me?"

Amalia's looked behind him with hope that she might see her in the prison cell with him. It was empty except for some fur bedding, a chamber pot, and a wooden plate.

Her mother had never even said goodbye before she left, nor did say a word to Amalia that she was leaving. She just woke up one day suddenly alone in the world.

"She is dead. He told me he found our cottage and then killed her." Then he peeked around her to see she was alone. "Run. Run while you have the chance. You must leave. You cannot be here."

"Why?" She hiccupped through her tears, confused and hurt. There was a painful swell in her heart. "What is happening? Are you really not a human? Who is he?"

She had so many questions, and she fell to her knees to be level with him.

"I am like you, Amalia." So, he really was a Witch. She had been lied to. "We changed your memories to think I was human. It was easier to hide. I am so sorry, sweetheart. We saw no other way."

"But why? Why did you do these things?"

What in her memories of her childhood were real? Her mind felt like it was shattering, like fragments of glass cracking along her skull. Reality felt skewed, and she didn't know what to believe anymore.

"Because... tonight you are to become corrupted." The shock of his words stopped her tears. "There is a proph-"

Before he could finish, the door behind her swung open with a creak. She gasped and turned to find the stranger.

Rurik laid shackled, bound, and unable to move.

His neck had been chained to the wall by a large metal collar while all of his feet were shackled together by chains, forcing him to lay down permanently. Even his dangerous tail hadn't been spared of chains.

Large, thick, coarse rope was tied around his snout, rendering it impossible for him to speak, or bite. Even without it, he wouldn't be able to unleash fire.

He could feel they had already hexed him.

He was unable to grow small, was unable to break the shackles that the strength of his kind should be able to. They hexed him, not just once or twice, but multiple times.

He was rendered weak and incapable of escaping. He felt as feeble as a human.

The room he woke in wasn't one he'd ever seen before. It appeared to be some form of dungeon. There were no windows, no bars, nothing but four walls of grey stone and a singular, heavy, metal door.

Where am I? He couldn't remember coming here, nor had he been awake to know he was being chained.

He would have fought otherwise.

He hadn't been picked apart, hadn't been visited since he awakened. He was left with questions as he tried to figure out how to escape. *Where is Amalia?*

Rurik feared for her safety. He wasn't sure if she allowed the male into his lair on purpose or not. *It is not something I think she would do. She would not allow someone such as he to enter my cave.* Someone who would harm him and possibly herself.

The area was uncomfortably silent. At least *he* couldn't hear anything. They may have placed a spell on him to dull his senses.

Why are they not pulling my scales from me? Usually, they would make quick work of Dragons. *This is unusual.*

Not only did they capture him, but they had relocated him from his lair. Typically, they would pull the Dragon apart in their caves, unwilling to carry them around alive.

No, something is different.

He was trying to figure out what.

He was angry, he was confused, and he was determined to escape. If he discovered that Amalia was in danger here, he would fight for her and escape with her in tow. *I cannot leave her here alone. She will not be safe.*

I must protect her at all costs.

"Have we had a nice conversation with daddy dearest?" The stranger asked with a grin, opening the door to her father's prison tower. He examined her teary state, and that grin widened. "Good, I can see you now believe your mind has been altered. Let us remove the spell."

"Leave her alone! She does not want this," her father yelled. "She has always been pure-hearted, leave her as she is. She will never accept you."

"I want what she will give me more than anything else in this world."

Then he stormed forward, his face of satisfaction never fading even when she tried to scramble back.

"Stay away from me."

She put her hands up to keep him away, but he grabbed her wrist and yanked her to her feet.

"No!" Her father yelled when they crossed through the doorway, and the stranger slammed the door.

Then he turned her with his features falling. "You will give me what I want." His voice was stern as he grabbed her face.

She tried to pry herself away with her hands, her cheeks squishing as she forced her head back.

"And what is that?"

"Everything will make sense when your memory is returned."

Once again, Amalia was pulled. She almost stumbled when she was forced to take each step back down the spiralling stairwell.

"I do not want to be evil." She attempted to twist her wrist from his hand when they reached the bottom step.

As he spoke, he took her to the other side of this hallway to another set of stairs that led to the second floor of this small castle-like mansion.

"Comparing what is evil and what is good is such a deformed approach to moral ideologies. What is chaos to the fly is natural to the spider. I am merely going to make you the spider in this world of tiny bugs."

"But if that means I will hurt others, then I do not want it."

"You did when you were younger. You were rather curious about what you knew you were going to become."

Once at the top of the stairs and on the second floor, he took her to a room that was overflowing with magical items. A wall to a second room had been knocked down to make it bigger so it could accommodate everything.

And it held much.

On one side there were more herbs, plants, and spices than she had ever seen – even more than in the Dragon's lair. Crystals and vials of strange liquids littered benches, and their strange colours of clear blue, red, yellow, and even silver captured her eyes.

On the other side there were four benches. Three were against the walls with one in the middle by itself to create a square shape. She would've been able to walk on either side of the bench standing alone in the middle with ease if she tried.

Everything looked healthy and alive, except for the hundreds of jars she could see were filled with different creature parts. She gaped at them in horror, able to make out a jar full of either pixie or fairy legs, while another was filled with wings.

There were jars of dead rats, bugs, eyeballs, and even random paws of different animals. Bile rose from her stomach to her throat when she thought she may have seen a human finger when her eyes finished scanning.

"Quite remarkable my collection is, is it not?" He said it with pride, placing his hands on his hips while he let his eyes sweep over the room.

"Remarkable is not how I would put it," she answered honestly before swallowing thickly, hoping the acid she felt in her throat would go back down.

Horrifying, disgusting, sickening; these were words she found more appropriate to describe this place.

"This incessant behaviour is beginning to unravel me."

He stormed to his benches to grab a jade green, marble mortar and pestle. Then he began to hastily move around the room, throwing different items into it, mainly herbs and spices.

Nothing that had once been a moving creature was added to the bowl.

Amalia watched him cautiously. She wanted to remember what was real. She no longer wanted to have false memories now that she knew she had them, but she worried about what she would see. She didn't want it to change her.

He used a spell to light a burner, adding water and spices until it was yellow and then he added the crushed-up items he'd obtained. Before long, what he was making was ready, and he poured it into a cup.

"Sit on the bench. Recovering your memories may cause you to become light-headed."

She complied, seeing no other way out of this.

He didn't give her the cup, instead he wanted to feed it to

her himself. It smelt sickly sweet when the wafting steam entered her nostrils.

She noted the length of his nails now that she was observing them up close. They almost appeared like short claws. She would imagine it would be easy to pry inside of things with them, like a piece of fruit... or the skin of something.

Once he drained the contents into her mouth by force, he nodded before cutting the palm of his hand open.

"This may be strange, but do not fight what you see. It is all real, it has all happened." Then he looked up to the ceiling, bouncing side-to-side as if he was deciding on whether or not he wanted to tell her something. He looked at her when he decided. "It may also hurt."

Before she could say anything, he slammed his blood covered hand against her forehead, and she was jerked back. Not by her body, but by her mind or soul.

She felt herself falling even though he was holding her up. The moment her eyes were closed, memories came flooding in. They flashed quickly, and she was barely able to hold onto them as they passed. Only a few held her focus.

She remembered being a little girl, no more than three, in a room while Witches moved about. It was a coven. She was playing on the floor, but her head lifted when she heard a screeching noise.

She turned to find her father who was standing at a bench with his hand out and waiting. He was given something crawling and squirming with fur. Three-year-old Amalia watched her father take a cleaver to its head and then drained its blood into a bubbling pot.

Someone came to add something else to the pot, a sprinkle of something, but she didn't know what it was. *My father was a Dark Witch.* She didn't see her mother.

The memory faded and Amalia was a year older, walking

between the legs of coven Witches as she held a toy. She was curious, trying to reach for things on the benches, but they were preparing for a ritual, and her father wouldn't let her.

Someone else picked her up and settled her on their hip to show her what she couldn't see. They chattered happily to her while showing her natural things as well as blood and pieces.

She wanted to pick up a wingless fairy, thinking it was a doll.

Young Amalia hadn't been frightened or horrified by what she was seeing since she was used to what was happening.

That memory faded also.

She was five in this new memory. She had met the stranger now before her, but she could see the coven was shaken up that he was there. They were fawning because they were afraid, and Amalia sensed this from them, sensed they were worried.

He took her into his arms and walked around to the benches. She pulled his long hair that was the same as it was now, but he was wearing it loose. He was being kind to her because she was a young witchling, and he desired all Witches to prosper, to obtain power and strength.

He gave her the body of a headless rat, and she took it, squeezing it as she pointed to the head of a fairy – once again, she thought it was a doll. He swung it by its long hair in front of her eyes, and at her giggle, he put it back down to grab another part of a creature.

"You are very curious child. One day, you will make a superb Witch."

She continued to see him in her memories. He wasn't always there, but he often went around to covens to meet them. The people around her talked about him in hushed whispers, saying he was searching for strong Witches who would be of use to him.

She knew she'd only aged another year in her next

memory. She had recently blown out six candles.

She was sitting on a table while the coven of Witches stood around her while uttering quietly. They were concerned but also excited as energy seemed to bustle between them.

Their eyes continued to return to her.

She was frowning in confusion until her father came to her with a comforting smile.

"You are going to be special Amalia," he said to her while bouncing her on his hip. *"You are a part of a prophecy that may change our future. You are going to birth something new to the world, and you will live a long time with that child."* She giggled, not understanding what he meant, but happy to see her father's smiling face. *"On the night of a black moon, you will steal the heart of a Dragon. We believe that you are to eat it, and it will extend your life, in the same way many of our kind seek."* Then he trailed his finger over the curve of her nose before bopping it. *"Most do not get the chance to, but it has been told that you are destined to take one. You will also birth its child and raise it."*

Even with all the memories regained of her mother, she had never been with the coven. She wasn't a part of it, but she was upset when her father took her to them when he visited them. All her memories of her mother were in a house that was not her cottage, but a place far away near the sea.

Her mother and father argued about the prophecy. She was concerned because, although Amalia was curious, she'd never harmed anything.

She had always been sweet.

Her mother was a white wielder, and Amalia often saw them fighting about his use of dark magic. He'd only recently begun to do this and hadn't been corrupted when she met him. Something turned him, and he became addicted to the power he knew he could obtain.

Amalia's mother hadn't wanted the same for her.

Her next memory was with the stranger, and he was speaking to her. He'd heard of the prophecy and had swiftly returned.

While he held her, he spoke to her father.

"She will become mine. If what is foretold is to happen, then she will become powerful, and I seek a woman such as this." Then he turned his head to her with a smile. *"You, little child, will one day become bonded to me and become my wife."*

The stranger remained by her side for years, telling her she would marry him, bond with him. The young and impressionable Amalia became infatuated with the person who told her he would one day love her and become her husband when she was older.

The memories began to flash quicker.

Her father had hidden this stranger's plans from her mother because he didn't approve, and he knew she wouldn't either. It was Amalia who told her when she was nine because she had been excited about the man she loved.

They argued in front of her, and her mother gave him an ultimatum – to let them run away by themselves or to change and come with them.

Since he didn't want to lose the woman and daughter he cherished, her father came with them and refused to use magic ever again except to take Amalia's memories and change them. It was the only time her mother approved of his use of dark magic.

He changed them to the cottage she thought she had lived in all her life and made her think he was nothing but a human soldier who would often leave. But he didn't leave to war, he left to make sure they were safe.

Amalia's love for the stranger had been taken by the change to her memory. Now that they returned, she strangely felt it again, as well as other emotions, confusion, shock, uncertainty.

As a child, she had reached for the prophecy because she wanted to become something. She had wanted to be strong. Her coven told her she would be admired for it, be loved for it, and what child didn't want to feel that way?

It was hard not to feel these things again when they were returned to her so vividly.

Once the spell came to an end, she was left with the real memories and the ones she knew were false – of her simple peaceful life in her cottage.

Her eyes came back into focus. Her head felt heavy as it swam when everything still tried to flash even though he'd taken his hand away. She was left with a terrible headache.

When her vision finally cleared, she saw the man in front of her, but he wasn't a stranger to her anymore. *I loved him.*

"You understand now, do you not?" he asked, his green eyes flicking between hers with tenderness and care.

"Yes, I remember everything."

"Excellent," he said with a welcoming grin.

Then his mouth was upon hers, pressing like he had waited eons to do so, and something inside her heart shifted for him. Amalia readily kissed him back.

Strolguil, Rurik sneered when the man entered his dungeon cell with an evil hint to his upturned smirk, humour brightening his eyes when they met Rurik's foul glare.

A growl came from his chest that was quietened by the rope keeping his mouth shut.

It faded when he saw her.

Amalia. She came into the dungeon behind Strolguil before he pulled her forward to be beside him. *She is here. I must escape with her.*

Her eyes found his before they drifted over his body, and the shackles and chains keeping him down. He could barely move, only shuffle slightly.

"I have been going easy on you, WitchSlayer," Strolguil said with a laugh. "Have been keeping you at bay for years."

Rurik answered him with a snarl. He knew he'd been taken over easily since he had been attacked with only one move that rendered him unconscious. He hadn't been prepared for such an attack, for such unimaginable power.

He has been letting me escape him on purpose.

Now he understood that he hadn't allowed the Witches to capture him in Mahesh's lair on purpose. He'd even been heartless enough to kill his own kind to prevent it.

"I have been waiting for this very night for the past twenty years." Then he pulled Amalia in front of him and wrapped one arm around her torso while his other hand came up to cup her chin. He leaned over her shoulder so that his head was next to hers with that evil smirk widening. "Did you have fun with my future woman?"

Rurik's head reared back as at his words, staring at Amalia who was being forced to face him.

"She is quite beautiful, is she not? I did not realise when she was younger that she would grow to be this lovely."

She knows him? Rurik couldn't stop his heart rate from increasing as confusion crawled into his chest. His stomach knotted.

"Although I have been with her for quite some time, protecting her, I knew I needed to wait in order to not get in the way of fate." Rurik's eyes flickered between them, at the forceful, yet affectionate, way he was holding her. She wasn't trying to escape. "But I have been with you for many years, have I not Amalia?"

"Yes," she answered plainly, her eyes falling away from Rurik's. "As Bala. As my cat."

Rurik shook his head. *It cannot be true.* Confusion crawled deeper to contort his gut in a disgusting way. *She is a captive. She is not here willingly.*

"I had to watch over her," Strolguil said. "There is a prophecy, you see, foretold when she was six. You know of this prophecy, do you not, my sweet?"

Her eyes moved to look at the wall behind him. It was as if she was bored of being there, her face blank.

"Yes."

Rurik's expression changed into one of horror.

She has tricked me. She has been waiting. His trust for the Witch was falling by the second, at each time she confirmed what Strolguil the Vast said.

"I did not know how things would pan out, but when you hunted me near her little cottage, I thought perhaps I was supposed to bring you together." He gave a bright smile, his crooked teeth showing his glee. "I wondered if the prophecy was supposed to begin before this day."

Rurik to let his eyes flicker over the cold, stone-brick floor he lay on as he tried to think.

This has been planned.

"I knew you would fall for her charm." His eyes shot up to see them together, to see the innocent looking Witch being held by his greatest enemy. The woman whose beauty had easily captivated him, whose softness had made him lower his guard. "I knew you would find her lovely, would find her caring and kind. That, as long as I did not intervene, did not turn her yet, you would be at ease with her if you ever found her. She was convincing, was she not?"

It... It was all an act? Those fragments of trust were beginning to fall away faster.

"Blood debts are a funny thing, are they not WitchSlayer?" He met Strolguil's burning gaze. "I brought her to you so she would heal you, and when they came to put her in fire, I knew you would save her."

Strolguil turned his head to Amalia to kiss her cheek, making her head turn up slightly. Her eyes lifted to the ceiling.

"I am sorry I had to let the humans burn you, my dear. It was necessary, but with the prophecy in place, I knew you would survive it."

Her breath hitched.

Rurik didn't know if that was at the mention of her time on the stake or because this foul cretin's lips were against her. They had dulled his senses – he couldn't smell.

He growled at her freely allowing Strolguil to touch her. She wasn't even *trying* to put up a fight to get away or flee. *I had been a fool!*

"Do you like my home?" The hand around her torso moved to gesture to the walls around them. "You are very tricky, WitchSlayer. I have searched for your lair for years and only knew you flew near these lands often."

Strolguil's eyes trailed over the side of Amalia's face before he brought them to Rurik's.

"I worried that I would not find you in time, but then she released the lightning, did she not?" A cold rush rolled through him. "I knew it had to be her."

She led him to me on purpose! She let him into my lair! She has been a part of this the whole time. The last fragments of trust faded, and Rurik began to fill with hate and anger for the woman.

"Tell him about the prophecy, Amalia. Tell him what you have known since you were a child."

Her eyes faded out as though she was thinking back with her gaze on the wall.

"On this night of the black moon, Amalia Swafford, daughter of Witches Gregory and Hellena, will steal the heart of the Dragon, Rurik the WitchSlayer, and one day birth his child. The child will be the first DragonWitch ever born and will be more powerful than either Dragon or Witch, will fly the skies without stolen wings while harnessing the power of both its parents. It will be the start to many born."

She pronounced it with boredom, like a well-rehearsed line. Rurik shook his head, not believing such a thing will ever be born. *It cannot be. I know she is not pregnant.*

Strolguil's hand came down to rest low on her stomach.

"I thought when you took her that she was to take your child sooner. I had not thought that she would need to take both your heart and seed this night." His eyes widened, horrified as understanding dawned on him. "I have removed that pesky little spell of yours, the one that stops her from getting pregnant."

She will ride me and cut out my heart. Rurik snarled with disgust. *I cannot let this happen.*

"And I will raise that child," Strolguil grinned. "I will raise that child of power with her. I knew she was meant to be mine, to give me it when I heard of what her future was. That once it was born, I would bond her to me."

Rurik frantically struggled in his chains, wanting to escape, to prevent this, and the sound of them clacked and chimed.

"Then, when it has grown and has become strong..." Rurik didn't like the dark humour that rolled in his tone. "We will consume that child for its unimaginable power."

His scales puffed, and he managed to shuffle back in abject horror. She wouldn't look at him, made no reaction to such a vile thought or plan. It was like she didn't care.

I bedded a monster.

A sick, disgusting monster that would pull apart her own child for more magic. Who would eat its flesh and blood.

He wanted to unleash his fire, wanted to claw at them, at her. He was filled with rage, the undeniable want to maim this hateful female he had allowed into his lair, had taken care of. *I should have let her burn!*

He hadn't thought it was possible for him to despise anyone more than he did Strolguil, but he had been wrong. He hated her more and was more disgusted by her.

She is vile, wretched, vicious. How did I not see through her lies, her façade?

"I think he understands his place in the world like you do now," Strolguil said to Amalia. "We no longer need to taunt him any longer. In a few hours, his life will be ended, and, like the new moon symbolises, one thing will die so that a new life can begin."

Hearing such words uttered made his eyes widen with shock. *She said such things to me! She has been playing with me, teasing me with the knowledge I did not know!*

He tried to rise so he could rid the world of these two disgusting vermin. These evil creatures who couldn't be allowed to live. His paws were caught by each other, and he fell snout forward into the ground with a distinct *thud.*

Then Strolguil yanked a silver dagger from a sheath against his belt. The handle was covered in black leather that swirled around it while a red jewel was embedded into the circular base of it.

"Come, my dear. I want you to gain your strength before tonight, you will do so if you drink his blood. We will start your new path now."

He handed it to her, and she willingly took it.

"The prophecy does not state that I am to gain power before I steal his heart," she said while looking at the hilt with little interest.

"Yes, but I see no harm in doing so. It will merely be a sip."

"How are you to know that this will not change things?" Her voice was dull and calm as she disagreed with someone most Witches would never dare anger. "Have prophecies not been broken before?"

It is because she is comfortable with him, has always planned to bond with him.

"Yes, they can be broken. But as I mentioned, I see no harm. You will eat his heart tonight, what difference does it make?"

She let her eyes move along the walls, refusing to look at him. *Yes, I would not look me in the eye either.*

"You told me he is my Dragon, so I should be allowed to do with him as I please." She handed the dagger back to him. "The prophecy states that I am to take his heart when the black moon has risen. If I take from him now, it may change things."

"I see that you are quite patient and determined to do this

by the way of the foretelling. It is true, simple things can break a prophecy." Strolguil took the blade from her with a proud smile of admiration. "Perhaps you are far wiser than I imagined. I am pleased."

She nodded in agreement.

"I have left him this way so that you may make a choice. Would you prefer to ride him as a Dragon or as a human?"

Amalia looked to the wall once more in thought.

"Although I do not care which form he is in, my opinion of him the same, it will be easier if he is human."

"Ah yes, very true. His skin will be soft for the blade. Once again you show me you are wise. I am sure you also do not wish to bed something as repulsive as this beast." He gave a chuckle with humour crinkling his eyes deeply. "I have always admired them for their power and strength, but it is hard to look past how ugly they are."

My kind is magnificent, you unseeing fool!

Strolguil turned to him.

"Contemplate the last hours of your life, WitchSlayer. You are to be a part of something bigger than yourself."

I will spend my time on plotting my escape, Vast. He tried to curl his lips over his fangs, barely able to do so because of the rope around his muzzle. *And when I am free, I will pull you both limb from limb,* he vowed.

They turned from him and left him in the darkness of the dungeon, seething and visibly shaking with fury.

She has betrayed me, has twisted me with trickery. Now he understood why she tried to convince him that she was pure. He understood why she had tried to convince him that she didn't utter lies.

It was because underneath what she was saying and doing, there was nothing but untruths.

She played soft and broken to make me believe she needed protecting, rather than killing. And he was disgusted in himself that he'd tried to comfort her through her tears.

She used her beauty to make me want her so that she could take my child. He was thankful that he placed the spell on her that prevented her from doing so – and never told her.

She had never desired him, she had desired power.

He didn't know how long he'd been there, waiting. However, it wasn't Strolguil or Amalia who entered hours later, but the three Witches he hadn't managed to kill in Mahesh's lair.

They didn't say anything as they strolled into the dungeon, but one of the two females hummed a jolly tune absentmindedly. Then they paused in a triangle around him, and he felt the pulse of magic against his scales when they began to chant in unison.

Rurik's eyes widened when he started growing smaller against his will and his body changed.

The shackles around his neck, paws, and tail became loose. His face morphed unnaturally, almost painfully, while his wings pulled inside him.

How is this possible? They were forcing him to shift from Dragon to human. He'd never heard of such a thing being done!

But this is my chance. Once the change was complete, the shackle no longer holding him in place, he ran forward to tackle the only male Witch in the dungeon.

He brought his fist down across his face and then leapt back before one of the women could grab him. His body was still hexed. He couldn't unleash fire, and when he tried to use magic, he was unable to do so.

I will not run. No, he would kill these people. He would kill them, find Amalia and strangle her neck with his feeble human hands. Then he would sneak up on Strolguil and stab him with the very blade he'd threatened him with earlier. *I will take their hearts instead of them taking mine.*

He lunged for the woman closest to him, knocking her against the wall and making her fall against it. She looked dazed from the impact, and he turned to the other one while the man was still trying to get to his feet.

They came to him as a group knowing he would be too small for the shackles. *They underestimate me.*

With a large, meaty fist, he punched the woman he was heading towards in the stomach before he cracked his other one across her cheek.

In his peripheral vision, he saw the man get to his feet, and Rurik tackled him to the ground so he could put hands around his throat. While he was squeezing it, he tried to slap Rurik's hands away.

Uck! Something long and thin wrapped around his own throat. With one hand still wrapped around the neck of his prey, he scratched at the coil around his neck until it tugged, forcing him to let go of the man he was on top of.

When he fell back, he saw that the woman he'd knocked against the wall had already recovered and was using a whip against him. She dragged him along the ground while he worked on unwinding it from his throat.

A moment later, a boot connected to his head. The other female was kicking him to knock him unconscious. Ignoring the whip, he grabbed her foot and twisted. She fell to the ground on her front.

She screamed when he rolled over and bit into the back of her calf hard enough that blood welled in his mouth.

A handful of different spices mixed with witchcraft was thrown over him.

He thought nothing of it, freeing himself of the whip and then crawled up the woman he'd bitten. With a growl, he grabbed her by the back of the hair and pulled. Then he slammed her head against the ground and heard a loud, but distinct, *crack*. She went limp.

He rose to his feet in preparation to fight the other two. His head and face were covered in yellow and red spices, and it stung his eyes and nostrils to the point they both watered.

The moment he was steady, he suddenly wasn't. He stumbled back a step. His sight quickly fogged and he shook his head to rid himself of it, which only made him dizzier.

What did they do? They didn't approach him, didn't move. It seemed they were waiting. Whatever they threw at him was working fast.

Stepping forward, he went for the man again, but his knee crumbled under him. *They got me.* They managed to subdue him.

He hoped he managed to at least kill the female still laying on the ground. If he managed to escape from this place with her head as a trophy, she would be his hundredth proven kill.

He tried to get back to his feet, shaking on raised arms, but they also gave out. His head hit the ground right before his mind went black.

Rurik woke lying down on his back facing a grand ceiling. The room was tall with high ceilings that had embossed floral like designs in it. Dust and spiderwebs covered an unlit chandelier dangling directly above him, and he noted candles were precariously missing from it.

He tried to lunge forward to sit or stand but he was pulled back by shackles around his human hands and feet. He'd been cleaned at some point.

He looked around to get a gauge for where he was.

I lay on a stone altar.

Around it, symbols had been carved into the stone floor in a circle. There was an outer ring drawn around those symbols and then an inner ring. Candles had been laid out and were lit, giving the room light as they melted against the broken and dirt-covered stone floor.

His eyes darted to the stone walls of this otherwise empty room, and then to the windows that told him it was night. They widened.

It is beginning.

The outside world was dark, no glow from the moon to give it light like how it often did.

He struggled against the shackles, determined to be rid of

them as the chains clinked together. He couldn't break them with the hexes on his body. *They have taken my strength.* They were prepared and made sure he couldn't fight.

The sound of a door opening in the direction of his head caught his attention, and he arched so he could tilt it back to see. It was the female coven Witch he hadn't managed to crack the skull of. She was glaring at him.

"Release me!" he shouted, knowing it was pointless, but he wanted to yell at her regardless.

"You will give Strolguil what he wants," she answered as the male Witch entered behind her.

"I must be hard for him to get what he wants, and I will not do so for that vile Witch!"

A cruel smirk lifted one side of her lips. It was only then that he noticed she was holding a shallow bowl in her hands.

"That was to be expected."

They both came to him, and the man grabbed his face with a tight grip. He forced his mouth open by prying his teeth apart, but he was careful. He knew Rurik would bite his fingers off if he placed them inside his mouth.

Once his lips were parted, she poured the liquid contents of the bowl into his mouth. With his teeth pried apart, he was unable to spit it out, but he did try to use his tongue to do so.

"Swallow it, Dragon. I will not release you until you do."

Rurik calmed and laid there to let the liquid sit in the back of his throat. He didn't have to drink it if he didn't want to. They couldn't force him to take it willingly.

When too much time passed, the woman flattened her hand and smacked him in the throat with the side of it. The impact made the liquid lift in his mouth. He clenched in reaction before he mistakenly took it down.

Blasted! He ingested it.

"Where is the other one of your coven?" He grinned with a sneer since he couldn't see her.

"You know you killed her," the female bit out. "You are lucky we are not allowed to harm you. Only Strolguil's woman can while you are living."

His lips curled back in distaste at her words.

Then his head suddenly shot forward. *No.* He felt it before he saw it, but he knew without a doubt that he was hardening when he felt the tingle in his groin. *Fuck!*

"Good. We will tell Strolguil that you are ready."

They left, and he once again struggled against his bonds but with far more desperation. But he knew. He knew he was unable to escape, that he was unable to do anything.

They will take from me what they want.

The two coven Witches returned a few minutes later before Strolguil entered with the vile Witch in tow.

She was wrapped in a black, silky cloak with the hood back to reveal her blonde hair. That sweet, innocent face still seemed to radiate with its lies to hide inner ugliness.

"The moon is almost at its peak, we must start this before the tea wears off," Strolguil said while leading Amalia to his feet.

He bared his clenched teeth in disgust when she looked at his body. She didn't react to him being forced down like this.

She lifted her hands to undo the ties around her neck. The moment they were undone, the silk black cloak rolled off her shoulders to reveal a bare and unclothed body.

His hands clenched, wanting away from her.

Yet, he didn't struggle when she climbed onto the altar near his feet, didn't try to get her off him. He knew there was no point. Instead, he held in his anger, waited until she was seated across his hips and against his legs.

She was straddling him, one of her hands resting between her breasts like she was pretending to be bashful. His eyes fell onto the three other people in the room with them, not buying her shyness when he could tell she didn't intend to back away

She lifted the blade higher, her knees rising to give her extra strength for when she came back down. She was sliding up his shaft. The higher she went, the more her hair pushed back.

He growled menacingly when she finally held his gaze.

She had eyes of determination and will power. Eyes that screamed they wouldn't stray from their path, wouldn't back down no matter what they faced. She was going to plunge the blade, her resolve was set on doing this.

He flinched when it came down, his body tensing at the impact.

Amalia knew when she climbed onto the Dragon's body that she wouldn't stray. She was determined for power, wanted it, *needed* it. She knew she was going to take his seed and plunge her blade. Nothing was going to stop her.

Strolguil had taken her to this main room sitting at the end of the hall not long after he'd taken her to the dungeon to taunt the Dragon. He'd pointed to the ground, to the symbols, and explained why they had been prepared. When she stabbed him in the chest and took his heart, they would use those symbols to force his body back to its scaly state while he was fresh of death so they could extract him.

After that, she'd been taken care of by one of the female coven Witches who helped to prepare her, had fed and then bathed her. She gave Amalia teas to increase her fertility. She was a grovelling woman who wanted to appease and pamper Strolguil's chosen woman.

At multiple times throughout the afternoon, Amalia could have run, could have escaped. She didn't want to. She wanted to stay here and was set on the path she was taking.

Then night fell. She'd been told to undress and to wear a black cloak to make things easier, quicker. She made no complaint, her shy self gone after everything she'd learned...

everything she knew she was about to do to the Dragon.

Amalia didn't hesitate to climb onto that altar to be with him, regardless that she was being viewed. She no longer cared.

The mention of burning did make her memories of the stake plague her, but it wasn't enough to get her to back down. The Dragon could say what he wanted, but she wouldn't falter.

And once she had ridden him and held that dagger, she pointed the tip of the blade hanging in the air towards his chest. She kept her eyes focused on him, her mind refusing to stray from her target.

Her hands didn't shake, her arms didn't feel weak.

Then she brought her hands down with all of her strength and she watched him flinch, watched him tense. She watched his eyes widen when that blade cut through flesh and muscle.

But it had not been sunk into him. Amalia had sunk that blade into herself.

Her back bowed upon impact and crumbled around the blade. She reefed it forward and dropped it onto the Dragon's chest with shaking hands. It made a metal clunking sound as it fell to the stone altar and then bounced to the ground.

She looked down at her aching stomach. Blood ran over her fingers when she touched the wound with trembling hands. Her heart was racing, her breathing shallow and short.

"What have you done?!" Strolguil yelled, taking a step forward.

Snapping out of her shock, Amalia raised her blood-covered hands and immediately began to chant.

She'd seen the symbols on the ground and knew she could use them to her advantage. She had known what she needed to do when she saw this room, this altar, those gouged marks.

A gust of wind circled around her between the inner and outer rings around those symbols. It pushed all those who were outside away when they tried to enter.

Blue flickers of lightning sparked throughout the wind, picking up dust and dirt, and it grew stronger by the second. They also made certain symbols on the ground flicker to life with blue fire as she called out.

Her head was tilted up as she desperately tried to remember the words she needed. She shouted the chant, pouring all her strength, all her will, all of the magic she possessed inside her into the spell.

Blood was running down her wrists. She felt pain, but she refused to stop. She didn't stop screaming those words, didn't end her chant until that gust of wind broke into fire and blasted outwards.

It slammed everyone on the outside against the walls.

For a single moment, they were down, the force of the impact making them immobile.

She didn't look at Rurik's face when the spell dissipated. Instead, she looked to where she placed her hands on his stomach, where the puddle of her own warm blood had begun to pool on his abdomen, and pushed herself off him.

Amalia then bolted for the door while cupping her wound with her hands.

Before she made it, she could see that Strolguil was already starting to rise. The coven Witches were still unmoving when she yanked open the door to run through it before veering to the left.

She didn't make it far before she was tackled around the waist, and both of them fell against the floor.

"What have you done?!" Strolguil yelled, grabbing her around the throat with one hand and fisting her hair with the other.

Amalia flailed underneath him, pressing her hands against him. She smeared blood across his face when his grip tightened.

"Get off me!"

The emotion that had shifted inside of Amalia's heart when he kissed her, had been pure and unbridled hatred.

Seeing her memories, seeing the fear everyone around her had for this man made her realise that he was terrible, was evil. If even Dark Witches feared him, thought the actions he took were too far, then he was an abomination.

If her mother had feared for her safety at the hands of him, had hidden her in hopes he would never find her, then she would trust in her parents' actions.

They did what they needed to in order to protect me.

He tricked her, had tried to force her to do something she didn't want to. Amalia knew he wouldn't have taken no for an answer.

And, since the moment the disgust and loathing had settled into her, she'd been trying to discover a way out. She played along with his plans, had returned every saliva-filled kiss he'd given her. She had hidden her fear and worry just to get to that altar.

"You will have that Dragon's child, and you will give it to me!"

"No!"

She pushed her hands harder against his face, and her fingers started to curl into his skin as her nails bit in.

He gave a bellowing roar of pain when steam came where she was touching him.

He jumped back to his feet while covering his face with his hands. When he pulled them away to look at her, she saw his skin had melted like he'd been touched with acid. One cheek had a palm print of melted flesh. Her other hand had been over his eye, and she'd melted that away, blinding him in on one side.

Amalia scrambled to her feet while he was distracted, and her movements caught his attention again.

When he ran forward, she turned her head to the side and threw her hands up in fear, only to hear a loud thud. When she turned her head back, she saw he'd been knocked back.

She realised she had shielded herself with a barrier.

She brought her bloodied and trembling hands in front of her face to gaze at them with uncertainty. *I am casting without chanting.*

Strolguil got to his feet with a teeth-baring glare of rage present on his face. It twisted his expression and made him appear undeniably *demented.*

"I will heal you of this wound and then you will ride that Dragon again." He reached into his pocket. "You will steal his heart, and you *will* be mine!"

He threw something small at the shield, and it shattered like it was nothing but glass. Then he was chasing her again before he tackled her once more to the ground. He struck her across the face with his fist, intending to make her go limp, but it only made her fight harder.

Both their heads shot towards the sound that came from the main room they were next to in this hallway. It was a roar – a loud, deafening, large, lung-filled roar.

"You freed him?!" She could tell that Strolguil was growing more furious by the second, to the point he was beginning to shake with it.

While his head was turned, Amalia kicked him off of her and sent him flying to his back. She scrambled back to her feet and took an unsteady step back when he started to kneel. Just as he was about to lunge for her again, another roar sounded before it was followed by a thud against the wall.

Strolguil paused to decide.

"You may run," he said with a spiteful sneer. "But you will not get far. I will contain your Dragon while you uselessly flee and then I will force you to take what I want from him."

When he turned his back to her, Amalia ran the other way.

Now that she was alone, trying to run up the spiralling staircase, she realised each leg lift ached her stomach. She stopped running when it felt like it was too much to bear and gave a sobbing cry as her fingertips found her wound to feel it. She wished she hadn't.

Trying to stop the bleeding that hadn't slowed, she used her free hand to press against the wall to help lift her up, to help her keep going. She smeared her blood along her path.

It was dark in the stairwell with no torches lit and no sun shining to brighten it.

When she made it to the top of the tower, she fumbled to find the doorknob. Her wound protested when she twisted the knob with her slippery hand, like her strength came from the muscles in her stomach.

She stumbled and placed a hand against the ward before she slipped to her knees, her body drained and weak. Blood had run down and between her legs while she ran. Now it dripped to the ground while she knelt there holding her aching stomach.

"Please..." she begged to her father. She didn't know who else to turn to. "Please help me."

Rurik watched the blade come down, but the path wasn't straight, the direction had been curved. His eyes widened in unmasked shock when he realised the Witch had sunk the blade into herself. He followed it when she yanked it away and shakily dropped it against his stomach before it fell to the altar and then the ground.

What is she doing? He expected death, not to witness her inflict a wound upon herself. *What game is she playing?* Was this some strange part of the ritual?

"What have you done?!" Strolguil yelled, taking a step forward, and Rurik's head shot to him in confusion.

Amalia raised her blood-covered hands in reaction and immediately began to chant. It caused his widened sight to return to her.

His eyes fell onto the wound low on her stomach and the blood he could see was already beginning to drip onto his torso. Then he looked up to her raised face.

She was shouting with her eyes clenched shut in concentration, her brows knitted tightly.

I know this chant. He'd heard her speak it before.

He felt something pulling from him, yanking out of his body, and he turned his head to his chest. Symbols were lighting up, glowing on his skin before they appeared to be lifting away.

They were being pulled from him, like tape, before they withered away like hot ash.

She is unhexing me. And she wasn't just removing one, but they were all coming away.

This required an unspeakable amount of power, required skill and experience to remove this many hexes in one go. The spell she was using generally needed to be repeated, taking them away one or two at a time.

He understood where she'd gotten this power from when he heard the crackling of electricity and saw the blue dragoncraft lightning moving through the gusts of winds surrounding them.

She has combined the use of her blood with the magic she stole from me when I came inside her. She had increased the strength of her magical capabilities to make sure she had enough of it to do this.

Why is she removing my hexes? Does she not know that this will free me? Then he would be able to take his anger out on her, would be able to capture and kill her. He had threatened her with fire, she should be afraid to release him.

He was too dumbfounded to move when the blast of energy exploded outwards from her spell. He knew everyone else was unconscious for the moment.

Rurik thought she would say something to him, explain what the hell she was doing, but she wouldn't look at him. She'd just gotten herself off his body and fled from the room.

His head followed her, seeing Strolguil leave to give chase, before he looked at his body. At the seed and blood and evidence that he truly hadn't imagined what he'd just witnessed.

Then his eyes narrowed as his brows drew together.

He shot forward to sit, breaking the shackles with ease since the hex restraining his strength was gone. He also removed the cloth around his mouth by tugging it down.

Rurik used the pad of his thumb to rub it over the side of his still semi-hard shaft, staring at it in surprise.

She cut her womb. There was no other way to explain the blood on him there. *Did she make sure my seed would not take or did she hit herself there on accident?*

I do not understand. He didn't get any more time to think.

The coven Witches began to stir.

Springing into action, he bent forward and ripped the shackles around his ankles free and spun off the altar. He blew a ring of fire above his head.

"Shift!" The flames came back to encase him.

By the time the Witches were on their feet, he was standing before them on his paws.

He stepped forward and unleashed flames towards the woman from his breath. She had just enough time to throw three dragonscales in the air to add to a shield to protect herself.

He continued to breathe fire, knowing that the shield

would eventually falter, and only paused to take a quick breath through his slitted nostrils.

To the side he could see the man running towards him with a clean sword. *I have seen him use a sword before, his magic is not strong.* He kicked sideways just as he slashed. They would not poison him if they wanted to keep him alive.

Rurik sent him flying across the room, but not before he managed to slice off the toe next to his pinkie. A loud, pain-filled roar escaped Rurik as blood gushed from his missing toe.

He charged forward while he blew his flames, startling the female who gasped, right before his head made impact with the wall. She was between them, and his strength broke that shield.

He impaled her with three spikes jutting around his head.

The man threw something towards him when he stepped back to shake her corpse from his head. When she was flung away, Rurik released more flames, burning away those spices from the air so they couldn't affect him.

He reached into his pocket, crushed a glass vial in his hand, and spread the blood it contained over his palm.

Rurik spun around to knock him with his tail since it would reach further, but he was blasted in the side. He hit the ground and was sent sliding. Breathing fire to distract him, he rushed to his paws so he could do so without being attacked.

Rurik followed his fire, his scaly head coming through it and startling the male. He slashed his sword forward, cutting against his chest deep enough to make him bleed.

Another roar fell from him, and he swiped his hand to the side, making the male go flying against the wall. He crumbled, the impact hard and heavy.

Rurik didn't give him time to rise. He followed after him and grabbed him in his paw to lift him. He bit around his head before he could even open his eyes to scream.

If there had been any more for him to fight, he would have struggled. If he hadn't picked them off at Mahesh's lair and then killed that other woman when they had forced him to be human, then Rurik wouldn't have succeeded so easily.

He was used to fighting one or two Witches. There was only one who had ever caused him to flee by themselves.

I must find Strolguil. He needed to kill him, needed to rid the world of his villainous life, the heart of the plague of Dark Witches.

Being so large, that would be near impossible to do. He would have to tear this building down first.

Not willing to turn himself human, he was just about to shrink his size when the exit door opened, and someone confidently sauntered inside the room. His lips curled back over his fangs as his wings tensed behind him. Even his scales puffed in aggression.

With a snarl, he turned to face him with deep-seated loathing. "Strolguil..."

Amalia bashed on the ward with one fist to get it to open. She'd smeared her blood across it, she even tried to add to it, but she couldn't lower it.

"Why?" she sobbed. *Why will it not come down?*

She wanted to leave this place, wanted to flee before the Dragon came to burn her, or the Witch came to corrupt her.

Her legs were trembling, her stomach ached. She knew she wouldn't be able to walk on her own anymore since she had used the last of her strength to come here.

Terrified, she dug her nails into it. She didn't know how to take this kind of magic away consciously.

"The ward in place is powerful, Amalia," her father said while creeping forward slowly. "I can help you lower it, repeat these words."

Amalia nodded, waiting for him to tell her what to do with tears dripping heavily down her cheeks.

"Ra. Cu. Til. Flou. Sei."

With a shaky voice, she repeated them with him while her hands remained against the barrier keeping them apart. From where her hands were placed, holes started forming. They spread away to create openings.

When it was gone, she fell forward and crawled to him.

He did the same.

He opened his arms to hug her, but the shackles between his hands wouldn't allow him to. Reaching out, she grabbed the centre of those chains in hopes that what she had done to Strolguil's face would happen again.

Fortunately, the links melted away, and she collapsed weakly into his arms.

"Please." She couldn't do this on her own anymore.

"I will help you leave this place," he answered, pulling her in tighter before he worked to get them both standing.

Then he removed his white, dirt-stained tunic and put it over her to cover her body. She'd forgotten she'd been running through the small castle naked.

She hadn't cared when all she wanted was to escape.

He put her arm around his neck while he snaked his own around her waist to keep her up. He held her wrist to securely keep her arm over his shoulders.

Amalia held her wound with her free hand, trying to stop the bleeding as best as she could. She was lethargic as he carefully walked her down the stairs.

"What happened?"

Shaking her head, she knew she couldn't answer. She didn't have enough energy left in her to speak and move at the same time. Instead, she hissed between each painful footfall.

They almost made it to the bottom. They were just walking next the lowest window to look down the hallway when the wall to the main room crumbled.

The Dragon had been thrown through it, causing part of the mansion castle to collapse on top of him.

"We cannot go that way," he told her.

It would put them in the direct path of the two people she was desperate to flee. There was too much chaos, and they would likely be swept up in it. Amalia also wouldn't put it past either of them to use her as leverage against the other.

Her eyes looked to the corner of her lids, and she saw his head moving around to find another way out.

"We will have to go through the window." The idea of crashing through glass wasn't comforting. Still, she nodded. "I will try to protect you."

He picked her up by squishing her flush against his chest and then he threw them against it. The glass shattered, the window tall and fragile.

She felt the heave of her body as they fell and the sudden nauseous pit in her stomach, like it was flipping.

They hit the ground with a disturbing thud, but her father kept his promise and protected her from the worst of the small fall. He took the impact on his back with her above him while cupping her head, so she didn't hit it.

He even shielded her eyes from the fractures of glass.

With her arm over his shoulder once more, he tried to get them to go at a fast and steady pace through the tall, itchy grass that surrounded the mansion. She couldn't keep up, her father often needing to lift her forward.

I ache.

"I cannot see," he muttered.

She'd thought the screaming darkness was just because she was dizzy.

Her father pressed his fingers against her wound. He drew two lines down her face as well as his own with her blood, from their foreheads to down over their eyes. He spoke a soft chant and everything got brighter.

She could see the tall grass they were walking through, could see that they were heading towards trees. He used her blood to better their sight.

As much as she didn't like the use of the magic and that he took from her without asking, she was relieved. It made fleeing feel less unsettling.

They made it to the forest and wind rushed as they passed

tree after tree. Her unsteady feet often got caught on the large roots and made her trip. She felt bad that her father had to keep saving her from falling, and that she was most likely tiring him out.

She didn't know where he was taking her to, and she doubted he didn't either.

Shivers crawled up her spine, and it wasn't because the air was cold. It felt as though they were coming from inside, sapping more and more energy from her each time.

Amalia also stopped being afraid.

The further they walked, the more those trembles crept along her entire being and the pain lessened. Her legs began to give out. He halted when he realised he was beginning to drag her.

"We cannot stop now. We are still too close."

"I cannot anymore," she said, her voice only reaching the loudness of a whisper.

I have bled too much.

She hadn't thought that she would be overcome this quickly when she decided to stab herself. She'd been hoping to be able to keep moving forward until she found a way to heal herself. Neither one of them had the herbs required for such a powerful spell.

"I will carry you."

Amalia shook her head side-to-side when she slipped from him and fell to her knees.

"It is okay." She tried to give him a smile when he knelt down next to her. "I do not think I will make it much further. You can leave me here."

She may not have been able to save herself, but at least she gave Rurik and her father a fighting chance to survive.

"Amalia, I would never leave you behind."

He cupped the back of her head when it was too hard to keep herself upright on her knees.

I want to lay down. Her eyes felt weighted, her mind and body lethargic. *I want to sleep.*

Looking up into his dark blue eyes, she could see he cared. They were filled with deep sorrow. They shook as they fell to her stomach where he lifted the tunic to look at her wound before coming back up to greet her own.

That sadness grew stronger, and she knew he understood that she was dying.

"I am not scared," she told him, once again trying to smile reassuringly. "And I am not in pain." Amalia felt numb, both inside and out. "I do not mind dying. This way, the Dragon cannot put me in fire and Strolguil cannot make me do as he wishes."

It didn't matter which one of those two won in their battle. Amalia would suffer, and she didn't want either fate.

In her death, she could truly escape. *I can be free.*

"It is better if I am gone."

If she was no longer in this world, then the prophecy would never come to fruition. No one could seek to use her again.

She could tell he wanted to convince her otherwise, that he wanted to fight her on this. There was no point. She wouldn't make it out of this forest alive, and she would much rather rest to her death than have it fall upon her because she was trying to run.

He seemed to understand that she wanted to go peacefully.

"I will stay with you." He gritted his teeth, trying his hardest to stem tears from forming. "My sweet daughter, how could I let this happen to you?" He gently pressed his forehead against her own, twisting his head side-to-side, like he was nuzzling her. "You did not deserve this."

No longer willing to fight it, Amalia let her eyes close so that she could finally sleep.

The last thing she heard was a loud, monstrous roar that carried over the distance. It was long and deep and would have been bone-chilling if she hadn't already been slipping away.

34

"Strolguil..." Rurik narrowed his eyes upon the man entering the ritual room.

Then they widened in realisation.

He has been blinded. He could see two palm print marks of melted skin, one eye sunken and useless. *Feminine* palm print marks. *Did Amalia injure him? Why would she do this?*

Rurik was beginning to think that not everything was as it appeared to be. The question was, what was truth and what were lies? He no longer knew how to feel. His trust had been broken, and Rurik didn't trust easily.

I must not think of such things right now. He needed to focus on the villain in front of him.

The exit was now blocked, not that he would have been able to fit his size through the door. He took a few steps back to give them space.

I cannot fight how I usually do. This was no coven Witch, and Rurik had already been defeated by him many times before. It was only in the past two decades that he'd been hunting this man.

It had never gone in his favour.

Strolguil had too many totems of his kind dangling under his clothing. He could see the wings hanging around his neck, could see the of bracelets of claws. He knew he must have tiny Dragon bones under his breast plate and chainmail skirt because he'd never been able to crush him.

Rurik knew unless he could get close enough to him with enough time to strike, he would be at a disadvantage in fighting him. Yet, getting close to Strolguil for a fatal attack always seemed like an impossible task.

He also had to be careful that a hex wasn't placed against him when he got close.

He has killed many of my kind, has drunk our blood to steal our essence for centuries. He'd grown so powerful that he often didn't need to chant, at least not out loud.

Fighting by fang and claw wasn't possible. Rurik knew he would have to fight magic with magic. He'd learned many spells and chants in his life, and although he didn't use them regularly, he would have to utilise what he knew.

No words were spoken between them.

There was no need.

Rurik knew what he wanted from him, and the Witch knew he wanted him dead.

Something small was thrown at him – a tiny fragment of bone Rurik had often seen him throw.

He brought his wing forward, forcing magic from his body into it to re-enforce it. A shield formed. When the bone hit it, he was knocked back a step, but at least it hadn't been as devastating as last time.

The difference between dragoncraft and witchcraft was that Dragon magic was more natural. It was easier to harness and execute.

Rurik wouldn't need to think long chants, but rather one or two words and would only need to focus on imagining what he wanted, rather than how to obtain it. The only time he needed to use phrases were for when the spell required higher and long-lasting amounts of power, such as his wards and removing hexes.

Vulnus. He lowered his wing and slashed the claws of his right hand through the air. Three blade-like slivers of air rushed towards Strolguil who dove to the side to narrowly miss them.

Rurik followed him around the room to stay the same distance apart and waited for an opening where he could charge forward. He wouldn't be able to kill with his magic, only incapacitate.

No, he would have to do that with his claw or fangs.

Releasing fire from deep within his belly, Strolguil cast a shield with dragonscales to protect himself from the flames. While it was up, Rurik stalked to the side to make them walk in a circle.

A pouch of material was thrown towards Rurik when he took a breath, and he blew more fire, planning on blowing whatever it was to smithereens. He regretted doing so when it exploded, his fire fuelling it and sending him flying back.

He crashed through the wall. It crumbled to pieces as he went through the hallway and into the wall of a smaller room. The second floor toppled on top of him when the inner walls of the room caved in.

Just as he was digging his way out of it, he heard the shattering of a window.

He didn't have the time to even look in its direction because the moment he pushed a slab of rock off himself, Strolguil was in front of him.

Rurik's lips curled back in a feral growl as he was slashed across the snout by ghostly looking claws. It was a projection of magic from the Dragon claws he'd stolen.

Rurik snapped his head forward to bite around him since he was so close, but Strolguil jumped back to evade his attack.

He brought a wing forward when Strolguil threw another one of those tiny bones at him and blew fire underneath it when the shield formed. He felt the impact of the bone, but the rocky foundation of the building that had toppled around him kept him in place.

With a roar, he leapt forward and unleashed more fire to keep him at bay, despite knowing it would never reach him. He just wanted time to get out from the foundations so he could slash his paw sideways.

Impetus. A gust of force came from the side.

Not expecting an attack to come from beside him, Strolguil was thrown sideways. Laying on his side, the Witch threw three small crystals into the air while concentrating heavily.

He is chanting.

What had been a random toss became targeted, and although they did not hold the same devastating impact as the bone, they hit hard into his body. It felt like the power of multiple punches against him.

I am too big of a target. He only managed to avoid being hit because of his shields. He also could not manoeuvre well with his large body tucked inside this small building.

Rurik spoke the lengthy chant in his mind while he used his wings to shield himself of anything Strolguil could throw at him. He felt impacts as he chanted, heard the shatter of a glass vial that slid off the shield and onto the ground. It began to bubble like acid on the stone at his feet.

When he finally drew his wings back, he had changed his size to that of the man in front of him.

Scuttering, he moved with swift and unimaginable speed on his small paws, now able to move anywhere in this building a human could with ease. If his wings caught on something, like a corner or a doorframe, they were flexible enough to withstand it.

"You are changing how you fight, WitchSlayer," Strolguil said when Rurik ducked around the corridor of the building to avoid being hit with one of the glass vials.

The liquid once again melted into the ground.

His eyes flicked to the main room just across from him. He needed to get back in there where he could see him and move.

"I learn from each of our battles." And he had. He became a much better fighter because of his defeats.

The only time Rurik never lost himself to his anger was when he was in the middle of a fight. He had trained himself to keep his emotions guarded in the heat of battle. The rest of the time he was a volatile, unpredictable bomb about to go off at any moment. He needed to remain focused since he could be angry in the afterlife all he wanted.

"It will not be enough to save you from me. You are only lucky I do not wish to kill you, that I am holding back." His voice was coming closer.

If he joined him in the corridor, he would be cornered.

Diving for the hole his body had created, he rolled into the main room. He uncurled himself to slide over his four paws to face the large hole in the wall.

As soon as Strolguil joined him, Rurik slashed the claws of one hand forward. *Vulnus.* Those blades of invisible energy slashed towards him through the air, and he followed it with a breath of fire, refusing to give him a moment to recover.

The dragonscale shield he created shattered on impact, and he had to quickly make another one for his fire.

What he didn't know was that Rurik had released another slash of air right behind his flames. When he lowered his shield to retaliate, he was cut across his torso and sent flying back.

Being evasive with long range attacks would do him little good. They were merely playing a game of duck and cover.

Rurik needed to think of a way to bring him down.

He is blinded on the left side. I must take a risk. He needed to seize his chance while Strolguil was distracted and on his back.

He sprinted forward quickly, his four legs giving him more speed in comparison to Strolguil's two human legs. When he got to his feet, Rurik was on his injured side and out of sight.

Startled, Strolguil turned his head, shocked when he hadn't been able to see Rurik in front of him. He didn't know he was so close and he stepped back just as Rurik slashed his real claws.

Thinking his slash was intended to be a death blow, he covered his throat and it gave Rurik the opportunity to slash across his face. His claws had been precise. He managed to cut into his other eye, rendering him utterly blind.

Without Amalia blinding him on one side, Rurik would never have had the opportunity to get this close to him safely. He tried not to think of that since he still didn't know why she'd done it.

The man was yelling, his hands tense as he tried to handle the pain. This was his opportunity!

Scuttling forward, he leapt for him with his claws poised to end this. He landed on top of a bubble shield and was unable to penetrate it. Strolguil had protected himself completely while he was trying to deal with being blinded.

Then, with his injured eyes clenched shut, he crossed his arms before throwing them open. The shield exploded with fire, sending Rurik hurtling across the room.

"You think because I am blinded that I cannot see?" he shouted, his face turned in his direction, but not fully. "I am done with this! You will falter!" He pulled a vial from his pocket, and Rurik readied himself to shield his body. "You will give me what I want!"

Strolguil drank the large vial of red liquid and threw the empty container against the ground to shatter.

It filled his nostrils with the scent of Dragon blood before Strolguil lifted his hands to the ceiling and began chanting out loud. Dark grey clouds formed against the ceiling, starting from above the Witch before growing in size.

His eyes widened. He couldn't fight against a storm!

He unleashed fire and Strolguil threw one hand forward. Red lightning crackled towards the ground, blocking his attack. It sparked towards the walls, trying to reach out while it cracked the stone floor with its force.

It remained until he stopped breathing flames.

Lowering both his hands, the storm he'd created in the room remained, and would continue to do so until Strolguil removed it or died.

Rurik had already dealt with this magic firsthand, and his wings had been broken because of it. He warily eyed the storm above, knowing he had to be careful not to be struck.

Strolguil turned his head to the side with his ear facing forward.

Vulnus. He released that slashing claw force, and Strolguil shielded himself.

He saw the attack?! It had been silent!

Rurik took in a breath for fire, and Strolguil's head and hand shot towards him. Red lightning struck towards him, and he rolled away to dodge.

The booming of thunder loudly echoed in the room.

How is he seeing me? Rurik had thought with his eyes gone that he wouldn't be able to strike with accuracy, but that lightning strike had been heading right for him!

Strolguil had his head turned to the side once more.

Rurik walked to the side, his claws clinking against the ground. Strolguil's hand shot to him, and lightning struck down where he was standing.

Rurik rolled away to doge it.

How? He had barely done anything but move a few steps!

The Witch didn't move, his head turned as if he was listening. Rurik waited to dodge an attack while he thought. Then he stilled completely when Strolguil didn't try to strike him where he stood. *He does not know where I am.*

He was listening to the sounds he made. His sharp inhale for breath when he planned to release fire, his paws and claws tapping against the ground.

If I move, he will hear me. That was how he was sensing his location.

Quietly, he lifted his paw and swiped it through the air sideways. *Impetus.* A gust of force formed to the side and headed straight for Strolguil. He wouldn't know it was there.

He threw his hands out in two different directions. One to shield himself from the force, the other was to try to hit Rurik with red lightning coming from above.

Rurik took the impact to his body because he hadn't been ready for it and gave out a roar. He heard something break, a rib possibly. Pain shot through him, and his eyes clenched shut against the blast.

How did he see me?!

He released fire to combat it, and Strolguil had to stop the lightning to protect himself.

The attack had been silent!

He rolled out of the way when another strike of lightning came towards him as the loud booming of thunder echoed against the walls. They were constant and deafening to his sensitive ears.

When he settled, he didn't move, didn't attack, and once more the Witch was listening. *He can hear my movements.* But how had he known the force was coming from the side and where it came from? *He is blinded, so how is this possible?*

Then his eyes widened. *He is sensing the magic!*

If Rurik didn't cast magic or breathe fire, Strolguil wouldn't be able to see where the dragoncraft was coming from. He was using a spell similar to the one Rurik used to change sight and see the tendrils of magic in the air.

I must make my attack silent, and it must be done without magic. With a fanged grin forming, he knew exactly how to do this.

Rurik began to scuttle across the room with quick steps, making sure that they were heavy and loud. Lightning struck to follow his path, Strolguil's hand following him wherever he went, but he was moving around the room too erratically.

Flapping his wings, he then sprinted towards the wall and started climbing it. His claws dug around the stone blocks as he used his wings to make himself lighter. He climbed up the side of it with speed, then he jumped to the wall next to the one he was on when he reached the ceiling.

Strolguil's hand only followed him when he landed, his claws creating a distinct crunch when they dug into the stone-brick wall.

Just before lightning struck, he leapt for the chandelier in the centre of the ceiling. The crystals hanging from it chimed from the impact, and it groaned from his weight. It swung, but he didn't stay on it long.

He used it to get himself to the other side of the room just before lightning struck it from all sides.

This time, he didn't cling to the wall, instead he bounced on it. Rurik tucked his wings against his body as his eyes narrowed on his target, with claws at the ready. His path was silent as he sailed through the air with his arms reaching out in front of him.

He didn't growl. He didn't make a noise as he descended... right into Strolguil who couldn't hear or see him coming.

Claws clutched around the Vast's arms and a sharp gasp of surprise left him when he was grabbed.

"No!"

Rolling with him, Rurik shot his head forward with his fangs bared before digging them into his shoulder and ripping it apart. Ghostly claws tried to strike back, slashing down his sides, but Rurik snapped his head forward again to bite into his chest.

He ripped bits of skin and muscle away, using his sharp and long teeth to eat into the man, as he twisted his head side-to-side in jarring movements to make it more damaging. He firmly held onto Strolguil while he yelled.

Ghostly fangs bit into Rurik's shoulder, but it was too late for the Witch. Rurik finally got the squirming opening he'd needed with his throat forward and exposed. He bit into his neck to pull his jugular from him.

It was enough to weaken him and prevent him from using his magic. Rurik bit into his throat again, this time pulling his windpipe from him and causing blood to splatter. He spat it out when he jumped back so he could free himself from Strolguil's hands.

Rurik refused to hesitate, to draw this out. He once had some grand fantastic speech prepared for when he finally managed to get to him like this, but it would be foolish to do so now that it was happening.

He jumped forward to place his paw against his face. Digging one set of claws under his jaw, he dug his other paw around his shoulder.

With a bellowing roar, Rurik pulled his arms apart to tear Strolguil the Vast's head from his body.

Just when he was done, a giant blast of force came from his headless corpse. It was a violent release of energy the Witch had been collecting and holding inside his body for eons.

Rurik was flung through the air. His body hurtled until he crashed into the other side of the room with enough force he broke through the wall. He found himself in the dark of night, and he slid over grass as stone blocks flung and fell around him.

Getting to his four paws, he could see Strolguil wasn't

going to rise. Rurik gave another roar, but this time it was triumphant. It was long and deep, the power of it so strong that he unintentionally released flames along with it. It was so powerful that his body tightened against it and forced him to his hindlegs as he released it.

Rurik let out his anger, his frustration, the hatred he'd held for so long for the life he finally destroyed.

Strolguil the Vast is no more!

He did it. He finally killed the most heinous villain to his kind. One that had pulled them apart by the dozens and had helped others to do so as well.

And it had been him! The WitchSlayer! He was the Dragon who took his life, who had experienced the delicious feeling of his skin tearing and the sucking sound of his head being pulled from his body.

His front paws touched the ground when he'd emptied his lungs on his bellow. A sneezing huff followed before he walked inside, determined to take his trophy, the proof of his kill.

Others of his kind would come far and wide to admire it in his lair. He gave a satisfied growl to himself. He would both love it and hate it. He would love to show it off with pride, but would hate to have his tunnels riddled with others.

He walked to Strolguil's head and rolled it so that it was facing him and then gave his sightless, eyeless face a sneer. *You brought me down on you today when you took me from my lair.*

But someone helped him to do that.

His head shot to the rest of the partially destroyed building. *Where is the Witch?* Where was Amalia?

He couldn't celebrate his victory when he had other matters. A lying, betraying woman... who also saved him?

Grabbing the head with his paw, he knew he wouldn't be able to carry it anywhere other than his stomach. He forced it down his throat since it was just small enough for him to do so at this size – although, it wasn't done comfortably.

Then he crawled his way through the hole in the wall to the hallway while sniffing at the ground and the air for the trail of her blood. He followed it to the left and was just about to climb the spiralling staircase when he stopped at a shattered window.

She stood here for a while.

His eyes walked up the stairs in front of him before they looked outside. He jumped through the window, using his wings to glide before he landed. Knowing he'd gone the right way when he could smell more droplets of her blood, he followed it with determination.

Rurik didn't know what he would do when he found the end of this trail, what he would do when she saw her.

Anger lashed him because she brought them to this place. Betrayal choked him because she lied to him, tricked him. Confusion muddled him because he had no idea what truly happened, why she'd done what she did.

He'd seen her in that dungeon. She'd seemed like she was a willing party to all this. She allowed Strolguil to touch her without any fight, had told him herself of the prophecy like it was well rehearsed.

She'd known what was going on as though she had always known. She didn't even bat an eyelid at the horrific things Strolguil admitted to or what his plans were.

Yet, Rurik felt admiration for what she had done, for stabbing herself to remove his hexes. She gave him the ability to fight for himself. The dragoncraft she'd stolen would have been completely used in that powerful spell. But it meant he also felt grateful because she had freed him rather than escaping by herself.

Because of what she had done, he was finally able to kill his enemy.

What was he supposed to do with these conflicting emotions? One part of him wanted to truly let her burn. The other wanted to make sure that the Witch who had once again given him freedom was okay.

The blood he was following wasn't as heavy.

Is it because she healed herself or because she began to run out of blood?

He ran harder.

In the distance between the trees, Rurik saw a man kneeling with Amalia across his bent legs while he held onto her. They were in a small opening of trees that was barely big enough to fit them.

Sliding against the grass and roots of trees, he came to halt a few metres away.

Who is he? Would he have to fight with another Witch to get to her? He could smell he was of her kind from the mix of it in his body scent.

"Give her to me," he snarled, baring his fangs that dripped with lethality.

The male turned his head up to him, his eyes dark in the night. He was cradling the back of her head with one hand and brushing his thumb over her cheek with the other.

Like he didn't care Rurik was there or the danger he faced, he tilted his head to look down at her face.

"Can you not see she has suffered enough? Let her be in peace."

He cares for her. Great, what was this? Some lover she didn't know about? *First the Vast, and now this?* The man looked older than her, but their life spans often made it confusing to gauge their age.

He stamped a paw forward in warning. He couldn't charge with him holding her the way he was. Rurik may hurt her in the process, and he had many questions for this Witch before he threw her into his prison cell.

"Hand her over," he demanded, lowering his head as if he was preparing to pounce.

"Leave me to grieve over my dying daughter, Dragon."

He brushed his hand over her hair while staring down at her face before he pressed his forehead to hers. He began rocking her like a child.

Rurik's eyes no longer narrowed, and his head reared back.

His daughter? The man was shirtless, making it easy for him to see his hands were bound by shackles. A handful of chain links were still attached to both.

"You are her father?"

He frowned as he eyed the man, unable to tell if it was true.

"Yes, I have been held captive by Strolguil the Vast for nine years."

"She told me her father was a human soldier!" Rurik shouted this at him, but he'd always known that she'd two Witch parents from how much magic her body naturally held.

He was angry because it was just proof of her lies.

The man laughed, his chest vibrating with it while he shook his head. "That would be because I altered her memories."

What? Once again, Rurik's head reared back.

"You altered her memories?"

That was dark magic, no white wielder could do this.

"Yes, I made sure she had no memory of what today was supposed to signify. Her mother and I had hoped this day would pass, and she would be safe. We were hoping if she did not know then he would never find her and force her to do something we knew she was too tame to do."

He brushed his hand up her cheek, over one of her closed

eyes, over her forehead, and then down the side of her temple to her ear.

"She looks so similar to her mother." Then Rurik heard the choke of someone trying to hold back sadness. "It is all my fault. If I had not desired to learn dark magic, the person who foretold the prophecy would not have visited my coven and met her. They would never have seen this day. I got my wife killed and led my own daughter to her death."

Rurik shook his head, unsure of how to process what he just heard. *Her memories were altered... Does that mean she never knew about any of this until now?*

Something more pressing entered his mind.

"Give her to me. I will heal her."

If she was dying, then Rurik needed to act fast.

"Why? So you can torture her for what she has done to you? Bring her back just so she can be put to flame or locked away?" He brought his head up to face Rurik with his teeth gritted into an angry glare.

"If what you say is true and she had no part in this, I do not plan to harm her."

If it is true... Then Rurik would have no reason to be angry with her.

She released me. Removed my hexes so I could fight. These were not the actions of someone who had been plotting against him.

"What-" her father started.

"I do not have time for this! Do you wish your daughter to die or not?"

Rurik was beginning to spiral, and his emotions became more chaotic. With the more he learned, the more he thought, the more he tried to reach for the possibility that she hadn't betrayed him. It meant he was beginning to fear for her, fear for himself that he would not see her live past this day.

"No," he whispered after a long pause.

"Good," Rurik said, before he approached him. Then he pressed his paw against his face and pushed him away from her. "Now get the fuck out of the way."

Once she was lying against the ground, Rurik crawled above her and pressed his scaled head to her chest. Her breaths were shallow and struggled while her heart beat softly, like it would cease any second.

She will not last much longer. Her skin was deathly pale, draining away from the tan he was accustomed to.

With careful claws, he lifted the tunic to check her wound to see it was barely bleeding. *I cannot heal her wound like this. I will have to change it.*

"Why do you care what happens to her? She is the reason you were brought here as a tool by Strolguil."

"Because she has been living in my lair for the past month and a half." He also had other reasons, emotions he didn't wish to face. He backed away from Amalia to give himself space. "I am going to increase my size."

He internally chanted the words he needed, and his body grew in height and width. Trees uprooted to move out of the way as he grew in a space that couldn't accommodate his size.

"Place her in my paw." He extended it out to him.

Her father scooped her into his arms and carefully placed her in it. Then Rurik snatched him with the other, earning him a yell as he lifted off into the sky.

Once he reached a height where he could see far over the land, he flapped his wings in a circle. *Which way is my-* He knew the scene. He had flown over it multiple times and could see his mountain close by.

The flight was short, barely a few minutes with the speed in which he had flown.

Strolguil was so close! He'd flown over that small castle many times and had never known.

"Do not try to escape, or I will kill you," he warned when

he hovered above his lairstep and tossed her father inside since his ward had been lowered.

He would just add his head to his collection and tell Amalia he didn't know what happened to her father.

When he landed on three paws, he demanded, "Take her, I cannot save her in my Dragon form."

He was too large, too unwieldly with his claws.

Although being in a much more vulnerable body with a stranger nearby, a Dark Witch no less, wasn't something he would usually do, he didn't have any other choice with Amalia on the brink of death.

The man took her from his paw and then he blew a ring of fire above his head to shift.

Not even a moment later, he'd stolen Amalia from her father's arms as he cradled her down the tunnel. He looked at the man from the corner of his eye before looking at the shackles on his wrists.

"Why were you a prisoner?"

"She was six when we had heard about the prophecy, and Strolguil told us he wanted to obtain what was foretold she would give birth to. He thought since she could carry such a thing that she would be powerful."

He followed Rurik into the alcove where Amalia would usually cook her food.

"When her mother and I ran with her, we knew he would search for Amalia. I would often scout the land to make sure the cottage we'd fled to had not been compromised. I was discovered. He was hoping to use me as leverage to get her to bond with him if she refused."

Leverage? So it had never been set in stone that she would bond with the Vast.

Rurik laid the Witch against the stone dining table and lifted the tunic she was in to expose her wound.

She made sure it was deep.

He filled his hand with magic before he blew a fireball at it. He made sure it stayed lit with flame.

"Please, WitchSlayer! She did not know anything. You promised me you would not harm her." Her father leapt forward to grab his arm in a futile attempt to stop him. "When she first came to my cell, she did not know who Strolguil was. She had not regained her memories yet. Please, I swear this to you."

Had she truly not known before today?

Rurik elbowed him out of the way as he placed his hand over her chest to feel her heart beating beneath it.

"Do not command me, Witch," he bit. "I told you I would heal her."

He shoved his flaming hand into her wound. She was too far gone to know he was doing something so horrendous to her.

The wound began to cauterise as her skin and organs melted around his hand when he pressed it deep. He wouldn't have been able to heal her stab wound, but he could heal a wound from flames.

Rurik was changing her injury to one that he could save.

His eyes widened, and he moved his non-flaming hand from her breast.

"Pump her chest. Her heart has stopped beating."

Her father immediately ran forward. Pressing his hands just above her breast, he pushed against her ribcage to massage her heart.

After he removed his flaming hand, he shook it in the air to remove the fire and then he placed it over the wound he'd created. He couldn't understand why his hand was shaking when usually it was so steady, but his mind was too rampant with her safety to fixate on his thoughts. He had to chant the spell he needed to fix her before he could do anything else, needed to utter the words out loud.

He concentrated, keeping his hand over it until he could feel the magic flowing. He could see the reversal of his flames lighting inside her and feel the warmth of it.

Keeping his hand against the lower part of her stomach to keep the magic fuelled, he leaned over and blew into her mouth. He gave her his breath mixed with magic.

He was thankful her father was here to help him pump her chest. He wouldn't have been able to do all three on his own, and if he moved his hand from her wound, it would stop healing.

When her wound was gone and he could no longer feel warmth or his magic being used, he lifted his head to double check. Like the spell had done to her legs, he managed to heal her completely.

Not even a scar marked her beautiful body.

Rurik had saved Amalia of her wound. Now he just needed to bring her back to life like once before.

With the wound gone, her heart should start beating. She should take a breath.

Yet, even after he gave her more of his own, she didn't.

The silence between them only aided to highlight their attempts in saving her. The horrible thumping noise her body gave as her father repeatedly pressed into her chest. His subtle grunting, and the sound of Rurik taking in a deep draw of strong breath so he could give it to her.

"It is not working, WitchSlayer," her father said, losing his enthusiasm for the task. When Rurik didn't respond, just continued to breathe into her mouth, the man shook his head. "She has given up. She told me she did not mind dying."

His hands slowed, his brows creasing into sorrow and grief, before he started to retract them.

Some sharp emotion tore through him. Fear? Helplessness? Anxiety? He couldn't pinpoint what it was when his heart constricted in a way he'd never experienced before.

No!

Rurik hadn't gone to all this effort, healed her wound and given her his breath, just to fail.

Slapping her father's hand out of the way, Rurik got on the table to kneel over her torso. He took over, determined to see her breathe again.

Come on, Witch. You are not allowed to give up.

He started to pump his arms, his eyes moving frantically over her pale face. Her head bounced with each push before it settled for the split second he released the pressure.

There was something haunting about looking down at this female who usually radiated beauty and warmth to find her ashen and cold.

To know that her parted bluish lips held no life to them, didn't gasp at the force he was shoving against her, and wouldn't turn into the enthralling smile that always made Rurik feel strange inside. Instead of shouting at him for what he was doing with a fierce glare, her lids were closed. The azure blue lagoon eyes he wanted to swim in were shut from the world, possibly forever.

You did not take my blood. He pushed against her chest. *You did not take my child.* Another push, his lips curling over his gritted teeth. *You did not plunge me with that knife.* Push. *You did not leave me defenceless to save yourself.*

He bent over and pushed his breath past her cold lips that felt as though they were freezing his own every time he did it.

He leaned back to pump his arms as his mind continued with its chaotic and erratic thoughts, his brows slowly furrowing together while he looked down at her.

You took that blade yourself. You removed the hexes on my body. You blinded Strolguil. You gave me the opportunity to kill him. You hurt yourself to save me.

Rurik was reaching for that trust he'd held for her before

this day, was trying to use what he had witnessed as well as heard from this man to rebuild it by himself. He *wanted* to trust her, wanted to have faith in her because... he had once felt something tender.

She had been his friend, had been a place of his desire.

He'd come to care for her.

You satisfy the rage in me.

Since she came to his lair, she had calmed his anger. Instead of his irritated huffs and snarls filling his tunnels, it had been her laughter – and his own. Rather than lying under his riches waiting for information, he'd found fascination in her, in this tantalising creature who had stolen all his attention – whether he was with her, or without.

If she truly did not know... Then her kindness towards him had been real, and the innocence and sweetness he'd liked in her... It hadn't been a façade.

Her father watched him while standing to the side, unaware of the swirling emotions twisting his stomach.

"She is gone, WitchSlayer."

Rurik's eyes crinkled into heavy bows because he *knew* he was right. This wasn't working.

Amalia had truly given up.

But I do not want her to die.

He couldn't stop picturing the moment she shoved that blade into herself rather than him. Or, that deep, wet sound of impact when she shoved it hard enough through her own womb that the hilt guard had been pressing against her skin.

And the more he did, the more something inside his chest twisted. A painful ache he didn't want to bear.

She would not have done that if she had been a part of it. He knew it was the truth, knew she'd had no purposeful part in what happened this day.

She'd been a tool to Strolguil's plans as much as he was. But she had also been the one to save them.

She caused harm to herself and would have known her death could have been a possibility in doing so... just to save him. Him. Someone who had threatened her with fire.

Looking back to when she had been in that dungeon, he thought she hadn't cared.

She tried not to look at me... Perhaps she could not have. Perhaps what he had seen wasn't a lack of care, but a desperation to pretend not to. She never said that *she* wanted to do the things that Strolguil wanted.

All she had answered were questions directed to her.

He'd asked her if she knew about the prophecy, and she said yes and then spoke it. *But if her memories had been returned to her before they came to the dungeon...*

She admitted to him that Strolguil had always been around as her cat, but she may have only just discovered this. *She had never been shy changing or bathing in front of him.* In the same way she hadn't been when she thought he was nothing but a lizard with wings.

Then she'd rejected the offer of his blood.

He could remember her face when they had been in his lair with Strolguil holding her hand. It had been a face of complete and utter confusion, pale and stricken.

She would not look at me. Amalia only looked at him completely in the eye herself when she was on the altar and had that blade raised above him.

Her look of determination had been bone-chilling. Now he understood she only had the strength to meet his gaze when she finally had the opportunity to save them.

And then Rurik remembered something... A detail he'd barely thought about at the time, something he'd ignored.

There, when she'd been riding him on the altar hidden behind her hair, he had felt two droplets fall against his chest. *She cried because she had not wanted to ride me against my will.*

But there had been no other way. She had needed the power of his dragoncraft to free him.

That painful ache in his chest suddenly twisted unbearably harder. Rurik's eyes crinkled in unyielding sadness at the utter loss he was feeling. *I... I do not want her to leave me.*

His hands flew from her chest to her throat, and he wrapped them around it. He wasn't choking her. They were just placed against her firmly with his thumbs trailing up on either side of her windpipe as the tips rested against the bottom of her jaw.

"What are you doing?" He ignored her father's shout, ignored him even as he tried to pry his hands off her.

Warmth radiated from his hands as strange, powerful, and ancient magic poured from them into her. His arms were shaking, trembling not with exertion, but with undeniable fear as he stared down at her face. Nothing would stray him from what he was doing.

If she does not breathe, I will incinerate the world. A rumbling, dark growl bubbled from his chest like thunder as his face morphed into rage, and fury, and resentment so deep he knew he'd never felt anything like this before. *If the world thinks I am hateful now, just wait until they see me if she is taken from it.*

It would rue the day it gave birth to him.

It would regret putting him on this earth, would regret giving him life, strength, a beating heart. It would *regret* giving him Amalia only to take her from him.

One last time, Rurik leaned over and gave her a deep breath while that ancient magic was being used – something he would never be able to do again if she lived.

Something he didn't want to do again even if she didn't.

A sharp gasp came from her, knocking him out of the way when her torso lifted. Her eyes snapped open wide while her body contorted, and her spine arched prominently.

Then she fell limp against the table.

Rurik released his hands and crawled down her body to press his ear against her chest. He stayed there when he could hear her heart beating weakly, listening to it flutter like the gentlest, shyest, smallest little butterfly ever imagined possible.

It fluttered relief through every part of his being, stealing his tension to leave a blossom of ease.

When he moved his head, he pressed his forehead against the centre of her chest while he slipped his hands under her. He held her against him as he nuzzled her sternum with his nose.

"Is she-?"

"Yes, she is alive," Rurik answered, his voice ladened with so much emotion that it was impossible for him to hide it.

He lifted to look at her sickly pale, yet beautiful, face with his heart aching in his chest.

She is alive, and she will stay with me.

She would live in his lair just as she had before, and he was determined to hear her laughter in it. He was determined to smell her cooking that always made him seek his own food. To hear the sound of a page turning, or her light feet pattering around.

He wanted to walk through his tunnels wondering where he would find her. To see her sitting by the entrance of his cave so that he could come to sit beside her in the sun – he wanted to share in that moment of tranquillity that was rare for a warrior like him.

But most importantly, Rurik hoped Amalia was still the same way she was before and wanted to be beside him. *I threatened her not knowing of her plans.*

There was a long pause before he backed off the table so he could allow her to rest peacefully. Like he had been waiting for him to move, her father rushed forward to check himself.

Every muscle in Rurik's body tensed at him coming so close to her precious form, but he didn't do or say anything as he checked for himself.

Watching him smile at her face before stroking her soft hair back, Rurik's eyes inspected him now that they were in the light of torches.

His eyes may be darker, but they were blue like hers, and his hair was blond. Even though his hair was tight with little ringlet curls whereas hers were large, almost straight around her face before they twirled towards the end, they had similar features. Even the tan colour of his skin was the same.

He is truly her father.

"You said her mother died. How did you know this if you were a prisoner?"

"Strolguil told me." Her father turned his head to him with a look of guilt clear in his features. "After he discovered me when I was patrolling the area, he knew Amalia must have been close. He found the cottage, and Hellena tried to fight him." He gave a laugh, but it held no humour. It was too forced and shaken. "Her mother was a white wielder; only I had wanted to learn dark magic. She stood no chance against him."

He stepped away from Amalia to stand on the other side of the table so that it was between them.

"I cannot express what I felt when he threw her head in my cell and told me he found Amalia."

Rurik *could* imagine what he felt as his eyes gently fell over the Witch who just moments before had been dead.

"Why did you change her memories to make it so that you were a human?"

He gave a shrug.

"We worried if she ever saw me use magic that it would make her remember. She would have been curious to know why I stopped, because once I took her memories, I never used witchcraft again until the day I was captured. Soldiers often leave their families for long periods of time, so it gave me an excuse to leave so I could scout the lands."

"And you made sure she did not know what Dragons or covens were so it would not remind her of the prophecy."

"Yes, exactly. We sheltered her to the best of our abilities."

Things were beginning to make sense. Amalia had never lied to him, she had just told him the version of the truth she knew. *Her mother had warned her of the black moon because of this very night.*

Rurik walked over to lift her head so he could see better.

"You used dark magic on her." Rurik couldn't contain the growl that left him at the two finger strokes of red liquid on her face, as well as his own. "You used her blood to cast."

Just knowing that made his skin *crawl*.

"We could not see!" he bit back. "And you do not get to cast judgement on me when you did not get her permission to do what you just did."

That growl grew as Rurik shot his head to him. His nose crinkled and tension shot through him.

"You do not get a say in what I do with her!" Then he approached him, his height only slighter taller than his. It was enough that he took a step back when he tried to tower over him with menace leaking from him. "You do not get a say when I saved her life, when you intended to let her die by doing *nothing.*"

He took another step back with unease, but Rurik could tell he was angry. His eyes were slitted while his teeth gritted.

"I allowed you to take her even though I did not trust you." When Rurik took another step forward, her father pointed to her. "She had not just accepted her death, she *wanted* to die!"

Rurik's brows furrowed. *She wanted to die?*

"She did not want to be taken by Strolguil again, and she was afraid of you. When I tried to carry her, she asked me not to. She even asked me to leave her behind!"

Then her father halted to stare him down. His cowardliness faded to boldness.

"I have been locked away for nine years hoping this day would pass, and I would not see her again. I worried when I was moved to that castle recently. I knew something was wrong. My own daughter came to me bleeding and pleaded for my help. Then, when I had been hoping I could save her myself, she could not go on, and I could see she did not want to." He had the audacity to point his finger at Rurik's face only a few centimetres away. "You do not get to make me feel more guilt than I already do. She wanted an escape from every terrible possibility because at the time, she knew one of you would win and come for her."

His eyes travelled to her once more.

She is afraid of me again.

His words on that altar rung in his head, and he visibly winced. He'd tried to punish her before she took his life, had wanted her to taste fear one last time. Rurik could only imagine what he would face when she woke.

"Instead of letting her die in my arms while talking to you, I let you take her when that is not what she wanted. The only reason I did was because you said you would not harm her once you healed her, and I hoped that you would at least allow me to be imprisoned with her so she does not have to be locked away alone."

"No." He stepped back, letting his own anger fade rather than grow. "You will be imprisoned by yourself, and she will return to walking inside of my lair like before."

"Why do you even care for her? She is a Witch. How did she come to know you before this day?"

Rurik sighed, seeing no point in answering the man's questions, but decided to do so in order for him to understand.

"She saved me and healed my wounds in her cottage when

I had been injured after fighting the Vast. Then she released me, setting into motion my blood debt to her that I did not intend to fulfill at first. Right after I left her cottage, she was taken to be burned on the stake, and I did not return in time when I knew something was wrong. She was burned, she died, and I brought her back to life with my breath like I did just now."

The man's face paled upon hearing this terrible fate his daughter had faced. Rurik waved his hand backwards towards her limp body.

"I brought her here so I could heal her legs because they had been eaten by fire, and she would not have been able to walk again. Before I got the chance to take her to a town, she saw my human face. Because of my stay in her cottage, I could see she intended no harm, so instead of killing her or putting her in my prison alcove, I let her roam free inside of my lair."

Her father frowned in thought as he brought his hand up to cover his lips and chin. "You did say she has been with you for quite some time."

"Yes." Rurik's eyes wandered slowly to the wall for a moment before they returned to him. "You will be imprisoned by yourself, but I will allow her to see you if she wishes to. I will not keep you from her."

He could imagine her begging him to see her father, and he didn't want to cause her any sadness. He just hoped she understood that he wouldn't be allowed to walk his lair like she could.

"You would not keep us apart?" His brows drew together tighter as he tried to understand why Rurik would allow this.

"No, and you will create a potion to heal her of the damage we have just done in bringing her back to life." Rurik had heard her ribs breaking and felt they were loose under the force of his pumping. "And then you will follow me there. I still have some questions for you, but I would feel more at ease if you were inside of it."

He also wanted Amalia to rest in silence.

"Do not fight me on it," he sighed since he didn't want to have to drag him there.

The man gave his own sigh. "Fine, I will help heal her and go there. One cell to another. At least in this one, I do not have to fear for her life."

He allowed Rurik to lead the way.

36

The moment Amalia could feel herself waking, her eyes flew open. She shouldn't be waking. She should be seeing darkness forever – or whatever place they went to in the afterlife.

Why am I alive? Anxiety picked up in her chest as she stared at the ceiling. *And why do I not feel pain?* Her hands flew to her stomach, finding no wound, not even a scar.

Amalia felt drained of life, like she wasn't supposed to be here. She had bled *a lot.*

Where is my father?

Her breathing quickened as she stared at the rock-covered ceiling before she finally let her eyes fall on the room. She went white with fear, the coldness of it rushing through her so quickly her skin prickled with goosebumps as a shiver ran up her spine.

She knew this room, this alcove. It was where she'd cooked her meals. *No! I am in his lair.*

Throwing herself forward so she was seated on top of the stone table, she continued to look around.

Where is he? He wasn't in the room with her. Wherever he was, she didn't want to be there.

She needed to run and hide.

Amalia turned so she could put her feet to the floor and

jumped down, but immediately lost her footing. She managed to save herself by falling to one knee. Her legs felt like nothing more than soft, cooked spaghetti.

Dizziness swam through her, but the adrenaline of fright gave her the strength to move. Getting to her feet, she made her way to the entryway and leaned against it to steady herself before she peeked her head out.

She could see the entrance to the cave, but she would have to walk past multiple alcoves to get there. *The ward.* He would have put it in place by now since he wouldn't let her escape.

That would mean she would have to hide inside of his lair until she knew he was gone.

Trying to keep her footsteps quiet, she checked that he wasn't inside each alcove when she travelled deeper inside his lair. She often had to right herself with the wall and stop so that she could breathe through the wavering dizziness trying make her collapse.

Shaking her head to clear her constantly wavering vision, she walked through the main room, thankful that he hadn't been inside of it. She made it to the fork in her path.

Her chest tightened with fear when she looked down the tunnel that led to his trophy room. The firepit that was usually unlit was bright with flames, and she swore she saw his moving shadow. *He is preparing.* She bit back a sob before quickly turning the other way.

Her knees tried to buckle with each step while her hands shook against the wall.

She managed to reach the cavern with the stream without being noticed and ducked behind the waterfall so she could crawl into the shallow hole. Amalia bent her legs so that she could rest her head against her knees while wrapping her arms around her shins.

The cold air made her tremble just as much as her emotions, and she prayed that she would just fade away.

I want to disappear from the world. She didn't want to be here anymore, had very much wanted to die.

Although she hoped Strolguil was dead and was relieved that she hadn't woken inside of that castle-like mansion, she hadn't wanted to wake here either. *I do not want to face fire again.* She dug her nails into her calves.

Her eyes threatened to close. *I feel so weak.*

Not wanting to rest, in fear she would be found when asleep, she peeked her head up to look at the water. She also checked the cavern entrance through the waterfall to make sure he wasn't there.

Her eyes drifted over the small path behind the fall where she had walked, and where she could possibly run to if she was found.

The stream wasn't in the centre of the cavern. There was a great and long space between it and the entrance, but the other side had just enough space that the Dragon would be able to lay there against the wall.

She also eyed the stream. She didn't know how to swim. *I could drown myself.* She would rather that than the agony she would feel.

Just when she was about to get up and try to do just that, she heard a noise. The sound of the waterfall rushing did little to hide the yell she heard. The yell of her *name.*

With a quiet squeak, she held her legs tighter and pushed herself further against the wall. She couldn't get deeper than she already was.

For a long while, she heard nothing.

Please do not come here. Please do not find me.

She knew what Glov had told her about being able to be found here. Amalia just hoped her scent was faint since she felt that way. That perhaps with so little blood inside her, she couldn't be followed.

But she did realise her mistake in coming here.

I could have bled myself.

She'd been in the cooking alcove where there had been knives. It wouldn't have taken her long to cut down her wrists and bleed the last of what she had inside her.

My death may have come peacefully as it was coming before. Now she feared it would be violent.

She bit back a cry, her stomach twisting when she saw him coming down the tunnel through the water. She expected to see a Dragon, not the human wearing leather breeches when he usually hated them.

Every swift footstep closer made her heart quicken and quiver in reaction, and she covered her mouth to hide the quick, high-pitched breaths that escaped her. She cringed when he stood at the entrance, his head moving as though was looking over the entire area.

The waterfall made it murky to see, but she could tell he was coming closer to the stream. Every time he took a step, her head shook. He was veering in her direction.

Before he could even duck his head between the waterfall and the wall, Amalia unfurled herself from her hiding spot. She backed up so she was on the other side of the cascading water.

She held her hand forward when their eyes connected.

"Stay back," she pleaded.

He didn't growl or snarl like she expected him to. He didn't have that hateful nose crinkle she'd seen him wear. She didn't expect him to halt when she asked him to, and he stayed still while peeking around the falling stream.

They were staring at each other, and Amalia didn't know what to do. She considered diving for the stream, but she knew it wouldn't matter.

He is faster than me. He will catch me. She couldn't stop the strangled noise that came from her at realising this.

He took a slow, deliberate step towards her and her heart

leapt to her throat. She backed up a step. When he took another, so did she, but she could feel her tears rising and beginning to fall. Her feet found the other wide space next to the stream and he seemed to come faster.

"Amalia." His voice was quiet, but she didn't know the emotion behind it.

Was it a warning? A threat? She was too afraid of him to register anything other than her fear.

"Please," she cried. Her weak legs tripped on her retreat and she scramble backwards on her backside. "I did not know."

But she knew Rurik wouldn't listen through his anger and would often ignore words to lash out first.

"I did not know who he was before this day! I did not know those people!" He was right near her feet when she covered her head with her arms and cringed. "Please do not burn me."

Hands grabbed around her forearms. Her chest tightened to the point she thought it would make her pass out, and she felt even more light-headed than before.

She wondered if her heart would stop beating in fright.

She even wanted it to.

When her arms were forcibly moved and she felt a hand on the side of her face and another on her shoulder, she clenched her eyes shut. She didn't want to face whatever was about to happen.

They fluttered open when his firm lips pressed against her own.

He was crouching down over her with a knee between her legs while his right foot was placed on the ground beside her leg. His hands weren't gripping her violently, and his mouth was gentle against hers.

His silver eyes looked into hers, but they'd never appeared so kind before. Her own were filled with a mixture of surprise and confusion.

He pulled back, and the hand on the side of her face gently brushed behind her ear and through her hair.

"I know," he said, making her bottom lip tremble. "I know you did not have any part in it."

His silver eyes flicked between hers as he waited for her to understand she wasn't in any danger. That she was safe. He kissed her to show her that he wasn't angry and didn't hate her.

Heavier tears pooled, and her face crinkled into one of pain and distress. Her hands tentatively came up to hang in the air, wanting to hug him but unsure if it was okay.

Seeming to sense this, he captured her in his arms. One crossed over her back while the other held her head to him so her face was pressed against his bare shoulder. He held her tight as she dug her fingertips into his back and cried.

"I am so sorry," she sobbed. Her lungs heaved as she tried to breathe through the emotions washing over her. "When Bala came to the entrance of the lair, I had been so excited to see him. I did not know he was him." Her voice broke into a higher pitch when she said, "I did not know he was watching me. I did not mean to let him in."

The words began to fall from her. He held her while she wept and tried to process all the guilt and shame that was radiating inside her. Amalia recounted to him what she'd done, what she'd learned, what she'd gone through to make sure she got to the altar without suspicion.

She'd worried that if she didn't pretend to play a part in Strolguil's plans and showed she was against what he was doing, then he wouldn't have allowed her freedom. She made him lower his guard, allowed him to think her memories, that still didn't really feel like a part of her, had changed her.

She'd created a mask of indifference to hide her disgust.

Rurik patted her hair, silently holding her while she released everything. She knew she was digging her nails into him now, but she couldn't stop the tension in her body or hide her regret as she spoke her next words.

"I am so sorry." She shook her head as she trembled all over. "I knew you did not want me to ride you, but I did not know what else to do. I knew I could not do it by myself. I knew I did not have enough magic to free you, and I did not want to leave you trapped."

Amalia made the choice to ride him, but she'd seen no other option. She wasn't knowledgeable enough with her magic to do it on her own, and she knew she would never have won against Strolguil. She'd made the choice and then had to bear the heavy weight of guilt from doing so.

"It is fine, Amalia." Hearing him say those words, hearing him understand why she had done it, that he'd forgiven her, settled her aching heart. "If it helps you to know, it felt good." His voice was filled with a combination of concern for her and humour at his own words.

Amalia laughed. She laughed until her sadness and guilt took her over again and then she just cried against him.

She had nothing more to tell him.

But she felt better. *He does not hate me.*

Relief sailed through her, and she started to calm. She didn't have a lot of energy to begin with and began to droop, falling limp against him.

"Come, you are not well. Let me help you to the other side of the waterfall and then I will carry you."

He lifted to his feet while taking her with him.

He turned her so that her back was against his chest. Then, he helped to keep her upright as they walked the thin path between the rock wall and the waterfall.

Once on the other side, he tilted his body one way to make her body dip. One arm held her up behind her back while the other slipped behind her knees to lift her until she was cradled in the cushion of his strong arms.

Unable to lift her hands to hold on, she tried her hardest in keeping her eyes open to stop herself from passing out.

Her focus was in front of her. She was looking at her legs, at her skin still stained with her own blood. Tracks of it twirled down and between her legs.

Realising she didn't like the sight of them, she turned her gaze towards his face to look over something more pleasant.

"Will you stay with me?" she asked when he carefully placed her on her bed.

"Strolguil is no more, he will not be able to come for you," he answered once he covered her with the furs. He looked over her with his gentle face beginning to frown. "That is not why you asked me to stay."

She shook her head. She just didn't want to fall asleep alone.

He turned to sit on the edge of the bed beside her and held her hand comfortingly. Amalia stared at him with languid eyelids. Now that she knew Strolguil was dead and that Rurik didn't plan to harm her, she felt safe again.

She had no reason to fear being alive anymore.

"Thank you for saving me."

Rurik stayed with Amalia until she fell asleep. Which was about all of five seconds before her breathing softened. He sat with her for a little while longer, silently watching over her like a protector.

Rurik had spoken with her father for some time while he made a strong, dark magic infused ointment to heal her shattered rib bones. He had been disgusted that he'd asked for some of his blood but had willingly given it so that it could help Amalia.

He applied it himself, observing as the strange, nose-tingling slime sunk beneath her skin before fading.

Then he took him to the prison alcove.

He asked him about her childhood, her real one, and about what he's learned being Strolguil's captive for years. Rurik had come to learn more of the villainous Witch's misdeeds.

At every coven and turn, he'd advocated for dark and blood magic use. He would teach every Witch he met how to increase their power, and would also force white wielders to turn, would go out of his way to corrupt them.

Her mother's pregnancy had been difficult, and they knew when Amalia was to be born that her mother would most likely not survive. Strolguil had been the one to teach her father how to save her and showed him the spells and ingredients he would need when the time came.

It was what turned her father. His love for his wife and his desperation to save her is what led to his corruption.

Once Rurik was done with him and closed him inside of his prison alcove, warding it as well, he'd turned to his trophy room.

If he waited much longer, his stomach would begin to digest Strolguil's head. When they changed size or form, their food would change as well since their stomach had magical properties inside of it.

Unless it was expelled, of course.

He'd shifted so that he could bring his head up, as well as the other two coven Witches he'd killed. Preparing them for later, he placed Strolguil's head on the stone workbench he had inside this room and removed his blazing red hair.

He was planning to attach it to his skull once he removed his skin and muscles. Rurik wanted to make it obvious that it was Strolguil's since he didn't want anyone to mistake his skull for the others he'd collected.

After he did this, he changed back into a human, knowing it would be easier to face Amalia if he wasn't a towering, scaly beast. He knew she would be afraid and would have to approach her slowly.

What he hadn't expected was, in the time he'd spoken to her father, removed the Witches from his stomach, and found pants because it would make her more at ease, that she would rise and be gone.

Rurik nearly had a damn heart attack when he'd walked into the cooking alcove to find she was no longer resting against the table.

She had fled, and after shouting her name, he'd bolted to the entrance of his lair thinking she had run away outside. He hadn't replaced the ward yet and thought she was truly gone.

When he couldn't find a trace of her scent outside, a deep frown had marred his features as he'd walked back inside to check each alcove for her. Her scent had filled the cooking alcove, softer than usual, but still noticeable to him even in his human form.

The moment it took him to the stream, and he looked around for her, he knew where she was. He was aware of the shallow hole behind his waterfall. He knew the ins and outs of his own lair as much as he knew every scale on his body.

Her fear of him had twisted his insides worse than any sword that had ever been sunk into his side. But he'd found her, he'd comforted her, and then he brought her here to rest. She was very pale, and weakness was easy to see in her trembling legs and hands.

She has lost a lot of blood. It may have been one of the reasons why he found it so hard to bring her back. Last time she was strangled to death.

Amalia hadn't been toeing the afterlife so hard.

She also did not want to return.

Now that he'd been told her side of the events that played

out, he knew she had been brave. She convinced them that she was a willing party in their plans to the point they gave her fleeting moments of alone time.

She could have tried to escape on her own, but she did not want to leave me behind. Warmth and pride spread through him.

As much as he wanted to stay with her, there were things he needed to do before she woke again. Now that she understood she was safe, he doubted she would wake for quite some time.

He went to the entrance of his lair and reapplied the ward that would prevent Witches and pixies from entering, no longer seeing the need to ward it further.

Then he made his way back to his trophy room to finish what he had started. He didn't burn the Witches to remove their flesh like he normally would. Instead, he skinned them and cleaned their skulls by his own hands, not wanting to add the smell of burning flesh into his home with Amalia inside of it in a fragile state.

Once he mounted their heads on the wall, he turned to Strolguil's skull and did the same. He'd once wanted to mount his entire skeleton in his main room, but when he had needed to search for Amalia, he hadn't cared at the time to also retrieve his body.

He still mounted what he'd taken in the main room of his lair, though, and it sat right above the tapestry of the tale of him killing his own father.

Rurik stared up at it for a long while and the hair he had attached to it. His kind would never forget him, the Dragon who had slain the Vast.

If I am not to hunt him any longer, who else must I search for? He had reached his peak of pride, nothing he did after this would matter as much.

I could kill the Witch King. But even that was a feat too

grand for Rurik.

He could not take on an army of Witches.

I have obtained a hundred kills before anyone else. I have killed the Vast. What other greatness can I reach for? After his last battles with him, Rurik hadn't thought he would ever see this day.

The Elders must be told. It was his job to inform them that the biggest threat to their kind was gone, and that there was a possibility that their numbers might begin to flourish rather than dwindle.

But he didn't want to leave Amalia. It would take him time to fly to them and they would want to have a lengthy discussion with him.

Even the great Dragon King will want to know of this.

Deciding on what to do, Rurik left his lair to fly to Falen's. She was only a few short hours from his, and he would be able to return quickly.

He made his request to her. It wasn't something Rurik had ever asked of Falen before, and even though she didn't want to, she agreed to find Glov for him. He didn't tell her why, only that it was important.

Glov was a tricky Dragon to get a hold of since he was never stationary, but Falen was a tracker and could find most if she wanted to. She also had the ability to scry for their kind by searching the lands and skies through her magic.

She was called Falen the Seer for a reason.

When Rurik returned to his lair, Amalia was still asleep.

She at least looked better than the last time he'd seen her. Her magic was trying naturally to push her further along in the process. She wouldn't be right for days, but it would have been much longer for a human.

Rurik stayed with her. She may have questions for him, and he needed to speak with her once she was awake.

He sat on the bed and leaned against the footrest while facing her. It was hours before she made any sign of waking, and he just thought about the day and night they'd gone through with all the information he now had.

He'd been rubbing his thumb over the tip of his fingers together in thought, his elbows resting on his knees, when she finally moved.

His brows knitted tightly together when her chest picked up in anxiety before she shot up in the bed reeking of fear. For a moment, she looked terrified to see him.

After a few panicked breaths, she eventually started to calm. She'd woken up disorientated and must have needed to remember their last interaction.

"Did you stay with me the whole time?" she asked after a few minutes, her brows crinkled in confusion at seeing him still there.

"No. I prepared some things and left the lair for a short while."

"How long was I asleep?"

"I laid you down when it was mid-morning, and it will not be long before the sun rises again."

He'd flown back to his home from Falen's in the middle of the night and had been sitting with her for hours since. He wouldn't be surprised if the sky was already starting to lighten.

"Where... Where is my father?" He knew this would be one of the first things she would ask him.

"He is here. I have put him in one of the prison alcoves."

She brought her hand up to her chin, eyeing warily. "Will you let me see him?"

"Yes." As he told her father, he wouldn't stop her from meeting with him.

"Can I see him now?"

His face crinkled into one of deep concern. "You are still quite pale and weak, Amalia."

"Please?" Her eyes pleaded him, and he couldn't deny her when she looked at him like that.

With a sigh, he nodded and helped her to her feet. She didn't change from the blood-covered tunic she was in, and she was still shaky on her legs and slow. Yet, she was able to make the walk down his tunnels on her own.

He rolled the boulder out of the way. When he was standing beside her in the entryway with his arms folded, he expected her to run into her father's arms with joy.

"Amalia." Her father smiled while taking a step forward.

"Stay there, please." Rurik's brows furrowed at her request before his eyes moved the short distance between them. Her father immediately halted, his smile faltering when she put her hand forward. "I wanted to thank you for helping me."

"Of course, you are my daughter. I would do anything for you."

Rurik could tell he wanted to come forward to embrace her, but he remained where he stood.

"You use dark magic." When he confirmed, her eyes crinkled with uncertainty. "When I got my memories back, I saw that you took me to your coven in hopes I would want to learn."

"Yes, I wanted for you to grow strong. Even though your mother argued with me about it, I wanted you to be able to protect yourself since white wielders cannot do so very well."

"I watched you pull apart creatures in front of me even though I was little." Her father winced while Amalia's expression began to grow into a distressed frown. She balled her hands into fists. "You harmed others that did not deserve to be harmed."

"I know but I changed when we took you to the cottage."

"No, you did not," she answered sternly. "You used my blood so that we could see. You did not hesitate to cast dark magic upon me, and you made the decision to do so easily. I do not trust you."

"Amalia, I-" He came to take a step forward again.

"No. *He* will not trust you."

Rurik's head shot to her when she placed her arm across his stomach. *What do I have to do with this?*

"As much as I thank you for your help and what you tried to do for me, I do not wish to see you again."

Both his and her father's eyes widened. Rurik thought this would be some conversation about bridging their lives back together.

Instead, it was her way of saying goodbye.

"I do not wish to be around someone who has allowed darkness to enter them. It is like a contagion, and I do not want to become a Dark Witch like you."

After long moments, his eyes looking at her beseechingly, he eventually sighed with a nod.

"I understand, and I do not blame you for making this decision. Your mother felt the same way. I am glad that my daughter is still alive, even if I will, regrettably, not see her again."

"Thank you," she said softly before she turned from the alcove and walked up the tunnel a little to wait for Rurik.

"Did you convince her of this, Dragon?" The man gave him a glare, and Rurik returned it.

"I am as surprised about this as you, but she has made the right decision."

Then he went to the other side of the boulder and pushed it back in front of the entryway to lock him in. He walked over to Amalia.

"If you do not wish to see him, then what do you want me to do with him?"

She nibbled on her bottom lip. "I do not know. He helped me, so I do not wish for him to die, but I also do not want him here. I do not want to know he is so close."

"I can give him to the Elders with that request. They have their own prison cells, and they try to rehabilitate Witches who have tried to turn back to the light. We have been experimenting to see if we can heal the corruption that has grown inside your kind for years."

"Would that be okay?" Her voice held a hint of uncertainty.

"Of course. I would prefer not to have a long staying prisoner."

Most who entered his cells didn't usually live for long. He didn't want to have to feed and take care of her father like he was some kind of pet.

She pulled at the edges of the blood-stained tunic she was in while looking down at it. "I need a bath and to change."

"Yes." His eyes fell to the wall. "And I must tell you something."

She tilted her head in question, but he shook his own.

He needed to show her first.

They made their way back through the tunnel to her room. His eyes often came to her while they walked. *I do not know how she will react.*

Rurik led her to the full-length mirror, and he stood behind her as he lifted the side of her jaw with one hand so she could see.

Across her throat, starting from the middle and trailing to the back of her neck to almost circle it completely, was a black mark. It was in the shape of a tribal Dragon.

Its tail started from the nook between her collar bones while its head came to the centre of her throat where his thumbs had trailed up the sides of her windpipe. Wings rose up to just below her jaw and fanned out to the back of her neck where his fingers had gone.

Amalia frowned as she leaned forward to see it better.

"What is it?"

"I have marked you." She turned to him with her light brows drawn together in a lack of understanding. Rurik gently lifted her chin so he could see it and give his fingers room to softly caress over it. "I have claimed you as my mate."

His eyes flickered up to her face. She stared up at the ceiling with her brows drawing together impossibly tighter.

"You bonded yourself to me?"

"Yes. It does not always work, but sometimes we are able to claim someone on the brink of death and bring them back."

It was generally a last resort, a desperate bid to save someone they cared for.

She stepped away from him as her head turned down from the ceiling. He could see tears forming in her eyes, and her hands were trembling more than they were a minute ago.

"I know I did not get your permission to do this but-"

"Take it back," she begged, shaking her head wildly and making her glossy blonde curls sway around her shoulders.

He could see she was growing more upset by the second when her breathing became sharper on quicker intakes of breath.

"I cannot take it back."

He hadn't known what she would do when he told her, but he'd hoped she would be happy. Rurik had *wanted* her to be happy. He hoped she would be overjoyed in being claimed by him, that he was bonded to her, that he was *hers*.

"Take it back!" she cried, stepping further away from him.

She shook her head more, and those tears started to fall in heavy drops. Each one stung his chest and bruised it.

She is rejecting me... She is rejecting my claim. Rurik didn't like the way her rejection tasted, didn't like how it twisted in his chest. He didn't know how to handle this feeling or the way it ate at him from the inside. *She does not want to be bonded to me.*

His nose crinkled in anger while his lips tightened over his teeth. "I cannot take it back, Amalia. It is done. You are my female now."

And he wouldn't allow anyone else to have her.

Actually, he was likely to possessively rip the eyes out of anyone that even dared to look upon her beauty.

He chased her when she kept backing away, like she could escape from this when she couldn't. His mark would never fade, and he couldn't mark another now.

She covered her face with her hands, and the sound of a shuddering sob came from behind them. He hated the pain he could hear in her voice and the way it choked him.

"And I *will not* allow you to forsake me," he growled as he stalked her. He *wouldn't* allow his own mate to abandon him, to spurn him!

"But I am a Witch! You are supposed to be mated to your own kind."

He gave a quiet growl as his anger rose further the more she tried to deny it. "It does not matter that you are a Witch. I have made my decision."

She will accept my claim! He had saved her. *Her life is mine. She is* mine! *For all of eternity.*

"You do not want this!" His steps slowed and his head twisted in confusion when her hands flung away from her face to hug her stomach. "You told me you did not want a mate or hatchlings. You did this to save me and have trapped yourself in doing so. You should not have if it meant you would have to suffer this. You do not want this from me!"

Rurik realised then that she didn't understand. That her tears were not for herself, but for him. She thought he'd felt cornered and would regret what he'd done.

He came forward with swift determination to wrap one arm around her back while the other pushed through her hair to fist it. He pushed her against the wall.

"I did not make this decision lightly," he said, forcing her to face him. "I would not have done this if I did not want you as my mate. You fulfilled part of that prophecy, Amalia."

"N-no, I did not." When she tried to avert her gaze, he shook her head and made her look into his eyes. "I-"

"When you shoved that blade into yourself, you took my heart, but not in the way they thought."

"What?" she gasped as her eyes widened in shock.

"Every time I look back on that moment... Every time I remember what you did to save me, I know that is the moment in which I made my decision."

He'd had to fight through his confusion, had to defeat Strolguil and save her first, but the more he thought on it, the more it moved him.

And it wasn't something he would *ever* forget.

The smell of her sweet copper blood. The sound of the blade giving impact and the small gasp of pain she'd made. Even now the chime of the blade each time it hit something solid before it cluttered against the ground still rung in his ears.

The more he thought about it, the more he realised that the tender and caring emotions inside him he hadn't wanted to accept had been turning into something for her. He'd lacked the trust in her to see it and would never have accepted her without it.

When she'd shoved that blade, she'd brought back the trust in her he had lost and then viciously shoved it over the edge. He'd fallen for her in one swift move.

On the night of the black moon, Amalia had indeed stolen the WitchSlayer's heart.

"You will not try to feel regret for me when I do not feel an ounce of it!" he yelled with such a deep sense of unwavering doubt it couldn't be ignored, not by her, not by anyone. Her tears started to slow, and she made another gasp when he gave a sharp tug on her hair. "So, you are going to tell me when you want to fulfill the second half of that prophecy." He moved his hand from behind her to snake it under the tunic to rest it against her stomach. "You are going to give me that child, but I will be the one to father it. To protect it and cherish it just as I will you."

He moved his hand up to wrap it around the back of her neck while the other pulled her head to the side so he could lean forward. He placed his lips against her throat, sharply nipping at her skin with his teeth.

"I am going to fill you with my seed whenever I want, and I do not care what you do with the magic that comes from it." He closed the last bit of distance between them so he could thrust his hips against her, letting her feel his hardening cock. "And I would do so now if you were not so weak."

He didn't care that she was still covered in her own blood and hadn't bathed. She still appeared remarkably lovely to him.

"And even if it means you will have to learn blood magic, we will find a way to extend your life, because I will not have my mate wither into old age and die hundreds of years before me!" He gave a growl against her throat when he could scent her arousal growing. His lips continued to move over her throat and the mark he'd put on her. "Even if you have to take it from me, or yourself, or another Dragon, I will have you with me until I fade from this world."

He wouldn't let her become corrupted, but they would find a way.

"If I did not want to bond with you, I would have let you die on that table and felt sad for your loss like I have felt sadness for the Dragons who have been lost, but I would have moved past it. I claimed you as my mate because I wanted you, and I did not give a fuck about asking you for your permission when all I wanted was for you to *live* alongside me."

Rurik had finally found the one female he truly wanted. He would do anything to keep her, to protect her, and the world would rue the day it ever tried to harm her because he would finally turn his unyielding rage upon it with an uncontrollable vengeance.

He would set fire to the world around him, but never let a flame touch her.

Rurik pulled his head back to bore his gaze into hers.

"Do you understand me now?" With her lips parted, she hesitantly nodded. "Do you still not want it?" She shook her head. *Good.*

He had one last question. He released the pull he had on her hair to gently cup her head so he could ask it softly. "Do you feel for me?"

Did she return his feelings?

"Yes," she answered, and he swiftly leaned forward to take her mouth, to kiss her with hard and unyielding need and force and the deep passionate heat he held for her.

She welcomed his lips, and he gave a silent groan when she gave a loud one. He reluctantly broke from the kiss before he got swept up and forgot she wouldn't be able to take him right now.

"Good, because you are the only female who seems to know how to handle me."

His words got her to laugh, but he knew it was the truth, and he had a feeling so did she.

Nobody, and he really meant nobody, male or female, human, Witch, or Dragon, knew how to calm him from his frequent bouts of rage. He was volatile and ill-tempered, and instead of barking back, she often redirected or replaced his anger with something else.

"There is one last thing I wish to show you."

But he didn't let her walk since he didn't truly want to separate from her. He scooped her into his strong arms so he could take her to the entrance of his lair. They both embraced the sunshine that bathed over them.

"Why are you taking me outside?" she asked when they were in the middle of the clearing in front of his lair.

She reached her hand up to place it over her brow to shield her squinting eyes from the bright light.

"You are no longer a prisoner in my lair," he answered, turning his head down to look at her in the sun and see her dull hair springing to life. "With my mark on you, my wards will not be able to hold you back anymore. They will see you as an extension of myself, and you will be able to pass through them without thought in the same way I do."

"I can go outside?"

He nodded.

If Rurik wanted to keep Amalia inside, he would have to concentrate on a shield at all times. It wasn't that he didn't want to waste energy or magic on doing so, he just no longer wanted to keep her trapped.

She reached up to cup his face with both hands, giving him the smile that always made his chest feel tight. Yet with the meaning behind it from his words, it also made him feel unbelievably heavy.

Now that he'd shown her she could go wherever she pleased, he took her back to her room. When he placed her on her feet, he pulled the tub to the centre and began to walk around it thoughtfully. *I hope I remember how to do this.* He also didn't let her fill it with water when she tried.

"What are you doing?"

He pointed to it. "I am not letting you in this alone when you are unwell. I fear you will fall asleep and drown yourself by accident."

He remembered the last time he healed her and had to bathe her while she was unconscious. She kept slipping inside it to the point he had to hold her up.

"It is too small for both of us, it will be fine."

She stepped forward, but he grabbed the rim of the porcelain tub and crinkled his brows in concentration. Rurik hadn't tried to change the size of something in a very long time.

The reason he'd never changed the size of his travel pouch when he'd fallen from the sky and eventually found himself in her cottage was because it was a difficult spell to do.

He had to feed his magic past his hands and wait until the entire tub was vibrating with it. He also had to change his eyes so that he could see it because if the tub wasn't completely imbued with it, the spell would fail, and he might shatter it instead.

Being a difficult spell to do, he had to chant the words out loud. He didn't need to yell, he just merely spoke them.

His arms pushed up when it grew, making it slightly taller and wider. It only changed in size by a small fraction, but he figured it would be suitable.

"There." He gestured to it. "You may fill it now."

Watching her fill it with water and then heat it with her own magic, it took longer than it usually did. Her witchcraft was just as weak as her body currently was.

He knew he'd made the right decision to make it bigger and join her when she appeared paler from doing so. She was even wobbly in the legs. It had taken some of the small amount of energy she'd gained.

After kicking off his pants, he slipped inside, and his muscles jumped at the heat wrapping around his waist.

I do not think I have ever had a warm bath before. He'd always dunked himself into cold streams and lakes. *It appears to be quite relaxing.* Already he could feel his body softening.

"Um, where am I meant to sit?"

Her tunic had already been removed, and she was covering her bare chest with one hand and her pubic mound with the other.

He blinked at the water. He thought the answer was obvious. "On my lap, of course."

Her face pinkened when she stepped inside between his legs and turned, coming to sit down on top of him. She was seated just above his pelvis, leaving the precious jewels of his groin unharmed.

With the size he made the tub and with her sitting on top of his body, the water came to just below her chest – where it usually came to when she was in it on her own.

She didn't have as much leg room, though.

After she settled, her muscles un-bunching from nervousness, she relaxed in the water. Once she did, he flicked his forefingers and middle fingers of both hands up while the rest held the tub edges his arms leaned on top of.

"Now do the leg thing," he commanded with a grin.

She turned her head to the side so she could look over her shoulder at him with a peek of humour. When she didn't do it, just stared at him, he made an impatient gesture with his head.

With a sigh, that peek of humour pestering into a smile, she leaned back against him. Then up one of her legs went as she brushed her hands down the side of it to wipe what she could of the blood off them.

His eyes perused the length of it before she brought it down and did the other.

I think perhaps I may like bath time with her. He'd liked watching it from the outside, but it was far better when he was a part of it up close. He even brushed his own hand down her calf and thigh to help her, feeling her wet skin under his palm.

She had to wash the blood from her feet when they were submerged.

"I have dirtied the water."

He didn't care about the quality of the bathwater when he had this naked female on his lap in it. He brought his hands to her sides so he could cup liquid into his palms and brush them over her shoulders.

"I think we need a bigger tub," he answered.

He wanted to do this again, but with a little more freedom to move. His chest was broad, his muscles strong. He took up a lot of the room.

With a small laugh, she shook her head like she couldn't understand him. Rurik hissed in a quiet breath as her core rubbed against his already hardened shaft when she leaned forward to wash her face.

He made no mention of it when she came back up to lean against him and her shoulders lost all their tension.

"I feel much better now."

They stayed in the tub just to soak in the relaxing heat together. After a long while, her head lolled to the side and backwards with her ear pressing against his shoulder.

"We have had quite the day and night on the black moon. How are you feeling?"

A night had passed while she was resting, and he wanted to know how she was coping. It took her quite a few days to break down after she'd been put on the stake.

He reached forward to turn her face towards him softly and her body twisted slightly to the side, making it easier for him to assess her.

Much had happened, both terrible and good. For him, he'd killed the man he'd been hunting for years and claimed this female as his mate, the in between was pointless to him now.

"Tired and light-headed mostly."

He snuffed his want to roll his eyes. He'd already known that. "That is not what I meant."

"Oh." Her brows knotted as she gave him pout. "I am not really sure. I feel upset that it happened, but I am also relieved that it is over."

Accepting her answer, he let her rest against him while he trailed his fingertips over her. He even occasionally massaged her shoulders to get the last of the tension out. She looked tired, but also like she was deep in thought.

Her fingertips came up to brush over her neck.

She is thinking about my claim.

Just when her eyes began to droop, and he was about to get them out so that she could rest in the bed again, he heard a noise.

Rurik brought his arm forward so he could wrap it around her breasts to cover them with his arm. This woke her a little from her trance.

He pressed his lips to the back of her neck with his head turned so he could see the entrance, and spoke softly when he said, "You do not need to move."

She didn't get the chance to ask him why before a green scaled paw came into their line of sight. She tensed against him, and her arms came up to cross over her waist. She even brought her knees up higher to hide her body.

"Witch," Glov casually greeted, poking his head in before continuing down the tunnel.

Then he suddenly took a step back and shot his head inside the alcove. His eyes widened, and he reared his head back far enough that it smacked against the entryway that was lower than the ceiling.

He shot forward to cover his head with a paw.

"Rurik?!" he exclaimed with surprise while rubbing his scaled head. "What... What are you doing?"

"Ha! Knew that would be hilarious," Rurik chuckled. "Obviously, I am having a bath."

"Yes, but you are having a bath *with* her."

His spiked brows drew together at the sight of them.

Amalia turned her head to him to whisper, "I thought you did not want anyone to know."

Instead of answering either one of them, he lifted one hand and pressed it to the side of her jaw. He tilted her head up, keeping his eyes on Glov until he unveiled to him what he needed to.

He revealed her neck like a display.

"You claimed her as your mate?!" Rurik could see the confusion in Glov's expression and the obvious aversion he had to discovering this.

He lowered his head to Amalia's ear to speak to her, knowing Glov would overhear.

"Although we usually mark the body, I marked your neck so that all my kind would see it even when you are clothed. It means they will all know you are mated to a Dragon and should not attack you if I am not around." Then he spoke out loud. "It would appear so, yes."

"You cannot do this! No Dragon has ever mated with a Witch."

Rurik was in too much of a good mood for the green Dragon to truly upset him.

"It is irrelevant, I cannot take it back."

"The Elders will not approve, Rurik!"

Glov stomped his paw forward.

With a growl, he lifted his foot until it rested on the edge of the tub and was clear for all to see. "I did not lose a toe for anyone to tell me they do not approve!"

"You lost a toe?" Amalia leaned closer to his foot to see he was indeed missing a digit next to his pinkie toe.

"Yes. I am falling apart, soon there will be nothing left of me."

Amalia laughed at how dramatic he was being, but he was quite fond of all his body parts.

"Is that why you called me here? To tell me you have done something as wicked as this and laugh about it in front of me while in a bath?"

Rurik brought his foot back into the water while a hand covered the mark he'd placed on Amalia.

"No. I had not expected you to arrive so soon. I often forget how skilled Falen is."

"Tell me what it is you want so that I may leave."

"I do not think you will want to leave when I tell you, but... if you were to walk down my tunnel into the main room-" Rurik turned his head in that direction. "You will see Strolguil the Vast's head mounted on my wall."

Rurik would need to speak with Glov now that he was here. He planned to inform him of both his and Amalia's accounts of the day so that he could pass the information to the Elders since he was unwilling to leave his recovering female by herself.

Rurik and Amalia had one last battle to face. He knew the meeting would be long and, if it didn't go in his way, it could end in him regrettably spilling the blood of his own kind.

Glov's eyes widened and the aggressive tension in his body left him to be replaced with surprise.

"You have finally killed him?"

"Yes. He is no more. And, with such a daring feat, nobody is allowed to command me or tell me that I cannot have what I want." Then he wrapped his arm across her neck so he could cup the side of her face to push her cheek against his own. "Especially when she is the one who helped me do it."

Three nights had passed since the night of the black moon, two since Glov's visit, and Amalia had finally woken up like herself again... mostly.

Each day she'd been gaining strength, especially the first where she spent most of her time coming in and out of sleep. She'd gained enough energy to do something, like bathe or cook so she could eat, before she started feeling drained again.

Like a puppy with a new toy, the Dragon hovered around her. She was unsure if that was because he had bonded with her or because she was unwell.

Glov had still been in the lair when she'd woken the first day, but he'd quickly been dismissed.

The night of Glov's arrival, Rurik had slept under his treasure, crawling into it since he hadn't slept since the night before the black moon.

This morning, she woke up alone.

Not in the mood for cooking, she made her way to the food alcove and just ate fruit while she was there. Then she went to hunt Rurik down, wondering where he was.

She didn't really need to look far. As she was walking down the tunnel, she could see a handful of books had been carelessly thrown out of an alcove. Her brows creased together in concern until another flew out as though it had been carelessly tossed.

Just as she was coming to the alcove and was about to enter the room, she had to duck when a book was tossed over his shoulder. She peeked inside when she heard growling.

"Blasted! Where is it?" Rurik cursed to himself in his human form.

He was crouching in the magical items alcove to dig through the chests of spell books he'd told her he didn't want her going through.

He'd obviously attempted to go through them slowly at first since he had a few piles of neatly stacked books, but his impatience took over because he'd started tossing them in anger. One chest was empty and the other only had a handful of books left. He grabbed one of the few remaining and flicked through it quickly.

"What are you looking for?" she asked, knowing he placed the book on the ground because she was in the way when he was done checking it.

"There is a spell book I wanted, but I am unable to find it," he answered when he reached in to grab one of the last two.

With an irritated huff, he eventually threw that one to the side. Then he grabbed the last one, took one look at the cover, and immediately knew it wasn't the one he wanted.

"What kind of book?"

She looked at the sea of them around her feet.

"It has white magic in it." He moved the books around on the floor to see the front covers as though to double check he hadn't missed it. He gave another rolling growl through clenched teeth. "I do not know what the spell is called!"

Nibbling her bottom lip, Amalia eventually told him to wait there before running back to her room. She pulled a handful of her books off the bookshelf and reached behind them to grab the one she'd hidden.

He might be mad. She'd kept this from him after all.

When she returned, he was still going through the books on the floor, tossing them back inside the chests after checking them. His nose was crinkled in frustration, and she figured he was a hair-trigger away from losing it like he often did.

"Is it this one?" She held the book with both hands in offer to him.

With a huff, he took it. He went through it quickly as if he expected it not to be it. Then he slowed before stopping at a page.

"Yes, it is this one." He flicked through it slowly. "Did I miss it?"

His eyes wandered over the books on the ground.

"Uh, no. I kind of found it in your collection and never told you that I did."

She tried to give him an innocent smile when he narrowed his eyes at her.

Instead of reacting, he became engrossed in it, turning page after page. Finally, he stopped and placed it on the bench and shoved his hand against the open pages.

"This, I want to do this." He gestured to a particular page. "I am not good with witchcraft spells. There are often special nuances your kind learn that are different from mine. I can only recreate concoctions. I want your help in doing this."

Once again, he gestured to the page by tapping it impatiently. She stepped forward to look at the spell.

"Rurik..." she gasped, her lips parting. "It is a handfasting spell."

"Yes, I know what it is. I just do not know how to do it."

"But this is a binding ritual that Witches use to bond with the person they love."

Her parents had done it, and both had the marks it created to prove it.

"So? You bear my mark. I shall have yours."

She picked up the book to inspect it closer before she put it back down.

"But you would be permanently marked with witchcraft with this." She didn't think he would ever be on board with the idea.

He gave an irritated huff, gesturing to the spell again with his hand. "I love you. You love me. It makes sense I should have your mark."

Amalia clasped her hands to her chest as quick tears pooled in her eyes. He frowned and immediately retracted his hand.

"You are so soft these last few days. I did not think this would upset or sadden you to tears." She could hear in his voice he was stemming the want to roll his eyes.

Amalia ran and leapt, wrapping her arms around his neck while her legs trapped his arms to the sides of his torso. He took a step back, startled when she impacted to cling to him.

"I am not crying because I am upset, you absurd Dragon. I am crying because you told me you love me."

Then she grabbed his face and crashed her lips against his to take his mouth in the way he often took hers – with hard, unyielding passion.

His hands grasped the underneath of her thighs to help hold her up when she began to slip. His mouth moved eagerly, and his tongue was quick to slip against hers.

She eventually pulled back but didn't get down.

"I thought I made that quite obvious."

He shook his head like he didn't understand how she couldn't have known.

"Yes, but you have never said those words to me." Sure, it had only been a few days, but he'd never told her directly. "My feelings are not new. I have felt them for a while."

She'd just never admitted them to herself because she hadn't seen the point before. She never thought he would return them. Once he told her that he'd chosen her as his mate, they'd bloomed freely.

Her words made him grin. "So, I will have your Witch's mark on me."

She turned her head to the book when she finally released him. "Well, when do you want to do it?"

"Today, if possible."

"Really?" she asked with a bright smile, walking over to the spell book to pick it up again. It was a fairly simple spell to do. She figured he worried about getting the words wrong. "All we need to do is tie rope to each other in the way we want the design to look and then we do the chant."

He stood beside her and pointed at a footnote. "It says multiple colours can be used. What do they mean?"

"Our marks will turn out black." She frowned for a moment. "I actually do not know if I will obtain the marking since I technically already have one, but the colours are for symbology. We can just use normal rope if you have it."

He nodded and started to go through his array of items before he grabbed a ball of brown twine.

"I will need to plait it." She tied a knot at the end of the three very long pieces and got him to hold the end for her while she did. Once she had a few metres of plaited twine, she explained the rest to him. "We find the middle and take turns wrapping each other's forearms. It can be simple, or it can be elaborate, knotted or unknotted. It really depends on what you want to see your mark look like on me. It makes each one individual."

With his hand balled into a fist, he thrust his forearm forward and waited. She laughed, realising he truly wanted to do this. Amalia was happy that he did. She wanted to return the bond that he had created with her.

Rurik watched her intently as she wrapped his wrist and then forearm while making crisscross patterns. He seemed to be absorbed in watching her work as she tried to design it how she wanted to. She double wrapped his wrist and occasionally made crossing sections thicker as well.

Her wrappings came up three quarters of his forearm.

"I was wondering, will others be able to see this on your scales?" she asked when he started doing her arm, having a little more trouble since one of his arms wasn't as free.

"Most likely since my kind's marks can be seen. If our scales are dark, like mine, it will appear much lighter. If they are light, it will appear darker." He paused to look at her arm, twisting it one way and then the other before nodding. "I am done."

She turned to the book so she could read the words she needed to chant. Only one of them needed to be a Witch in order to fuel the spell, but they both had to chant the binding vows.

Repeating each word after she said them, in the way she said them, the plaited twine began to glow multi-coloured. Glittering magic came from it and cascaded over their arms.

When they stopped chanting, she could feel it tingling her skin. It continued to radiate magic since the spell was still working to complete itself.

Holding up his arm in the air, he shook it, making her connected arm shake as well.

"Now what?"

"It will turn brown again in twenty-four hours."

His brows drew together. "I have to be connected to you like this for twenty-four hours?"

I probably should have mentioned that first. She'd forgotten to tell him.

He reached forward to touch the centre string separating them to inspect it since it was still glowing. She made sure to give them both enough room to be able to move, but now she worried that the distance was too short.

"Yes, and we cannot break it otherwise we will have to do

it again from the beginning and there is a chance it will not work if we try a second time. Sorry, I should have mentioned this to you."

"So, you are attached to me for a whole day?"

He turned his gaze away from their arms to look at her. She grimaced when she wasn't sure if he was upset or not.

"Yes."

To her surprise, he grinned.

"That means you cannot run away from me, and I can see you are feeling better."

Amalia knew the look he was giving her. He often chased her around his lair with that particular heated look.

She squealed when he grabbed her bound wrist with his captured arm. He used it to toss her over his shoulder with her stomach laying against it.

Even though she was kicking her legs and beating at his back, Amalia laughed as he carted her up the tunnel over his shoulder. *I am glad I am feeling better. I would have had to say no otherwise.*

Rurik pulled up the skirt of her dress until he exposed her backside and grasped it with his free hand. Then he bit one arse cheek!

"Ow! Why do you always bite me?"

"Because I like you so damn much."

At his admission, Amalia hung on him with her eyes bright with a smile.

He'd been biting her for a long time.

Rurik grinned as he carted Amalia up the tunnel over his shoulder.

She'd been like a thorn under his scales for the past few days with her occasional tears at the strangest of things and her sleepiness. He'd been patient with her since she needed to rest and recover, but she'd also turned him on at the simplest of tasks.

Rurik wanted to play with his new mate. He hadn't gotten the chance to since he'd claimed her.

The time afterwards was supposed to be for touching, not him chasing behind her because he worried she'd fall asleep without a moment's notice. She'd fainted once while standing, and he'd barely had the time to catch her before she hit the ground.

He knew the day before that she was beginning to feel better. And, when he saw that her colour had returned completely when she offered him the spell book, he decided he no longer wanted to wait.

Firstly though, he'd wanted to do the spell, not knowing that it would work to his advantage in the way it did. *She cannot run from that bed for twenty-four hours.*

His mischievous grin widened.

Plopping her against the mattress, he made sure to hold his hand to her wrist so that there wasn't any pressure on the twine. Then he stood above her while forcing her hand to be raised in the air.

"It appears I will have to rip you out of that dress." He shook his arm again, enjoying the fact she was trapped to him. "We should have done this with you unclothed."

Rurik bent over so he could use his teeth and free hand to begin a tear in the sleeve of her dress. Then he ripped it from her arm before he tore the centre of it.

She is exquisite.

His eyes walked a path over her bare body. The slender legs he wanted to separate with his hands so he could see more. Her hip bones he wanted to grasp so he could pin her down. Her tucked in waist he wanted to hold so she wouldn't bounce when he thrust. They trailed over her palm-sized breasts that were firm and barely drooped, but he knew without a doubt were quite soft, dusted with pink nipples he wanted his mouth to permanently stay attached to.

She let him take his time with the appetising scene before him.

His gaze roamed over the lightly tanned skin he wanted to sink his teeth into. The mark he had placed on her was so dark against it that it always caught his eye and was easy to see, no matter how she turned her head.

Finally, they fell to her face to look over the soft features she had that always made her appear guiltless. Her lips and blue eyes, her blonde hair like a halo around her head making her appear even more sinless.

Rurik always thought he liked women that looked mean, bitchy even. That was until this woman came along. Now he realised he preferred the opposite because it was so damn *hard* to be angry at something that looked this unbelievably sweet.

When he could tell she was becoming more aroused by the second, he used the rope connecting them to get her to sit on the bed until she eventually had to kneel. He brought her hand to his black breeches, and she immediately understood that he wanted her to remove them.

She was careful with the four buttons, and she tugged them down when she was done. His already hardened cock sprung to action.

Running his fingers behind her ear into her hair, he held the base of his cock with his hand that was connected to her.

"Open your mouth," he demanded, his shaft pulsating when he brought it closer.

He'd been waiting for the chance for her suck him.

Her head had been level with his navel. She had to bend forward and lean against the bed with her free hand to reach him as she placed the bound one against his hip so she didn't fall.

Then she licked her lips and parted them as though she was hungry to taste his cock.

The moment the tip slipped against the wetness of her tongue, he couldn't stop himself from pulling her head forward until it reached the back of her throat. Rurik shuddered, his nose crinkling on one side for a second. His jaw fell slightly.

He felt her tongue move when she tried to swallow the saliva that collected in her mouth while he was inside it. The muscles in his abdomen bunched.

This is not going to last long. Even the slight sensation of her swallowing had felt remarkable.

He pulled his hips back so his shaft would slip away before he came forward again, showing her how she would need to move. When he stopped and pulled his hand away so she could take over, he realised she looked nervous.

"You cannot do this wrong, Amalia. I have never had it before."

Rurik rarely fucked in his human form, and he'd never trusted a female enough not to bite his cock off in retaliation for something he had done before he got to this stage.

He didn't expect her face to turn bright red, but he could feel that the corner of her lips turned up. She was pleased that she would be his first with this. It also seemed to calm her that he couldn't compare it to anyone else.

Then she started to move, and his head fell back. It was slow, but he hadn't realised that he would be able to feel the different textures of her mouth.

He could feel her lips stroking around his cock and pulling the taut skin back-and-forth. It took her a while, but eventually she started to lap that wet little tongue against him. He could even feel the small ridges in the roof of her mouth against the tip of him, the sharpness of her teeth when it caught against the rim of his broad cockhead.

Her mouth was deliciously warm.

His head tilted forward to watch when she spun her tongue around the tip for the first time, and a quiet groan fell from him. She made a sound of enjoyment that she'd gotten him to make a noise and did it again.

She started experimenting with him.

She tentatively brought her captured hand to the side to wrap it around him, adding to what she was already doing with her mouth by stroking. She rubbed the head of his cock between her upper and lower teeth by sliding him against her cheek before she drew him to the back of her throat. Then she slipped and dabbed her tongue against the slit in the tip of his cock.

The second time she did it, she took a welt of his semen with it.

His breath started to shallow as his eyelids drooped. Different muscles around his groin twitched and bunched at what she was doing to him. His abdomen would twitch, then his thighs would before they sent a shudder down his legs to make them shake at different intervals.

She realised that he would react more if she did something to the head of him, that he was more sensitive there. She started to focus on it.

When she actually suckled it, making the pressure in her mouth tight, his hand that had only been resting through her hair, fisted it.

Fuck, this feels amazing.

Just when he thought he was about to come, she pulled his shaft from her mouth, and he didn't know if he was angry that she had done so, or excited for what she would try next.

That flare of anger faded when she licked him from the base all the way up to the tip and looked up to see if he liked it. He answered her with a pant with dazed eyes, more pre-come welling and waiting for her to take.

She makes me feel crazed. She was lapping her tongue up the sides of him and around the sensitive tip. She even started just kissing down the length of it, like she appreciated this part of him, moving her lips over him and making the sweetest sound.

She wasn't just sucking him. She was loving on his cock.

He hadn't thought she would be so attentive, not bringing him further to release but making sure he didn't stop toeing the agonising line he was at.

His breathing began to shallow further when he throbbed harder, his mind getting frazzled at her mouth's movements. He wanted back inside, needed back inside. He'd been close to spending before, and she was keeping him on the edge and making him ache.

She is teasing me. He didn't think he'd ever been teased properly before.

She pressed her lips against the broad head and spread them over it. He thought she was going to bring him back in slowly, and he thrust his hips forward to quicken the pace.

What he didn't know until it happened, was that she'd been intending to surprise him by slamming her mouth around him. To give him a hard press, like he usually did inside her core.

Instead of what she intended, slamming him against the back of her throat, his sharp movement sent it past that point and down it.

Fuck! His eyes snapped open wide. Both his hands shot forward to wrap his arms around her head and ripped her hand from his cock. His entire body clenched.

It was tight, it was firm, it was hot, and he let out a loud strangled groan. Her tensing from it made it worsen.

He pulled his hips back when she pushed against them, but he didn't let her pull her mouth away. He held her face where it was because in one stroke, his balls finished drawing up and he began to come *hard*.

She stopped trying to push him away when she felt that he was spending. His muscles tensed with each burst, another, louder groan coming from him. Then she started lapping her tongue against him and that groan caught in his chest.

Fuck yes. She is so fucking perfect.

When he finally pulled back, she brought her hand up below her mouth as though she feared it would spill.

"Swallow it," he demanded while huffing wildly, *wanting* to watch her drink him down.

Her throat expanded when she did as she was told. He pried her mouth apart to check before he grabbed the back of her head to make her rise higher on her knees.

He kissed her with much force when he leaned over to grab her so he could lift and pull her further across the bed. There was this dangerous feeling rising in his chest of unmistakable lust from what she had just done to him, of how hard she made him come.

Rurik didn't even care that he could taste remnants of his own seed against her tongue when he twisted his against it. The moan she made when he slipped his softening length against her core as he laid her down made that dangerous feeling deepen.

I will make her do that to me again, that is for sure.

Kneading her backside, he lifted her so he could thrust harder against her, uncaring that he was barely even erect.

Amalia's head tilted back when Rurik broke from the kiss to press his lips under her jaw. Then her back arched when he bit her neck, and he made a small noise as he did.

He seemed more turned on than he did before, his hands sweeping down her body to grab at her skin like he was desperate to touch her everywhere. She let her hand connected to him follow without resistance, allowing him to take control of it, so they didn't snap the rope.

While moving lower, he trailed kisses along her chest and over the mound of her breast. He didn't even wait before he brought her budded nipple into his mouth and sucked on it hard enough that she felt both a spike of pleasure and pain from it.

The moment he freed it, he lashed his tongue across the other one in a wet stroke before bringing that one into his mouth to do the same. She gasped when he nipped it with his teeth.

She was just about to tell him he was being too rough, but he lowered his body even further. He brought his lips down over her abdomen, across her stomach, and then down her hip.

He made sure his body was tucked between her legs, but he pushed them further apart with his hands so he could fit his snapped open wide. He quickly shot forward to be on his knees.

"I came inside you!"

He rolled her to her back and knelt over her.

"That was what I was trying to tell you!"

He quickly put his hand against her stomach to place his thumb below her navel. He concentrated on the spell he needed to stop her from getting pregnant, hoping it wasn't too late.

The spell wouldn't take if she already was, and he sighed in relief when it worked. An orange magic symbol lit against her skin before fading, telling him that her body accepted it.

He would have to replace it once a year.

Thank the heavens. I am not ready for whatever monstrosity it is we will create.

It took Amalia a long while to fully wake since her body was languid and comfortable.

They'd barely left the bed and only occasionally got up to eat. He'd taken full advantage of the fact that Amalia was trapped to him, and although a lot of their time had been about sex, there had been other moments of intimacy.

Ones where he just wanted to touch her or hold her. She'd felt like she was falling under some kind of spell in those moments as tenderness fluttered inside her belly.

There had also been a lot of playfulness and laughter – as well as the occasional growl from him.

Even though they'd spent days similar, the meaning behind them had been about desire and lust. This time, he'd made her feel different, like she was cherished and cared for. She couldn't help smiling now because of it.

Laying on her side, she let her eyes flutter open.

He was laying on his side, facing her as she was him, with their legs tangled. They both had to keep their upper bodies apart because of the handfasting rope in the way, but his hand was firmly clasping hers.

Amalia frowned a little before she brought her face closer to his slowly, being careful not to jostle the bed.

Is... Is he sleeping?

Indeed, he was. Rurik was asleep next to her. Not even in his Dragon form had he ever fallen asleep in her presence, and she'd known he was completely averse to the idea in his human one.

Even after everything that had happened on the night of the black moon, he'd come to trust her. She couldn't help the silent tears that welled and fell as a smile grew on her face. They didn't take long to fade, the heavy spike of joy calming so she could just look at him.

He looks so peaceful. His dark lashes were long, fanning shadows over his soft and calm expression. The scar that ran across his face wasn't as puffed – like he had always carried tension in his features – while his inch-long hair was like a small black pool around his head in the dim light.

He really does have a lovely face.

She wanted to touch him. She wanted to caress her fingertips over the curve of his nose, his lips that were just parted, his cheek bones. They wanted to whisper over the scar she liked, making him look rogue and rough, which was exactly how he could be.

But Amalia didn't. She didn't want to disturb him, didn't want to rob him of sleep or herself of this moment.

Her arm was tingling with magic, and she just took in this moment of contentment, of peace.

Many things had come to pass over the nearly two months since he came to her as a strange little flying lizard in her cottage. Sure, there were some things that she really wished she could change, but she wondered if she would do them again just to see him sleeping next to her with trust like this.

Amalia had never thought her life would turn out this way, or that she wouldn't live in her cottage forever.

My life is different, but I prefer it this way.

She had a Dragon who couldn't seem to get enough of her,

and she may have just as deep of a craving – although she often tried to pretend she didn't. She couldn't help giggling, in those times, at his face of dumbfounded disbelief.

It was like he couldn't believe he wanted her more than she did him. He'd almost seemed offended. *He is either too egotistical or he is truly insecure.* She would put her money on the former rather than the latter. *He is a rather arrogant bastard,* and she'd told him that many times.

But he could also be very sweet and charming. *And he is soft for me.* Looking around at the room he carved, filled, and given to her, she realised he'd had a soft spot for her for a while and neither one of them noticed.

He'd also made her feel safe when she had very much felt the opposite.

Her eyes fell back to his face just in time to see it tense slightly. Then his eyelids lazily flipped open, revealing those silver eyes of his that often made her feel at ease.

"Why are you so far away?" he mumbled groggily, before he reached out with his free hand and tried to pull her forward. It forced their connected arms to go straight up against the headboard with a thud.

"That might be why," she answered when he seemed annoyed that it happened.

"You woke before me. I did not expect that." He grabbed a handful of her hair, lifting it into the air before letting it fall.

"Yes, and no matter how much I shook you or yelled, you refused to wake."

Her lips were pouted into a playful smile.

He frowned with his lips pursing. "I thought you did not lie."

"Only when I am not jesting."

She let out a quiet squeal when he rolled them over, so he was on top of her.

"You further my belief that you are actually wicked."

"Is that a joke?" It had to be.

"No, I am being quite serious. You may possibly be the most wicked."

He brushed the hair that was covering her face, her arms trapped by him and making it impossible for her to do it herself.

"I was certain I melted the most evil's face on accident."

Rurik gave a warm chuckle. "That you did, but you should not tell others it was an accident. It may not bode well for your reputation."

"Then what else am I to say? And I do not have a reputation to care for."

"I have now seen you, multiple times, spin conversations your way so you do not utter a lie. You do it quite splendidly. I do not think you will have any trouble finding a solution." Amalia let out a laugh when she felt something growing against her. "Yes, it often makes me hard thinking about your skills. The right kind of trickery is quite appealing to me... as long as you do not do it to me."

"Then I will expect a snarling and cranky, ill-tempered Lady Lizard?"

"I am not a woman! The fact you ever confused me as so is insulting."

"Then perhaps you should stop being so pretty when you are a Dragon?"

Rurik gave her a small huff.

"Compliments make it hard for me to stay angry with you," he said before he brought his mouth against hers. "And you are lucky I find you irresistible."

Rurik didn't compliment her often, but each time he did, it made her heart flutter. Her eyes closed, returning his kiss with a little moan.

Just when she felt he was about to enter her, like he truly couldn't seem to get enough of her even though she knew she was quite tender from their multiple bouts of sex the day before, he froze. Her eyes shot open to see his were wide even though his mouth was still against hers.

Pulling back as his nose began to crinkle on one side, he looked over her face, then down their bodies to look at their chests pressed against each other's. Finally, they landed on their bound wrists.

"Blasted! This could not have come at a worse time."

Rurik got to his knees above her with his straining erection obvious. He threw his free hand up in the direction of the entrance to his lair while seeming to focus incredibly hard.

"What is going on?" she asked as she crawled out from underneath him.

"The Elders have arrived. I did not expect them to come so soon." Then he eyed their bound wrists again. "Or for them to do so while I cannot morph."

She pulled her hand forward to look at her arm. The spell would complete soon as their twenty-four hours were almost up. Although she'd enjoyed every moment they'd had together doing this, she couldn't help becoming crestfallen.

"If... If it is important you shift, we can remove it if you want."

They would have to do it again, but there was always a possibility it wouldn't work the second time, and definitely not a third.

He gently caressed the side of her face with his palm while shaking his head.

"No, I do not wish to stop the spell, it is too important. I only intended to speak with them as a Dragon because it meant I would be better able to protect you. Come, I have shielded the entrance so they cannot gain entry until we are ready."

"What do you mean, ready?"

His eyes slipped down her body, heat once more seeping

into his features before he shook his head of his aroused thoughts.

"Although my kind would not care, you do not wish to be naked in front of multiple others, do you?"

She paled. No, she did not.

Rurik had to follow her as she quickly put on a dress, shoving the sleeve she couldn't get on into the side of it. She was surprised he put breeches on.

"How come we cannot hear them, like when Glov usually arrives and could not get through your other ward?"

"Because their shouting would have irritated me. I put a sound dampener at the entrance as well. The old are impatient and noisy."

She bit her tongue to stop herself at making fun of him as she often did. *Are you sure you are not old then?*

"I am supposed to meet them at the entrance of my lair, but we shall have them come inside to the main room. They will not appreciate following behind us like this."

He led her there and they stood under Strolguil the Vast's tale and mounted skull. She couldn't help noticing his protective stance when he made her stand a little behind him.

"Are you in trouble?"

She wanted to know what they would be facing.

"No," he chuckled. "But I will be."

A moment later, the slow but heavy footsteps of multiple large creatures echoed down the tunnel.

Glov was the first to enter.

"I have done as you asked," he said to Rurik quietly before walking to the other side of the main room.

The next to walk in was a dark Dragon whose scales shimmered with red when hit with torchlight. Rurik gave a small growl to that Dragon as it walked past. Amalia couldn't tell if it was a male or a female as they made their way over to stand next to Glov.

"You are supposed to invite us into your lair, WitchSlayer," a male, with such light lavender scales that he almost appeared white, said to them when he came into the room.

He stood before them a few metres away, but not near Glov or the other Dragon, as two others followed in behind him. A dark blue one and a golden one. Neither one said anything to Rurik, but they stood on both sides of the pale lavender one.

Amalia blinked when she realised she could actually tell that all three were old, especially the one in the middle. Their scales appeared to droop from their bodies and faces while eons of time seemed obvious in their tired eyes.

"It is also customary that you shift when you are in the presence of the Elders," the lavender one said.

Amalia's hand had been resting between Rurik's shoulders and she dug her fingers lightly into his skin.

"Customary, but not law," Rurik rebuffed.

All three of the Elders tried to look around him to see her.

"So, this is the Witch you have been allowing to roam free in your lair," the dark blue one said, revealing to Amalia that she was a female.

"And the one who helped you take down Strolguil the Vast," the golden one added, his voice deep.

At the mention of the Dark Witch's name, their eyes lifted to stare at the skull mounted behind them.

"It is true! You have really slain the Vast," the blue one said before her mouth morphed into a fanged grin. "I would know that red hair anywhere."

"Before we truly begin the discussion, I will warn each and every one of you in my lair." Rurik's head turned to each of them, even to Glov and the dark red Dragon standing off to the side. It was obvious they weren't a part of this. "That if you are to unleash fire in my home, I will not hesitate to retaliate."

Amalia's face paled, only realising now that she was standing around five Dragons who could cook her alive.

41

Rurik could scent Amalia's fear. He knew his words had caused it, but he didn't turn to her. No, he kept his eyes focused on the three old Dragons in front of him.

He paid no attention to the other two. They were merely witnessing because they wanted to. Anyone was allowed to view a meeting with the Elders as long as they remained quiet unless spoken to.

The golden one on the left was Aneirin the Great. His title came from a vicious victory against a human army that any Dragon would have struggled against. His magic and strength were known to all. It was also because he'd been a hundred and seventy at the time, a very young dragon who hadn't long left his parents.

The dark blue one was Nayana the Loathsome. She obtained her title by lashing out at almost every Dragon, Witch, and human she'd ever come into contact with. Most believed she would be mateless until it was discovered that a particular male Dragon happened to like her vicious tongue and claws. Apparently she'd been quite beautiful when she was younger.

Rurik often related to her anger, although she was one of the main Dragons that got under his scales the quickest.

The lavender one in the centre, who was in fact the oldest and held the highest place in their trio, was Fionnlagh the Hidden.

His title didn't come from being cowardly, but from having the ability to hide himself in any place. He'd killed many Witches and humans in his time by leading them into traps until it was too late for them to realise he was right in front of him.

He was respected by all. Unfortunately, he was stubborn and unmoving in his opinions as an Elder.

These three were the oldest of their kind that cared enough about their laws and traditions to want to become an Elder. More could join them and any one of them could step down.

There could even be just one Elder, but no Dragon liked having one deciding all fates without there being a fair chance for a trial. They often worked for the Dragon King and would speak to him about trials and events that went on over his people.

"You dare threaten us, Rurik?" Nayana sneered, stepping a paw forward in anger.

"I do believe I said it as a warning," Rurik growled back.

"Enough," Aneirin interjected calmly, knowing both Rurik and Nayana were quick to argue. This wasn't his first time in front of the Elders "We have come here for a reason."

"Yes, we have come to discuss the night of the black moon," Fionnlagh commented. His eyes went back to the skull mounted on the wall behind him. "We have decided to have another tapestry made in your honour, but we believe your current title is already fitting for what you have done."

Rurik thought there may have been a chance his title 'the WitchSlayer' could have changed. He was relieved it would remain the same.

"You are one of the few who will have more than one tale hung in the room of great histories," Nayana added.

The room of great histories was a place every Dragon could visit to see the greatest deeds of their kind. It sat in the temple of the Elders at the top of a central mountain no human could walk to or Witch could get to without wings. It was guarded and any who weren't of their kind were quickly killed even approaching the lands from the sea.

Most knew it as the mountain of death. Its real name was the Pinnacle of Dragons.

There were other rooms, like a great hall for trials, a place for banquets, even rooms to spar. It was a place of growth and tradition.

"We have also decided to give the Witch a title after what Glov has told us," Aneirin said, each one of them seeming to want to take a turn speaking. Rurik frowned since he hadn't expected this – no Witch had ever been given a title by them. "We have been told her name is Amalia. From now on, she will be known by our kind as Amalia the GoodWitch."

"That is until she turns and then the title will be stripped," Fionnlagh cut in, telling Rurik he wasn't on board with the idea.

"Although she has used blood magic, she did so in order to release you from your captivity. She also did not extract this power from anyone else, nor did she cause harm to anyone, bar herself. It was blood magic," Aneirin said, looking at the other two Elders who began to nod. "But we have decided to not consider it evil magic in this instance."

Rurik's shoulders lost their tension. He didn't think the discussion with the Elders would go this way. He also wasn't blind to how it still could turn out. There was a reason he was standing in front of Amalia protectively.

"We are also pleased with your tale of your fight. Glov has relayed what you told him, and we wish to discuss it further when you come to the Pinnacle of Dragons to tell the weaver of your story," Nayana said as her eyes fell onto the tapestries around the main room.

"But we have some concerns about the prophecy that was told," Aneirin said, making Rurik's shoulders bunch in tension. "For it to be foretold that she was to take your heart and birth your child does not sit well with us. No Dragon and Witch has ever birthed such a creation."

"We are now concerned if you two remain together with this knowledge, then what was foretold will come to light. That she will turn on another black moon," Fionnlagh said. "Since you allow her to walk freely within your lair, making it obvious that you trust her to some degree, we have decided that when we leave today, we will be taking the Witch with us."

"No," Rurik answered. His arm came back to touch Amalia's side when her fingers dug harder into his back. "She is to remain in my lair."

"You will not disobey us, Rurik," Fionnlagh barked before snapping his jaws forward. "She is not to remain here with you. This is what we have decided. All three of us have agreed, and you must adhere to the law of our word."

With a wicked hint to his grin, Rurik suddenly spun Amalia so that she was in front of him. He kept their bound hands hidden between them, but he pulled her so that Amalia's back was against his front with his head next to hers.

Grasping her chin and jaw, Rurik forcibly lifted her head to reveal his mark against her throat.

He specifically asked Glov not to reveal this to the Elders. He knew once Glov spoke with them that they would come here, and he would be able to do it himself.

All Dragons in the room gasped and took a step forward, except for Glov who was already aware of this. Even the dark red Dragon who wasn't an Elder reacted.

"You have taken her as your mate?" Nayana said with surprise, her silver eyes blinking wildly, and her head slowly rearing back.

"Yes, I have chosen Amalia as my female."

He bit her on the jaw to show his affection for the kind Witch against him.

"You cannot do this!" Fionnlagh roared, his old, wrinkled scales shaking from the power of his yell.

Rurik pointed to them. "I have gone over the tomes. There is no law in place that states I cannot choose a Witch as a mate."

There wasn't. He and Glov had gone through the ancient texts Rurik held when he visited after the black moon.

"It has never been done!" Fionnlagh yelled again.

The other two Elders remained quiet for long moments while sharing looks between each other. They were concerned about this, but they didn't appear enraged. It wasn't their place to get in the way of a Dragon's decision like this.

"He is right, there are no laws that prevent this," Aneirin said as his eyes trailed over them. Amalia was frozen, and he could scent her fear worsening by the second. "But I also do not approve of this bonding."

"This is no longer an appraisal of heroism. This is now a trial," Fionnlagh bit out. "You are to shift so this can be discussed!"

"I am currently unable to." Rurik grinned before finally bringing their bound hands forward to show them. "Since I am currently in the middle of a Witch's bonding."

This time, every Dragon in the room, including Glov, took a step back in either disgust or shock.

"She has tricked you into marring your body with witchcraft!" Fionnlagh exclaimed, his paw coming up so he could point a claw at them. "She is already trying to fulfill the prophecy, and you are blinded to it. She is trying to get you to trust her with this."

Rurik shook his head before bringing their bound hands up

and forward over her head so he could wrap his arm around her waist. He made sure not to put pressure on her shoulder by doing so and was thankful the length of twine between them was long enough to make it easy.

"She was not the one to ask for this, I did."

Nayana's brows came together in thought while Aneirin's head twisted as he observed them.

"She had my mark, I wanted hers." Then Rurik turned Amalia's head so he could gaze into her face with tenderness radiating from him. "She has already completed the first half of the prophecy. We know that when Witches foretell a future, they speak what they have seen as it is happening and then forget it. She did not take my bloodied heart with a knife, instead she took it softly when she plunged that dagger into herself for me."

"You love her..." The dark red Dragon off to the side muttered.

Everyone turned their heads to her.

"Yes, she stole my heart this way."

He wasn't afraid to reveal to anyone his feelings for this Witch.

"He has been mating with her already," Aneirin commented. "I thought I mistook the smell, but now that I understand he has marked her, the scent is obvious."

"Once again, this is proof that she is trying to trick you now that she has obtained her memories! She wants to obtain that child for herself. That is why she helped you kill Strolguil," Fionnlagh growled.

Rurik gave a laugh. "I have been bedding this Witch for the past month, *before* she obtained her memories."

The Elders turned their heads to Glov. "You did not tell us of this."

His eyes were wide, and he shook his head in disbelief. "I did not know. This has been kept from me."

Now that the proverbial cat was out of the bag, Rurik felt no reason to keep any other secrets.

"That strike of lightning you saw racing towards the sky was her."

Glov's jaw dropped before he took a step forward with a snarl. "You have been lying to me!"

"Of course, I did. I was hiding how she obtained such magic." Rurik's eyes fell to the Elders once more. "How Amalia obtained dragoncraft from me."

"She has stolen your essence! This is forbidden. Witches who steal blood from Dragons must be eradicated, not mated with." Fionnlagh shook his head, his snout bunching when his lips curled over his fangs.

"The lightning was blue, not red. I would never have allowed Amalia to drink from my blood." When they were about to accuse him of lies, his hand moved to rest low on her stomach. "She obtained my magic with my seed. She took it incidentally and obtained it purely."

"Is it true? Was the light you saw blue?" Aneirin asked.

Glov's eyes flickered to the wall as he thought back before they widened in realisation. "Yes, it had definitely been blue."

"I am sure Glov explained to you that Amalia had chosen to ride me on that altar." All eyes came back to them. "She had two reasons for doing so. She did not have that dagger in her hands yet, and she needed to take my magic in order to increase her power so she could remove the multiple hexes on me in one go."

"I did not know Witches could obtain magic this way," Aneirin whispered as he brought a paw up to cup his snout in thought.

Once again, Rurik's eyes found Amalia's face. She looked incredibly uncomfortable being presented like this. Her lips were pursed together, her eyes crinkled in embarrassment and worry, her brows furrowed. *Still so beautiful.*

"And once she had taken what she needed to save me, she had pierced her own womb to make sure my seed would not take and could not grow that child without my consent." Rurik let his eyes fall back to Fionnlagh in particular. "You accuse her of trickery, but if she really wanted it for evil purposes, she would not have made sure it was not possible. They gave us both teas to increase our fertility. It would have been her perfect opportunity."

"This does not matter. You cannot have this Witch as your mate and we have already discussed that we do not want a DragonWitch to be created," Fionnlagh said. "Even though we are not supposed to intervene in a matehood, we still cannot allow you to keep her."

"You will not take this Witch from me!" Rurik snarled while throwing Amalia behind him again. He'd been trying to explain this calmly, but the pale lavender Dragon just wasn't listening. "I have chosen her, and she is *mine!*" He brought his free hand forward with tension in his fingers, wishing he had claws to threaten with. "I did not kill Strolguil and then watch her die for anyone to tell me I cannot have her. I did not bring her back to life with my mark for anyone to tell me that they will not approve of this union."

Rurik took a step forward with a dangerous growl emitting from his chest, his anger rising quickly and steadily. He was running out of patience, and he barely had any to fucking begin with!

"I did not go through my own broken wings, being forced to take the life of my own kind in mercy, and then used as a toy in the Vast's plans while he mocked and threatened me with a horrible fate, just for you to tell me no. I did not complete my blood debt to her by saving her from the stake, something that is just as painful as our scales being removed, for you to tell her no. I did not lose a toe-" He was still rather upset about losing it. "And think that this Witch betrayed me so that I threatened her with what she fears the most, for anyone to tell us that what we have suffered together is not enough proof that our matehood is pure!"

Rurik kept Amalia behind him as he shouted at the Elders, none of them stepping back in shock at his anger. He did watch Fionnlagh's snout bunch more though while Nayana's and Aneirin's brows came together in thought.

"I have defeated and taken the head of our most wretched villain." Rurik pointed to the skull behind him. "I have obtained my goal of a hundred kills, plus the kills I do not count because I did not grab their skulls to mount on my wall as proof. What I have done is far greater than the tales you three have accomplished in the long years of your lives put together."

His lips drew back. He gritted his teeth, his nose crinkled to the point he could see his own scar blocking a part of his vision.

"No one is allowed to tell me what I can have or what I can do when I have done all this, done what has seemed impossible to our kind for centuries." He put his arm behind him to hold Amalia closer to his back. "I will have the child that is promised to me, and if any of you try to get in the way, I will rip your hearts from your chests and feed them to her so that she can live as long as me!"

"You are talking about extending her life with blood magic," Fionnlagh gasped with horror.

"If there is no other way then so be it! But I will not have her die before me. I will not have her age and wither away, leaving me to take care of that child. If I cannot find another way to do it, then I will find an old Dragon and rip their heart from their chest after they have taken their last peaceful breath, and I will make sure she has it." Then Rurik pointed to them. "Unless you anger me enough to take yours as vengeance for trying to separate us."

"You are serious. You wish to keep this Witch alive as your mate, even though you once swore to us that you would never lay such a hand on our kind unless in mercy," Aneirin said, but his voice lacked any kind of anger.

"You once told us that you held the lives of Dragons so sacred that you would rather one kill you than to kill it," Nayana added. "That, no matter your short, ill-mannered temper, you knew you would never allow yourself to take the life of one of our own in anger or revenge."

"Does that not prove to you then that I am determined about this? That I have made my decision on her, and I will not falter from it even with my own beliefs against me?"

Rurik backed up to be closer to Amalia protectively when Nayana came forward. A snarl so vicious fell from him that even he thought it sounded awfully barbaric.

She didn't approach them directly, but she did come to stand next to them. Then she turned around and sat, facing the other two Elders.

"I have chosen my side. I will allow my son to have this bond and the child it will create," Nayana stated, her eyes coming to the corner of her lids to look at them before they fell back to the other Elders.

It was true, Nayana the Loathsome was indeed Rurik's mother.

It was believed he got his temper from her, as well as his thoughtful nature. His mother was dark blue while his father was bright red, creating the purple in his scales. His strength came from both of them since his parents were strong and formidable.

His eyes fell on Nyotakara who was standing to the side. She must have been with his mother when Glov arrived to tell them of Strolguil's death.

It was why she was often with the Elders.

"You cannot mean such a thing. You are only siding with

him because he is your son. You are meant to be unbiased!" Fionnlagh shouted.

"She is your mother?" Amalia whispered softly, and he could feel that her body had turned to face her.

"Yes, I am this brute's egg carrier," Nayana answered while leaning her head to the side to be closer when she spoke.

"I disagree," Aneirin said to Fionnlagh before he took a step forward. "I believe she has made the right decision." He came to stand on the other side of Rurik and Amalia before turning to sit. "I see no problem with this bond. If Rurik will be alive to father the child, then I see no issue with it being born. We feared it would be taken and corrupted as a power against us, but he would never allow that to happen."

"I will not step down from my opinion on this," Fionnlagh roared.

"That does not matter," Nayana sneered. "I joined the ring of Elders to prevent your stubbornness."

"And I joined to prevent no trial ever being completed because you two disagree on everything," Aneirin added. "The decision has been made, Fionnlagh. Two Elders have sided with the defenders. Rurik will be allowed to keep the Witch as his mate and the child, watched carefully, will be raised."

"But now that she is marked, his wards will not keep her here. She is not a prisoner. She is not safe to our kind like she was before, and she will try to escape."

"I do not wish to leave." The voice came from behind him, so soft and hesitant. The two Elders beside them turned their heads to Amalia. Rurik stubbornly attempted to keep her back when she tried to come forward, but she slapped his hands away. "Although I could not consent to his mark, I consented to the Witches bond when he asked me. He has kept me safe and protected and makes me feel cherished."

Rurik turned his head to her when she stood beside him to

speak, but he was ready to grab her and shield her with his own weak human body if anyone were to try to harm her.

"I did not leave him behind because he did not deserve to be tortured and I took that blade to myself because I already loved him." Her face began to grow pink as Rurik's eyes widened. He didn't know that she'd already fallen for him before the night of the black moon. "That was the only reason I got the courage to do it. I do not wish to leave Rurik, and I am afraid of humans." Her averted gaze came to Fionnlagh's so she could meet his glare. "And I do not trust my own kind to the point that, even though he helped save me, I do not wish to see my father again because his hands have touched dark magic. I do not wish to harm or be without the only person I trust and care for."

"That still does not change my mind, Witch," Fionnlagh sneered, his eyes narrowing on her further.

Nayana's wing came up to block their view from the last Elder standing in front of them. "It has been decided. This trial is over, and your argument has lost. Any more words about the topic are in vain."

"Fine! By the order of the Elders this bond has been recognised and any or all products of it allowed," Fionnlagh bit. The wing came down to reveal that the lavender Dragon sat as well. "Now that it has been decided, and all discussions we had hoped to commence are done, we are to leave."

He only wanted to leave because he was angry he didn't get his way.

"Actually, I have a request," Rurik interjected.

Now that a new discussion was coming into place, the two Elders came away from beside them to stand next to Fionnlagh.

"Speak your request," Nayana snapped, no longer being kind now that she was being indifferent of the topic.

"Amalia's father is here and neither of us want him to be.

He has tried to return back to the white path for the sake of her mother and her so, therefore, he should not meet his death."

"You wish for us to take him from here?" Aneirin said with one of his brows cocked. "She truly does not wish to be with her father?"

"She has asked me that he does not remain here."

"You want us to take him to our prisoner cells so that we can see if we can rehabilitate him," Fionnlagh stated.

"Yes."

When all three began to nod slightly, Fionnlagh spoke again. "Yes, I believe we would all prefer he does not remain here."

"Agreed," Nayana said before Aneirin answered with, "I third the proposal."

"It is done. Let us take him so we may leave," Fionnlagh said before eyeing them warily and adding, "Unless there is anything else you wish to tell us?"

He was asking if Rurik had any more secrets.

Not any that I wish to share.

"No, that is all." Rurik turned his head to Glov. "Would you mind assisting with this?" He held up his arm to show that he was bound to Amalia. "I believe I will be too slow."

"I will do it!" Nyota squealed, quickly turning around to walk down the tunnel to his prison alcove.

Fionnlagh and Aneirin turned to follow behind his sister as her dark red tail bounced with excitement.

Nayana, his mother, and Glov walked over to approach them. Amalia stepped back a little to shelter herself from them with his arm.

"You have found a female that is willing to bond with you, Rurik," his mother said with a tone of disbelief and mocking humour. "I truly thought that you would be mateless with how easy you come to anger... or that you would die before you found one."

"If father can tolerate your spiteful, barbed personality, then Amalia can love that in which you gave me, your spiteful, barbed personality."

"You do not get your temper from me!" she yelled, proving to all that he truly did. Then she huffed, shaking her head as if to rid herself of her anger.

She managed it better in her old age.

Rurik thought that both his parents had about two hundred years left before death of old age came for them. They were considered old because not many of them lived this long.

"Why did you not tell me of your actions?" Glov asked as he eyed them both over.

"Because you were being intolerable about it. You tried to burn her, you thought she tried to drown you when she did not and then you refused to let it go. You did not allow me to trust you."

"But I can see now that this is what you truly want." Then his neck stretched to the side so he could see Amalia better. "And that she is of no harm to you, quite the opposite in fact."

"Ah, Rurik?" Amalia said, lifting their arms so she could touch the bit of rope that connected their wrists.

Where she touched began to turn back to brown before it slowly spread up over their wrists and the strapping over their forearms. When the multi-colour glow faded, the string pressed against their skin began to mark their arms like it was seeping into their bodies.

"The spell is completed," he answered, turning to her so he could watch until the plaited twine was no longer glowing, and he couldn't feel the magic from it anymore. "What do we do now?"

He knew Glov and his mother were watching their interaction, but he didn't particularly care. He'd rather focus on this, something he cared very deeply about.

"Well, we are able to remove it now."

Rurik frowned before lifting his arm higher than hers so that it would shake when he shook his own.

"But I am rather fond of being attached to you like this."

I will try to convince her to remove it later. Possibly in a year... when he was done being obsessive about her. *That will not happen, I will always be obsessed.*

He knew it was the truth.

"And we can sense why," Nayana chuckled.

Amalia's face turned bright red.

Rurik pointed to her without removing his eyes from Amalia. "You... will shut your trap about such matters."

"I will expect to see that child before I die, Rurik." His nose crinkled, averse to the idea of being anywhere near her – whether that was with his child or not. "And possibly the others that follow."

His eyes widened in realisation. He hadn't considered he could have more. *I can have as many as I want.* He didn't know if he was horrified by such a fact or delighted.

Their heads lifted when the other Elders entered the room. Aneirin held Amalia's father in his front paw, and she turned to look away.

"Your sister will attempt to stay. I will make sure I take her with us so that you may continue your fornication with this poor female."

"I said to shut your trap!" he snapped, seeing that Amalia was becoming more uncomfortable which would make it harder for him to do such things with his often bashful woman.

"We are leaving," Fionnlagh bit as he passed by. "But I will be watching you and her and the creation you will have closely."

"You will be dead before long so I doubt you will," Rurik answered back, seeing this Dragon was close to the end of his life.

He curled his lips back over his fangs with a small growl, then he walked out of the main room and up the tunnel with Aneirin close behind. He and her father exchanged glances, but he was being glared at, more than he thought he would be. He'd already told her father that he planned to have him taken.

Perhaps it is because I forgot to feed him yesterday.

This is why Rurik couldn't have prisoners as pets. He raised his bound arm to show him that he'd been distracted by his daughter with a malicious grin.

Nayana decided to put her snout right in front of them and her silver eyes, like his own, were bright as they shone directly near their faces.

"You, little Witch, will speak to me in the future." Amalia turned towards her but jumped when she realised how close she was. "I am interested to know about you. My son may be irritating like an infected scale-" She gestured her head towards him. "But, he does have a good sense of character. If he believes that you will never become corrupted or harm another, even though you were born as that which he detests the most, then I am to believe him."

She pulled her head back with a face that told him she wouldn't allow his interference in this. He would try to interfere, but he had a feeling Amalia would get upset if he were to fight with his mother in front of her, especially since they both easily liked to whip their claws out.

"Nyota!" she yelled with a stern motherly tone. "You are to come with me. Do not remain here and annoy your older brother."

"But–"

"No!" Both Rurik and Nayana shouted at the same time.

"Fiiiiine," she whined, giving a huff and an annoyed swish of her tail before she turned to leave the main room.

Nayana followed behind her to make sure she actually left.

"Glov," Rurik growled in warning.

"No, I can see that I am not to remain. I only came because of the Elders," he answered, but he did duck his head to the side to look at Amalia. "After the events of the black moon and what I have learned today, I can see that I was mistaken about you. I will attempt to make amends with you on a later date."

Amalia didn't respond, but Rurik nodded his head. He was thankful Glov wouldn't be an irritant in the future.

And then they were all gone, leaving Rurik and Amalia standing alone in the main room of their lair.

"Well, that was awfully scary," Amalia sighed as the tension in her shoulders lessened.

"I asked Glov to bring them here with the intention of revealing all this, but I had hoped to give you warning about it first. I did not think they would come so soon. Being old and often disagreeing upon discussions, the Elders usually take their time."

Rurik could see that she looked worn, not physically, but emotionally.

She is upset. He lifted his arm to inspect the binding to see that his arm had been blackened in the markings of the design she had put on him. Then he grabbed her arm to check it, seeing that her marking was very light, barely noticeable, but was indeed there.

She inspected it as well.

"I did not know if you would be able to mark me with this kind of bonding since you already did one." Amalia reached up to touch under her chin so her fingertips could flutter against the tribal Dragon against her throat. "I am glad that we can still see it, though."

He hadn't been sure either, but multiple male Dragons could mate with a singular female. It didn't often bode well, but it was possible. He thought since they could be marked by different Dragons, he might be able to mark her twice.

She will not be receptive to me right now. Rurik also didn't want to pressure his mate when he could see she was upset. *Perhaps I can take her for a walk through the forest since she has not done so yet.*

Rurik wanted to watch this woman be her witchy self in the woods and flitter around within the nature her kind often like to revel in. He thought it would please him to see her be herself, and he thought it may also cheer her up.

Or...

"Perhaps you may like to take a flight with me?"

Now that she was his, he saw no issue with taking her up on her request. It would be something she would continue to ask him for, and he wanted to offer it as a gift rather than for her to plead with him for it.

Tenderness filled his chest when his question was immediately met with a bright smile. He returned it with a grin, a devious plot unveiling itself within his mind.

42

Rurik had flown with Amalia gently at first, making sure not to suddenly bank too quickly or dip their height. He hadn't wanted to frighten her or further upset her.

It didn't take him long to realise she was rather content and comfortable with him, and that he could be bolder.

And it was after the first time he twisted in the air, momentarily placing her upside down and she let out a squeal of excitement, that he understood she trusted him fully to know he wouldn't endanger her.

He checked on her occasionally by looking over his shoulder. Kneeling between his shoulder blades with his wings behind her, the bright smile she was giving to the sky with her eyes closed had sent a tremor through his body.

The wind was cutting through her purple dress, making it flutter behind her as it moulded to the front of her body, showing all of her curves to him. Her long blonde hair wisped behind her and seemed to glow in the bright sunlight that shone directly upon it.

The enjoyment he could see as she held onto two of his spikes for safety while her head was tilted back, allowing him to view his mark on her completely, had been beautiful, breath-taking even.

Looking at her now, not a single part of him doubted his decision of claiming her.

And he hoped she was ready because he no longer wanted to wait.

With that thought in mind, Rurik headed back to their home. When he dove for the entrance of their lair, Amalia gave a high-pitched, girly squeal. The sound of it elated him and caused a rumble to vibrate through his chest.

He landed right in front of the mouth of the cave, not wanting to frighten her if he glided through his tunnel walls.

He reached behind him with one of his front paws, lifting it so that she could slip into it. He carefully placed her on the ground.

"Rurik!" Amalia exclaimed, spinning to throw her arms around his neck to hug him and bury her face against his shoulder. "That was so exciting. Thank you!"

He curled his head around her and brought one of his paws up to return her embrace with his claws curling around one of her shoulders.

"For you, Amalia, anything."

She leaned back to look into his eyes, her smile just as bright as it was when she was in the sky.

"You were right! Clouds really are made of water."

Rurik had made it his mission to fly through every single one he could find. Her giggles had been part of the reason, the other was because the condensation of them caused her clothing to wetly cling to her.

"But why are you suddenly so small now?" She looked over his face and then body to see he was the same size as her. "You are rarely this size when you are in your Dragon form."

Rurik typically liked to remain his full size when he was in his lair. If he needed to be small, he found it easier to have full dexterity with his human hands.

"You are mine, Amalia," he said, taking a step forward and

licking across his snout while heat flared through him.

Her brows drew together in confusion. "Yes, I know."

Parts of him clenched at her unhesitant admission.

"And I will have you in any way I want." Her little brows drew together even tighter as she retreated into their cave, taking them out of the sunlight. "In any form I can take."

Her eyes drew wide, and she stumbled back a step before tripping to land on her backside.

She pressed her hand against his shoulder when he crawled above her and pressed his snout against the crook of her neck and shoulder. He let out a deep expire when he took in her scent directly against her skin, unable to stop himself from licking to taste it.

"Wait. Can we talk about this first?"

"Why?" He took in another taste of her, refusing to allow her to push him away. He did, however, pull his head back to stare at her with a small frown. "You seemed content with the idea when we spoke of it."

"That..." Her face grew blistering red. "That was because you were inside of me!"

"And you came around me when I told you I would take you like this."

Somehow, her face grew even more flushed. It caused a deep chuckle to rumble from him.

"That was only last night. I–I just need a little more time to adjust to the idea."

"I thought you said I was handsome in my Dragon form." A spike of uncertainty lanced his gut to twist his insides. He took a step back, and his jaw clenched shut before it relaxed. "I thought that you would desire me like this."

She averted her eyes to the side.

"I do." He would have thought she looked away from him with misgivings, if the subtle smell of arousal didn't lift into her already mouth-watering scent. "But how do you know you

of their cock was fully gloved. The heat around it caused a full release from deep inside their bodies. It was as though the female's body heat was demanding all of its due for a successful mating.

She turned her head up with a cute little pout.

"Really? So, we can only do it once a day like this?"

"You are safe for now."

For now, he thought with a grin.

For a long while, Rurik just took in the feel of her beside him in silence with bliss radiating from him. His eyes became half-cast and were lowering by the minute.

"Rurik?"

"Hm?" he answered with a dozy voice.

"What will you do if we are not able to extend my life?"

His arms tightened around her in tension.

"Do not speak of such ill things. I will make sure you are with me until I take my last breath."

He would make sure of it. As he told the Elders, he would give her a Dragon heart, if need be, but he would not have Amalia wither away hundreds of years before him.

"You would be so selfish as to leave me here by myself?"

He gave a snort of humour.

"Yes. I do not think I could bare to spend a day in this world without you." Rurik released her arse cheek to tenderly cup the side of her face while being careful of his sharp claws. "But if you do not wish to be alone, you could always come with me, and we could walk to the afterlife together."

"You would kill me yourself?"

"No, I doubt I would have the strength in my old age before death. But it is not an uncommon request among my kind to ask for assistance from another Dragon. When you have spent most of your eight-hundred years with someone, it is hard to imagine your life without them."

Yet, Rurik knew there was also another possibility.

One where he could return home on a hunt so injured that he knew he was going to pass not long after. There would be no time to ask another Dragon for assistance, and he would make the offer to do it himself if she didn't want to be without him.

It would pain him, but there was a spell they could do that required both of their assistance to perform it. Grief was a heavy burden to bear, and he didn't want to leave Amalia on her own to try by herself.

I do not want to leave her on her own.

If she wanted to live on without him, he would be content as long as he got to take in her scent with his final breath and she was the last thing he held onto – whether that was in his large paw or in his arms. Rurik wanted her voice to be the last thing he heard, and her radiant beauty and innocence to be the final thing he saw before he left this world.

And yet, she has almost left me twice.

"I am sorry," he said to her softly.

Her lips pursed as she frowned.

"For what?"

"I have not been able to spare you of pain."

She cupped his scaly face again and gave him a small smile. "I did not mind sacrificing my life to give you a chance at escaping, Rurik."

He shook his head as he untangled his claws from her hair before he reached down and gently drew them over her leg. Not a day had passed where Rurik hadn't regretted not preventing her from being placed at the stake.

"If I had not been so hateful of your kind that night, even though you had done nothing to receive my hatred, I would not have left you to be taken by the humans." His eyes searched her face with the need to drink her in. She was alive and well with him now. "You had gone out of your way to save me, and I had intended to abandon you and my blood debt to you when I knew something was wrong. I should have fought to protect you then when I could see you were kind."

The tears that began to well in her eyes pained him, but he refused to look away from her. She brushed her thumbs over his scales on his cheeks, and despite her tears, her expression appeared so gentle.

"I am glad you did not."

He gave a humourless laugh. "I thought you did not utter lies."

"Rurik, I would have willingly placed myself in that fire if I knew I would be able to have a moment such as this with you."

"But your fear..." Even now he could smell it subtly rising in her scent.

"Yes, but would you have brought me here if I was not in need of healing?"

Rurik thought for long moments as his eyes fell away.

"No. I would have killed those human soldiers and then left." He slowly brought his gaze back to her. "But I would have also revealed what I was to you. I may have taken you regardless."

"And what if you did not? I am here now, and I am happy with you. I no longer care how I got here, or what pain I had to suffer through first."

"I love you, Amalia."

With every piece of his fiery heart.

"I love you too, Rurik."

The regret that had been subtly gnawing on Rurik eased, and he drew Amalia closer. He would never allow harm to come to her again.

She is mine, and she will be with me always.

Epilogue

60 years later

Rurik lay in the main room of his lair facing a handful of the tapestries.

Amalia wasn't with him. She was laying in his main treasure room reading or doing something... he wasn't sure this day. He'd transferred everything from her original alcove into it decades ago – after carving to make it bigger to accommodate her furniture, of course.

He hadn't wanted to be without his riches when he wanted to sleep as a Dragon, but he also hadn't wanted to be without his mate.

The soft female had made no complaint since he had carved the room to account for everything inside it, ensuring she could walk around the pile with ease. Rurik often found entertainment in finding coins that rolled away under furniture to be thrown back onto the pile.

It took a few years, but they discovered that they couldn't extend her life any other way than for her to eat the heart of a Dragon and to do the incantation required.

They were still trying to find other ways, but Rurik had made the request to an old Dragon, who had been surprisingly charmed by his Witch when meeting her, if they may take her heart for such use when she was to pass.

After getting her approval and then presenting this to the Elders, who were made up of four now with Fionnlagh long dead, they had allowed it.

With the way her kind aged, she didn't look a day over a human's twenty-eight years with the heart she'd taken and unhappily consumed. While Rurik himself didn't look much older, perhaps only a few years.

It hadn't changed her, just as he knew it wouldn't. Her pure heart was still uncorrupted. He thought that might be because it hadn't been taken viciously, but rather gifted.

That was nearly thirty years ago, and he knew that they had a hundred years from that day before she would begin to age. They would wait for her to catch up to him and then he would obtain another if no other solution had been found.

It was always on his mind, as Amalia often was.

If only there was a spell in which I could entangle her lifespan to mine. It would be convenient if it were possible. He often spoke with those of his kind who were more adept with their magic to research if there was a possibility.

In the meantime, Rurik kept himself busy.

He often left to hunt Witches and had added to his collection of skulls quite nicely. Now that Strolguil was no longer a plague upon the world, he was being more careful in who he was hunting. He made sure the Witch he came across was truly evil before he took its life.

If there were other white wielders like his woman, then he didn't see the need to eradicate them. And there were, he had found a very small handful of them.

He no longer killed indiscriminately, but indeed remained apprehensive and hateful of them.

Then, when he was in his lair, he often chased his woman around his home, still obsessed with the pretty female he had in his keeping. That would never fade – as it often didn't for his kind. Even when she was old and wrinkled with bland blonde hair, she would be aged the same as him, and he would still want her.

He also had one other thing that often took his time.

It irritated him, aggravated him. A noisy, terrible little gremlin that often got on his nerves and fried his already small patience.

Currently, he was speaking to it. He was telling it of the tales of his kind by retelling the stories of the tapestries in front of them while it was climbing his back. It was making guttural noises, holding onto his spikes so that it didn't fall.

When it made a noise of struggle, desperately holding onto a spike and kicking against his back to get purchase, Rurik turned his head to face it.

"If you fall from me, your mother will be mad," Rurik told his son, who just answered him with a grin while he hung from the highest point of his back.

Haelan was his name, and a lot about him was a mystery to both of his parents. They often estimated his age because he didn't age the same as either one of them.

He'd been born forty years ago, but he wasn't the equivalent of a four-year-old boy like his kind would be at this length of life. He also wasn't in his twenties like he would have been if he were of Amalia's kind.

No, he appeared to be eight or nine.

His hair was a dark purple like his own, but he had light blue eyes that were even softer than his mother's. They often caught the light and appeared metallic blue, like fragments of silver were easy to see.

He had many of Rurik's features. His own parents often told him Haelan looked similar to how he'd been as a child when he was seen in his human form.

Haelan didn't obtain his bad temper, though. He was more like his mother in personality with his easy kindness and playful nature, which is how Amalia was with Rurik.

That was to the relief of most.

Many hadn't liked the idea that this child could have been a hateful, angry thing upon the world with the kind of power it was foretold it would have. Power Rurik had seen him produce. Like Rurik, he had a deep sense that was already easy to see. It'd been proved with his quick ability to learn.

But this child could harness both witchcraft and dragoncraft. He also had the ability to shift to a Dragon even though he hadn't been hatched from an egg. He was smaller, though, since his height was obviously stunted.

With how large Amalia had gotten carrying him, Rurik had thought he was going to have to extract an egg from her belly and perhaps save her life again.

He was thankful he hadn't needed to.

No, he'd been born human-shaped, stayed in the womb for a year, and both mother and child had lived through the birth. This had also been one of Rurik's fears.

His scales were dark purple like his own, but he really was a spectacular child. He could form wings, claws, and fangs while human, something no other Dragon could do.

He was different, and he was being observed very carefully.

"Tell me more stories!" Haelan laughed, managing to get a hold and climb up to his spine.

Much to Rurik's irritation, he climbed up to his head so that he may sit on it. He sat with his legs wide, one on either side of his brows.

Rurik had been booted in the eye a few times by the boy who turned absentminded when playing. No matter how many times he roared at him for doing so, Haelan often forgot when he became engrossed in what Rurik was talking about. His son was very fond of him and the tales he had to share.

"Get down!"

Rurik bucked his head back, but the child's grip was strong enough that he merely flailed.

"Noooo," he squealed with laughter.

When it didn't work because Rurik didn't want to hurt the boy, he pawed at his snout. He had to stem the urge to throw him across the main room and into the wall.

He is my son. He is my son. I cannot harm him. I cannot bite or claw him. Amalia will be angered with me again if he injures himself because of me. This wasn't the first time Rurik had mentally muttered these words to himself like a mantra, although he'd never intentionally harmed the boy.

Giving up, Rurik let him sit on his head like he was a living hat.

There had been many discussions between Rurik and Amalia about when the child would set off on his own. His kind would leave after a hundred years from their hatching place and their parents when they were the ripe old age of ten-year-old equivalent.

They were usually stronger and wiser than a human and they spent many of their first years out of danger, shaping their own lair to live. With little claws, it often took a long time after they found a suitable cave to their liking.

It also made them strong in form from doing so.

Rurik had left his parents when he had been one hundred. He expected for his own spawn to leave around the same age.

Unfortunately, to his dismay, Amalia wouldn't allow the boy to leave until he was at least an adult. *Why must I give her whatever it is she wants?*

Rurik cringed, knowing he was going to have this child in his lair for longer than he wanted. With how fast he grew, he'd been hoping he wouldn't have to put up with him for a hundred years.

Many were bewildered by Rurik's interactions with his own child. He often got on his nerves, but he loved the boy without question and was violently protective of him.

He taught him to fight, taught him dragoncraft. He was determined to make him strong, not just in body, but in will. Rurik wanted him to live a long full life.

He cared for him, and like his mother, he was soft for him.

The problem was, he often found him in places he didn't want him to be in – like in his trophy room touching a skull. He'd broken one and Rurik had been infuriated at him for doing so.

There was also the number of times he'd been trying to bed Amalia to find him at their alcove entrance wanting something. It often got Rurik booted away from the female who would stress that they had been caught in the middle of being intimate.

A cloth now hung over the entranceway with a soundproofing spell, but she wouldn't allow Rurik to shield the boy out in case he needed something serious – which he never did.

Other times, Rurik would wake in his human form sleeping next to Amalia while this tiny creature had his small arms and legs wrapped around his back when he wasn't supposed to be there. He had his own alcove!

It made him uncomfortable because the child could sneak up on him with silent little footsteps, and it disturbed him because he'd been vulnerable and asleep.

That didn't stop him from grabbing the child with one arm to yank him over his body to tuck him between himself and Amalia. Many mornings were often spent cuddling with the only two creatures he could truly tolerate.

But there were times that Rurik truly felt something deep and tender for the mate he had chosen and the child they created.

Times when he would watch over them in his Dragon form as they walked through the forest hand in hand. Amalia would be showing him something to do with nature and witchcraft, and his child-like stare of wonder would be engrossed as he smiled up at her.

It was a sight he often liked to see, a mother and child together.

Then there were the times when new visitors would come to their lair. Although every Dragon knew of the WitchSlayer who had killed Strolguil and mated with a Witch, they were always wary of her.

Just as she was of them.

Haelan would stand in front of her as if he could protect her in his child body from the wrath of a spiteful, full-grown Dragon. The protection was unneeded, no one would harm her, but it still made his chest bow with pride.

"If you will not tell me more stories, will you take Mother and me flying again?"

"No, she is in a foul mood."

Amalia wasn't happy this day, much to Rurik's confusion because he knew he wasn't the reason for it. *At least I do not believe so.*

"But she has been in a bad mood for the past two weeks!" Haelan exclaimed, falling back to lay against his head and almost hitting him in the eye with a foot when he bounced. "And I want to go flying todaaaaaay."

Rurik had already tried to see if going for a flight with him would cheer her up as it usually did.

"I have already offered. She rejected it."

Haelan groaned with unhappiness.

"Is it because of the child? I do not wish for a sibling if it will already annoy me."

"She is just feeling unwell-" Rurik's head reared back, and he almost sent his son flying. "What do you mean because of the child, the sibling?"

Haelan rolled up to bend forward so he was looking into

his large eyes.

"You did not notice?" Haelan gave him a frown. "I sense something in her stomach when I cuddle with her, magic that is unfamiliar." Then he shot up with a laugh with his head flinging back. "Maybe I am wrong then!"

This was just another case of the strange magic his son wielded. He could feel magic with his hands. He often told them he felt the waves of it like tiny vibrations against his skin.

Rurik bent his head forward so that Haelan would fall and land into his paw. His back lay against it as he looked up to him, grinning from the exhilaration of being tossed.

"You have sensed something different with your mother and did not inform me?"

Rurik then put him down on his feet so he could get to his own.

He blew a ring of fire so that he could shift and then went to the chest that was now kept in this room to acquire pants. The child didn't care. He was used to seeing him unclothed like most of his kind. Amalia was against it.

With the child in tow, following him around his lair constantly like a lost puppy, Rurik sprinted to their room.

She was resting against the bed as she read. Her collection of books had grown since Rurik often hunted for more for her. It was one of his favourite tasks when he left their lair.

She squealed when he came up to her and lifted her dress.

"What are you doing? Get out from under there you perverted scoundrel!" She tried to push him away. "Our son is watching!"

"Quiet Amalia, I wish to sense for something."

Once he was under the skirt of her dress, he tried to scent her stomach. His eyes widened. She indeed smelt slightly different – a barely noticeable change.

He filled his skull with magic so that he could change his

sight to view the tendrils of magic. He could see hers as well as another's. He couldn't see the spell he had to place on her once a year – the one that prevented her from getting pregnant.

Did I forget to place it? He winced. He should have done it quite some time ago, a few weeks, perhaps even a month. It wasn't the first time he had forgotten, but he usually remembered... eventually. *I have taken her recently in my Dragon form.* Which would have guaranteed her pregnancy.

"No wonder you have been foul with me!" he yelled before bringing his head out from under her skirt to face her. "I have forgotten to replace the spell."

Amalia rolled to sit up with her brows furrowing.

"Wait, that is why I have been feeling unwell?"

Much to Rurik's pleasure, her body required dragoncraft to carry a child that would be born from both of them. It would drain her witchcraft otherwise, sapping it from her to compensate and leaving her weak.

It took them a while to realise this at first.

"Blasted! Not another one."

Rurik groaned as he fell onto the bed face first next to her.

"Ha! You did not want another, but I did and then you forgot. You have no one else to blame but yourself."

She'd been hounding him about it for the last five years.

Indeed, she was right.

He could feel it, a fit of rage about to burst from the seams.

"If you could," he tried to say calmly while rising to his knees with the intention of leaving. "Make it a girl... because I do not think I can handle another son."

Perhaps he would be calmer with a daughter. She would remind him of Amalia, and she might soothe him whereas their son often got under his scales.

His son was playful, but he was a male. Rurik didn't often think him cute, whereas Amalia was adorable with her feminine giggles and attempts to stare him down like she could best him. When his son tried to playfully go toe-to-toe with him, he often wanted to throw him across the room for trying to be more dominant than him. A common male Dragon trait.

Rurik got to his feet and walked to the entryway to their alcove. He palmed Haelan's back to push him forward into the room.

"Stay with your mother. I need to vent."

He headed down the tunnel to make his way to the cavern with the stream before it exploded from him.

They were right. I do not have the patience for children. And he was about to have another, meaning his time with them would be prolonged.

Rurik was excited, he didn't completely regret this. It would be something else for him to love, to protect, to watch as it interacted with its mother – those moments often filling him with contentment and joy.

He just wanted to keep his Amalia selfishly to himself. He was tired already of being restricted and having to be understanding of something that was learning.

Not even halfway down his lair, he gave a bellowing roar in frustration, nobody else to be angry with but himself. Amalia's giggles at him echoed down the tunnels.

Blasted!

Also by Opal Reyne

DUSKWALKER BRIDES
A Soul to Keep
A Soul to Heal
A Soul to Touch *(Coming February 2023)*
A Soul to Guide *(TBA 2023)*
A Soul to Revive *(TBA 2023)*

WITCH BOUND
The WitchSlayer
The ShadowHunter *(April 2023)*

Completed Series

A PIRATE ROMANCE DUOLOGY
Sea of Roses
Storms of Paine

~~THE ADEUS CHRONICLES~~
This series has been unpublished as of
20th of June 2022
(May be republished in the future with revisions)

Made in the USA
Las Vegas, NV
20 January 2024

84682084R00319